BLOOD BROTHERS

A Family Divided

Ronald E. Pressley - Nancy P. Holder

1122 Creations
Knoxville, Tennessee

ISBN: 978-0-578-55666-6 (hard cover)

Forward

"And ye shall hear of wars and rumours of wars . . . ."
Matthew 24:6

When war is experienced only as a chapter in history, a segment on the evening news, or a political argument waged by well-paid pundits from the comfort of a padded recliner, it is not real.

Only when you lose someone you love does the insanity of it cut through the façade of "the greater good," or "heroic sacrifice."

In this book, we attempt to introduce characters who will live in the reader's mind so that both their joy and despair will feel real.

We hope that the following quotes will be worth remembering.

"It is well that war is so terrible, or we would grow too fond of it."
Robert E. Lee

"When the rich wage war, it is the poor who die."
Jean-Paul Sartre

"War does not determine who is right – only who is left."
Bertrand Russell

"All war is a symptom of man's failure as a thinking animal."
John Steinbeck

Introduction

If you are a citizen of the United States but do not claim direct ancestry from the indigenous people of the North American continent, you are either descended from voluntary immigrants or involuntary abductees.

Most voluntary immigrants to the southern colonies came from Western Europe and they were probably sent with a military commission, a land grant from the King, to fill needed trades positions, or they made passage in exchange for a period of indenture.

The history of indentured servitude on these shores actually precedes the introduction of slavery and began to grow during the decade following the settlement of Jamestown by the Virginia Company in 1607.

The American South would develop the largest need for indentured labor with the introduction of tobacco as the main cash crop. The conditions of indenture evolved from total control of the indentured person by the Leasing Company to sale of contracts by Shipping Agents to land owners.

Most indentured workers did not survive their indenture period. Those who did, received only their freedom after paying an additional fee.

Some landowners were farsighted enough to offer a parcel of land at the end of the indenture period. This *enlightened self-interest* was an investment in the growth of the land owner's work force, guaranteed economic growth of the community, and continued income from shared crops.

The following pages chronicle the story of one young man who came to North Carolina in 1830 with nothing but a contract of indenture and belief in his ability to create a better life for himself. What happens to him and the family he builds in that place is based loosely on a Pressley family legend. The story is told of three brothers who chose different paths during the American Civil War and what became of the one who defied his family and friends to join the Union Army.

Any similarity to actual persons living or dead is unintended and the authors apologize if possibly familiar names used for the fictitious characters is found to be offensive.

Table of Contents

Sunday Dinner

Chapter 1

It was the year of our Lord 1858, and the rumblings of secession and war permeated the air.

Sitting under a large oak tree in the front yard of the Roaring Fork Farm, John Wesley Henderson was engaged in a lively conversation. Buck, Johnny, and Will Presley were listening as Henderson spoke. The circuit-riding Methodist minister was quoting the words of Jesus.

"Blessed are they who mourn, for they shall be comforted...... Blessed are the peace makers, for they shall be called the children of God."

Buck Presley spoke up, "But Preacher, we cain't jist let 'em Yankees take over 'er land an' ever'thang else. We gotta stand up ta 'em."

Maggie, one of the younger sisters of the Presley brothers, walked over to the group and said, "We've got dinner on the table. Come on in tha house and eat."

The four men entered the house and sat down at the table. The other four younger Presley brothers were already seated. (As was customary, the men ate first and were served by the women.)

Sally Presley, the matriarch, directed her two daughters, and her two daughters in-law as they placed bowls of mashed potatoes, green beans, boiled corn, and fried chicken on the table.

"I shore do wish Mrs. Henderson cudda been with us taday, Pastor John," Sally smiled.

"Yeah, me too," Henderson answered. "Nellie jist wuddn't feelin' well taday."

"How are Ralph and Sarah doin' this mornin, Preacher?" Martha inquired about her brother and sister-in-law.

Henderson had preached the Sunday morning service at Old Yellow Creek Church. He then travelled to Roaring Fork where he would hold afternoon services after enjoying dinner with the Presley family. Ralph Johnson, Martha's brother and his wife, Sarah, attended the Old Yellow Creek Church.

Answering her, he said, "Ther' doin' well. Ralph thanks he's got a good crop a 'backer' this year."

After dinner, the men went outside to sit under the big oak tree in the front yard to continue their debate.

Sally didn't tolerate it very well when people smoked in her house, not even the preacher. Henderson liked to smoke cigars and Ralph Johnson always gave him one when he preached at Yellow Creek. He saved it to smoke after dinner on Sunday.

Buck Presley and his wife Martha lived in the two-story house his father, J.W., had built after Will was born. J.W. got permission from Charles Graham, the land owner, to build it. As the family grew, he added two bedrooms on the back, and, later, the second story.

Johnny and his wife, Willadeen, now lived in the same log cabin that was J.W. and Sally's first home at Roaring Fork farm.

Buck and Martha, at Sally's request, had moved into the larger two-story home with her, along with Will and the younger children. Buck was the oldest and head of the family now that J.W. had gone on to his reward in Heaven.

(At least Sally hoped he was there.) J.W. did like to drink the corn whiskey he made in his "still" up in the woods. He wasn't much for church-goin' either. Preacher Henderson harped too much on the evils of alcohol.

The hilly terrain of the two hundred acres they farmed was not conducive to raising cattle, so most of the farmers in the area raised tobacco as a *cash crop*. Situated along the banks of the Nantahala River, the soil was fertile and produced bountiful crops of tobacco.

Chestnut, oak, poplar, and walnut trees were abundant in the wooded hillsides of southwestern North Carolina. With two major cash crops, tobacco and timber, everybody in the area prospered.

The girls, Maggie and Lizzie, had plenty of chores to do. They helped their mother with the garden, canning, milking the cow, churning butter, and the other household jobs.

Because the family raised tobacco, the girls helped with the harvest and *cure* of it as well. Exporting much of the crop to Europe, everybody, including the farmers made a good living.

Tennessee residents, just over on the other side of the mountain, called the river the *Little Tennessee River*, but the North Carolinians preferred the Cherokee Indian name of Nantahala-meaning land of the noon-day sun. Because of the high ridges overlooking the valleys, it was said you couldn't see the sun until noon.

Charles Graham, who owned nearly one thousand acres of the mountainous region, referred to the families as *tenant farmers*, but out of earshot of the people who worked for him, called them *share croppers*.

A saw mill, a Feed and Seed store, and a general store were also owned and operated by Graham in the little town of Graham, North Carolina.

The Graham family was a very prominent group in North Carolina. Charles' brother, William Graham, owned several thousand acres in the Lincolnton, N.C. area.

William served a term as a United States senator, and a term as governor of North Carolina. Later when the Carolinas seceded from the Union, William, a graduate of West Point, was commissioned as a general in the Confederate army.

The Supreme Court had issued a ruling in the **Dred Scott** case the previous year, 1857. That ruling opined that slaves were property, not people, thus adding fuel to the flame.

Abolitionists were a very small minority of the voters in North Carolina.

Preachers *justified* slavery by quoting Bible verses from Paul, the apostle, describing how slaves should be treated by their owners.

Politicians proclaimed the doctrine of *states' rights* that was still being debated eighty years after it was supposedly settled by **Hamilton** and **Madison** when they framed the Constitution.

Although there were not a lot of slaves in North Carolina, land owners generally sided with their fellow land owners in South Carolina, Georgia, Alabama, and Mississippi.

After dinner, under the white oak tree in the front yard of the Presley farm, the heated discussion continued. Reverend Henderson was adamant that Jesus *did not* condone slavery. "Jesus taught us that we should do unto others as we would have them do unto us."

Buck interjected, "Now Preacher, there's a whole book that the Apostle Paul wrote about how a man should treat a runaway slave. He didn't say nuthin' about *freeing slaves*, just that slaves shouldn't be beaten nor killed. I believe it was the book of Philemon."

"Well Buck, I do declare, I believe you *have* been reading the Bible, but you better be careful, *a little learning is a dangerous thing.*"

"Now Preacher, I ain't got much larnin', but I heerd Governor Graham talk about Philemon in a speech over in Asheville here a while back of this."

"Yeah, I heard him say that the *damned Yankees* didn't have no right to come down here and tell us what we can and caint do, too, Buck. But this debate has been goin' on for nigh on to eighty years now.

"Alexander Hamilton and James Madison argued about it as they were writing the Constitution way back in 1787. It is a fact, though that they didn't consider the teachings of Jesus, just their own preconceived notions of things."

Will listened intently, then spoke. "Preacher, I don't believe that one man oughta' own another man. I heerd you say the we're *all* children of God no matter where or when we were born. Ain't that right?"

"Yes, Will, Jesus said 'Love your neighbor as you love yourself' is the most important commandment that God gave us," Preacher Henderson retorted.

"But *still* Jesus didn't tell us that we couldn't own slaves, did he? He just said we should love them." Buck insisted.

Will, usually the quieter of the Presley boys, began to get agitated. "Buck, we ain't much mor'n slaves our own selves. Mr. Graham practically owns *all of us*."

"Now Will, that ain't right. You can leave anytime you want to. Momma wouldn't like it, but I ain't got you bound with no rope, and Mr. Graham ain't neither," Buck was yelling.

Sally walked outside when she heard the loud talking. "Now you two boys just calm down, it's about time to head to church. Billy Bob and Pete, you two go hitch the mules to the buggy. I'm goin' to church.

That stopped the argument for the moment.

Worship Service

Chapter 2

The unpainted clapboard-sided church at Roaring Fork had been built in 1840 to serve four of Graham's *tenant farming* families or *share croppers* as he would normally refer to them out of ear shot. Although he provided the building materials, the actual construction was completed by the men in these four families themselves.

Above the double doors at the entrance, a placard identified the building in large black hand-painted letters, ROARING FORK METHODIST CHURCH.

Sitting on a bank above a creek that ran into the Nantahala River, the little church could accommodate the members of all four families.

As worshipers climbed the front steps and entered through the double doors, they had a choice of twelve wooden pews on either side of a center aisle which led to a simple raised platform and the pulpit.

Each long interior wall on the left and right of the aisle featured two windows with wrought-iron candle sconces on either side of each window. A small cast-iron pot-bellied stove warmed the church in cold weather.

Reverend John Wesley Henderson anticipated each Sunday meeting and carefully prepared his sermons with his audience in mind. He considered his appointment to the ministry as a grand opportunity to teach and lead, a status to which none of his immediate family members had risen.

Fully aware of his limited formal education, Henderson continued to submerge himself in all available written material to enlarge his mental resources and enrich his ability to communicate.

He was an impressively tall and muscular man of fifty with a loud booming voice, a thinning head of once dark curly hair, and a full beard displaying streaks of grey below his engaging smile.

He had learned to make the best use of his God-given voice to command attention in any crowd. Henderson took pride presenting himself in a professional manner. His suits were always freshly brushed, and his white clerical collar was immaculate.

He held his large frame erect without being stiff and he was careful to use his hand movements judiciously. Conscious of his dominant voice, he modulated the tone for emphasis while delivering his Sunday message.

When everyone was settled into their regular pews at the church, Henderson stood up.

"Everybody get a hymnal, and turn to page number 142. A preacher friend of mine announced to his church that he would be leaving them at the end of the month.

"He explained, 'the Lord led me to come here, and now he is leading me to leave.'

"An old Elder stood up and started singing, *Oh Why Not Tonight.*"

John Wesley howled with laughter, but Buck leaned over to Martha and whispered, "he tells that same old joke every time we sing this song." Martha smiled and nodded her assent.

Henderson was fond of beginning each service with a humorous remark, but he often could not recall which joke he had *used* at each location.

Both Johnny and Will were good musicians. Johnny played guitar and Will played a fiddle. Buck played a harmonica and used to join his brothers in accompanying the singing, but he quit when the Preacher started harping on the evils of slavery.

"People have always had slaves," he thought. Why is everybody so upset about it now? Tha Yankees ain't got no right to come down here and tell us what we can or cain't do. Mr. Graham said so, and I think he's right."

"Open your Bibles to Galatians 5:13-14," Henderson announced. Then he began to read.

"For, Brethren ye have been called unto liberty. Only use not liberty for an occasion to the flesh, but by love, serve one another.

"For all the law is fulfilled in one word, even in this; Thou shalt love the neighbor as thyself. But if ye bite and devour one another, take heed that ye be not consumed one of another."

"Martha, didn't he preach this same sermon last month?" Buck whispered.
"Yep, but he read a different passage of scripture. I think it was somewhere in Matthew," Martha answered softly.

"Yeah, but it's still the same sermon ain't it?" Buck complained.

"Now Buck, if it's in more than one place in the Bible, maybe he's right," Martha interjected.

Buck folded his arms across his chest and stiffened his upper lip but didn't say any more until the service was over.

Standing at the front door shaking hands with the people, Henderson was smiling and acknowledging the praise of his members.

As Buck approached, he steeled himself for the onslaught, but Buck just dropped his eyes and shook the preacher's hand.

Indentured

Chapter 3

LONDON 1830

"How long do I hafta be aworkin' to pay fer me ticket on the boat to 'merica," J.W. asked the agent.

"Mr. Graham demands an indenture of naught less than four yeahs," the booking agent answered.

James William Presley had just been released from a debtor's prison in London. After serving two years for refusing to pay for a horse that had died of disease only five days after he bought it. He was eager to get out of the city.

Not wanting to return to the family farm he had left behind in Dublin, and hearing about the New World in America, it seemed like a place to make a new beginning. Serving a prison sentence, even a debtor's prison sentence, would make it difficult to *get ahead* in England.

Some of his relatives had already emigrated to America. His sister had read letters to him about the wonderful life they had found overseas. As his heart raced at the prospect of a four-week voyage on the ocean, he imagined himself as a big land owner over there....... *Eventually.*

"What 'appens afta them four yeahs?" J.W. quizzed him.

"Well, if ye done a good job, and make 'im money offa tha farhm, Mr. Graham'll grant ye twenty-five acres ta farhm as yer own. Of course, he'll expect ye ta keep on aworkin' fer 'im a few more years, but you could end up owning a lot of land yerself."

"Aye that's exactly what I'm athinkin'. Might even find a bonnie lassie and raise me a passel of kids."

"O.K. Put yer X on tha line right 'ere. Ye can carry two copies of tha Indenture with ye. Keep one fer yerself and give t'other ta Mr. Graham when ye git ta North Carolina," the agent directed.

"What's an Indenture?" J.W. was confused.

"It's just a contract that says ye'll work fer Mr. Graham fer four yeahs ta pay 'im back fer yer passage on tha ship. E's paying fer yer ticket.

"In addition, he'll provide ye with a place ta live, and tha supplies ye'll need ta operate tha farhm fer 'im – a wagon, two mules, a plow, cross-cut saws ta cut timber, shovels, and hoes ta work with.

"Ye'll have a house, a shed fer the mules, and plenty a land ta work on - about 200 acres on this farhm, me thinks.

"If ye want 'em, e'll starht ye with a flock a chickens and some pigs ta feed ye. Ye'll have to maintain 'em and breed 'em on yer place," the agent explained.

"Great, that sounds like tha farhm I grew up on. Now, if I can jist find me a pretty wife to help me raise some young'uns, I'll have everythin' I need," J.W. grinned.

"Well, a fine-lookin', hard-working young'un like yerself shan't have no problem with that," the older man winked.

"Go upta tha port at Southampton, report ta the ship called **Queen Shipping Lines**."

"Do ye mean I hafta sail outta here on a freighter?" he was surprised.

"Aye, but I've booked a lotta young'uns for Mr. Graham, and I ain't had no complaints yit. You might even git a job hepin' load tha ship and pick up a l'il extra money ta get by on 'til ye get ta Graham.

"Over at the Market Place you might could catch a ride on a wagon haulin' a load ta tha port. Good luck and God speed, J.W."

Shipping Out

Chapter 4

"Thank ye fer the ride, sir, I'm much obliged ta ye," he thanked the man driving the wagon.

"Happy to be able to help ye, Laddie. Now be careful on that big ship and take good care of yerself over there in 'merica. That ship they're loadin' right down there is the one ye want."

"Yeh, whadda ye want, boy?" the man loading the ship asked J.W.

"I'm lookin' for the cap'n," he tentatively answered.

"Well, whadda want with 'im?" he quizzed.

"I've booked passage on this ship to 'merica, sir," he politely answered.

"OK, but he's really busy right now tryin' to get this ship loaded. I don't know if e's got time to talk to ye, boy," the grizzled old sailor scowled.

"To tell ye tha truth, I thought he might hire me ta help load out," he replied.

"Aye, we're gonna need some help on this trip. It's getting' harder and harder to hire merchant sailors these days. All ye younger boys wanna go to 'merica. Ain't got no loyalty to merry Ole England no more."

"Hey, Cap'n, you wanna hire me some help ta load this ship?" the sailor yelled at the captain.

"Is he warm and breathin'?" the captain joked.

"Aye he is *right now*, but he might not be when I finish workin' 'im," the sailor shot back.

J.W. was going to enjoy this trip. He liked to laugh and joke with the people around him.

"Well, whatta ye waitin' fer, boy, git to work," barked the sailor.

"How much ye gonna pay me," J.W. asked the captain with a straight face.

"We'll pay ye what you're *worth, boy*," was the quick reply.

With just a hint of a grin, he snapped. "Hell, I caint work tha cheap. I've gotta have some cash when we git ta 'merica."

"Get your ass ta work, boy, and quit trying to be funny," the captain yelled at him. But he knew he would like this kid.

Two days later at daybreak, the captain ordered the anchor to be raised and J.W. was on his way to America.

Arrival in Charleston

Chapter 5

Four weeks at sea was not easy for a country boy on his first voyage. Two hours out from Southampton, as the waves billowed and the ship swayed, his stomach churned.

The first mate in charge of the crew had assigned J.W. the job of swabbing the deck. As he scrubbed with the large, heavy mop, his arms began to tire quickly, but he pushed himself and kept on working. If he could concentrate on mopping, maybe the uneasiness in his stomach would subside.

As the wind picked up and the ship rolled with the waves, he could hold it no longer. He threw down the mop, ran to the rail, and proceeded to vomit violently. When he caught his breath momentarily, he looked up and saw the other crew members howling with laughter.

Alan Underwood, his bunk-mate on the ship, walked over to console him. "Don't fret it matey, it gits better."

"How long does it take to git used to it?" J.W. queried.

"Aww, maybe two or three days if yer lucky. I've seen mateys be sick fer the whole trip."

"Ow long does this trip take?"

"Well, we're sailin' the southerly route down past the Azores. We'll pick up the westerly winds an' current once we git there. This four-master rig'll really pick up speed then. It'll take four or five weeks fer the whole trip. It depends on whether we hit bad weather er not. Don't worry mate, ye'll 'ave your 'sea legs' by then."

The next day J.W. got a new assignment. The first mate told him to go down to the galley and work for the chief cook down there. Cleaning the pots and pans, dishes, and cutlery made for long days. The crew of forty- two men had to eat in shifts. By the time breakfast was over, preparations for dinner began, then, for supper. Cleaning up the whole mess occupied him until almost bedtime.

Staying busy in the galley made the days go by faster, and being below deck, the ride was not as nauseating. (Perhaps he had his *sea legs* now).

Alan, J.W.'s bunkmate, worked on deck manning the sails and taking turns in the *crow's nest*. He always talked to J.W. as they lay in bed at night.

"Where ye goin' when we git to Charleston, J.W.?"

"Gonna catch a stagecoach to Columbia, then on to Asheville. I've been tole ye can git a freight wagon on down to Graham from there. Made enough money the two days I spent loading this rig to pay my fares all the way ta Graham."

"Sounds like ye got a good plan. Ye got a good head on yer shoulders fer a young'un," Alan bragged on him.

"Aye, and I'll git more money in Charleston fer workin' on this rig," he boasted. "Might even have enough to catch me a sweet girl."

The days dragged on, but finally the word spread over the ship from the *crow's nest, "Land ahoy. Land ahoy."*

Alan went running down to the galley to tell J.W. "Are ye gonna stay and hep us unload mate?"

"Nay, I'm anxious to git to Graham. Besides, with my loadin' out money, and what the cap'n owes me, I'll have enough to git me started good."

"OK mate. Good luck to ye. If ye ever give up on fahmin', ye can always find a job as a merchant sailor. Use my name. I'll vouch fer ye."

Preparing to land, J.W. packed his few clothes, then reached up in under the mattress on his bunk where he hid his loadin'-out money, *it wasn't there*. "It's Gone," he screamed.

"What's gone?" Alan appeared surprised.

"My loadin'-out money, Alan. Somebody's stoled it."

"Ye gotta be careful, kid. Ye never know who might take advantage of ye."

"Aye, a bloody bloke in London sold me a sick horse. When I refused to finish payin' fer it, they sent me to debtor's jail."

"Aye a pore man ain't got a chance. We just hafta spend our whole life workin' fer the big money man."

"Gonna go see the cap'n and get my money. I'm outta here, Alan."

"OK kid, be careful and god-speed to ye."

J.W. found the captain checking the cargo manifest. "Mornin' to ye Cap'n. I'm headin' out to Graham. Can I git paid and be on my way? "

"Aye, let's see kid. OK here's ye wages fer this trip."

"But Cap'n, Alan told me how much ye pay everybody else. This ain't near that much."

"Aye kid, but you ain't reg'lar help. I paid you as casual labor. These other boys 'll stay with me."

"Now that ain't right Cap'n," he protested

"Take it or leave it, kid. Now I'm busy unloadin' here. Be on yer way."

J.W. just learned one of many life lessons.

His Daddy used to say, *"Some things ye just have to learn by living."*

The Stage Coach Ride

Chapter 6

"The stage coach line is down that street right there," the dock worker answered J.W.'s question. "It's 'bout a mile or so, but ye can easy walk it."

"Thanks, good Buddy." His mother had told him to be polite to strangers.

Walking up to the ticket office at the stage coach company, he was a little bit *nervous*. Not having as much money as he had counted on, he wondered, *"Will I have enough?"*

"How much fer a ticket to Asheville?" he asked the ticket agent.

"Well, I can sell ye a ticket to Columbia. Ye'll have to buy a ticket from there to Asheville. Ticket to Columbia is three dollars. It'll be two dollars more to Asheville. Stage to Asheville runs tomorrow. Ye'll have to stay the night in Columbia. They's a hotel right beside the stage office.

"Ye can get a clean room for fifty cents, and a little female companionship for a dollar more. Thought a strappin' youngster like yerself might be interested. Tell her Ralph in Charleston mentioned it to ye."

Riding to Columbia, J.W. figured out his money. Only getting fifteen dollars from the captain on the ship changed everything. Usually laborers were paid one dollar per day for labor. He was on the ship thirty-two days, and worked as hard as he could every day. Fifteen dollars was less than half of a *fair wage*. It didn't help any that his two dollars for loading out was stolen by someone on the ship.

"Three dollars for a ticket to Columbia, two dollars for a ticket to Asheville, fifty cents for a hotel room in Columbia, that don't leave but nine fifty. Oh, I forgot, I'll have to eat suppa at the hotel, too. That'll git me down to nine dollars. J.W. grinned as he thought, "I'll have to pass on the female companionship."

Entering the door to the hotel lobby, the first thing he saw was a pretty woman standing at the front desk. With her hands on her hips and a smile on her lips, she spoke to him.

"Hi stranger, what brings ye to town?"

"On my way to Graham to work on a farhm. Just got off a ship in Charleston."

"Were you on the ship for a long time? Must be lonely on a ship for over a month without a little female companionship."

"Aye pretty much so. Ye must be Ralph's friend."

He looked closely at the woman. She was somewhere in her twenties with an ample bosom, (which she proudly displayed). Pretty brown eyes and long dark hair made her eye-catching. He thought she would be prettier without so much *paint* on her face, and lips. Of course, he was used to seeing girls who lived in the *country* - farm girls. They didn't use so much *paint*.

"Do you know Ralph?" she smiled.

"Nay, not really. We just talked fer a few minutes when I bought my ticket."

"Well, when you get checked in, I'll come up and keep you company for a little while."

"I reckon not ma'am. Ain't got much money."

"Didn't you just tell me you were on a freighter for over a month?

Surely they paid you for working."

"Aye, but not much. You're a pretty woman, but I cain't afford ye."

"Are you telling me you ain't got five dollars for some time with a willing woman?"

"Five dollars? Ralph told me one dollar."

"How much money you got boy? Maybe I'll give you a better price. You look like you'd be a lot of fun."

"I'm sure we'd both have fun, ma'am, but I'll have to pass this time."

"Ok, but if ye change yer mind, I'll be around fer a while."

Arising at daylight, he packed his bag, and went downstairs to the front desk. Stopping before he got there, he reached in his pocket and fished out a silver half- dollar. Walking up to the front desk, he laid it on the counter.

The desk clerk looked up and said, "Thanks, young man. Ye have a safe trip to Graham."

As he walked out the door he thought, *these people sure know a lot about me. Maybe I talk too much.*

"Stage leaves at seven o'clock sharp. Stay here close by and don't miss it," the stage coach ticket agent admonished him.

Those mountain roads had gotten a lot of rain and there were ruts in the road everywhere.

Arriving a little past six in the evening in Asheville, he was tired, but needed to try and find a freight wagon heading toward Graham. Inquiring at the stage ticket office in Asheville about a ride to Graham, J.W.'s *heart sank.*

"The last south-bound freight wagon left here at noon today. Won't be another 'til about seven o'clock in the mornin'."

"I ain't got much money left," J.W. realized he was telling too much again. "Cain't afford a hotel room."

"Well, you might go down the street to the Methodist church. They might let you sleep on one of the pews in there. Ain't like a bed, but you can lay down and stretch out. Tell Bishop Cooper I sent you down there. He's my pastor."

Guessing that the house adjacent to the church was where the Bishop lived, J.W. knocked on the door.

An older woman with a sweet grandmotherly smile, opened it. "Well hello young man, what can I do fer ye?"

"Hello ma'am. I was talkin' to the ticket agent at the stage coach office. He told me ta come down and talk to Bishop Cooper. Said he might be able to help me."

"Wait just a minute, young man. I'll go git him. *Robert*, come out here," she shouted. "There's a young man here to see ye."

"Good afternoon, young man. What can I do fer ye?" the Bishop inquired.

"Aye Sir, the gentleman at the ticket office said he was a member of yer church, and that ye might help me."

"Tell me what ye want young man. By the way, what's yer name?"

"Sir, I'm J.W. Presley, and I'm a heading down to Graham. Gonna take over a farhm for Mr. Charles Graham."

"Oh, is that his place at Roarin' Fork?"

"Aye, but how'd you know?"

"My nephew, **Reverend John Wesley Henderson** rides the circuit in Graham. Sent him there myself. He's my sister's boy. Figured he'd fit right in with them mountain folks. We're gittin' ready to start another church at Roarin' Fork. They's lotsa folks around there with growin' families, and with ye a movin' in, I'm convinced we need another church."

"Aye Sir, I reckon ye cain't have too many churches, what with thieves and cheats everywhere ye look takin' advantage of folks. **John Wesley Henderson**, huh. Sounds like a good name for a Methodist preacher."

"Yep, my sister, John's mother, wanted him to be a preacher. She thought with a name like that, he couldn't help but be one."

"Well, I'm shore lookin' forward to meetin' him, Bishop."

"What can I hep ye with right now?" the Bishop asked.

"Need a place to sleep tonight. Gonna try to catch a ride in tha mornin' on a freight hauler headin' south. The ticket office man said ye might let me sleep in the church on a pew."

"Yep, I reckon we can do that fer ye being as how ye'll be a parishioner of John Wesley. Wait here just a minute and let me tell my wife what we're a doin'."

When Bishop Cooper returned, he was carrying a pillow and a blanket. "These might make it a little easier to sleep on them pews."

He handed the pillow and blanket to J.W., and said, "Wife said supper'll be ready in 'bout an hour. Yer welcome to eat with us if yer hungry."
"I shore do 'preciate that, preacher. It's real nice ta meet some good folks fer a change."

Waking before daybreak, he had to look around and figure out where he was. Momentarily, he had forgotten.

Jumping up quickly, he ran outside and back to the stage coach office. Knowing freight haulers would be picking up packages from the arriving stages, he figured he could catch a ride with one of them to Graham.

Speaking to the driver of the first wagon he asked," Er ye a goin' ta Graham?"

"Naw, son," the old driver replied. I just go ta Waynesville. Second wagon back behind me. He makes that trip ever day. Lots of stuff goin' in ta Graham."

"OK thank ye, sir," his mother had taught him very well to be polite.

"Pardon me sir, er ye a goin' to Graham this mornin'?"

"Shore am. Ye lookin' fer a ride?" When J.W. nodded his assent, the driver asked, "can ye handle a rifle? We be goin' through Injun country. Gen'lly don't have no trouble, but ye never know 'bout them Injuns."

"How long'll it take ta git down there?" he wondered.

"Well, if we don't have no trouble, 'bout five hours. We ort ta be there 'bout dinner time."

"How much ye gonna charge me fer the ride?" He held his breath.

"Just handle that rifle fer me and they'll be no charge. Ye might wanna help me unload when we git there."
He breathed a sigh of relief and sat back to enjoy the ride.

The road was rough and full of ruts, but the scenery was *beautiful*. Trees and flowers like he had not seen since leaving Dublin were in abundance. He remarked to the driver. "Shore is purty 'round here, what with all the trees and flowers."

"Yep, I reckon. We kinda get used ta it, and don't' pay it much mind."
"We ain't seen no Injuns yet," J.W. observed.

"Don't go ta braggin' too quick. We ain't there yit. Judging by the sun, we're 'bout a half hour out."

As they finally arrived in town without encountering any Indians, J.W. was a bit surprised at what he saw.

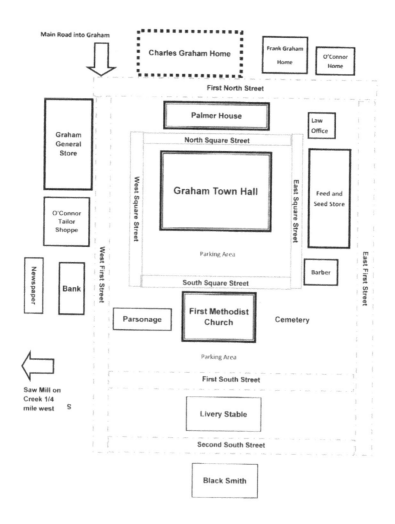

Main Road into Graham

Charles Graham Home

Frank Graham Home

O'Connor Home

First North Street

Palmer House

Law Office

Graham General Store

North Square Street

West Square Street

Graham Town Hall

East Square Street

Feed and Seed Store

O'Connor Tailor Shoppe

Parking Area

West First Street

Barber

South Square Street

East First Street

Newspaper

Bank

First Methodist Church

Parsonage

Cemetery

Parking Area

First South Street

Saw Mill on Creek 1/4 mile west   S

Livery Stable

Second South Street

Black Smith

Graham, North Carolina

Chapter 7

On the north end of town, before they reached the town square, two streets were lined with large, two- story houses. The largest house, a three-story, was prominently located on the corner of First North Street and Main.

Pointing it out to J.W., the driver explained, "That's Mr. Graham's house. Next door to him is **Frank Graham's** house, and next door to him is the **O'Connor's** house.

"Wow, them's *some fine houses*." He was impressed. "Who's Frank Graham, and who er tha O'Connors?"

"Frank is Mr. Graham's nephew. He runs the Graham Gen'ral Store. The O'Connors run the Tailor and Seamstress shop. Mr. O'Connor's the tailor and his wife's a seamstress.

"Mr. Graham paid ther fare on tha ship to git 'em to come here. Word is he wanted 'em here so bad, they don't hafta pay him back."

"How come they don't hafta pay him back, but I hafta work fer 'im fer four years to pay mine back?"

"They got *skills* and yer jist a dirt farmer, I reckon."

"Aye, I reckon, too. Anyways, I signed up ta work, and I was learnt by my Maw and Paw ta keep yer word."

"The O'Connor's has got a real purty little red-headed gal named **Sally**. She's got green eyes and nice wide hips. She'll make somebody a good wife. She 'll make purty babies. Ye oughta check her out."

"Aye, I will when I git a chance."

"She works fer Mr. Graham in the Gen'ral Store. Sells piece goods and fabrics. Sends a lotta work right next door to 'er Maw and Paw in ther shop. We'er a gonna unload at the back door of the Gen'ral Store. I'll interduce ye ta 'er."

As the wagon continued on into the middle of town, J.W. got his first glimpse of Graham.

Standing squarely in the center, was the Town Hall, a two-story clapboard building painted white. Built in a perfect two-hundred-foot square, the four facades faced North, East, South, and West. Commercial buildings faced the Town Hall on all four sides. Doors on each façade of the building opened to the inside, providing easy access from any direction.

Graham's General Store sat on the corner of Town Square West on the north end of the square facing Town Hall. A two-story building, it was the second-largest commercial building in town. Owned by **Charles Graham**, it was managed by **Frank Graham**, a nephew of the owner.

Moving south, down the west side, sat **O'Connor's Tailor Shop**, operated by **Patrick O'Connor** and his wife, **Eunice**. They had learned their trade in London and were recruited for Graham by the same agent who recruited J.W. Presley.

Next door to the General Store, their shop was conveniently located. Their daughter, **Sally**, worked in Graham's General Store and referred many clients to her parents.

Adjacent to the O'Connor's shop was the **First State Bank**. A college classmate of Charles Graham, **Ulysses Winslow**, owned and operated the bank.

Immediately behind the Bank, a small unimpressive building housed a printing press. It was in this make-shift operation that

George Whitfield Eubank produced a sporadic weekly newspaper he named *The Graham Gazette*.

George was the son of the Bank's **Vice President, Elias Dawson Eubank**, who had arranged, with encouragement from Charles Graham, the financial backing necessary for this addition to the town. Graham residents had previously received their printed news from the Raleigh Register delivered by mail. Although received as progress by most, in truth, the news remained just as dated.

The South side of the square was occupied by the **First Methodist Church**, and a parsonage for the minister, **John Wesley Henderson**, and his wife, **Nellie**. On the other side of the church was a small cemetery. In the coming years, it was destined to become *filled with the bodies* of many young residents of Graham.

First Methodist Church was built to accommodate three hundred people, but rarely was more than half full. Bishop Cooper had hopes that the fast-growing town would soon need that much space.

A large open lot behind the church was left vacant to provide space for wagons, and hitching posts for mules and horses on worship Sundays. Behind the parking area, the **Livery Stable and Wagon Shop** were situated.

Jim Murphy operated the Livery Stable. He was born in **Murphy's Landing**, and learned his trade serving in the U.S. Army. As a member of a cavalry unit in the *War of 1812*, he was taught to build wagons for every conceivable purpose.

It didn't take a lot of brains to shovel horse manure and tend horses, but he was *proud* of his wagon-making skills. Mr. Graham had offered free land, but Murphy was a proud man. "I don't want to be beholden to nobody, I'll *pay for my land*," he declined Graham's offer. He did, however, agree to bring his shop and talents to the center of commerce in Graham.

Immediately behind the Livery, the **Blacksmith Shop** had been built. **Bertram Wills**, the blacksmith, had moved to Graham from

Waynesville. Large hands and forearms were needed to *blacksmith*, and Wills was well endowed with the necessary physique. **Vernon**, Bertram's teen-aged son, sometimes did odd jobs for Charles Graham.

A fast-growing town would present many opportunities for service-providing businesses. Then, too, Mr. Graham had **donate**d enough land to build the shop and a dwelling house for the operator. Wills felt very good about the *deal* he had arranged with Graham

On the east side, south-end corner lot sat the barber shop. A small two-story building, where the upstairs provided living space for the barber, **John Perkins**. John was a short, stocky, man with a ruddy complexion. He stood on a small crate in order to reach the top of tall men's heads. Cutting hair and providing shaves took most of his time, but occasionally, he did a blood-letting for medicinal purposes.

Adjacent to the barber shop, a feed-and-seed store was located. Owned also by Charles Graham, it was operated by **Fenton Murphy**, the son of the livery stable owner.

Moving north on the east side of the square, the lawyer, **William Mahan**, had an office. Getting a law degree at the University of North Carolina in Chapel Hill, he believed it would be easier to establish a practice in a small town, and Graham was eager to have a classmate be a local lawyer in his town.

Located in the northeast corner of **Town Hall**, the sheriff had his office. Two cells with bars and locked doors were at the back of the building.

The sheriff, **John Calvin (J.C.) Schultz** had several years of experience in law enforcement, working for the high-sheriff in Knoxville. He was a large man, six feet four inches tall and weighing close to three hundred pounds. Intimidated by his sheer size, most of the townspeople were compliant and law-abiding. His wife, **Carolyn**, was a sister of Reverend Henderson. Sheriff

Schultz had a son, **Joe**, who served as his deputy, and a raven-haired daughter named **Savannah**.

A relatively quiet town, the jail cells were seldom used. Sometimes on Saturday night a youngster would drink too much at the saloon and get rowdy. An over-night stay in jail always handled the problem.

Conrad Palmer had moved to Graham to operate a hotel, *The Palmer House.* Learning the trade in Atlanta while working in a hotel there, he was another classmate of Charles Graham at the University of North Carolina at Chapel Hill. Graham built the building but sold it to Palmer for a low price as an incentive to get him and his wife, **Laura Taylor Palmer**, to move to Graham.

Occupying the entire north end of the square, the hotel rose to an imposing four-stories. On the first floor, the lobby boasted four separate seating sections. Plush upholstered chairs bought from a North Carolina furniture builder, adorned the area. Large Grecian-style urns were strategically placed to be eye-catching as one entered the lobby. A large ballroom, upscale restaurant, and a saloon occupied the remainder of the first floor. It was really impressive for a small town, but Palmer believed that, "to become a big town, you had to look like one."

Charles Graham, a forward-thinking man, had seen the necessity to provide a place where the needs of the farmers could be met. His younger brother, **William**, had been quite successful developing the land he owned over in Central North Carolina.

"It's worth the effort to help the farmers establish their homes and families on your land," he told Charles. "When they have roots, they'll stay, and you'll prosper, too."

This family philosophy of *enlightened self-interest* was embraced by Charles Graham and became his operating strategy for the growth of his town.

Driving the wagon around to the back of Graham's store, the driver banged on the door. "Delivery Mr, Graham," he shouted.

Frank Graham opened the door, and spoke to the driver, "Just put that stuff over here in this corner. Sally, your fabric from Knoxville is here."

Smiling as she hurried into the stockroom, Sally almost bumped into J.W. "Oh excuse me," she blushed. "Don't believe I know ya, sir,"

"J.W. Presley ma'am. Pleased to make yer acquaintance." He took off his hat and smiled back at her.

"Oh yes, Mr. Presley, are ya takin' over the Roarin' Fork place?"

"Name's J.W. ma'am. Mr. Presley's my grandfather. But aye, I am taking over 'at place ma'am." He did like her green eyes and her shapely curves..

"Mr. Graham's office is upstairs. I'll go tell him you're here." Sally volunteered.

"I shore 'preciate it, ma'am," he smiled at her. As Sally started up the stairs, he nodded to the driver, "Aye, she is a beauty."

Winking at J.W. and looking at Frank Graham for his approval, the driver replied, "If ye play yer cards right, ye might git ye a good helper on 'at farm. Come on, let's git this stuff unloaded afore Mr. Graham gits here."

"Hello J.W., I'm Charles Graham. Welcome to our little town. I'm lookin' forward to workin' with ye. When ye finish unloadin', come on upstairs and we'll talk a bit."

Charles Graham was a tall, handsome, well-dressed, aristocratic gentleman. Wearing a long coat with a white cotton shirt, a silk brocade vest which hid the gallouses he used to hold up his pants, he was an imposing man. A silk ascot covered his neck and filled the space from his open collar. Although not an officially-titled **Blue Blood** himself, his ancestry was filled with such people. Articulate, intelligent, and educated, he was a bit intimidating to the young Mr. Presley.

Pausing at the top of the stairs to catch his breath, J.W. then walked over and knocked on the door of Mr. Graham's office. "Yes sir, Mr. Graham, I brung ye the papers yer man in London told me to give ye when I got 'ere."

"Great, let's have a look."

"He told me that after four years. I'd 'ave ye paid off fer my trip. Then we'd start a workin' on **halvers** fer the crops I raise to sell. What'ye plan on a raisin' sir?"

"Well, most people 'round these parts raise tobacco. This river-bottom land grows it real good, and it brings a good price. We're exportin' a lot of it back to England. Of course, I'm sure ya noticed the stands of trees we got growin' here. My saw-mill here in town produces a lotta good lumber for constructin' buildin's and houses. We buy a lot of timber from all the farms in these parts."

"You mean yer buyin' timber from yer own property?" J.W. smiled and nodded his head. "That's a purty smart thang right ther."

"Yes, and for the farmers, you don't haffta transport it very far."

"Sounds like a good deal ta me. Don't have to worry 'bout sellin' it neither." He liked Mr. Graham and what he was doing for the farmers.
"J.W., it seems there's been a bit of misunderstanding about your indenture."

"What kinda misunderstandin', Mr. Graham?"

"Have a seat next to me, and we will review your Contract of

Indenture." Once seated, Graham began pointing to conditions written in the document that J.W. had signed. Because it was likely that he wasn't very adept at reading, Graham carefully explained each point.

"The time required to repay your passage from England to America is the four years your Agent was speaking about. If he failed to explain the details, I am very sorry. Because I am setting you up with everything you need to get started in your new life, it will take you several more years of working to cover my upfront expenses."

"How many more years until I'm paid up and get my 25 acres, Mr. Graham,?" he asked with a worried expression on his face.

"Now that's another misunderstanding, Son. After you have worked out all the expenses related to travel and additional costs of setting you up, which may be another 3 – 4 years, you will receive 10 acres of your own to farm, not 25."

"But Mr. Graham, that's not anything like what that Agent told me back in England."

"I feel badly that the conditions of the Indenture Contract were not clearly explained to you before you set out on that long trip, but don't get discouraged. You are a strong and healthy young man with a bright future ahead of you. I am making a considerable investment in that future and plan for you to be successful," Graham replied.

"I am grateful, Sir, but since I left England, bad things jist keep happenin' ta me," he said in a defeated tone.

"You've made the right decision to seek a better life for yourself so don't let yourself get dragged down in the dumps. Let's talk about all the things I am making available to you to help you start over in a new land."

Wanting to turn his thinking toward the future, Graham began to repeat the list of resources, and to paint a vision that would hopefully revive the young man's hopes and dreams.

"You're going to have a cabin with a bed, table and chairs to start out living. Outside is a shed for the two mules I'm supplying. You'll have a wagon and all the tools necessary to begin working." As he spoke, he watched J.W.'s face for signs of acceptance.

"I'm setting you up with a line of credit at my general store, at the livery, and at the feed store so you can get all the provisions necessary. Because you're all alone, I'm also giving you a worker for the first few years to help you with all the heavy work like logging," Graham added.

J.W. began to hold his head up and listen as Graham continued. "That's not all. You'll also have a boar and 4 sows so you can raise some pigs for food. There'll be a rooster and 10 hens for meat and eggs. After you start your family, I'll add a milk cow.

"After you get settled in at Roaring Fork, you might go across the creek and meet your neighbors, the Johnson family. They came to Old Yellow Creek under an indenture contract. They can give you an idea of how things have worked out for them.

"Now it's gettin' pretty late in the day so I'm gonna' put you up in the hotel tonight and make sure you have supper. Before you leave, go downstairs and let that young lady you met help you make out your list of supplies. You can load out in your new wagon tomorrow morning. How's that sound?"

"Thank ye, Sir, **I am** a bit tired and hungry. What did ye say that young lassie's name was?"

"Her name is Sally O'Conner. Right pretty isn't she?"

"Aye, she **is**, Sir. She **might** jist be tha one I need."

Returning to the first floor, he found Sally busily unpacking the new fabrics she had just received from the Dry Goods Wholesale Company in Knoxville.

"Pardon me, Miss Sally, Mr. Graham said I might git ya ta help me with a list of supplies I'ma goinna need out on tha farhm," he had his hat in his hand.

"Of course, Mr. Presley. Just give me a coupla more minutes here, then I'll be right with ya," Sally smiled.

"I shore 'preciate it ma'am. I cain't write much. I'ma gonna need a list fer the feed store and tha Livery, too.

"OK, **now** Mr. Presley, I can finish workin' on this in tha mornin'. Let me get a pen and some paper to write on."

Sally began to write the list for the General Store first. "Let's see, sheets and a blanket for the bed. Knives, forks, spoons, dishes and cups for the kitchen. Pitcher and bowl, wash cloths and towels for the wash basin," she continued listing. "Ya'll need some flour, meal, and sugar. OK, I'll gather this all together in the mornin'.

"Now ya can get a plow, shovel, hoe, hatchet, and axe over at tha feed store. They'll have some feed for tha mules over there, too. Get some corn seed. Ya can still raise that **this** year. There'll be plenty of time before first frost to do that. Ya'll need it to feed the mules this year.

"Mr. Murphy over at the Livery can get you a team of mules. He'll have a wagon and a set of harnesses. I'll write a note to him and tell him Mr. Graham said to charge it to him. His son, Fenton, runs the feed store, so I'll write him a note, too."

"I'm much obliged to ye, Miss Sally. Ye shore 'ave made this a lot easier."

"Happy to be of service to you, Mr. Presley. Mr. Graham asked me ta help you all I could. There's a lotta details when you're just getting started. I still remember when we first came here from London about ten years ago. I was just seven years old, but I had to do a lotta work myself."

"Thanks ag'in Miss Sally. I'll take these notes over ta tha Livery and tha Feed Store. Do ye think it's alright if I tell them I'll pick it up in tha mornin'?"

"Yes, that'll give them time to check with Mr. Graham if they have any questions. Pick up tha wagon and mules first; that way ya'll be able to load out quickly." she smiled, "And it'll give me some more time to get all this stuff here ready for you."

After walking to the Livery and the Feed Store, he headed for the hotel. *"Wow this shore is a fancy place. Ain't never stayed in nuthin' nice as this afore"* he thought. *"Maybe my luck's achangin'."*

As soon as J.W. left and before she closed out and headed home for the day, Sally began gathering all the items on his list that were on hand in Graham's General Store.

"Momma," Sally chirped inside the O'Connor home, "Guess who I met today?"

"Must of been somebody nice from the look on your face, girl," Eunice O'Connor grinned.

"Yes indeed, Momma. I met the young man who will be farming the place at Roaring Fork. He is ever so polite and he's good lookin' too."

"Now young lady, don't you be gettin' any ideas on a first meetin'. You had best be lookin' for a husband with better prospects than a poor dirt farmer," Eunice advised her with a scowl.

"Who would that be, Momma? There aren't many young men around here not already married," Sally replied.

"Well for one, there's Mr. Fenton Murphy over at the Feed Store. Now Sally, you need to be thinkin' more practical and not getting' all swoony over the first young man ye meet," Eunice said.

"Aah, Momma, you're talk like you were never young."

Supplies

Chapter 8

At seven A.M., when Jim Murphy arrived to open The Livery, J.W. was sitting by the front door on the ground waiting for him. Murphy, a tall, wiry man, about forty-five years old, with graying, curly hair and a close-cropped beard, greeted him.

"Mornin' J.W., yer out mighty early."

"Aye, Mr. Murphy figger it'll take me more'n one trip to haul all my stuff. Don't know exactly where I'ma goin' neither.

"Well, that's easy enuff. Jist head North straight outta town. Bout nine miles out, ye'll see the big crick runnin' inta tha river. That ther's Roarin' Fork Crick. Take that fork in tha road right ther', bout half a mile on ta tha house. It'll take me bout ten minutes ta git tha mules harnessed an' hitched ta tha wagon."

"Alright Mr. Murphy. I'ma goin' first ta tha feed store and pick up over ther'. Is tha Mr. Murphy at tha Feed Store any of yer clan?"

"Yep, that's Fenton. He's my oldest boy. He's a workin' fer Graham right now, but he'll take over this place when I quit. I'ma learnin' him to make wagons now. He comes over at'er he closes the Feed Store, and he'ps me work on 'em. We do fixin' work, too. If ya ever need sumpin' fixed, we can do it."

"Figgered I'd git tha heavy stuff first, then go see Miss Sally fer the house stuff. She shore is a purty thang."

"That she is. Think Fenton's had his eye on 'er fer a while now. Told him she could shore make some purty babies, what with them nice wide hips and all."

"Thank ye Mr. Murphy. I'll be seeing ye around town. Headin' over ta see yer boy, Fenton."

Be careful, and good luck to ya boy. Stop in and see me anytime yer in town."

Walking into the feed store, J.W. spoke, "Hello Mr. Fenton. Ye got me ready ta load out?"

"Almost ready, J.W. That stack settin' there b'side the door, I've got wrote down on tha bill. Ya can go 'head an' start loadin' it. I'll be finished writin' this other stack, then help ya load."

"Aye, thank ye sir. I might have ta come back this afta'noon, an' load out over at Mr. Graham's place. That Miss Sally shore is a sweet lady."

As they loaded the wagon, Fenton frowned "Yep, ya got that right, and she makes a mean apple pie, too. Got ta eat her pie at tha last pie suppa. Hadda pay fifty cents fer it."

"When do tha "ave "em pie suppas, Mr. Fenton?"

"Oh it's gen'lly 'bout October affta tha crop harvest. Las' year tha had a daince on Sat'dee, an' tha Pie suppa on Sundee'.

"OK, I got sev'ral weeks ta save me up some money. Ima gonna buy Sally's pie this yeahr," J. W. was thinking. "See ya Mr. Fenton. Ima headin ta the farhm."

Pulling the loaded wagon, the team of mules moved slowly. The ten miles to the farm took over an hour. Working by himself, it took J.W. about another hour to unload and find a place in the shed for everything. It was nearly noon when he got back to town, although the mules moved faster pulling the empty wagon.

"Mornin' J.W.," Sally smiled as he walked into the store. "wondered what happen' to ya. I was lookin' for you this mornin'."

"Hadda make two loads, Miss Sally. Hope I did'nt cause too much trouble a waitin' on me."

"No trouble J.W., it just gave me more time to get your stuff together. Mr. Graham wants to talk to you before you leave. Somethin' bout a helper to do loggin'.

"Momma's got some dinner fixed over in the shop. Wanna go over and have some dinner with us? I know Momma'd like ta meet you."

"Thanks, Miss Sally. It's mighty nice of ya to invite me. Ar' ye shore yer Momma won't mind?"

"Oh no, I told her I was gonna ask you."

"OK, but do I need ta talk ta Mr. Graham first?"

"Yes, go on upstairs and knock on his door."

J.W. knocked on the door and Graham quickly opened it. "Mornin', J.W. come in and have a seat. Did you find everything ya needed in the stores and at the farm?"

"Shore did, Mr. Graham," J.W. smiled. "Miss Sally, Mr. Murphy, and Fenton made shore I got all I'ma gonna need out ther', and the farhm is a purty place what with them trees and all."

"Good. You are gonna need a helper to get started with the loggin', and I'd like to see you get started on that the first of next week. **Vernon Wills**, Bertram's boy, over at the blacksmith shop has agreed to help you for a while. He's a good worker and has done some loggin'. It's too late to start a tobacco crop **this year**, but you can do that next year. And you can get a crop of corn planted to feed the livestock. Don't wanna have to buy feed for too long. We need to get some revenue started to get your indenture paid off as soon as possible."

"Aye, that we do, sir. I know what 'appens when a feller cain't git his bills paid."

"Go on home young man. Get settled in at your place and rest some this weekend. Vernon'll be there Monday mornin' at seven o'clock.

"Good luck, J. W. and be careful; loggin' can be dangerous work."

"Thank ya very much, Mr. Graham," J.W. said as he closed the office door and started down the steps.

Sally was waiting for him at the bottom of the staircase and she felt a slight tingle watching his now familiar crooked smile.

"J.W., let's double check your supply list before we head over to have dinner," Sally said as she returned his smile.

"Oh, I trust ya, Miss Sally. I know ya got it all together fer me and I really do appreciate yer help," J.W. said as he admired Sally's shiny red-brown tresses which for some reason were hanging loose around her shoulders today.

"Well if you're ready, lets head on next door and eat a bite. Momma should be ready for us."

 J.W. held the door open as Sally put on her bonnet and walked through ahead of him. He was somewhat nervous about meeting Sally's Mother and more so her Father.

"What will they thank of me, a poor dirt fahma, comin inta their house with ther purty daughter?" he thought.

As they approached the tailor shop, Sally said, "We'll be walking through the store part to the back room where Momma'll have the table set for us."

Eunice O'Conner was the first to see them when they opened the door to the shop. She was a short woman of medium build with streaked hair showing a bit of grey and a kind smile much like her daughter's. She was wearing a brightly colored dress under a clean white apron.

"Hello, you must be Mr. Presley, the young man who'll be working the farm at Roaring Fork," she said as she held out her hand to greet J.W.

He suddenly felt self-conscious about his soiled clothing but he took off his cap and quickly rubbed his right hand on his pants before extending it to Mrs. O'Connor. "Yes Maam, I am. Please call me J.W. It's so kind of ya ta have me in fer dinner."

"We're glad to have you. It's good to know who your neighbors are gonna be," she replied with a grin." Come on back and meet Sally's Daddy."

As they walked through the shop, J.W. noticed the expertly tailored suits and dresses in various stages of completion. The shelves along both side walls held bolts of fabric and several tables held tools of their trade along with sundry notions.

Patrick O'Connor stood about six feet, was broad shouldered, and mostly bald except for a fringe of salt and pepper that matched his full beard. At first glance, he seemed less friendly than Mrs. O'Connor but when he spoke, J.W. finally relaxed.

"Welcome, Mr. Presley, I understand you're getting set up to farm the place out at Roaring Fork for Mr. Graham."

"That's right, Sir, and everybody in town's been very helpful. It's so nice of yer family ta invite me in fer a meal when ya don't hardly know me," J.W. said.

"We remember what it's like being in a new place not knowin' anyone nor what the future holds, young man. We were in tha same position ten years ago when we first got here from London. Mr. Graham helped us get set up in our business and we're glad to pass on that help to newcomers to our growing community," O'Conner replied.

"Stop all this yakin' now and sit yerselfs down for dinner. This young man is hungry and has a long way to get back to his place," Eunice said.

Everyone laughed as they made their way to the small table at the back of the shop. Eunice had set places for four and there was a plate of side meat with potatoes, corn, and beans next to a stack of corn bread. J.W. could feel his mouth watering for a home cooked meal, something he had not enjoyed for longer than he could remember.

While they were eating, Patrick probed J.W. about his history and his decision to make the difficult journey to a new land. J.W told him about leaving his family farm in Dublin with hopes of a better life in London only to face one bad situation after another.

"I figgered that if I was ta have any chance fer better days, I'd have ta take a try at the indenture offered by Graham's agent in London. Fer a time, I was feelin' like I'd made a bad mistake. Nuthin' was turnin' out like tha agent promised. But now, I'm startin' ta feel more hopeful agin'," J. W. explained.

"What are you hoping to do after you get set up down there at Roaring Fork, Presley," O'Conner asked.

"Well, I got a long road ahead to pay back Mr. Graham for tha indenture plus all the supplies I'll be a needin'. Afta that, I'm a plannin' to buy me fifteen more acres of land and build me a nice house fer the wife and family I oughta have by that time," J.W. said with a smile and a glance at Sally.
"You might oughta take that last part a little slow, young man. A wife and family is a big responsibility," O'Conner frowned.

"Yes Sir, yore ever so right but I'm a hard worker and I can be trusted to do my duty, Mr. O'Conner."

After they finished dinner, Sally began helping her Mother clean up the small kitchen area of the shop. Mrs. O'Conner told her to wrap up some corn bread, potatoes and corn for J.W. to take with him.

"Mr. and Mrs. O'Conner, I wanna thank you ag'in for yer hospitality," J.W. said as he prepared to leave for his ten-mile trip back to the cabin at Roaring Fork.

"Wait, Sally said, I'll walk with you back to the store so you can load up all your supplies. I have ta get back to work anyway."

Eunice handed J.W. a basket with the leftovers wrapped in a linen towel. "Take this home with you, J.W. It will give you something to eat before you turn in tonight."

"That's so kind of ya, Ma'am," J.W. said as he looked back to catch O'Conner eyeing him very seriously.

Sally was smiling and talking as they walked together back toward Graham's store where he had left his wagon and mules.

"I hope you'll try to come to the harvest get-togethers in October. That's just a little over two months from now. There's always a fun dance on Saturday and a pie sale after church on Sunday. It'll be a good time for you to meet other folks," Sally said excitedly with a smile.

"I don't know much bout dancin'," he said looking at the ground with a lock of his sandy hair falling on his forehead," but I'd shore like ta see ye a'gin, Miss Sally."

Her pale skin began to show signs of blushing and she added, "You needn't worry about that. I can show you the ropes and you'll have fun."

Patrick and Eunice shared their impressions of J.W. as they finished cleaning up to return to work in the shop.

"I hope Sally isn't getting any funny ideas about that boy," Patrick said." He can't be thinking about marrying and raisin' a family when he just got here without nothing to his name. "

"You worry too much, Patrick. He seems like a nice boy with big dreams but also common sense," Eunice replied. "Let the young folks enjoy just being Sfriends for a while."

Back at the store, J.W. loaded his wagon, said goodbye to Sally, and began his trek to the cabin. He found himself whistling and thinking about his future.

Setting Up at Roaring Fork

Chapter 9

By the time J.W. reached his cabin, the sun indicated it was mid-afternoon. He knew he had much to do before dark to get everything unloaded and set up and be ready to start all the work he could do alone over the weekend.

Monday he would have to turn his attention to logging as that was a priority for Mr. Graham who had said to expect his helper, Vernon Wills, at 7:00 am the first of the new week.

He started by unhooking the mules and leading them to the shed where he had laid out some hay and a large trough of water earlier in the day after unloading the wagon on his first trip from town.

Remembering how helpful Miss Sally had been in making a list of the important things he would need, he smiled again.

He carried in his tick mattress and blankets and arranged them on the iron bed frame, which now looked much more inviting with the soft bedding material.

Placing the basket of leftovers given to him by Mrs. O'Connor on the small wooden table, he thought, *"This old place is startin' to look like home."*

Next he carried in the Dutch oven, an iron kettle, tin plates, cups, and other utensils Sally had insisted he should have. He set the pitcher and bowl next to his newly made bed, then thought it would be smart to pull up some water from the well, so that he could wash off a bit before retiring.

After he finished unloading and placing all his belongings where he thought they should be, he sat down on one of the two chairs to survey his new place.

The cabin was only one room, but it was the first place he could call **his** since leaving his family farm. He day-dreamed about how he could turn it into a pleasant place to come home to every night especially if there was a pretty little wife waiting for him.

With the Dutch oven and kettle in the fireplace, the freshly-made bed, and the table set for supper, he recalled the long trek he had made to this point. He told himself, *"I'm gonna be a land owner one day and have sumpin' of value ta share with my wife and kids. My Mama back in Dublin will be prouda her boy."*

He went outside to collect small pieces of fallen limbs for kindling. He wanted to be able to start heating water for coffee in the morning.

Checking on the mules, he then returned to the cabin to enjoy the supper he had carried home from dinner with the O'Connor family. Even cold, the combination of corn, beans, potatoes, and cornbread tasted wonderful to him.

As he pulled out the last piece of cornbread, he discovered something else in the bottom of the basket. It was a small leather-bound book. He held it up to the light of a candle that he had lit on the table and could see some lettering.

The sun was setting and darkness was falling outside the little cabin, and he suddenly realized how tired he was.

With the small book in his hand, he made his way to his bed, almost collapsing into it. He placed the book under his pillow and sighed, *"Miss Sally, I shore wish I could read this book caus'in ya gave it ta me."*

He could feel the rays of the rising sun shining through his window and licking at his forehead as he slowly opened his eyes and stretched. It took a moment for him to remember where he was.

"I need ta git cracken," he thought. *"Only got two days to get a corn crop out afore I got ta start loggin them trees for Mr. Graham."*

He poured a little water from his pitcher into his bedside bowl, splashed his face, and put on his trousers.

The remainder of the water drawn last night from the well behind the cabin was dispensed into the iron kettle along with half a tin cup full of coffee beans. He lit his pile of kindling and while he waited for the water to boil, he made a trip to the outhouse to inspect another necessary facility.

Back inside, he smelled the welcome aroma of coffee. When he tried to pick up the kettle, he quickly realized he would need a towel or some type of cloth to protect his hand. He sat down to savor the warm welcome liquid while planning his morning activities.

It occurred to him that he had consumed all the food he brought home from the O'Connor's last night. If he wanted to have something to eat today or in the days ahead, he needed to figure out how to cook something.

Cooking was not a skill he had learned while helping on the family farm. The only experience he had was watching the cook on the ship and washing dishes.

"A man best lern ta feed his self afore anythin' else'll be possible," he thought and laughed at his own joke. *"Sum time soon, I need ta git me a wife ta help me with the household chores."*

A vision of Sally preparing supper for him briefly entered his day dream before he set about fixing the limited items at hand. *"I've got ta start plowin' then plantin' the corn tween now and Monday mornin',"* he reminded himself.

He loaded the Dutch oven with a few cups of dried beans, then went back to the well drawing more water to cover them for the long slow cooking process. He put a handful of potatoes, also covering them with water, in the other iron pot that he would hang on the movable arm above the fire.

Next, he went out searching for additional kindling and small logs so that he would hopefully have a stack ready for use next week.

He was able to find enough wood on the ground to keep him supplied for at least two days but he thought, *"Monday, I'll have Vernon help me cut some small trees, saw them into usable logs, and stack them near the cabin."*

By now, it was mid-morning and he was already feeling some hunger pangs but he needed to start on planting the corn before he could rest. He made a check on the beans and potatoes to be sure there was no danger of fire and headed out to the shed.

The mules seemed to be rested from yesterday's trips and he selected the larger of the two, whom he decided to call **Jake**, to hook up to the plow. His plan was to finish the plowing before dark.

He would take a break half way, change mules find something to eat, then continue until nightfall.

He selected a flat area and walked off a space of approximately 100 by 50 feet for his corn field. With Jake hooked to the plow, he began the process, one row at a time.

To break the monotony, he whistled and periodically talked to his mule. "Jake, ole boy, you an me gonna make Roaring Fork Farm a show place. Jist stick wit me an I'll treat ya right."

When the sun hit the two o'clock spot in the sky, he pulled Jake back to the shed, refreshed the hay and water, and went into his cabin to cool off and regain his strength. He could smell the beans cooking and the potatoes were bubbling in the iron pot.

Moving the iron pot away from the fire, he carefully removed a few potatoes and put them on a tin plate. He reheated the leftover morning coffee and sat down for a meager meal of potatoes and a very strong dark mug full of coffee.

"All right, **Miss Agnes**, it's yer turn," he said to the other mule as he hooked her up to the plow to finish the day's work.

As the sun was kissing the top of the mountain ridge, he was just finishing breaking up the clods of dirt in the final row of his would-be corn field. "Ya done good, Miss Agnes, now we both need to rest. Tomorrow is corn-plantin' day."

The beans, even without any seasoning, were welcome to his growling stomach. Mixed with the potatoes, he thought, "Not bad for a youn'un with no cooking 'sperience."

He rinsed off his plate and cup in a wooden tub, packed down the remaining embers, washed his hands and face, and fell onto his tick mattress with a feeling of accomplishment.

"Tomorrow, we plant our first crop," he smiled as he drifted off to sleep.

Sunday brought with it another clear warm day of scheduled work. After drinking two mugs of his coffee, he headed out to the shed to load a bucket with seed corn. *"Mr. Fenton tole me this 'ere kinda feed corn'll be ready ta pick in bout sixty days, 'nuff time ta beat tha first frost."*

Since there were still beans and potatoes left, he didn't need to spend time fixing more food and could get in a full day of work.

"Good Mornin', Jake and Miss Agnes Hope ya both slept good. Ya got a day a rest ahead a ya. I gotta do all the hard stuff taday," he laughed.

With a bucket full of seed corn, he headed out to his cornfield and methodically sowed the seed using a hoe to cover them with dirt row by row.

Although tiring, the seeding process went faster than the plowing and he was finished by early afternoon. He stopped for a half-hour or so to eat and rest.

Then he went out to the shed to organize his tools and supplies in a manner that would make for easier access to what he might need.

While he was taking inventory and rearranging his newly-acquired property, he untied the mules and let them have a bit of roaming exercise.

With the sun headed toward the ridge, he secured Jake and Miss Agnes in the shed, returned to his cabin, ate his leftovers, cleaned up, and turned in early for the night.

He had started to develop a routine. He felt **proud**, and was beginning to feel like he was home.

Logging Begins

Chapter 10

The Monday morning sunlight danced across J.W.'s face. He yawned, stretched, and pulled himself out of bed thinking of his new challenge of the day.

As he was pouring himself a tin mug of coffee, he heard sounds of what he believed to be the neighing of a horse outside the cabin.

Eager to actually talk to someone other than Jake and Miss Agnes, he opened the cabin door with a smile at the first knock.

"Good mornin', ya must be Vernon," he said with a lilt in his voice.

"Yup, and I recon yer J.W.," Vernon responded. "Here, I brung ya some biscuits," he said handing him a small sack.

The two young men who were close in age sized each other up for a few moments.

Vernon stood about five feet ten, had a broad chest, muscular arms, dark brown hair and eyes, and sported a small beard of the same hue.

J.W. was only slightly taller with a slender build, light almost blond hair and beard both of which had not been trimmed in months. His eyes were sky blue and his complexion was paler than Vernon's.

"Thank ya fer tha bisquits. Sit down a few minutes. Let's have us sum and a cup a coffee whilest we git our plans together."

"Don't mind if I do," Vernon smiled.

J.W. quizzed Vernon about his logging experience and admitted, "This is mostly new ta me. I've cut up sum logs inta firewood but I haint neva actually cut down no large tree."

Vernon said, "Don't worry. We gonna take it one step at a time. We'll cut us a path fer pulling them big trees down the side of the ridge by startin' wit the smallest uns. Onest we git the li'l uns outta the way, we'll start on them hardwoods."

Filling his Dutch oven with more dried beans and water, he lit the fire, then said, "Cum on over ta tha shed and git the tools we gonna need, I'm anxious to get started".

"Vernon, this here's Jake and Miss Agnes; they's done a good job helpin' me. They had to carry me to an' from town two times Friday. Then they took turns plowin' the corn field on Sat'adee. I let 'em rest a bit on Sunday when I was a plantin' that corn," he added.

"Aw, they's gonna make up fer it when they start pullin' them big trees down the hill and haulin' them logs to Graham's mill," Vernon snickered.

J.W. gladly followed Vernon's lead as they began to chop down the smaller trees creating a pathway into the heavier forested area of the ridge.

With a yard full of fallen trees, Vernon said, "We'd best stop fer a spell and start takin' tha small limbs offen them we already cut. That'll make ya sum good firewood."

As they were working on reducing the fallen trees to firewood and logs of the proper size to take to the mill, the two shared a little more of their backgrounds as well as their dreams for the future.

Vernon learned why J.W. had been in debtor's prison in London and why he had taken a chance to start from scratch in the new world under an indenture contract.

J.W. was surprised that Vernon was not all that interested in following his Father in the blacksmith business. Instead, he had visions of buying his own land and becoming a farmer.

"Vernon, why would ya not go inta a ready-made fer ya line a work?" he asked. "Seems like thatta be the easy way ta git started."

"I jist wanna be my own man. "

"I kin understand that, Vernon. Guess that's what I be being by and by," he said wistfully.

"We best be stoppin' fer a bit and git sumpin' to eat," he said suddenly. He was wishing that he had something besides beans and a couple of leftover biscuits to offer.

As they sat together in the cabin eating the meager meal with stale coffee, they gave their sore muscles a rest and J.W. began to realize the extent of the difficult work ahead.

"Vernon, I'm mighty glad Mr. Graham arranged fer ya to help me git started. Don't know how I'd a done it wit out ya."

"Graham's apayin' me but I'm glad ta help ya. It's the neighborly thing ta do," Vernon replied with a grin. "I been thinkin', though, ya gonna need sum other tools and a gun."

"When I git back ta town, I'll tell Mr. Graham that ya gonna need a trailer ta hook ta the wagon fer carryin' the timber to the saw mill and ya gonna need a gun fer huntin' and fer protection."

"I cain't pay fer no trailer and no gun," J.W. said worriedly.

"Oh, Mr. Graham'll jist add it ta yer bill. That's how ya'll be gitten everthin' ya need til ya work off yer indenture," Vernon replied with an expression that implied he knew more about how things work than did J.W.

"At that rate, I be indentured fer life," J.W. said as he shook his head. The weight of his contract began to slice through his enthusiasm for a better future.

"Ah, I'm jist messin' wit ya. Don't git down. Ya got a much better chance under Mr. Graham than ya did in London from what ya tole me," he replied as he smiled and slapped J.W. on his back.

The two young men returned to the work of the day. By the time they had trimmed all the fallen trees of their small limbs, stacked them near the cabin for firewood, and cut the trunks into pieces that would fit into the wagon, the sun was heading toward late afternoon.

"I best be gitten home fer tha day, but I'll be back first thing in the mornin'."

J.W. shook Vernon's hand and replied, "Be careful ridin' back, I don't want nuthin' to happen ta my good helper."

J.W. checked on Jake and Miss Agnes, let them roam for a while, and refreshed their feed and water. After securing the mules and putting the axes and saws back in the shed, he settled into the cabin for the night.

Tuesday morning, he was up early and had the coffee ready and waiting for Vernon's arrival. A sound night's sleep had restored his energy and some of his optimism.

Arriving on schedule, Vernon brought another sack of biscuits, a small crock of molasses, a slab of seasoning meat, and four apples. "Mr. Graham said ta tell ya he wants to keep up yer strength being as how he's specting a load a lumber by the end of the week."

"That's a wonderful surprise," J.W. said with a puzzled look. "I don't know much bout cookin' so not shore what ta do with all them presents but I 'preciate it."

"I haint no cook neither, but I kin show ya how ta make them beans taste a lot better and how ta make griddle cakes outta the corn meal. With molasses on top of them cakes, yer gonna like it," Vernon promised.

The weather cooperated and they made the most of the daylight each day. By Friday, they had cut many of the smaller trees and cleared a path leading toward the hardwood on the ridge.

They talked as they worked and gradually became pals - two young men, each with dreams of building a future life that included their own land, wives, and children.

On Friday afternoon, the two loaded the wagon and readied it for the first trip to the saw mill on Saturday morning. J.W. was excited to think about showing Mr. Graham what he had accomplished in only one week.

Market Day

Chapter 11

Every Saturday from spring until early fall was Market Day in Graham. Farmers brought their fresh produce along with a variety of home-made goods to sell from wagons parked behind the town hall.

It was an opportunity not only to add variety to the diets of town folk and rural farmers but to share all the community news and gossip.

For young folks, it was one of the few chances they had to get to know each other. A young man might catch a glimpse of a pretty girl in church but on market days, it was easier to mingle and strike up conversations.

J.W. started his trip to town before 8:00 Saturday morning knowing that Jake and Agnes would have to pull the heavily loaded wagon at a slow pace. When he reached Graham's saw mill, it was around 9:30 a.m.

With the help of **Steve Henderson's** boys, **Chris**, **Joey**, and **David**, he unloaded the results of his work. (Steve was the manager of the saw mill.) He received a receipt and five dollars in cash to take to Mr. Graham. He felt proud of all that he had accomplished in one week's time.

Only a short time ago, he was fleeing a dismal situation in London and embarking on a hazardous trip across the ocean. Now, he was settled in a new world, in his own little cabin on land that would one day would be his. He had a few new friends including a helper and a pretty girl who had been very kind to him.

When Graham opened his office door, he saw an excited young man dressed in work clothes with a shaggy head and beard in need of a barber. "Good mornin', Sir, I'm bringin' you the receipt and cash fer tha first load ta yer saw mill," J.W. said almost panting.

"I'm pleased you got off to a good start," Graham exclaimed. "Word got back to me that you'll be needing a trailer and a gun. Guess that means you plan on staying a while," he joked.

"Why yes, Sir, I'm gonna pay ya back ever'thang', buy me sum more land, find me a wife, rise us sum young'uns, and build us a big house down by the crick," J.W. boasted.

"I like a young man with dreams and ambition. Yer gonna make a fine addition to the town of Graham."

"Thank ya, Sir. Guess I best be gitten down stairs. I want ta see what them folks have over ta tha market place afore I head back ta Roaring Fork. See ya next week, Sir," he said as he opened the door.

As he descended the stair into the store below, he spotted Sally talking to a customer. He thought she looked even lovelier than he remembered with her shiny auburn curls sneaking out of her bonnet.

Knowing this might be his only chance to speak with her for at least another week, he pretended to be examining some merchandise while Sally finished helping her customer.

Sally spotted him and came over to offer her help. "Is there something you need today, Mr. Presley?" she said with an alluring smile.

He thought for a moment. He knew what he really wanted, but instead he said, "Yes, Miss Sally, I need a bit more coffee and maybe sum salt."

"I'll fix you right up. How's it going out at your place?" she asked.

"The loggin' work's harda than I thought, but Vernon's a fine helper," he said. "I got tha corn planted and brought ma first load of logs ta the saw mill this mornin', so I think ever'thang' is goin' purty good outside. I haint too good wit inside work tho," he said in a hushed tone.

"Whatcha mean?" She asked.

"Well, I don't know much about cookin' and house keepin'. Been eatin' mostly beans, taters, and coffee so far," he replied with his distinctive crooked grin.

Sally thought for a moment and then said, "Why don't you write me a list of what you think you'll be needing next week and I'll have it ready when you get here. Maybe I'll show you a few easy cooking tricks too," she smiled.

"That's nice of ya, but I haint much for makin' no lists, Miss Sally," he said looking at the floor.

When he continued to remain silent, she began to understand that he might have a problem with writing and maybe even reading.

"We'll be having services tomorrow and it'd be nice for you to join us and meet other folks," she said. "The services are the second and fourth Sundays in town. You'll pass the church on your way ta the market place."

"Thank ya, Miss Sally. I'll thank on it," he replied while thinking of his shabby clothes and unkempt hair and beard.

Sally put the coffee and salt in a burlap bag for him. As he was bidding her goodbye, she reminded him of the fall dance and pie supper to be held in late October. He intended to attend both and would be sure to get a haircut, a clean shirt, and some polish on his boots before then.

After checking out the produce being sold by farmers from their wagons, J.W. spent $0.74 for a peck each of potatoes and corn, a pound each of lard, butter, and dried apples, a dozen eggs, and a loaf of bread.

"This was a fine day," he thought as he loaded his wagon and got Jake and Agnes headed for home.

"Got to pay on my bill. Got compliments from Mr. Graham. Got to meet sum nice folks at the market, picked up sum good thangs ta eat."

Mostly, I got ta talk wit Sally." He whistled and hummed the whole way to Roaring Fork.

The next few months became routine. J.W. arose each morning, made coffee, put beans in the Dutch Oven, and sometimes started the big pot simmering some potatoes.

Vernon was always punctual and ready to work. Often, he brought some biscuits and occasionally a piece of side meat.

The young men shared a mug of coffee with a biscuit or piece of bread that J.W. toasted over the fire before they went out to begin each day's logging work.

Every day revealed the progress they were making at removing the small trees and cutting a path up the ridge to the hard woods. Vernon instructed J.W. in the most efficient way to cut the trees down, strip off the limbs, and cut up the trunks.

Working so closely each week, they gradually became comfortable enough to share more of their private thoughts and dreams for the future. You might say they were becoming friends.

J.W. asked one day, "Do ya have a young Lassie, Vernon?"

"Naw, I'm not good at strikin' up conversations wit the ladies. How bout ya, ?" Vernon replied slightly embarrassed.

"So far, I only met me one Lassie, but she shore is a purty one," he said smiling.

"Er ya talkin' bout Miss Sally,? Ifen ya er, ya got sum comp'tition," Vernon said, glad to get himself out of the spotlight.

"Who'd tha be, Vernon?"

"Fenton Murphy ova ta feed store has his eye on er fer one. He's gonna have tha livery afta his Daddy's gone," Vernon explained with an air of being in on things.

J.W. got very quiet but thought, *"I guess I best be gitten' better acquainted wit Sally afore I miss ma chance."*

Each Saturday, after unloading his logs at the saw mill, and taking the receipts and cash to Charles Graham, J.W. made a point to have something to say to Sally. Sometimes it was just to pick up a few staples in the General Store; other times they talked about the fall harvest festival.

Sally never failed to remind him of the schedule of church services nor to invite him to attend. He thanked her and flashed his now familiar smile as he thought of a new excuse each time for not having darkened the doors at the First Methodist Church

Harvest Time

Chapter 12

O n the first Saturday in September, J.W. made his usual delivery of logs to the saw mill then drove his wagon into town to pay Mr. Graham and hopefully catch Sally's eye.

"Be sure to stop at tha livery to pick up yer trailer before headin' home," Graham said. "You can find yer long rifle waitin' on ya downstairs. Best get Vernon ta show ya how ta use it. Don't need ya killin' yerself before tobacca plantin' time," he laughed as he shook J.W.'s hand.

"I shore thank ya, Sir," he responded. "Y'ave been eva so kind ta me whilst I's getting started."

Down stairs, J.W. found Frank Graham, Charles Graham's nephew, and manger of the General Store. "Pardon me Sir but I believe ya have sumpin fer me," he said politely.

"Who are ya, boy? "Frank Graham said looking at him with curiosity.

"I'm J.W. Presley, workin' the farhm at Roaring Fork fer Mr. Graham, Sir."

"Oh yeh, I do have a package fer ya. Just gotta be shore who I'm handin' guns ta, ya know. Guess ya'll be wantin' sum ammunition too, "Frank replied.

With his new rifle in hand, J.W. walked to the domestics' area where he found Sally straightening shelves.

"Good Mornin', Miss Sally. Nice ta see ya agin."

"Why Mr. Presley, I didn't see you come in," she said with surprise. "How are you doing out at the farm?"

"We're makin' headway on them trees," he smiled. "I'll be pickin' up my trailer afore goin' back. That'll help hauling them hardwoods when we git ta 'em."

"Is Vernon still helping you out there?" she asked.

"He shore is, and we's become good friends workin' togetha," J.W. smiled. "In fact, Vernon's tha one that tole Mr. Graham I needed this here rifle fer huntin' and pertection," he added as he stood as tall as possible thinking Sally would be impressed.

"I haven't seen you in church yet. Are you planning to join us this month?" Sally asked.

"Well, I've been purty busy tryin' ta git all my work done, but I'll shore try makin' it ta the pie suppa. When was tha agin?" J.W quickly replied trying to change the subject.

"The Harvest Dance will be October 9th and the Pie Supper is the next day after church services," she responded emphasizing that he was expected to attend church **first**.

"I won't be forgettin' tha date, Miss Sally, and I wish you'd start callin' me J.W. stead of Mr. Presley," as he flashed his charming smile at her.

On his way to the livery, he dropped in to ask the barber the cost of a haircut and a shave. He was planning ahead, so he would have enough money to make himself presentable at the dance, at church, and especially the Pie Supper on October 10.

After Jim Murphy attached a hitch to his wagon and secured his new trailer, J.W. headed home remembering the twinkle in Sally's eyes as he bade her goodbye.

The rest of September passed quickly. J.W. had to tend to his corn field which had flourished. The crop provided additional feed for Jake and Agnes as well a few ears each week to be roasted over the fire.

Vernon was happy to show off his shooting prowess as he instructed J.W. in the use of his new long rifle. He often repeated his mantra, "Safety first in shootin' and loggin'."

The first Saturday in October would be a busy day for Presley. In addition to his weekly delivery of lumber to the mill, payment to Graham, and talking with Sally, he intended to spend some of his remaining $8.26 to purchase a clean white shirt, a haircut, and a shave.

He knew that he would then have only $7.18 left to his name, but he considered it an investment in his future.

After all, he thought, *"I caint expect a purty Gal like Sally to git interested in a farhm boy wit dirty clothes and a shaggy head."*

He grinned hoping his magically unusual smile would make up the remaining difference between him and his competition.

Sally had reminded him before he left the general store, "Now don't forget the dance is coming up next Saturday. I'm hoping to see you there."

"I'm plannin' on droppin' in, Sally, but I haint gonna be doin' no dancing," he grinned.

"We'll see about that," Sally said with a lilt in her voice.

The next Saturday morning, he arose with anticipation. He had a small breakfast of coffee and griddle cakes, did his morning chores, then washed himself from head to toe from a large bucket behind the cabin. He also cleaned and buffed his boots.

After hooking Jake and Agnes to the wagon, he went inside to dress. He pulled out the second set of clothing brought with him from London but not touched since arriving in Graham.

The brown britches and matching vest looked nice with the new white shirt he bought last week in town. He inspected himself as best he could without a mirror and joked," I aint no Prince Charmin', least not tha Prince part anyways."

When he arrived at the saw mill, the Henderson boys gave out a whistle. "Lookee who's here," said Chris, "and he's bout four hours late today."

"What's with the new shirt and vest,?" asked David.

"Who ya wantin' ta impress,?" added Joey.

"Ah, come on fellas, I'm goin' ta tha harvest dance an jist had to clean up a bit," Presley said with a flushed face.

"Didn't know ya was tha dancin' type, J.W.," Chris said with surprise.

"Well, I aint, but I was invited ta go, so I'm givin' it a try," he sighed. "Now, whoya know that'd be invitin' ya," asked David. "Yer purty new to town to be havin' a gal."

"Bet it's Miss Sally ova ta Graham's store. Ya musta been visitin' her right regular," guessed Joey.

"Don't ya'll be spreadin' no rumors bout Miss Sally. She's a fine Lady and was just nice and friendly to me causin she thought I should try ta meet sum more folks," J.W. said worrying that people might start to talk. "Just git me unloaded and I'll be on my way."

At the General Store, Graham said, "Yer lookin' mighty fine, young man. Are ya plannin' on comin' ta the dance?"

"Yes, and thank ya, Sir. I did the best I could wit what I had," he grinned. "Do I look alright?"

"You look just fine, and I hope you'll have a great time this evening."

"Where exactly will the dance be, Mr. Graham?"

"It'll be set up in the ball room over at the Palmer House hotel. The Pie Supper's gonna be there too after church tomorrow," Graham replied.

J.W. parked his wagon close to a water trough behind the Palmer House, secured his mules, and made his way into the hotel where he spotted Conrad Palmer giving instructions to his staff before the crowds began to form.

He knew he was early, so he watched as the hotel staff and the musicians finished setting up the room. Two young men were practicing dance tunes with a guitar and fiddle at the far side of the long room. Several people dressed as hotel servers arranged a long table at the opposite wall with autumn foliage and gourds, jugs of cider and plates of sweet and savory treats.

Standing back against a side wall in the ballroom, J.W. observed the town residents entering in a wide range of attire. There were gentlemen in frock coats and ladies in fancy dresses. Non-city dwellers and farmers came in plainer styles.

Since he didn't recognize anyone other than Conrad Palmer, he just stood quietly as people began to arrive. He noticed that he was beginning to tap his foot in time with the music. It had been many months since he had heard music of any kind other than birds singing outside his cabin.

Finally, a familiar face entered the room. "Vernon, I'm mighty glad to see ya," J.W. said as he raced across the room to greet his friend.

"Just seen ya yesterday," Vernon said with a big laugh and patted J.W. on the back.

"I'd like ya to meet my father, Bertham Wills, and my brother, Neville," Vernon said.

"Glad ta meet ya folks. Vernon's been a good helper an friend whilst I'm startin' up," J.W. smiled.

Gradually, the room began to fill with town residents and farm folks. John Perkins and his wife, Hazel, came in and seemed to know everyone. J.W. guessed it was because he was the barber.

Preacher Henderson and his wife, Nellie, arrived and made a tour of the room greeting everyone by name. When he came to J.W., he stopped.

"Don't believe I've had the pleasure of meeting you. I'm John Wesley Henderson, minister at the First Methodist Church here in town."

"Yes, Sir, I heerd bout you from yer uncle in Asheville, Bishop Cooper. I'm J.W. Presley an I'm workin' fer Mr. Graham at the Roarin' Fork farhm."

"Yes, my uncle mentioned that I might have a new parishioner, but I haven't seen you in church."

"I'm sorry, Sir, it's been a busy time jist gettin' set up and started with the loggin' and all, but I plan ta be there tomorrow fer shore," he said trying to quickly save face.

Several residents whom J.W. had met arrived and greeted friends as they moved about the room. Jim Murphy from the livery with his wife, Mary, and son, Fenton, from the feed store acknowledged him.

The Sheriff, John Calvin Schultz, entered with his wife, Carolyn, daughter Savannah, and son Joe. "We best be hopin' all the hooligans are in here so as I kin keep my eye on 'em," he roared to announce his presence.

Charles Graham made a grand entrance with his wife, Isabella, and several friends. Included in his social circle were Ulysses Winslow, the banker, and his wife, Emily, and William Mahan, the lawyer, and his wife, Imogene and daughters, Ruby and Pearl.

Charles Graham's nephew, Frank, arrived directly behind the larger group with his wife, Sarah.

The Graham party were all given special greetings by Conrad Palmer, another of Charles Graham's college classmates.

When his wife, Laura, joined the group, Palmer delegated management of the party to his restaurant and bar manager, **Thaddeus Dickenson** who was aided by his wife, Elsie.
Steve Henderson from the saw mill appeared with his wife, Connie, and his three sons who had chided J.W. earlier in the day.

Joey said, "Where's your sweetheart, J.W.?"

"That aint funny. I tole ya not ta be talkin' like that. Sum folks might take it serious," he said sternly.

Anxiously watching the door, waiting for a glimpse of Sally, J.W. was stunned by a vision. The O'Connor family were together but all he could see was a beautiful young woman dressed in emerald green to match her eyes.

Her auburn hair was pulled back from her face with fancy combs, but a few ringlets escaped to fall on ivory shoulders partially bared by the wide neckline of her party dress.

Sally spotted J.W. and came forward to greet him. "I'm so glad you decided to come to the dance after all," she said with a warm smile and twinkling eyes.

J.W. was unable to speak for a moment. He knew Sally was pretty, but he had only seen her in everyday work clothes, an apron over a high-necked dress, and her hair tucked into a white bonnet.

Standing before him was an unusual beauty who could probably attract a man of substance and stature.

He felt inadequate. When he finally spoke, it was in a slow soft voice. "Miss Sally, ya look like a princess tanight."

Sally blushed and quickly changed the subject. "Have you met everyone? I can introduce you to anybody you don't know," she offered. "The dancing music will be starting soon. Are you gonna give it a try?" she added.

"I'll most likely jist watch fer a while, ifen that's alright," he murmured still feeling a bit intimidated.

"Well, I won't let you just stand around all evening," she laughed.

She excused herself to speak with some friends she had just noticed. J.W. sighed remembering something his Mother used to say, *"Maybe*

I don't have a chance but ya don't never know unless ya try."

The two musicians struck up a familiar country tune and took turns calling out the dance sequences. Couples began to form squares and seemed to know the dance moves.

J.W. watched with interest as Mr. and Mrs. Graham led off the first dance. Gradually, other squares formed.

From across the room, Fenton Murphy approached Sally O'Connor and asked her to join him in a dance. She accepted, and they joined three other couples in a square.

J.W. noticed that Sally was smiling and obviously having a good time. He remembered that Vernon had warned him of competition. *"I don't know nothin' bout dancin', he thought. "I must be dreamin' ta think Sally'd be choosin' me ova them town boys which got manners and all."*

As he was edging toward the hallway with intent to quietly excuse himself and avoid further humiliation, Sally ran over to him and said, "Come on now, no more standing against the wall."

"But, Sally, I cain't dance," he said staring at the floor.

"J.W. Presley, I'm not having any more of that nonsense. Take my hand and just follow me," she protested.

He was afraid to argue, and to his surprise, he found himself moving to the music, slowly at first but then with enthusiasm as he saw Sally's eyes light up.
The musicians called a free-form set next, which did not require changing partners, and Sally remained with J.W. - gently leading him in the moves.

This gave him the chance to have her to himself for a few minutes and he tried to make the most of it. As they talked and laughed, he felt a bit of confidence returning.

Watching from a distance, Isabella Graham whispered to Charles, "Who is that young man dancing with Sally O'Connor?"

"Oh, he's my new tenant farmer working out his contract at Roaring Fork. He's only been here since early August but seems to be settling in nicely," Charles answered.

"Well, I can't imagine that the O'Connors are any too pleased to see their only daughter cavorting with a dirt farmer," Isabella said with a sneer.

"Don't be judging a book by its cover, woman, that boy's got a lot of spunk," Charles smiled.

Sally told J.W. that she needed to be sociable, so she would probably be dancing with different partners. She was quick to add with a giggle, "Don't be slipping out the door when my back is turned."

He took her admonition as encouragement, and he remained through the evening. He and Sally had several additional dance sets together. They also shared refreshments and conversation. At the end of the evening, he told Sally he would see her in church tomorrow.

"I've had tha best time. Thank ya fer invitin' me, "J.W. said.

"Glad you decided to give dancing a try, J.W. For a beginner, you did very well. Bet you got music in your bones," Sally smiled as they said good night.
He was tired on the ride home but almost too excited to sleep after taking care of his wagon and mules. *I'm gonna see her agin tomorrow,"* he thought as he drifted off to sleep.

Sunday morning, he arose, had coffee and leftover toast before going out to feed Jake and Agnes. He let them both wander free while he bathed himself and donned the better of his two sets of clothing, the one he had worn to the dance.

Putting $1.18 of his remaining cash in the pocket of his trousers, he was thinking, *"I gotta be gitting tha pie taday."*

Entering the First Methodist Church, he doffed his cap and looked around to see who was inside. He spotted the Graham family on the first row and several other families he had met the previous night directly behind on both sides of the church.

As he slipped onto a seat in the last row on the left side, he felt that sense of insecurity returning. *"Ever body's got family but me."*

The O'Connors entered and seated themselves about half way back on the left. Sally saw J.W. and motioned to him to move up and sit with her family. Although he wanted very much to do that, he was reluctant, not knowing what Sally's parents would think.

Halfway through the service, Preacher Henderson, had the congregation greet each other. Eunice O'Connor walked back to greet J.W. and said, "Why don't you come sit with us, son."

Worshipers were each greeted by Preacher Henderson as they left the church. "Nice to finally have you actually inside with us, Mr. Presley," Henderson said with a grin,

"I tole ya I'd be here," J.W. sheepishly replied in a hushed tone.

"Just glad to have you, " the Preacher laughed. "I'm just messing with you."
"Guess I'd best git used ta folks messin' wit me," J.W. grinned.

The ballroom of the Palmer house had been rearranged for the pie supper when people began to arrive. The long table on the side wall was laid out with platters of fried chicken, roasted vegetables, and fluffy biscuits.

On the opposite wall was a table filled with a variety of fruit and custard pies. The baker of each pie was identified with a small label. Ladies could be seen checking the placement of their contributions. Some seemed pleased, while others smirked at not being on the front row center of the table.

Before getting in line at the supper buffet, J.W. walked past the pie table to locate the one he was planning to win. The plan included winning more than a pie, he smiled to himself.

Most people waited their turn in line and then found a seat at one of the smaller tables which were decorated with fall foliage. J.W. noticed that the Graham family seated themselves without passing through the line. Palmer house staff brought each of them a plate and served them coffee, tea, or cider.

J.W. asked Vernon for permission to sit with the Wills family. He felt comfortable talking with Vernon, and Mr. Bertram Wills had been very friendly when they met.

This was the best meal J.W. had eaten since lunch with the O'Connors. In his mind, he was thinking of a future time when he would have good food every day prepared by a pretty wife who would sit close to him and talk about the day's happenings.

Vernon said suddenly, "Snap out of it. The Pie Auction's 'bout ta start." J.W. sat up straight and saw the lawyer, William Mahan rise and address the crowd

Mahan called out in a voice of authority, "Get your money ready cause there's some mighty fine pies to be had today. The ladies of Graham have done themselves proud, boys, so don't be shy."

"Mrs. Elsie Dickenson will be selecting the pies one by one and the bidding has to start at least at $0.15. Real bargains here, and the real prize is that the lucky bidder gets to sit and share a slice with the baker."

J.W. was on the edge of his seat as the process began, waiting for his chance. Sally's pie was number five in line for bidding. He almost jumped out of his seat when Mr. Mahan announced, "The famous apple pie of the lovely Sally O'Connor. What'll you give, boys?"

"Fifty cents, Sir," J.W. heard himself shout out. "Well now, this must be some special pie," Mahan laughed.

Then another voice said, "Sixty." J.W. turned around and saw Fenton Murphy smirking at him.

"Sixty-five," J.W. quickly retorted.

"This is getting to be fun," Mahan smiled. "I've got sixty-five cents for Miss Sally's apple pie. Any more bidders?"

Fenton shouted, "Seventy!"

Sally was starting to blush, and her father was looking worried.

"Seventy-five," J.W. said in desperation.

"I've got seventy-five once, twice," Mahan paused and looked around toward Fenton.

"Going, going, gone to our new neighbor, Mr. J.W. Presley.

"Come get your prize, the pie, and the pretty lady," the lawyer laughed.

The Courtship

Chapter 13

The remainder of October and November became mostly routine. The two loggers cut and trimmed trees Monday – Friday. Saturdays, J.W. took his loaded trailer of logs to Henderson's saw mill where he was certain to receive a bit of ribbing from Chris, Joey, and David.

With receipt and cash in hand, he headed to the General Store, paid Mr. Graham on his debt, and spent as much time as she could spare talking with Sally.

There were three opportunities to see Sally in church and he was also invited to eat supper with the O'Connor family on the fourth Sunday in November.

After supper, he asked permission to take a short walk with Sally and her parents consented. "Don't you be going far or staying too long," Eunice reminded them.

"I'll be shore an stay close, Mrs. O'Connor," he promised.

As they ambled toward the river, Sally asked him., "Are you starting to feel at home?"

He replied, "I'm feelin' a bit more easy, bein' as how folks 'av bin so nice ta me 'sept fer sum teasin' from the other boys."

"That just means they like you, J.W. Everybody likes you," Sally smiled.

"Does ever'body 'clude ya, Sally?" he asked hopefully.

"Sally, ya member tha book ya giv ta me?"

"Of course, I remember. Did you like it?" she asked.

"I liked hit causin' ya giv it ta me, Sally, but truth tell, I haint too good at readin'," he mumbled.

"Well, we can fix that. How about letting me help you with reading and writing both?" Sally proudly proposed.

"Then you'll be making your own lists of supplies and checking the balance on your indenture, too. You'll be getting a good start on becoming a gentleman farmer," She smiled at him with a twinkle in her green eyes.

"That's mighty kind of ya, Sally. Jist let me know when ya 'ave time an I'll show up."

The ride back to Roaring Fork didn't seem so long that afternoon. All he could think about was spending more time with Sally and becoming a gentleman farmer.

As they went about their logging each week day, J.W. and Vernon talked and joked with each other. It made the hard work pass quickly and they learned that they liked and trusted each other.

Vernon would tease J.W. about his obvious interest in Sally. J.W. would warn Vernon, "Ifen ya don't git crackin', I'll be a married man afore ya even git a kiss."

Eunice and Patrick O'Connor cautioned Sally about getting too attached to this young man although they could see that she appeared to be smitten.

In their brief meetings and conversations with J.W., Sally's parents could clearly see that he was honest, hard-working, ambitious, polite, and very charming; however, he would be deeply in debt for several years.

He would not be able to provide Sally with anything close to the life style in which she had lived for some time. Sally was the O'Connor's only child and they wanted the best for her.

On the first Saturday in December, J.W. made his regular trip to the saw mill and the General Store. When he took the receipt and cash to Mr. Graham, he got the courage to ask a favor from his boss.

"Mr. Graham, Sir, could ya see yer way ta lettin' me have a few dollars in cash and add it ta my bill," he asked with hat in hand.

"Why do you need cash? You can get whatever you need now added to your bill? "Graham quizzed.

"Well, Sir, Christmas time's a comin' up an I'd like ta buy a present fer Miss Sally. She's been so helpful ta me ever since I first came ta town," he explained.

"Don't suppose it has anything ta do with her being a pretty young Gal, does it, boy," Graham snickered.

J.W. began shuffling his feet and staring at the floor.

"I'm just giving you the business. You're a good worker and an honest man. I'll be happy to help you out. How much do you think you need?"

"Four dollars would be great ifen ya can see yer way ta that much, Sir."

"Must be a right nice present you have in mind, boy. Here you go. Just don't spend it all in one place."

He was day-dreaming about handing his gift to Sally at Christmas time as he descended the stairs into the General Store. Losing focus, he stumbled and missed two steps at the bottom and landed on his knees. Sally heard the noise and came running to the staircase to see what was happening.

"Are you alright, J.W. You could have broken a leg," Sally said with a worried tone.

"I'll be fine. Jist gimme a minute ta catch ma breath," he said after a long pause. He was trying to hide his embarrassment.

The timing could not have been worse because two of the Henderson boys unexpectedly appeared laughing and pointing at him. David said with a grin, "Look at that, Chris, the boy 'aint been here a year and he's proposing to a pretty girl."

Sally was startled and began blushing. "It's not a laughing matter. He could have hurt himself bad," she said and turned her back on them.

J.W. pulled himself up and walked toward David and Chris. "Don't ya boys got nutin' better ta do than roam around town startin' trouble?" he said with a deadpan serious stare.

To ease the tension everyone felt and avoid any possible violence, Sally reminded him that she had the supplies he ordered ready for him to carry out to the wagon whenever he was ready.

"Thank ye, Sally. I'm sorry 'em boys caint seem ta hep themselves from jabbin' at me wheneva they git tha chance," he said with his head tucked.

"It's alright. They don't mean no harm. They just want to have fun," Sally said quickly as she led him to his stack of supplies.

"I've got some good news for you."

"Well, I'm always ready ta hear good news," he replied. "What is hit?"

"I was talking to my momma and daddy about helping you with your reading and writing and asked them where we might find a quiet place to do that," She said with excitement.

"Momma first thought of asking Preacher Henderson if we could use the church when it is available, but she thought people might talk if we were in the church just by ourselves."

Hardly pausing for a breath, she added, "Daddy heard us talking, and said we should just use the work room at the Tailor Shop. There's a flat counter space, a desk, and some chairs that might work."

J.W. was listening and wanted to ask a few questions about when and how to make this happen, but Sally did not give him an opening.

"I've always dreamed of being a teacher," she said wistfully looking into space. "This is my chance to give it a try. If it works good with you, I might get some other students and become a real teacher. After all, I've got more education than most anybody in town except Mr. Graham and his college friends."

When Sally finally stopped talking for a few seconds, he asked, "When would we start and how would that work?"

"Well, I think we could start next Saturday after your regular weekly stops in town. That Sunday will be church services and you could have dinner with my family and stay for a few hours for a second session.

"Then, I would give you an assignment to work on during the week to review when you come back the next Saturday. We could do the same thing every week including the Sundays with no church services. The first and third Sundays would give us a longer lesson," She rattled on.

He was feeling dizzy with all the details. It was as if Sally had been planning this for years just waiting for her first victim.

On his trip home, he started worrying. "What ifen I caint learn? Sally might be findin' out how dumb I really is and she wont want ta have nutin ta do wit me no more."

Jake and Miss Agnes began snorting as if to say, *"Oh how ya do go on, J.W. Ya can do whateva ya make up yer mind ta do so shut up and git us ta home."*

The next Saturday as he was driving his lumber to the saw mill, he was focused on two things. First, with Christmas only a few weeks away, he needed to be finding that special present for Sally. Second, this would be the beginning of his reading lessons.

He was apprehensive about both. *Would his $4.00 be enough for a nice gift and how would he go about purchasing anything in the General Store without Sally being aware of it? Would Sally be disappointed when she learned that he would need to start at the beginning in learning to read?*

He wished he had planned earlier and found a nice gift from one of the craftsmen on Market Days before they ceased for the winter.

Entering the General Store, he attempted to stay out of the piece goods area so as not to be spotted by Sally until he had a chance to look at the ladies' accessories. He was certainly a novice and out of his comfort zone inspecting bonnets, aprons, shawls, and gloves.

Out of the corner of his eye, he saw something gleaming. As he got closer, he spotted a display of hair combs and ornaments. Something emerald green caught his attention. It was a lady's hair comb made of bone and inlaid with small pieces of green glass which looked like gem stones.

"How beautiful that would look in Sally's auburn hair,"he thought, "but I probably cain't 'ford hit."

Cautiously, he approached the clerk, pointed, and whispered, "What will ya take fer tha hair comb?"

"Oh, that's a nice one, and it goes for $5.00, young man."

"Can ya do any better than tha fer a new fahmer still gittin' started?" he asked with a smile.

"Don't know that I kin. Would have ta ask Mr. Frank Graham," the clerk replied.

"Well, kin ya at least hold it fer me ifen I give ya a $2.00 deposit? I'm on my way upstairs fer sum business wit Mr. Charles Graham," he said hoping to gain some credibility with the clerk.

"I suppose that'd be alright."

In Graham's office, he delivered his weekly proceeds from the saw mill and the receipt to be applied to his account.

"How is it going now that winter's setting in, J.W." Graham inquired.

"Not too bad. Vernon an me got plenty of kindlin' an fire logs set by fer tha cabin. The loggin' is gitting sum harda causin' 'em big trees take longa ta tackle," he said shuffling his feet.

"Is there something else on your mind, boy?" Graham asked noticing the nervous behavior.

"Yes, Sir, I hate ta ask anotha favor of ya since ya been so nice an all, but could ya ask Mr. Frank if he could see his way ta lettin' me have tha nice comb I spotted fer $4.00 instead of the $5.00 the clerk tole me?"

Graham laughed out loud. "Boy, you've got it bad now aint ya?"

"I give 'im a $2.00 deposit an I can give 'im the otha $2.00, but I don't know how ta come up wit tha rest," J.W. said looking at the floor as he often did when embarrassed.

"Tell you what, Boy. I'll take care of it, and have that comb here for you next Saturday. You are about to get yourself into some real trouble, aint ya now," Graham laughed.

J.W. expressed his gratitude and left the still snickering Graham to find Sally and start his first assignment. She was waiting for him saying, "Let's go over to the shop and get started."

Inside the O'Connor's Tailor Shop, Sally pulled out a slate, a few slate pencils, and a sample page of upper and lower-case block letters.

"I think we'll start here with sounds," she said. "Just tell me if you already know something and I will move a little faster."

Sally wrote the word, BOOK, on the slate and asked him to pronounce it.

"I think I've seen tha afore, but cain't rightly 'member, " he said with obvious embarrassment.

"That's alright. We all have to start someplace," Sally said reassuringly.

"The word is BOOK, and you will soon be reading the best one ever," Sally promised.

"What's the name a tha one?" he asked.

"Why it's the one you already own," she smiled. He looked confused.

"Remember, the book I gave you to take home after we had our first supper together?" she asked.

"How could I forgit tha, Sally? I love hit but I cain't read hit."

"J.W., that is a Bible, or at least the most important parts, the New Testament and the Psalms. That's what we are going to use to help you learn to read. You'll be learning more than reading. You'll be learning the Good News," she added.

Thus, began the formal education of J.W. Presley and the practice teaching of Miss Sally O'Connor. This would be a mutually beneficial arrangement.

Each weekend, she would review the previous lesson with him. At first, the lessons focused on sounds, letters, short words and phrases.

She carefully selected verses that were special to her in hopes of passing on her faith. She started with John 3:16, *"For God so loved the world . . . . . ."* The first assignment she gave to him was to learn this verse and write it on his slate.

She spent time sounding out each letter and putting them together to form words. "G-O-D = God, L-O-V-E-D = loved," she enunciated slowly and had him repeat several times.

The fourth Saturday in December was Christmas Day. Most of Graham was shut down for the holiday celebration which would continue through Church Services the next day. J.W. had been invited to have Christmas Dinner with the O'Connor family and he was anticipating giving Sally her gift.

As a small token for his hosts, he loaded his wagon with enough kindling to last the O'Connor family through the winter. He dressed in his better set of clothing, put on his coat, and headed to town before noon.

The O'Connor home was decorated for the holidays with evergreens, pine cones, and red berries. The aroma of roasted foul and bread baking filled his nostrils as he was greeted by a smiling Sally at the front door of her parent's home.

"I've brought somethin' fer yer Momma an Daddy, but I'll need 'em ta show me where ta unload hit," he said excitedly forgetting to even say hello to Sally.

"And a Happy Christmas to you too, J.W.," Sally said as she flipped her curls in a sassy manner. "Best that you show me what the big surprise is, and we'll ask them."

"Oh, I'm sorry, Sally. Happy Christmas ta ye and yer family, and thank ya very, very much fer invitin' me ta share this special day wit ya," he said, trying to recover from his faux pas. "I brung ya a loada kindlin' ta last tha winter."

Patrick O'Connor heard the voices at the door and came to see what was happening. "Well, hello, J.W. and Happy Christmas to you, young man. Don't just stand in the doorway; come on in here and sit a spell. Dinner will be ready soon," said Patrick with a holiday lilt in his voice.

"J.W. has something for you and Momma." He seems to be more interested in that than talking with me at the moment," Sally told her father in a slightly agitated tone.

"I'm very happy ta be here an want ta talk wit all of ya, but I thought I might oughta take care of unloadin' the kindlin' first," he explained afraid that he had made a mistake.

O'Connor sensed the tension and cheerily said," What a wonderful surprise. I'll come outside with you and help with the unloading."

As the older man helped J.W. place the kindling next to the rear door, he smiled at him. "Don't worry, boy, it takes time to understand women. Sometimes they seem to get up in airs about nothing. Just act like everything is fine when we get back inside."

"Thank you, Sir. I ain't spent much time talkin' ta ladies, but I heerd somewhere tha practice makes perfect."

Sally was helping her mother assemble the feast on a sideboard and she lit two candles that had been placed in the center of the dining table.

As she turned around, J.W. was behind her. "I have a small gift fer ya, Sally. Can I giv it ta ya now," he requested almost pleadingly.

"Certainly, what is it," she asked.

He handed the small gift-wrapped box saying, "I want ta thank ya fer all yer kindness and help."
Sally carefully untied the red ribbon and opened the box. She gasped at the lovely comb with the shiny green stones. "Oh, J.W., **it's beautiful**."

Patrick O'Connor winked at J.W. and said under his breath, "Good timing, boy."

The year of 1830 ended on a positive note for J.W. What a difference twelve months had made in the life of an Irish immigrant.

Learning and Loving

Chapter 14

A young man not yet twenty left the only home he had known on a family farm in Dublin to try his luck in the big city of London. There he met with nothing but misfortune culminating in a term of incarceration on dubious charges.

Upon release from Debtor's Prison, he took an even larger risk by leaving Europe for a chance in the New World. He entered into a contract of indenture to a landowner in North Carolina that would hold him in another type of bondage for the next ten years. Due to illiteracy and naiveté, he accepted the false advertising and signed his life away with dreams of becoming a landowner.

Arriving in America with not much more than the clothes on his back and a few dollars earned through hard labor on the ship, he relied on his wits and the kindness of strangers to finally reach his destination.

There he learned the facts of his contract. Despite his disappointment, he found his benefactor and indenture holder to be a kind man who encouraged and helped him to achieve some success during the first few difficult years.

He had gained self confidence in his ability to do the work necessary to gradually reduce his debt. Starting his new life without family or friends was lonely; however, he had made several friends in his age bracket this year.

He had gained respect in the eyes of his boss, business people in town, the local preacher, and most importantly a beautiful young lady who had taken him under wing.

On New Year's Day 1831, J.W. Presley made a resolution that he would work hard to make this year just as memorable.

Sally continued to work with him each weekend unless there was a family obligation. He never missed a session and he always tried his best to complete each week's assignment before meeting with Sally the next Saturday.

There were a few occasions during the first few months that J.W. became discouraged. "Sally, I'm 'fraid that I might not be smart nuf to ever read good," he confessed one weekend.

"Now don't you be quitting on me, J.W. I've got my future reputation as a teacher riding on you," She smiled.

When he was tired or frustrated from the studying, he sometimes told himself, "This whole teachin'an learnin' thang's more about what Sally wants ta do than bout me."

When he was rested, he was thankful that someone had taken enough interest in him to help him become a better man, *"'specially a purty someone"* he smiled to himself.

Spending quality time together each week and sharing a project naturally led to a closer relationship. The O'Connors kept close watch on these developments and worried privately that it could become too serious.

"It's going to be hard for Sally to catch the eye of a more promising prospect when she spends all her spare time with a farm boy," Eunice said to Patrick one evening after supper.

Patrick thought a moment and replied, "That's true, but I am proud of her for helping this young man to improve himself."

"I am too, Patrick, but how do the long walks they've been taking after lessons improve him?" Eunice asked.

"Look at it this way, Eunice," Patrick suggested. "Any two people who spend that much time together for a year, either ends of hating each other or finding out that they are a good match."

"Let's hope it's the former," Eunice snickered.

"Now, Old Woman, did you forget what it's like to be young and only dream of all the good things that can happen?" Patrick chuckled.

"After all, we have had him in our home many times and we know more about his character than we do about these mysterious *"better prospects"*of which you speak," Patrick said as he put his arm around Eunice.

"This boy doesn't come from money and he doesn't have any fancy education, but he has goals, he works hard, he is honest, he is courteous and polite, and he obviously thinks a lot of our daughter."

"Alright, Charles, you win. I'm not saying nothing bad about the boy. It's just that Sally's our only child, and I want her to be happy," Eunice sighed as she leaned against Charles.

Work at Roaring Fork continued to progress throughout the year. J.W. got the tobacco crop started on time and, with Vernon's help, had it cut and dried early in the fall.

Charles Graham was pleased with how productive his young protégé was becoming both in farming and logging.

J.W. was proud of how far he had come in living up to the expectations of his benefactor/boss.

He was even more proud that he had not failed to learn basic reading and writing skills under Sally's tutelage. With his confidence increasing, he was able to joke with Sally instead of being embarrassed by a mistake.

When presented with a multi-syllabic word, he told her, "Ye're gonna havta giv me a hammer to crack tha one."

J.W. planned ahead for Christmas of 1831. He had discovered a lovely hand-carved keepsake box during Market Days which he purchased and saved secretly for months.

On Christmas Eve, he found a private time to give Sally her gift. She was so excited that she grabbed him around his neck and kissed him without thinking.

"Thank you so much. I love this and will put only my special things in it. I don't know what got over me. I guess it's just the Christmas spirit," she blushed.

"I'm a hopin' that spirit's gonna last way past Christmas," he said with his special grin that Sally had learned to love.

"I've got something for you this time," Sally replied. "Let me go inside and get it for you."

She came running back with something that looked like a large book. It was bound in leather and on the first page, Sally had carefully hand-lettered in ink,

THE ACCOUNT BOOK OF JAMES WILLIAM PRESLEY.

He could feel moisture welling up in his eyes as Sally babbled on.

"Now that you can read, write, and cipher pretty well, you can start keeping your own records. You can write down the price of everything you grow or log for Mr. Graham.

"You can keep track of how much you've paid on your debt. The line down the middle of the pages will help you stay up-to-date on the balances.

"You can know where you stand without having to ask anyone else. You will be in charge of your own future, Mr. J.W. Presley of Roaring Fork."

When she ran out of breath and paused for a few seconds, he said, "Thank you, thank you very, very much." Then he grabbed her and kissed her like he meant it.

The Proposal

Chapter 15

On New Year's Day 1832, J.W. made a major decision. He would ask Sally to become his wife, but he knew that he would first need to speak with her father, Patrick O'Connor.

Although January 1st was a Sunday, it was not church Sunday in Graham and he would be staying at Roaring Fork all day. He would have time to think while he went about his routine chores outside the cabin.

He decided to run his plan by Jake and Agnes for practice. If he could hear himself say the words and measure the reaction of his mules, he might gain the confidence to approach Mr. O'Connor.

Imagining the way in which he would approach Patrick O'Connor, he said first in his head and then out loud:

"Mr. O'Connor, Sir, I have come ta ask ye fer sumthin' I ain't rightly worthy of, but please hear me out. "

"When I cum ta Graham a year an a half ago, I was fresh offa ship from London, an didn't know nobody.

"One of tha first people I met was Miss Sally O'Connor. She was so friendly an kind ta me. She hep'd me ta git my supplies togetha. She invited me ta eat wit yer family.

"She got me ta come ta church. She learnt me ta read and 'rite purty good. She tole me I could do anythin' I made my mind up ta. She hep'd me to keep goin' when work on the fahm was a gittin' hard.

"You an Mrs. O'Connor been eva so nice ta me, makin' me feel ta home in Graham. Now I know Sally is yer only child, an' yer wontin' tha best fer her. I'd feel tha same ifen she was my girl.

"I cain't 'spect ya ta think I'd be tha best, being as how I'm jist a fahm boy payin' off an indenture.

"On tha plus side, I've got big plans fer tha fahm at Roarin' Fork. Ther's gonna be a fine two-story house an' fifteen more acres of land that I'll be ownin' my ownself. Ya can ask Mr. Graham bout my work an' my characta. Now that I'm a readin' an' 'ritin' man, I'm gonna be a up standin' memba of the Graham community.

"I respect Miss Sally an' I love her. I'd see tha she has eva thang she **need**s even ifen I cain't get eva thang she **wants** at first. Ventually, she'd be tha lady of tha house at Roarin' Fork. Ifen she'd hav me, I'd be a good husband ta her, I promise."

He stopped his long monologue to gauge the response from his audience. Jake snorted, and Miss Agnes looked sleepy. "Guess, I best shorten this speech a bit," he said under his breath.

He thought about the timing for his talk with Sally's father. He hoped to catch Mr. O'Connor in a good mood. He thought he might approach him at the Tailor Shop and ask to talk with him in private.

Then he thought it might be better if he caught up with him after Sunday dinner when he was feeling all warm inside from one of Mrs. O'Connor's delicious meals. He would have to be subtle so that Sally did not see or guess the nature of the conversation.

He attempted to calm his nerves and convince himself that he had a full week in which to hone his salesmanship. He tried to remember what others had said about his positive attributes.

He thought out loud, *"I know I ain't got no higher learnin' or city ways bout me fer shore. On tha otha hand, I got a rep'tation fer being honest an hard workin'. Fer sum reason people seem ta like my crooked smile,"* he remembered with a grin.

During the week, he considered telling Vernon of his plans, but discarded that idea because gossip has a way of spreading quickly in a small town.

Saturday came and went with the usual activities. Only J.W. knew that something important was about to happen.

He delivered the weekly load of logs to the saw mill where he received the regular kidding from the Henderson boys. He gave the receipt to Mr. Graham and paid on his debt. He picked up a few supplies from the General Store while chatting with Sally.

As they bade goodbye, she reminded him, "Don't forget about church tomorrow, and you'll be staying for Sunday dinner."

"How could I fergit tamorra," he said with his famous smile which this time was laced with special meaning.

Sitting in the First Methodist Church, he knew he should be paying attention to the sermon, but his mind strayed to what he was planning to do after church today.

As they shook hands at the church door, Preacher Henderson observed, "You seem to have a far-away look in your eyes today, young man. Are you planning something?" J.W. was startled back to reality and tried to look as if it were just another day.

At the O'Connor home, he held the door for Sally and Eunice and asked Patrick if he could be of any help before dinner. "You are always polite and considerate, J.W. For today, just relax and enjoy a good meal with us," Patrick smiled.

Eunice, with Sally's assistance, presented another delicious feast which he tried to enjoy, although he sensed a queasiness in his stomach and sweating in his palms. When they finished eating, Eunice said, "You men go on into the other room and visit whilst Sally and me clean up."

He knew this was the long anticipated and dreaded moment. *"Please, Lord, don't let me mess this up,"* he prayed silently.

He was thinking of how he would react if Mr. O'Connor became angry. What could he do if his dreams were dashed without even a second chance? He had been dreaming of having Sally by his side building Roaring Fork into a home and family, but it could all end today if her Father refused to consent.

"How are things going at the farm?" O'Connor asked as he settled into his comfortable chair.

J.W. had worked himself into such a frenzy that his answer came out in a high-pitched squeal, "Oh, I guess as good's kin be 'spected."

"Is something bothering you, boy? You've seemed a bit edgy all day," O'Connor asked with concern in his voice.

"Could I talk wit ye outside fer a minute," he mumbled.

"Sure, we'll act like we're getting some kindling while the women finish in the kitchen," Patrick suggested.

Standing by the rear door next to the pile of kindling, J.W. was shuffling his feet and stalling for the courage to begin.

"Mr. O'Connor, Sir, I have come ta ask ye fer sumthin' I aint rightly worthy of, but please hear me out."

He managed to get the first sentence of his rehearsed speech out, but then became tongue-tied. The two men stood silently facing each other for what seemed like hours, but was less than a minute.

Men don't do well staring at each other in silence, so O'Connor filled the space. "Boy, are you asking me for my blessing?"

"Yes, Sir, how'd ya know?"

Patrick chuckled, "I ain't as dumb as I look."

With the air cleared, J.W. gained his composure and shared the rest of his prepared speech with Patrick O'Connor.

"Well, I can see that you've put a lot of thought into this," Patrick laughed. "You've mentioned many of the reasons I might have to object, but you forgot the more obvious one."

"What'd I fergit?"

"How about the fact that you are not yet twenty years old, have no experience with women let alone a wife and children?" O'Connor inquired seriously.

"You've only had a little over a year farming on yer own. You've yet to deal with crop failure due to weather. You haven't had to worry about anyone but yourself living in that cabin. You haven't had to argue about what's important with another person. You just think every day will be all love and flowers. I'm here to tell you, boy, marriage has its ups and downs."

He listened intently and finally responded. "I understand what yer atellin' me, Sir, but I do ave 'sperience dealin' wit tha unknown.

"I took a chance ta make tha long trip from England alone wit no money an' no real skills. I had ta liv wit bad weather, wit people who tells ya only half of tha truth, wit thieves that ya thought were friends, an' wit being the butt of jokes even right here in this town. But 'spiten' all tha, I 'membered what Momma tole me; be honest, be kind, be polite, work hard."

"Yes, I can see that your Mother taught you well, and she would be proud of you," Patrick said consolingly.

"Here's what I think we should do. Today, while you're having a lesson with Sally, take the opportunity to see if she feels the same as you. Meantime, I'll talk with Eunice and get the lay of the land around the home front."

"Thank you, Sir, I'm feelin' much betta now's we've talked," he sighed. "Not so fast, boy. You've got the hard part ta go."

"What'd ya mean?" he looked puzzled.

O'Connor laughed out loud. "You're proven my point, boy. You ain't never asked a simple question to a woman only to get a hundred asked back at you."

"What you boys been doing out back so long?" Eunice asked.

"Oh, just solving the problems of the world," Patrick answered with a smile.

Sally began the weekly review and assignment in her usual organized manner. J.W. attempted to pay attention without success. At one point, he interrupted her. "Sally, can we stop fer a minute? I've got sumthin' to talk wit ye bout," he asked.

"Of course. What's so important.?"

He got up from his chair and walked toward her. He gently took her hands in his and began. "Sally, ya must know how much I think of ya an how grateful I am fer everthin' ya done fer me since we first met in tha General Store in August last year."

"Yes, I know by how hard you work on your lessons, and that you appreciate my help. Is something wrong? You seem so serious today," she asked.

"Sally, I'm not tha best wit words, but I'll try ta tell ya what's on my heart. I more than 'preciate ya. I love ya, Sally. I love ever thang bout ya. Yer purty, yer smart, yer kind ta ever one, yer a hard worker, yer helpful. And did I mention, yer purty?

"So, what's the rest of your speech?" She quizzed him with a smile. "Miss Sally O'Connor, would ya marry me an' be my wife?"

There was an awkward silence followed by a gasp.

"Yes, Mr. Presley, I will marry you and be your wife. However, I have a few questions."

He sighed, "Your Daddy warned me bout that."

Sally began her litany.

"How soon were you thinking about us getting married?

Where?

What did my Daddy say?

Where would we be living?

Would I still be able to work at the General Store?

Could you support us if I stopped working?

Does Momma know?"

"Slow down a bit, Sally," he begged. "My head's a spinning 'bout all yer questions.

"I'll start wit yer last un first. Your Momma most likely knows by now. Yer Daddy was gonna talk wit her 'bout it when we left.

"Bout supportin' ya, I promise ta do my very best ta giv ya ever thang ya need and try ta make ya happy. Guess ya could keep a workin' at tha Gen'ral Store ifen ya wont ta, least til we have sum young'uns ta home." He smiled a special smile at the thought of little folks underfoot.

"Now as ta tha timin' an' place, I'd leave it up ta ya an yer Momma. I was a thinkin', though, we might git hitched at tha end of July. We'd ave known each other 'most two yars by then. I'd be pushin' twenty an you'd be bout nineteen. In some places that'd be 'most an old maid," he laughed at his own cleverness.

Sally was not really impressed with his humor, because she was already focused on planning a wedding. Even in humble settings, a wedding is a big event for a young girl. Many decisions and details would need her attention if a wedding were going to take place in a little more than six months.

"I need to talk with Momma," Sally said not hearing anything else he had to say. "Come on, let's go back to the house."

Inside the O'Connor home, the atmosphere was ominously serious. Eunice instructed the young couple to sit down for a few moments before J.W. would need to return to Roaring Fork.

Sally was exited and eager to begin talking; however, Eunice said, "I have something to say and some things for the two of you to think about this week before anyone else knows what we have discussed today."

He was worried. Were her parents getting ready to withhold their blessing? Should he say anything or sit quietly and await the verdict? A few moments earlier, he was the happiest man on earth. Now he was sweating and fearful.

Eunice continued, "I am told that you want to marry our daughter, Mr. Presley. From the smiles I saw when you came through the door, looks like she thinks she wants that too.

"Patrick and I think highly of you, young man, but we are afraid that neither one of you has taken time to think about the difficulties ahead."

Sally opened her mouth but was stopped short by her father. Patrick picked up where Eunice left off, "We know you like each other, and you've gotten even closer since the lessons began."

He added, "When two young people spend so much time together working on a goal, it may seem natural to take it to the next step. I know that you don't want to hear this, but being married is a lifetime commitment. When bad times come, and they will, a person can't just say, I've changed my mind.

"Eunice and I want you to take the next few weeks to really think how this decision will affect the rest of your lives. During that time, we suggest that you not tell anyone else what you are planning. That way, there will be no embarrassment if you decide to postpone any decision."

Eunice addressed J.W., "Son, I want you to understand that Sally has always lived in town where she has had other young ladies with whom she could socialize. She has never worked on a farm and knows very little about maintaining a home in a one-room cabin. How do you think she is going to feel after the bloom comes off the rose?"

Patrick directed his next statements to Sally. "Daughter, we love you and want you to be happy. This week, I will borrow a buggy from the livery, and we will make a visit to J.W.'s cabin at Roaring Fork. You have never even seen where you might be living. He can show you around the property and explain the type of work he is doing, what he plans, and what he might expect of you.

"If you still feel the same way by January 22nd, we will meet with Preacher Henderson after church and begin making plans," Patrick ended the discussion.

Eunice handed J.W. a basket filled with leftover chicken, biscuits, and a slice of lemon-custard pie for his supper.

"Take care of yourself, Son, and we'll be talking with you again soon," she said as he walked outside with Sally.

Sally looked disappointed. She said, "I was hoping they would be excited for us."
In a hushed voice, he responded, "They's only lookin' afta ya, Sally. I want ya to be shore before ya give me yer hand, too. Much as I luv ya, I don't want no regrets."

"Guess we'll be seeing each other this week out at your place," she said as she hugged him goodbye.

The trip to Roaring Fork seemed much longer this evening as he thought of all the reasons why Sally might change her mind. He remembered the questions Mrs. O'Connor had posed concerning the different life-style Sally would encounter at Roaring Fork.

He had grown up on a farm doing hard labor. He was used to having dirt on his hands and in his shoes. He had to admit that he knew very little about what it took to make young ladies happy. He was starting to fear the visit from Sally and her Daddy.

After he unhooked Jake from the wagon, refreshed the food and water for his mules, and put everything away for the evening, he looked at his surroundings with new eyes. "All she's gonna see is a one-room cabin wit hardly no furn'tur nor nuthin' purty to look at," he put his head in his hands.

"She's not gonna see what I'm 'maginin' down tha road a few yars. I need ta git my words togetha an' paint 'er a pitcha of how thangs kin change fer the good. Guess I best pull sum a tha ole blarney stone outta my mem'ry," he told himself.

When Monday morning came, and Vernon arrived ready to begin the logging, J.W. was unusually quiet. He wished he could share his hopes and fears with his friend, but recalled the instructions to keep the possible engagement secret until something definite was decided.

Vernon noticed his sullen mood, but did not say anything until they stopped for lunch. "Is sumthin' wrong today?"

Struggling to think of a response that would not invite more questions, he finally said, "I'm jist thinkin' bout my ciph'rn' lesson Miss Sally giv me. She makes it harda ever week."

"She mus think yer purty smart, ifen she keeps uppen the ante," Vernon laughed.

At the end of the work days on Monday and Tuesday, J.W. did his best to straighten up inside the cabin and move any tools not needed for the logging out of sight into the shed.

He wished he had asked Mr. O'Connor what day to expect the visit.

Shortly before noon on Wednesday, he and Vernon spotted a buggy pull up and stop close to the cabin. "Who'd that be?" asked Vernon.

"I think it might be Mr. O'Connor and Miss Sally. They said they mite visit sum time," he ad libbed.

He laid his tools by a large tree and jogged down the hill toward the cabin with Vernon not far behind. "Good mornin' Mr. O'Connor an' Sally. What a nice surprise," he shouted out in hopes they would catch his meaning.

Patrick whispered to his daughter clarifying the situation then turned to J.W. and replied, "We thought we'd come and visit this farm we've heard so much about from Mr. Graham. He speaks very highly of what you accomplished so far."

Playing along so as not to make Vernon suspicious, Sally added, "I came along to see where my prize student does all his study work."

When Vernon greeted the visitors, O'Connor said, "I hear you've become the right-hand man out here, Mr. Wills. Are you thinking about doing something different from your Daddy's line of business?"

"Yes, Sir, I am that," Vernon answered. "Blacksmithin's not fer me."
"Your Daddy is a fine man and does good work in a much-needed trade," O'Connor said sternly. "However, I know you young guys always want to make your own mark."

J.W. gave Vernon a chore so he could have a more private meeting with the O'Connors. "Vernon, why don't ya start cuttin' down sum a 'em limbs inta small logs for haulin' ta tha mill whilst I giv these folks tha tour.

"Cum on inta tha cabin an I'll tell ya bout my plans," he tried to say with confidence. He noticed that Sally's eyes were wide, and she wasn't smiling.

"Now ever one's gotta start sum whar afore they kin git ta whar they's a goin. This here lil cabin ain't much at this point but I've got me big plans ta make hit more home like. Course a lady'd be a big hep in makin' that 'appen soona," he smiled at Sally.

"In no mor'n a few yars, ther's gonna be a big house over ther on tha hill wit two floors. When I git my 'denture paid back, I'm gonna buy fifteen more acres from Mr. Graham. That's fer shore causen he an me already discussed hit."

O'Connor was listening politely, and Sally was walking off the floor space as if she were measuring for furniture placement. She also checked out the cooking equipment, still saying nothing.

J.W. continued painting his picture. "Me an my wife's gonna be real land owners, I kin promise ya. We'll hav ever thang we need an most ever thang we could be awantin' fore ya know it.

"When we gits ta being on halvers wit Mr. Graham, our part of tha loggin' business plus our backer crop will giv us plenty a cash ta buy nicer thangs fer tha house. Ya gotta admit it's a mite purty place ta liv an raise a fam'ly. Jist listen to tha babblin' crick an'look at 'em rollin' hills. It's so quiet n peaceful like . . ."

O'Connor stopped him before he could go any further. "Boy, you've certainly got dreams and the gift of gab about you. I believe you will work hard to see that picture come to pass, but don't be forgetting that every coin has two sides. You've gotta realize that things happen that may not fit your plans and these are *'the times that try men's souls' as they say."*

Exiting the cabin, O'Connor suggested they take a short walk to the creek and around the perimeter of the ten acres that J.W. would own at some future date. "It's a nice day to stroll about the property."

"Jist be mindin' whar ya step," J.W. admonished. "Ya know I've got mules livin' here." He first directed his guests to the shed and introduced his four-legged friends. "This her's Jake an Miss Agnes. They's the only ones I kin talk wit when Vernon ain't here," he joked.

Sally patted the mules on their snouts and appeared to like them. "How much of the talking do they do?" she asked.

"Not much, but they's real good list'ners," he answered.

"It's nice to have animals around," O'Connor added. "They do become part of the family."

As they walked toward the creek bank, "J.W. said proudly, the soil's nice n rich here. The backer an corn dun real good so far."

"We best be getting back to town. Eunice will be worrying about us," O'Connor said.

"Kin I offa ya sum coffee an corn cake afore ya leave?" J.W. asked hoping to prolong the visit and get some sense of their reactions.

"Thank you, but we need to get on home. Eunice will be expecting us," O'Connor said without discernible inflection.

He walked with them to the buggy and helped Sally climb up on to the seat. He smiled at her and said, "I hope ta be seein' ya when I take my receipts ta Mr. Graham this Sat'adee."

Sally said, "I'll be working in the usual place. Will you be needing any supplies?"

"Maybe jist sum coffee," he responded knowing that would give him an excuse to stop and talk with her.

As the buggy pulled away from his cabin, he had a sudden pang of sadness. "What ifen I've lost her? What ifen her Daddy tries ta talk her out of it? What ifen she thought ther's no way she'd liv in such simple surroundin's," he was working himself into a frenzy.

Vernon saw them leave, ran over and asked, "Kin we eat sumthin' afore gittin' back ta work?"

J.W. did not answer immediately. He was still lost in his dark day dream.

"What's matta wit ya,? Did Miss Sally put a spell on ya?" Vernon laughed.

"What'd ya say, Vernon?" he mumbled.

"I said, kin we eat sumthin'afore startin' the loggin' agin? Ya seem as ifen ya heerd sum bad news, tha way yer actin'."

He pulled himself together and said, "Shore we kin eat. I got sum beans an' corn cakes inside. Let's sit a spell."

As the two men went into the cabin and prepared to have lunch, J.W. was preoccupied. He wished he could share his concerns and worries with his friend, but he knew he had promised Mr. O'Connor to keep everything private until the family was ready to announce a possible engagement.

"Ya shore seem farway," Vernon said eating his beans and drinking leftover coffee. "Is sumthin' wrong? Why 'actly did Mr. O'Connor n Sally cum out here taday? Is sumthin' up?" Vernon was pushing for an explanation, but J.W. remained non-committal.

"Ifen yer thru wit givin' me tha business, let's git ta loggin'," he said suddenly as he rose from his chair and carried the plates to a bucket of water he kept by the hearth.

"Thought I's yer best friend an ya wont even talk wit me. Must be sumthin' portant," Vernon said with a sneer as they picked up their logging tools and proceeded with the day's work.

The rest of the week dragged on and his imagination ran wild. He asked himself what he did wrong and what he could do to make things right when he saw Sally again.

Saturday finally arrived with the usual trip to the saw mill followed by a visit to Mr. Graham. "How's it going, boy? You don't look like your usual happy self today," Graham remarked as they logged in the weekly debt payment and calculated the balance due.

"Oh, the loggin's goin' purty well, Sir. Vernon and me got a routine now. We're makin' good time and gitten closer to tha hardwoods," he responded trying to smile. He did not want any more questions that he could not or should not answer.

Shaking hands with Graham, he said, "See ya next Sat'adee, Sir." Then he quickly descended the stairs to look for Sally. He spotted her helping a customer select fabric and stood unobtrusively away so as not to interfere with her work.

When he saw that she was free, he walked over to her and said, "Good afta noon, ya good-looking thang, ya. How's yer day goin' so far?"

"Oh, hello, " Sally said as she looked up from the bolts of fabric that she had been straightening.

They stood staring at each other uncomfortably, each one waiting for the other to speak. He could not stand it any longer and spoke, "Sally, I've been worried all week tha ya and yer Daddy didn't like wha ya saw at Roarin' Fork an that ya mite ave changed yer mind."

She took his hand and said, "I haven't changed my mind about wanting to marry you if that's what you mean. But I am having a hard time picturing myself in that cabin with so little to work with and so far away from everyone and everything I know."

He didn't know what to say so he listened as she added. "Daddy wants me to be happy and he thinks you are an honorable young man, but he thinks we may be asking for trouble. He thinks maybe we should wait 'til you are further along in your plans."

"What could we do ta make things betta fer ya sooner?" he asked feeling like the air had been let out of his dreams.

"I'm not sure, but I think it would help to add some better cooking tools and some pretty things to look at," Sally quickly suggested as she could sense his depressed mood.

"Also, it might help if I could find a way to keep working at the store for a while or at least come to town more than once a week and visit my friends and Mamma and Daddy," she tried to sound hopeful.

"I think we'd be able ta do those thangs," he said quickly. He muffled his voice to avoid drawing attention to them in a public place.

"Kin we walk outside fer a few minutes so as I kin finish what I want to tell ya?" he asked.

Sally told Frank Graham that she needed to go out for a few minutes, and he gave her permission.

Once outside of the General Store, he began to talk. "Sally, I'd be willin' ta do anythin' to have ya as my wife. I luv ya so much an I want ya ta be happy. I think we kin work togetha ta make a won'erful life. Yer so smart an I'm a steady hard worker who's made up his mind ta be succesful. Most important, I luv ya." Sally smiled at him and resisted the urge to kiss him on the cheek.

"We got ta tell yer Daddy next weekend ifen we still want ta get married," he reminded Sally. "I know tha I do," he added definitely "What's yer answer, Miss Sally O'Connor?"

"Yes, J.W., I want to be your wife," she said tearing up a little.

"Then, we jist need ta let him know and ask fer his blessing. That's all there is ta hit," J.W. said confidently.

"Well not quite, Mr. Presley," Sally grinned. There's a whole wedding to plan and I'm betting you don't know much about those things."

"Guess yer rite 'bout that un, Sally, my love."

The next six days seemed to drag on, but he was in a much better mood. "She still wonts ta marry me. I'm a lucky man. Now we jist gotta 'vince er Daddy," he told himself and Miss Agnes on Friday the 20th.

Vernon, noticing the change in J.W.'s attitude, said, "Don't know wha 'appened over tha weekend, but I'm shore glad ta ave my ol' friend back."

Saturday finally arrived and he was rehearsing his talk with Mr. O'Connor trying to anticipate objections as most salesmen do.

It had been planned that he would stop at the Tailor Shop on his way back out of town to confirm, postpone, or cancel his proposal of marriage. Sally had prepared Frank Graham that she would need to leave the General Store early on Saturday to take care of some family business.

Charles Graham also noticed a perkier presence in J.W.'s walk and even his voice. "Glad to see you feeling better this week, boy. Guess the love bug's still bitting," he laughed.
J.W. simply smiled and bid Graham goodbye, "I hope ya 'ave a won'erful week, Sir."

Sally arrived at the Tailor Shop before J.W. and nervously awaited the meeting with her parents. When the last customer of the day left, O'Connor put the "closed" sign on the door and motioned to the back room where J.W. had first had lunch with Sally's family.

Eunice sat opposite Patrick around the small table leaving the other two chairs for the young couple, thus separating the young lovers but allowing them to look directly at each other.

"Well, you have had two weeks to consider the serious nature of your intentions," Patrick began the conversation.

Eunice chimed in, "There is no shame in changing your mind after all this is a mighty big step you two are considering."

Sally blurted out quickly, "We haven't changed our minds, have we.?"

"No, Ma'am, I most ce'tainly 'ave not changed my mind," he smiled in gratitude at Sally.

J.W. said humbly, "Mr. and Mrs. O'Connor, I know I ain't got now what ya would wont fer yer special daughta. I know yer worried tha 'ers makin' a big mistake. I kin only promise ta luv 'er mor than anythang an' ta put er needs 'bov my ownself. I believe Sally an me'll make a good team an we'll ave a good life togetha." He stopped and waited.

Sally had tears running down her cheeks. Eunice and Patrick were quiet for a few moments then they turned to Sally. "And what do you have to say, Daughter?"

"I love J.W. and want to be his wife. He has treated me with nothing but respect since the day we met. He has told me his life story, one of overcoming hardship and disappointment. Despite being lied to and mistreated, he has never given up on making a better life. He has not become bitter against the world. He makes me laugh each time we are together, and I would like to help him work toward his dream," Sally said choking back a sob.

Eunice spoke first. "We just heard a beautiful story of love, Patrick. What do you think we should do?

"O'Connor paused, cleared his throat and announced, "I guess we best be meeting with the Preacher tomorrow after church."

Sally rose from the table and moved to stand closer to J.W. He stood next to her and put his arm around her shoulder. Addressing her parents, he said, "Thank you, Sir and Ma'am. Thank you, thank you very, very much."

The Betrothal Period

Chapter 16

Sunday morning was cold and crisp. He could see his breath as he bathed and got himself dressed for church. Despite the January chill, he felt warm inside.

"Think I'll be lettin' Miss Agnes take me ta town t'day. Seems only fittin' that a lady should be takin' me ta meet my bride," he mused to himself.

When the Preacher greeted him with an unusually broad smile upon entering the First Methodist Church on January 22nd, he was unaware that the secret now included a fifth person.

Patrick O'Connor had already told Preacher Henderson in confidence about the engagement to prepare him in advance for the meeting with the young couple.

J.W. sat with the O'Connor family during the service but was unable to maintain his attention on the sermon. He was imagining what Henderson would say to him and worrying that this could be an additional obstacle to overcome.

When the service ended, and Henderson had shaken every hand and listened to every need and complaint, he made his way to the O'Connor home for dinner as planned.

Eunice and Sally were busy in the kitchen while Patrick sat with J.W. in the keeping room waiting for the Preacher. His fidgeting was quite noticeable.

"Don't fret, boy, Preacher is just a man. He'll most likely have many questions for you, but he's harmless," O'Connor grinned.

The Sunday Dinner was even better than usual today as if it were a special occasion; however, he was too nervous to think much about the food.

While the ladies began clearing the table, the men retired to the keeping room where O'Connor lit his pipe and stoked the fire.

Preacher Henderson looked straight at J.W. and said, "Young man, rumor has it that you are fixing to get yourself into even deeper trouble than you already got." J.W. was speechless for a moment before he realized that once again, someone was "messing with him."

Patrick and the minister let out bellows of laughter. "He doesn't know we've both been through this, does he?" Pastor John asked. Then he added, "Not only have I been through it on a personal level, but I've lived through it vicariously several times. Let me warn you, what seems like a simple decision, very rapidly becomes a complicated process."

Sally and Eunice joined the men and Henderson took charge of the discussion. "I am given to understand that you, Sally, and you, J.W., have decided to enter into the bonds of holy matrimony. Is that correct?"

He looked puzzled and said, "I don't rightly know tha word. Ya mite havta giv me a hammer fer it but ifen it means we wanta git married, that's the truth." Everyone laughed which cleared the air and eased the tension.

"What did I tell you, Daddy. He makes me laugh every time we are together," Sally smiled proudly.

"Let's get down to specifics," John Henderson said taking out a pad on which he would make some notes as he asked questions. "First, how soon did you plan on marrying?"

J.W. spoke up, "We kinda thought sum time in July. That'd give us six months ta plan an git thangs ready."

The Preacher consulted his calendar and said, "The weekend of July seventh and eighth would be my normal schedule for services at First Methodist. Do you want to have the wedding at the church on Sunday? We could combine it with our regular service."

J.W. looked at Sally for an answer. He didn't really care about the details, he just wanted to be married, to his love as soon as possible.

While she was still thinking, the Preacher offered his opinion.

"It's been quite some time since we have had a wedding in Graham, and I imagine the town folks will be excited and eager to be involved. They are used to coming to church on the second and fourth Sundays, so they would be there anyway. We might as well make it a special event."

Sally had not yet spoken but she looked at her parents for advice. Patrick said, "Yes, I think July 8th at church would be a wonderful time, and we can have a nice party after the service. This will be my only chance to be the Father of the Bride, so we should put our best foot forward."

"Good. We've got the place, date, and time decided. I'll leave all the other details to you good folks. I know there will be talk about clothing, flowers, music, food, and other things that don't really need my involvement. If you think of something that you want to add to the service, let me know. Otherwise, it will be a standard Methodist ceremony." Everyone nodded in agreement.

"One more thing. It is customary for the Preacher to meet with the engaged couple several times prior to the ceremony to discuss the meaning and responsibilities of the commitment. The best times for me to do that would be after church services," Preacher Henderson explained. "We can begin that process on February 12," he added checking his calendar.

"Unless there is something else, I need to get home to my bride, Nellie. Believe it or not, after all these years, she still likes to see me," he grinned as he made his way to the door.

Eunice looked at Sally and said, "You and me girl have got a whole lot of planning to do."

Sally giggled and said, "I'm so excited I can hardly stand it. Thank you, Momma and Daddy."

He thought for a moment that Sally had forgotten about him as she turned her attention to the wedding. He asked hesitantly, "Can we tell anyone now that we're fixing ta git hitched? I been wontin' ta tell Vernon so bad. He's my best friend and I think he 'spects I'm up ta sumthin'."

Patrick answered, "I think it would be best to tell Mr. Graham first seeing as how you and he have a contractual relationship. If it would make you feel a little easier, I would be glad to go with you to make that announcement."

"Oh, yes, Sir, that'd be eva so kind of ya. When could we do that?"

"On a Sunday afternoon, Charles is probably at home and resting after a fine meal. Let's you and me take a walk up to the Graham house and see if he will give us an audience," O'Connor suggested.

"Do ya think he'll git angry 'bout us int'ruptin' him ta home," J.W. asked worried.

"Under normal circumstances, he might, but I'm guessing he'll understand this is not normal. I'm also guessing he'll be pleased for you," O'Connor smiled. "Let's go, boy."

It was a short walk from the O'Connor's to the Graham home, but the frigid afternoon air was biting at J.W.'s nose giving him a flushed appearance. Ascending the front porch, O'Connor took the lead as he could see J.W. 's nervousness taking hold of him.

"I'll start the conversation, boy, and give you some time to calm down," Patrick offered.

"Thank you again, Sir. I ain't neva been in a fancy house like this un," he said slightly trembling.

Mrs. Isabella Graham answered the bell and said, "Good afternoon, Patrick. May I help you? And I see you have a young man with you, Mr. Presley, I believe."

"We would like to have a word with Mr. Graham if it's not too much trouble, Ma'm," Patrick asked politely.

"Come on into the parlor, and I will go get Charles," she said with a smile.

Charles Graham appeared at the door with a quizzical look on his face. "To what do I owe the pleasure of this Sunday afternoon visit, fellows," he said with a smile.

"For heaven's sake, Charles, ask them to have a seat," Isabella demanded.

Sitting on the richly upholstered settee did not relax J.W. in the slightest. He suddenly realized his humble position in this setting and that his future did depend on staying in the good graces of his benefactor. Fortunately, O'Connor began.

"Mr. Graham, we are here to share what we hope you will receive as good news. You are the first person outside of our family and Preacher Henderson to know that Mr. Presley has asked for the hand of my daughter, Sally, in holy matrimony."

J.W. was silent. He watched Graham's face for any signs of approval or the opposite but could detect neither. Isabella remained in the room without comment. J.W. was not certain if it was his turn to say anything; therefore, he did not.

O'Connor decided to fill the silence with additional details. "Eunice and I have given our blessing and we have met with Preacher Henderson who will be counselling with the betrothed. We are planning a July 8th wedding date at church with a party following, maybe at the Palmer House."

Graham walked toward J.W., who had not said a word, and commented, "Looks like you are taking on an even bigger responsibility than you already have, Presley. How do you think you are going to be able to take care of a wife and perhaps children at this point in life?"

He looked at the floor for a moment feeling as if he had been punched in the heart. Then he stood up and looked straight into Mr. Graham's eyes and said, "I know I kin handle tha 'sponsibility, 'causen I believe in myself, Sir. It's partly cause of Sally tha I know I kin do what eva I need ta do."

Charles Graham began to laugh, not in a mocking way, but in acknowledgement that he was looking at a young man of strength, conviction, and character.

"Well, congratulations, Presley, you have won the hand of our town sweetheart. You are a lucky young man. I've worked with you long enough to know you will do what you promise to do. I wish you both the best and I'll be here to help you if you need me, " he said extending his right hand.

"Thank ya, Sir. I 'preciate yer blessin' an yer confidence," he said standing proudly next to his future father-in-law.

When their unexpected company left, Isabella looked at her husband with confusion. "I cannot believe that you congratulated that poor young man on what is destined to be a big mistake."

"Now Isabella, I think you've lost all sense of romance in your old age," Charles laughed as he hugged his wife.

The ride back to Roaring Fork seemed to be shorter this evening as he was lost in thoughts of the new life he would have by mid-summer. After securing Agnes along with Jake, he stoked the fire, heated the leftover coffee, and sat down with a sigh.

"I kin see I'm gonna hafta make sum changes in this lil cabin ta make room fer my beautiful wife; but I'm not gonna worry 'bout it tonight. No, Sir-ee, I'm gonna go ta sleep dreaming of Sally."

Monday morning came and he could barely wait for Vernon's arrival. "He's gonna be so surprised, an I'm bettin' a lil jealous," he thought. Just then he heard Vernon getting off his horse.

"Come in here, Vernon, I got sum big news," he said with excitement.

"Yeah, I know. Ya an Miss Sally's gitten hitched this summer," Vernon replied in a tone devoid of affect.

"How'd ya know?" J.W. asked with considerable disappointment.

"Ain't ya 'ware Graham's a small town, boy?" Vernon replied with that "know-it-all look" he often proudly put forth.

There were two more weeks before they would meet with Preacher Henderson for their first counselling session; however, there would still be trips to the saw mill and the General Store. He had been invited to stay for supper on each Saturday, giving Sally's parents time to acquire a more in-depth knowledge of their future son-in-law.

As he and Vernon continued their weekly routines, he occasionally drifted off into thoughts of how different life would be after the wedding. Of course, his day-dreams only included the positives.

"I'll ave Sally by my side day an night ever day. We'll ave breakfast togetha. Whilst I'm aloggin' wit Vernon, Sally'll be bustlin' roun the cabin fixin' ever thang an' parin' our suppa. Afta suppa, we'll sit by tha fire an talk fer a spell. She may keep my lessons up so's I don't fergit what she learnt me.

"Cause tha days'll be longa in summer, we may go fer a stroll down by tha creek. Best of all, when we git tired, Sally's gonna lay down by my side."

He was lost in reverie one afternoon when Vernon yelled out, "Watch wha yer doin', boy! Yer 'bout ta cut my arm off. I've tole ya an tole ya tha safety's tha first thang a logger should be a thinkin' bout. Don't know wha yer thinkin' 'bout but it shore aint safety nor even loggin'."

After his deliveries on Saturday, he stopped at the O'Connor house for supper. Both Eunice and Patrick greeted him with smiles and put forth every effort to make him comfortable in their home.

Passing the cornbread, Eunice asked him, "We know most of the story of your adventures in coming from the old world to the new, but we, or at least, I, know almost nothing about your family. Tell us something about the home life you left behind in Dublin."

He was slightly stunned to realize that he had given little thought to his family since leaving for London almost five years ago. He had been working so hard to start a new life that he had turned his back on the old one.

"What kind a son leaves home neva ta return an don't even try ta make any contact," he thought with a feeling of shame running down his spine.

Pulling himself together, he began the tale. "My parents, Colleen and Ian Presley, live on a small farm outside a Dublin where they barely managed ta eke out a livin' fer the eight of us."

"When I got big enough ta realize there'd be no future fer me on tha farm, I headed fer London and ya know how tha turned out fer me."

"The first born to the Presleys was my sister, Mary Margaret. She's purty smart; kin read, 'rite, and ciper better than Momma an Daddy. She's a big help ta 'em in alotta ways. My oldest brother, Ian, is named fer our Daddy and he's a farmer at heart. I 'spect him take over when Daddy passes on."

"Next is me, James William Presley, am tha third in line and didn't git no real learnin' til Miss Sally heped me. Guess ever one thought we boys didn't need no ed'cation ta work in tha dirt. Not knowin' how ta read nor scribe, nor figure made it hard fer me ta git any kind a work in London."

Eunice broke in, "You said eight, but you've only told us about five family members. Please continue."

"Afta me, my brother, Sean Michael, was born. Then two sisters finished the family, Sarah Elizabeth, and Anna Cathleen. Anna'd be 'bout ten yars old now by my reck'nin'."

"From now on, I plan to call you **James**, Mr. Presley," Eunice smiled. "I can't tell everybody my daughter's marrying a man with no Christain names, just initials." Everyone laughed and the tension he had been feeling eased.

Sally was not to be outdone. "I'm just gonna call you, **Jay**. That'll be my special name for you," she beamed at him.

"As my Daddy used ta say, call me anythang ya wont 'septin' late fer suppa," Presley added.

Patrick had been listening closely without commenting. He looked directly into J.W.'s eyes and said, "Boy, you need to write to your family. They need to know that you are alive, well, and planning on becoming a married man."

"Well, I wernt able ta write till recent. Momma an Daddy cain't read good, so I jist ain't thought too much 'bout hit," he confessed.

"You said your sister, Mary Margaret, could read. She can read your letter to your family," Eunice said encouragingly.

"There's no reason left now that you cannot write a letter to your family, and I think you need to do that immediately. If you need help with it, you've got Sally," Patrick admonished with considerable firmness.

"When you get home start writing what you would like to say to your Momma, Daddy, Brothers, and Sisters. If you want me to read through it for you before posting it, bring it next Saturday and I will help you," Sally promised.

On the ride home, he thought, "Looks like marryin' inta ed'cated folks has its' downside. They's gonna 'spect me ta come up ta their standards. That's a lot a pressure fer a simple man, but I reckon it's a good thang."

Settling into his small cabin after securing his mules and the wagon, he sat down for the evening by the glow of his oil lamp to think about what he needed to accomplish in the next six months.

He picked up the stack of paper Sally had given him, and began jotting his list in no particular order.

"Sally'll hep me put thangs in order. Sum a them's gonna take more time and sum a them's gonna 'quire more money.

I'm gonna need ta talk wit Mr. Graham askin' bout addin' a few thangs ta my debt. Vernon kin hep wit sum thangs ifen he's a mind ta."

Must do 'afore July 8, 1832

By J.W. Presley

1. Write ta my family in Dublin like Mr. O'Connor said

2. Whateva Sally needs ta make her happy livin' wit me

3. Clean up tha cabin an make it more purty inside an out

4. Maybe add a room ifen Mr. Graham'll front me wit materials

5. Git me sum weddin' clothes

6. Git a weddin' ring fer Sally

The weight of what he would be taking on was becoming clear.

"Let me try ta start wit tha letter. That'll be 'nough fer one day," he consoled himself.

January 28, 1832

Dear Momma and Daddy,

I have learnt ta scribe a bit an wont ta
let ya an tha family knaw I'm alive an
well livin' in America. Got ta tha tawn of
Graham in tha state of North Carolina
in August 1830.

London waint rary good fer me. Many
bad thangs happened an I took a chance
on a new life in tha New World. Signed
a contract wit a kindly landawner ta
work his land return fer my passage here
an fer settin' me up til my debt's paid
up.

I'm workin' real hard an in a few yars,
I'll be a landawner my awnself. It's a
purty piece a land wit green mount'ns
like ta home an nice rich earth fer
plantin' along tha creek. It's called by
tha name, Roarin' Fork.

The best part is tha I found me a purty
lassie. She learnt me ta read an write.
She's a smart sweet girl an she's 'greed ta
marry me July 8th.

Wish ya could meet her. I knaw ya'd love
her jist like I do.

Hopin' yer proud a yer third-born son.

Your loving son,
James William Presley

"How come yer lookin' so worried ?" Vernon asked on Monday
morning.

"Jist thinkin' bout all I need ta git dun afore weddin' day. It's a turnin' inta a bigga project than I 'spected," he responded looking at his shoes and shaking his head.

"Takin' on a wife's always a big project and that's jist the beginnin' from what I heerd," Vernon laughed.

"If ya'll let me, I'm open to hepin' ya. Tell me what ya think ya haffta do n we'll take one step atta time," Vernon suggested.

I 'ready dun tha first un. Least I tried. Sally'll prob'ly do sum correctin' ifen I'm guessin'. Wrote me a letter ta my family in Dublin cause Mr. O'Connor said I had ta do that 'mediatly," he said.

"Let's see tha letter. I din't even know ya could write," Vernon said with surprise.

He handed his letter to Vernon as he explained, "Sally's bin learnin' me ta read n 'rite fer a bit n I'm gittin' fair ta middlin' at puttin'words together."

Vernon read the letter aloud and looked at him. "Good job. I'm mighty proud ta know I'm a working' wit a gentleman an a scholar."

J.W. beamed, "I ain't as dumb as I look."

As he shared the other items on his "TO DO" list, Vernon listened closely. "I cain't hep ya much wit fancy home fixings, weddin' clothes, nor Miss Sally's ring, but I'd be proud ta hep ya add a room ta yer cabin ifen ya can git Mr. Graham to spot ya a loan for tha building materials," Vernon offered.

"That's mighty kinda ya, Vernon. Yer a true good friend ta me," he responded quite in awe of the generosity.

"Let's do sum measurin' and make us a plan fer tha new room. Then we kin give Mr. Graham a estimate of the wood an' other necessary thangs so as he'll know wha yer askin'."

"Good idea, I was thinkin' bout knockin' out maybe eight feet on tha north wall an goin' out maybe ten feet. Wit three walls an a new roof, I'd have me a bed chamber fer Sally an' me. Then we could make the rest of the cabin a nicer place fer sittin' n eatin'," he told his friend with expansive arm gestures.

"I kin see ya've bin thinkin' bout this serious like. Ifen we's gonna do it afore weddin' time, we best git movin'."

All week during brief rest periods from the logging, the two friends honed their plans for their building project. They used stones to lay out an outline on the north side of the cabin and they estimated the logs and boards that would be needed to enclose the three sides of the added bed chamber and extend the cabin's roof over the additional space.

They made a list of everything including tools and smaller items, so J.W. would be able to give Mr. Graham a well-thought-out plan when asking for additional financial backing.

He planned to speak with Graham after making his weekly delivery of lumber to the saw mill. He practiced his speech as Jake and Miss Agnes pulled the heavily loaded wagon and trailer to town on Saturday morning. By the time he left the Henderson boys, who as usual gave him the business, he was feeling his muscles becoming tight and his throat felt dry and scratchy.

He spoke loudly enough for his mules to hear his practice session. Jake occasionally snorted but Miss Agnes remained silent. He was not certain if that was her way of approving or ignoring him.

Inside the General Store, he paused to speak with his sweetheart, then made his way to Graham's office.

"Good morning, young man," Graham said extending his hand.

"Good morning, Sir. Hope yer havin' a good day," he responded with his signature smile and a firm handshake.

"Afta I giv ya tha receipts an pay on my debt, I'd like to talk witcha fer a bit ifen ya have time."

"Of course, I have time for you. Have a seat and tell me what's on your mind," Graham said pointing to the leather chair in front of his large imported desk.

"Well, Sir, ya know that Miss Sally an me gonna tie the knot this summa, an I'm a lil' worried bout her movin' inta tha small cabin wit hardly no room fer her thangs."

"Yes, I understand your concern, do go on."

"I figger down tha road afta my debt is paid, I'll be buildin' me a big house on my ten acres but tha cabin'll havta do fer tha first few yars. Now ifen it was jist me, I'd be perfectly happy, but I 'spects a lady'd like ta have sum private space away from the gatherin' room."

"I believe you are very right, so what's your plan?"

"I was tellin' Vernon my concerns and we cum up wit a solution, but it'll depend on yer hep, Sir."

"Vernon says he'll hep me add a small bed chamber on the north side atha cabin. Me an him measured out tha space and ciphered tha materials and extras needed. Here's our list. Him an me kin handle all the labor and not short change ya any on the loggin'," he finally exhaled.

"You boys have been busy, now haven't you? Exactly what are you needing from me?" Graham asked waiting for the other shoe to drop.

"Sir, ya know I cain't pay fer the buildin' supplies taday but, I'd shorely pay ya back ova time ifen ya'd see yer way clear ta add them ta my bill. Ya know I hain't goin' nowhere," he answered with his eyes on the floor.

"Boy, I didn't take you to raise, but I'm starting to think you best be naming your first born after me," Charles roared and slapped him on the back. "Leave that list with me and I'll see that you have what you need within a few weeks."

"Mr. Graham, ya've bin like family ta me an I cain't thank ya enough."

He was feeling ten pounds lighter as he descended the steps two at a time into the General Store.

"Sally, I wrote my letta to my Momma an Daddy like yer Daddy said I had ta do. Kin ya kindly look it over an hep me make it look proper?" he asked handing his efforts to his sweetheart with a smile. "This is my first time writin' anythan 'sept my name and yer lesson," he added with both humility and pride.

Sally read quickly and with a tear in her eye said, " I wouldn't change a word. It's lovely and I'm so proud of my first student. I'll post it for you if you will give me the best address you have."

"The best I know is: Mr. and Mrs. Ian Presley, Greenfield Farms, Dublin Ireland," he said.

"That will be fine, and we'll put a return address so that we will hopefully know if the letter doesn't get to the right place," she suggested.

"Next Sun'dee, we'll be startin' our official betrothal time," he smiled at Sally.

"Oh, you mean because we have our first serious meeting with Preacher Henderson?" she asked.

"Yes, Ma'am, guess he's gonna set us straight on what's what," he laughed. "But 'tween yer Momma an Daddy, Mr. Graham, them Henderson boys, an my friend Vernon, I a'ready bin tole how much trouble I'm a facin'," he chuckled and winked at Sally.

"So, everyone thinks I'm trouble? How insulting!" Sally shouted with her nose in the air.

"They's jist messin' wit me, Sal, anyway yer worth it," he said as he turned her around with his irresistible smile and gave her a quick kiss on the cheek.

Saturday, February 11, he made his usual delivery to the saw mill and took his cash and receipts to Mr. Graham where he learned that some of his supplies were ready for him to pick up on his way home. The next day was second Sunday and church services at First Methodist in Graham.

As had been arranged, he met the O'Connor family at the Tailor Shop to walk with them to church. Patrick asked him to come into the shop where he insisted on measuring his son-in-law-to-be for a proper wedding suit.

Although he protested that he could not afford a fine suit, Patrick prevailed. "I don't want to see you standing at the altar in what you're wearing now. Those clothes are good enough for regular church, but not for my daughter's wedding."

Noticing that he looked embarrassed, Patrick quickly added, "You and Sally will have enough days ahead to be practical. I want that one day to be special, and it's my pleasure to make a suit for the son I never had."

Dinner at the O'Connor home followed the services, and, as usual was abundant and delicious. Preacher Henderson and his wife, Nellie, joined the family for the meal. While the ladies gathered in the kitchen for the cleaning away of dishes, the gentlemen sat in the front room to talk.

J.W. felt conspicuous as if both older men were waiting or making assessments of his worthiness to join this family. He was relieved when Sally appeared in the front room to rescue him. "Where would you like to meet with us, Preacher?" Sally asked.

"Patrick, can we use the back room at the shop?" Henderson asked.

"Of course, let me go with you to open the door and light the stove since it's getting a bit colder. When you're finished, I'll go back and shut everything down," Patrick replied.

Seated around the small table in the back room of the Tailor Shop, Preacher Henderson began.

"You two young people have expressed your love for each other, and your desire to be wed in the Church this July. Is this still the case," he asked?

Both looked slightly shocked but answered "Yes" at the same time.

"I'm glad to hear that since you have had a few weeks to think about the serious step you plan on taking. Let me explain the process I use in preparation for the ceremony of Holy Matrimony."

They listened attentively.

"We will have one meeting in each of the next five months after church on the second Sunday starting today, and continuing through June. We will then have a final meeting on June 24th prior to your wedding day to review all that we have discussed."

"What's we gonna talk bout at all 'em meetins," J.W. acted confused. "After all, we dun tole ya what, why, when, and where," he added trying to impress Sally.

Henderson laughed out loud. "Calm down boy. I know you're anxious to get on with it, but I don't think spending six hours spread over six months preparing yourself for what will last the rest of your lives is too much of an imposition."

J.W. looked at the floor and said in a whisper, "I guess not."

Henderson continued. "We will discuss the meaning of Christian marriage including the commitment and the responsibilities of husband and wife. We'll cover some of the challenges you will eventually face including management of your resources, raising of children, dealing with disagreements, handling illness or possible disability, and preparation for old age.

"Lastly, we will discuss the actual ceremony itself and the details involved.

"You will have questions for me during this process and I will not have all the answers nor will anyone else. Some things you just have to learn by living."

The Wedding

Chapter 17

The winter months with short days and long cold nights seemed to drag on forever, at least in J.W.'s mind. The tiring work of logging kept his mind focused until dusk each evening. After completing the usual evening tasks, he would day-dream about married life with Sally until his sore muscles finally demanded rest, and he fell into actual dreams.

With Vernon's help, he continued the usual logging work and used Saturday afternoons and non-church Sunday's to work on the bed chamber addition. His helper did not charge for the weekend work so as not to increase the debt to Mr. Graham. By this time, the young men were best friends, and Vernon considered his assistance to be his wedding gift to the couple.

After building the foundation for the new room and a base flooring layer, they boxed in the three sides with logs and began to install rafters for the roof extension. For protection from the cold air, they postponed cutting an opening into the new room until the roof was complete.

One weekend, Vernon brought a jug of corn liquor with him and the two shared a few drinks during rest periods.

Vernon was careful to offer a warning , "Ya cain't be a drinking while loggin'. I tole ya many times tha loggin's dangerous business an safety first's my motto."

J.W. agreed and added with a chuckle, "Sal'd most likely be frownin' on tha jug anyways."

Early in March, it was time to set out tobacco plants covered with cheese cloth for protection, which meant that the work load increased. With the logging, tobacco tending, and cabin expansion at Roaring Fork, plus the meetings with Preacher Henderson, J.W. didn't have much time to think about other details related to the wedding. He left most of that to the O'Connor family.

As spring eased herself into Graham, people spent more time outside visiting with one another. Announcement of the first wedding to be held in town in many years created excitement among the ladies.

Isabella Graham, with the assistance of her two daughters, Molly and Maureen, began planning an event which would give town folk an opportunity to express their best wishes and to assist the young couple in setting up their new home.

To her husband's pleasant surprise, Isabella had come around to a more generous attitude toward this unlikely match. "If you can't fight 'em, join 'em," Isabella joked as she and her team made lists of both durable household items, consumables, and physical tasks to help folks think of ways in which they could help according to their means.

The date was set for a community gathering at the Palmer House on June 10th after church. Preacher Henderson was informed and given leaflets to distribute after church services in April and May.

"I am so happy that folks in town seem to be pleased for us. Their being so generous to want to help us makes me cry," Sally said while walking with J.W. after an April counselling session with Preacher Henderson.

"I cain't really know how ta thank ever'un," he said with a lump in his throat."

"Not even two yars ago, I was a stranger ta folks in Graham an first good thangs I eva bin lucky nuff ta know started happ'nin' ta me. Yer the first an best thang tha eva happen ta me, Sal." Now Sally was sobbing quietly into her handkerchief all the while smiling sweetly at Jay.

Whenever townspeople gathered in church, at the General Store, the Feed Store, or other common areas, there was talk of the big doings being planned for the betrothed bride and groom.

The Graham daughters entertained themselves gossiping with their girl-friends about decorations for the June party and the July wedding. At their weekly get-togethers, they would embroider pillows, table cloths, and hand towels with the initials, **SPJ**, for Sally and James Presley. They naturally added sweet little love birds and flowers giggling as they worked.

All the happy chatter enhanced the sense of community and gave everyone something joyous to anticipate. People selected their own special ways to honor the couple.

Charles Graham encouraged the local craftsmen to use their individual skills to create useful gifts. Jim Murphy at the livery built a blanket chest which would be filled with hand-made quilts made during quilting bees by local matrons.

Vernon's father, Bertram Wills, fashioned a metal cookstove and assorted sizes of pots, pans, and kettles. Frank Graham had his staff gather a collection of sheets, towels, and dishes to be wrapped as gifts in large woven baskets which could also serve as permanent storage.

Thaddeus Dickenson and his wife, Elsie, told Mr. Graham that they would take charge of setting up the Palmer House for both parties. Elsie was looking forward to making the wedding cake and said she would talk with Eunice O'Connor to determine the proper menu. Ladies in the community would certainly want to contribute their best dishes for the gatherings.

Eunice and Patrick were overwhelmed and humbled by the out-pouring of love they felt from the town of Graham. They stopped in to see Graham one morning before starting work in their shop.

"Mr. Graham, we cannot tell you how it has touched our hearts to learn of the generosity being shown by you, Mrs. Graham, and many other folks in town toward Sally and J.W.

"You are making it possible for their wedding day to be much more special than we could have ever done alone," Patrick O'Connor said offering his hand.

Eunice daubed a lace handkerchief to her eyes, tried unsuccessfully to hide her emotion, and simply said, "You are good Christian people and dear friends to us."

Graham shook hands with O'Connor and replied, "The two of you are important to this community. You brought a vital trade and skill to our town making it a better place to live.

"How many beautiful suits and dresses have you made for other young folks in town both for celebrations and for everyday wear? How many garments have you mended or refashioned over the years, often without even charging?

"People of Graham love you and love Miss Sally. We want her to be happy. We know that the young couple are starting out married life with limited means but unlimited dreams," Graham concluded with a broad smile.

"It is a pleasure for your neighbors to be involved in this happy event. Plus, everybody loves a party," he laughed and patted O'Connor on the back.

"I am interested in your motives, Graham," Winslow inquired with a suspicious sneer. He was a large, thick-waisted, man, with a full beard who cleared his throat every time before he spoke.

Four men were having a leisurely lunch the first Wednesday in June at the Palmer House.

Charles Graham, Ulysses Winslow, Conrad Palmer, and William Mahan were not merely college classmates, they constituted the unofficial Graham Town Council. They met monthly to discuss the economic conditions of their town as well as any pressing issues that might affect the general welfare.

"Say what you have on your mind, Winslow. Don't beat around the bush," Graham responded as if he had been challenged to a duel.

"Why in God's name are you going out of your way to promote the union of the O'Connor girl with that dirt farmer out at Roaring Fork? Miss Sally comes from a family of skilled tradesmen, she has more education than most folks in town, and she is obviously both intelligent and beautiful while Presley is practically an ignorant nobody," Winslow threw down the glove.

Taking a few deep breaths, Graham began his response attempting to restrain his temper. "Winslow, you are a short-sighted fool and a snob to boot. Allow me to enlighten you by filling in the obviously absent part of your fancy education."

Standing up from the table to make his points, Charles outlined what he considered a common-sense strategy.

"Winslow, your bank will not prosper if our community fails to grow a population with sufficient resources to open accounts or take out loans that they repay with interest."

Turning to look at Mahan, who had been sneering along with Winslow, Charles added, "Mahan, you'll have a lot of time on your hands if your clientele consists of only this table and a few other folks with enough money to pay your exorbitant fees.

"Don't think you're off the hook, Palmer." The hotel owner was a tall, handsome man with a small moustache.

"How many rooms will you rent, how many meals will you serve, how may special events will you plan, if this town does not continue to grow in population and commerce?

"As for myself, I am smart enough to recognize that I need the folks who farm my land and cut my timber to produce families. Those children will grow up to provide additional labor, increasing the yield from the land, and they will be consumers of all the goods available in my stores.

"If you cannot see the connection between happy growing families and the overall success of our community, I think you must have missed a few classes at the esteemed University of North Carolina."

As he sat down, Charles concluded his lesson with, "In summary, Sally has chosen J.W. to be her husband, her parents have given their blessing, Reverend Henderson is counselling with them, and I intend to do everything in my power to ensure that this union is successful."

Winslow swallowed hard and said, "Lunch is on me today."

As time drew nearer to their big day, the young lovers found it increasingly difficult to focus on their daily work. Someone was always reminding them with roars of laughter, "married life's jist round ta corner, so ya best be enjoyin' yer freedom whilst ya kin."

J.W. asked Sally one Saturday, "How cum folks keep gittin' hitched ifen married life's as bad as they say?"

"I think they are just having a bit of fun with us," Sally giggled.

Wrapping her in his arms, he said, "Sal, I'm a guessin' we best be doin' our part for tha town by addin' sum babies soon's possible."

Surprised, but charmed by his knowing smile and the warmth of his arms, she replied, "Oh, how you do go on."

As he was leaving the General Store on May 5th, Sally told him that her father wanted him to stop by the Tailor Shop before going home. For a moment, he was worried.

"Am I in trouble?"

"Of course not. He wants you to try on your wedding suit," she laughed.

Having a suit hand made for him was more than he could comprehend. He had grown up wearing his brother, Ian's, hand-me-downs.

Since leaving his childhood home in Dublin, he had only owned two sets of clothing bought off the shelf in a general store plus the new shirt he bought for the Harvest Dance almost two years ago.

O'Connor greeted him and said, "Let's try these on to make sure I measured right. I'm still working on the vest."

Standing behind a curtain for privacy, he removed his trousers and felt the soft wool of the dark blue round-about jacket handed to him by O'Connor. "This is too nice fer me, Sir. I'm a bit scared I mite git hit dirty," he said.

"Nonsense, boy. You are going to look wonderful next to my beautiful Sally. The color really sets off your light-colored hair and makes your eyes even more blue."

As he stepped into the matching trousers and put his arms through the sleeves of the jacket, he exclaimed excitedly, "It fits jist perfect."

"Come out here and let me see you and stand in front of my looking glass," Patrick demanded.

When he saw his full image for the first time in many years, his mouth fell open.

"I look a'most like a 'spectable gent'man," he uttered with great surprise.

On the cutting table lay the pieces of a blue silk-damask vest which Patrick explained he would need to pin to his chest before stitching it together. "Vests fit closer to the body and have less room for error." He also showed him the bone buttons and the silk cravat that would complete the outfit.

"We just need to add a fresh white linen shirt and shine up your boots, boy. You will be a real lady killer in that outfit," Patrick said with pride.

"Not interested in 'pressin' no other ladies. I got me the one I wont," he responded. Glancing at his image one more time, he added, "Purty nice, an I'm athankin', she's gonna **like** it."

"One more fitting in a few weeks should take care of **your** wedding clothes. Sally's dress is taking longer because she and her mother don't always agree," Patrick chuckled. "Women folk are more particular about their clothes than us men. Best get used to that, boy," Patrick warned.

He thought to himself, *"I ain't gonna let the older folks skeer me bout married life. Me and Sal's gonna do jist fine . . . betta than fine, we's gonna be the perfect pair. The only thang I gotta do is git Sal a weddin' rang and finish fixin' the cabin."*

Eunice was creating a dress for her daughter that would be both special and practical. The extra adornments appropriate for the wedding could be removed allowing the same dress to serve thereafter for church or other special occasions. She had not seen the cabin but knew from all reports there would be a minimum amount of room for clothing.

Although she and Sally had not come to an agreement about the details of the dress, they had chosen the material. Pale yellow silk-damask for the base with emerald green silk appliques at the hem, and sleeves.

The wedding dress would feature short gigot-style sleeves, a fitted high-waisted bodice with a deep curved neckline, and a full pleated ankle-length skirt.

For modesty, a light-weight gauze caplet would cover Sally's neck and shoulders during the church service, but could be set aside for the party at the Palmer House.

White hand-tatted lace would be basted at the neckline and sleeve cuffs. Eunice was adding a small close-fitting bonnet in green silk with more white lace trimming on all sides. The cap, like the capelet, would be put aside after services for the party. Eunice would confer with Reverend Henderson as to whether it was necessary to cover the lower arms in church. If so, she would add additional removable gauze sleeves to the bottom of the gigots.

Much love went into each stitch of Sally's wedding dress. Eunice had to work around her customer needs but had found space in the evenings to complete the job in ample time.

Each fitting of the dress left a lump in Eunice's throat and tears in her eyes. "I can barely handle the idea that my only baby will be leaving me soon," Eunice sobbed.

"Oh, Momma, don't be **sad** for me. I'm so happy, and Jay is a **good** man. Besides, we will only be ten miles away, and I'll still be working next door until we start a family," Sally tried to console her mother.

"From the look in James' eyes, that will not be very long," Eunice said with a wink.

"Oh, Momma, I can't believe you actually said that," Sally said with a gasp.

"Girl, I wasn't born yesterday," Eunice said with a swagger and they both laughed out loud.

On Saturday, May 26th, J.W. entered the General Store to deliver his lumber receipts and cash to Mr. Graham, but was stopped at the bottom of the steps by Frank Graham.

"There's a package for you over at the post office, and it looks like it's from far away." "

"A package? I hain't eva got a package afore," he responded with puzzlement.

Walking over to the corner of the General store where the Post Office was separated by an iron gate, he wondered what he would find. The attendant handed him a small box wrapped in brown paper and asked him to sign for receipt.

"Shore am glad I learnt to 'rite," he thought to himself. Even though his curiosity was grabbing at him, he decided to wait until he was alone to open the package.

Climbing the stairs into Graham's office, his mind played all sorts of guessing games on him, but he resisted the urge to tear off that brown paper.

"Afternoon, Boy," Graham said. "What're you carrying there"?

"I don't rightly know, Sir. This was awaitin' fer me down at tha Post Office an thars a post mark stamp from Dublin at tha top."

"Well, if you would like to open it here in my office, I will give you some privacy," Graham offered.

"Thank ya, Sir, tha mystery's a killin' me."

"Take your time. I'll be over at my desk doing some work and you can sit by that table."

Inside the package was a letter and a smaller box. He opened the letter first.

Dear Son, James William,

Your whole family was so happy to hear from you. It's been over three years and we were beginning to believe we would never know your fate.

The long hard trip to America was a brave undertaking for a young man all by himself. We are so very proud of you for facing each challenge without giving up. We are also much pleased with the new life you describe and your prospects for the future.

We wish we could meet the sweetheart who will soon be your wife, but the distance is too far. Since we cannot be there for the happy occasion, I wanted to send you something that you could give to your bride as a gift from her husband's family.

The small box holds the wedding ring that belonged to your Grandmother, Sarah Elizabeth Presley.

Please write to us again and let us know more about your new family. Your Father, Sisters, and Brothers send their love to you and Sally.

Your loving Mother,
Colleen Presley

He tried to hold back his tears as he opened the small box.

Holding up the plain gold band, he noticed an engraving inside –
IN LOVE ABIDE.

Charles Graham could plainly see the emotion on J.W.'s face and
inquired whether it was good news.

"Oh yes, Sir, tha best. Would'ye like ta read my letter?"

"I'd be honoured if it is alright with you, Son.

"I'm so glad that you wrote to your family and received a response.
They must have had much worry with your being gone so long
without word," Charles said.

"Well, Mr. O'Connor tole me I had ta write ta 'em afore any more
time passed an I did jist wha he tole me being as how he's allowin'
me ta marry his only daughter," he responded with a smile.

"I knew you were a smart boy," Charles laughed. "Let me see this
ring.

"That is a beautiful ring and a wonderful saying inside it. Where
are you planning to keep it until the wedding?"

He thought a moment, and said, "I don't rightly know. I'm a bit
skeered of losing hit tween now and then."

"How would you feel about leaving it my lock box where it will be
safe, and let me bring it to you on the morning of your wedding?"
Charles suggested.

"That'd take a load offa my mind, Sir. Thank ya so much. I was thinkin' bout showin' hit ta Sally, but didn't know what ta do wit hit afta that."

"Why don't you show the letter to Sally, and let the actual ring be a surprise on the big day?" Charles posed.

"Oh, ya thank of eva'than', Sir," he added gratefully.

As he was leaving the General Store, he stopped in the piece goods department to speak with Sally.

"Do ya ave time fer me ta show ya sumthin', Sally?"

He proudly presented his Mother's letter and watched as Sally read it aloud.

"Oh, Jay, that is the sweetest thing I ever read. I wish I could meet your family in person," she said with tears streaming down her face.

"Where is the ring?"

"Mr. Graham's keepin' hit locked up fer safety til our weddin' day," he told her proudly. "He even tole me he knew I was smart fer doin' wha yer Daddy said I oughta, and fer marryin' ya, of course."

She smiled and kissed him on the cheek before bidding him goodbye for the week.

There would be two more Sunday dinners with the O'Connor family and two more meetings with Reverend Henderson before the big pre-wedding party.

J.W. used the five weeks wisely, with Vernon's help, to complete the work on his cabin improvement. When they were able to cut the opening from the cabin wall into the new bed chamber, both men were amazed at what they had accomplished.

"I cain't believe how much bigga hit seems wit jist one more room," J.W. said in awe.

"Yer new bride's gonna be a happy girl," Vernon predicted.

"I'm hopin' so, an' cain't hardly wait to show 'er. Wit out yer hep, I coulda neva dun this. Ya's my best friend." They shook hands and hugged.

The first weekend of June was an eventful period for J.W. and Sally. They were both excited and nervous as they pondered the prospect of being the hub of conversation in the town.

Saturday was the usual delivery to the saw mill and payment to Mr. Graham.

Sunday was singularly amazing.

After Church services, everyone headed to the Palmer House, which had been decorated with spring flowers and ribbons by a group of young ladies. Thaddeus and Elsie Dickenson had laid out a buffet luncheon with ham, vegetables, breads, and deserts all courtesy of Mr. Graham.

The betrothed couple were given a special seat in the middle of the large room and were ushered through the buffet line first.

When everyone had finished the meal, Isabella Graham stood, and announced that the town of Graham had come together to celebrate this happy occasion with a showering of both useful and decorative gifts all given with their blessings for a long and happy wedded life.

As the treasures were presented one by one, Sally and J.W. were overwhelmed with surprise and gratitude.

There were items of hand-made furniture, kitchen implements, blankets, linens, pillows, curtains.

Some folks brought bags and baskets of food staples: flour, meal, beans, potatoes, coffee, and sugar.

The artisans in the group brought examples of their crafts: wreaths, pottery, decorative baskets and wood carvings of animals.

With help from Vernon and the Henderson boys, J.W. loaded the larger items in his wagon for the trip back to Roaring Fork.

Patrick O'Connor made plans to bring Sally and the more delicate gifts in his buggy on Wednesday, giving Sally the opportunity to decide on the arrangement of all the gifts in what would be her new home.

He was both excited and nervous as he unloaded the wedding gifts from his wagon and carried most of them into the cabin. Mr. Wills' cookstove was a bit more than he could lift and carry alone. He would ask Vernon to help him in the morning.

It had been a most exciting but tiring day, and after taking care of his mules, he headed straight to bed.

"I need yer hep agin," were the first words out of his mouth as his friend knocked on the cabin door bright and early the next morning.

"Boy, I guess I'll havta move in wit ya and Sally, ifen ya cain't live wit out me," Vernon laughed.

"It's that cookstove yer Daddy made fer us. I cain't lift hit by my ownself," he mumbled with some embarrassment.

His pal chuckled, "Let's git it over wit so we kin git on wit the real work."

With considerable effort the heavy piece was positioned in front of the chimney, and they sat down to rest and survey the living space.

"Why, ya got this place 'most lookin' like a home. I see ya moved yer bed inta the new room wit the blanket chest at the foot. I'm guessin' tha room's gonna git worn out right straight, "Vernon said with a wink.

"I shore hope Sal'll feel tha way. Tell ya the truth, I got a knot in my gut worryin' bout this Wednesday when her Daddy brings er out chere."

"Take hit easy, boy. Ifen she's like most ladies, she'll want lots a changes later on, but right now, she's jist 'cited bout bein' a bride," Vernon consoled him.

They had been cutting lumber when they heard a wagon pull up in front of the cabin around mid-morning on Wednesday.

"Good morning Sal and Mr. O'Connor, he said as he helped Sally down from the wagon. It's so kind a ya to drive out chere bringin' a load of gifts fer us."

O'Connor replied, "Sally and I were both anxious to see her new home again."

Vernon offered a hand to unload the wagon and said, "Jist tell me whar ya wants eva'thin' to go."

J.W. thanked his pal and added, "Sal needs ta tell us, afta she has a look around."

Sally and Mr. O'Connor walked into the cabin and noticed immediately that things were different from their first visit.

"Oh, Jay, what have you done?" she said as she spotted the new room. It looks bigger, and there seems to be more sun light with the new window over the bed."

She whirled around and spotted the cookstove and all the new kitchen implements neatly stacked on the floor.

When she realized that he had placed some wild flowers in a cup on the table, she almost cried. "This is going to be lovely once we get all the pretty things laid out proper," she said as she flitted from one corner to the next.

"What'd I tell ya?" Vernon whispered to J.W. who was quietly standing out of the way.

He sat and watched as Sally deliberated placement of the remaining gifts she and her Daddy had brought in their buggy.

"I think this pillow's going to look mighty nice in that chair and I'd like to hang that lovely wreath over the fireside," Sally said talking mostly to herself.

When she was satisfied with her décor, the four of them sat down to enjoy some freshly made bread and sliced chicken Eunice had insisted they bring.

Walking her back to the buggy, J.W. took Sally's hand and asked, "Do ya thank ya kin be happy here, Sal?"

"Yes, Jay, we are going to be happy and very soon," she whispered sweetly in his ear.

Waving goodbye, he was all smiles.

"Betta close them lips afore the bugs git ya," Vernon laughed.

"Let's git back ta work so's ya'll stop givin' me tha business," he patted his friend on the back and whistled as they headed out to the trees.

Sunday, June 24th, would be the final meeting with Preacher Henderson before the wedding.

Continuing to question himself, he thought *"Could a poor 'dentured farhm boy wit no otha prospects really make a fine lady like Sally O'Connor happy? Wha ifen she changes 'er mind at tha last minute?"*

The drive to Graham seemed to become longer, and his imagination was not being his friend as he secured Jake behind the First Methodist Church. All through the service, he kept glancing at Sally trying to determine whether she was having second thoughts.

Even during dinner with the O'Connors, it was almost impossible for him to focus on the conversation at hand. Several times, he had to ask people to repeat their questions.

"Are you alright?" Sally asked.

"I'm sorry, Sal, I jist 'ave a lot on my mind t'day."

Preacher Henderson walked with the couple to the Tailor Shop where they would have their final pre-marital counselling session.

After a few opening comments in which he summarized all the issues covered in previous meetings, the Preacher asked, "Do either of you have any reservations about the commitment you are about to make to one another?"

Sally looked at J.W. and he looked at her. Both were nervous and reluctant to speak first.

Finally, Sally broke the silence and said, "No, I do not have any reservations. I understand that my life is going to change forever, and that I will have some difficulties adjusting, but I love Jay and I trust him."

It was J.W.'s turn; however, he found himself unable to speak because of the lump in his throat.

After several awkward moments, he blurted out, "I'm tha happiest man in tha world. Why'd I ave any resa'vations? Jist look at wha I'm gitten." Everyone laughed and Preacher Henderson offered them his blessing.

The sun shone brightly on **July 8th** and he drove to town earlier than usual to change into his hand-made wedding suit at the Tailor Shop. O'Connor had suggested it might be a good idea not to risk driving from Roaring Fork in the new clothing, so he met privately to assist him.

Sally was at home with her mother carefully stepping into her beautiful dress. Although she normally wore her hair in a modest braid on the back of her head, today she was determined to look her best. She wanted her lustrous red-brown curls to show during the ceremony even though she would be wearing a cap at church.

Eunice carefully attached the cap so that several long ringlets spilled out on either side and lay on her shoulders.

Standing back in front of the looking glass, Sally was quite pleased with herself, and Eunice had tears streaming down her face.

"Momma, please don't cry in church," Sally implored. "I don't want Jay to think you are unhappy for us."

"I'll do my best, girl, but I'm entitled to be both happy and sad when my only child is fixing to leave home." Then she handed Sally a small posy of daisies tied with lace matching her bridal costume.

Preacher Henderson greeted the congregation by saying, "I am humbled indeed that the whole town decided to come out today just to hear me preach." The room was filled with good natured chuckles.

He quickly added, "I'm guessing that you might be here for another reason, so I'm going to cut the normal service to the bare minimum, and get right to the main attraction."

After a few opening prayers and a well-loved hymn, Reverend Henderson asked the couple to join him in front of the altar. Reading from the standard Methodist marriage rite, he led the couple through the usual responses.

At this point, Charles Graham stood from his front row seat, and approached J.W. handing him something wrapped in a linen handkerchief.

J.W. unwrapped the gold band, took Sally's left hand, and gently slipped the ring onto her finger. "This is a gift for you from my family in Dublin, Sal. It was my Grandmother's wedding ring and inside it reads, *In Love Abide*."

Tears were streaming down Sally's face as she leaned into his kiss.

Before pronouncing them man and wife, he admonished the large crowd of their responsibilities as a community to support this union with Christian love.

"I now pronounce that James William Presley and Sally Ann O'Connor are man and wife. What God has joined together, let no man put asunder."

"Now, let's gather at the Palmer House for some good eatin' and fun." The congregation applauded.

Elsie Dickenson had done herself proud. The Ballroom at the Palmer House was resplendent with flowers and wonderful food, much of which were offerings from the community of their best dishes.

In a central place of honor stood Elsie's magnificent multi-tiered wedding cake.

This was a day to remember in Graham, North Carolina.

Building a New Family

Chapter 18

After changing into their regular clothes, the newlyweds packed some of Sally's other clothing and personal items and headed to the bridal suite at Roaring Fork.

Sally chattered for most of the hour's drive extolling the kindness of the Graham family and the town for all the gifts and good wishes. She remarked about the wonderful food, the flowers, the music, and the blessings.

"I'll never forget this day, Jay. It was perfect."

He, naturally, was thinking that this was to be their wedding night, and hoping that would also be perfect. He remembered how he had been admonished by both Preacher Henderson and Mr. Graham to be patient and gentle with his new bride.

Hurriedly taking care to feed and water Jake and Agnes before entering the cabin with his bride, he found that his palms were sweating and his heart was beating much faster than usual.

At the door of the cabin, he swooped Sally into his arms, kissed her soundly, and carried her into her new home.

Startled by his sudden bravado, She giggled with glee.

"Welcome home, Mrs. Presley," he said with pride. "Yer tha prettiest gal I've seen all day."

"Let me get my things out of the wagon and put them away, then we can have a piece of that wonderful cake Mrs. Dickenson insisted we take with us," she suggested.

"Jist don't be dawdlin' 'roun, Sal. "The sun's agoin' down an I was plannin' on us gitten a bit more familya, ifen ya knows wha I mean?" he winked at her.

As one might imagine, there was not much actual sleeping accomplished the night of July 8th; consequently, the first rays of sunlight dancing across the bridal bed on July 9th startled J.W.

"Vernon's gonna be chere afore I git dressed ifen I don't git on hit," he told his bride with a kiss on the cheek.

"Why didn't you tell him to take the day off?" She asked half-awake.

"I cain't 'ford ta lay offun my job causen I owe it ta Mr. Graham an now to ye," he said as he quickly pulled on his clothes.

"I'll start the coffee an keep Vernon outside 'til yer decent," he said patting Sally gently on her porcelain derriere, which he could see glistening in the morning sun.

"So, I'm no longer decent? Guess it's all down-hill from here," she chuckled as she slowly pulled herself out of bed and reached for her clothing which, for some reason, was in a pile on the floor.

"Holler when it's safe to bring Vernon in fer coffee," he said as he rushed outside determined that he would not be caught still in bed.

"Tha ol' Boy'll neva let me hear tha end of hit ifen I ain't ready ta work t'day," he mumbled to himself.

Sally stumbled into the living area, and began fumbling through assorted dishes and kitchen tools they had received as gifts. After a few false starts, she managed to get griddle cakes going, and set the table for three.

"You boys can come in to eat," she called through the open cabin door.

"Why Mrs. Presley, ain't ya lookin' lovely this mo'nin'?" Vernon said with a knowing grin. "Must be sumthin' in tha air out chere a Roarin' Fork."

"That's nuff, Vernon. Ifen ya want sumtin' ta eat, ya'd best not make tha lady a tha house mad atcha," J.W. said winking at Sally.

As the three friends finished their coffee and griddle cakes, they chatted about the events of yesterday.

Sally said, "I'm so thankful to all the folks of Graham for the love they showed to us on our wedding day."

"It were a real blessin' tha day I landed in Graham two yars ago," J.W. spoke wistfully.

"Most folks in Graham is 'good people'," Vernon declared.

Sally thought for a moment and said, "I think Mr. Graham can take a lot of credit for that. He and Reverend Henderson both set good examples of how folks should treat one another, like it says in the good book."

Vernon very meekly asked, "Guess wha 'appen' ta me causa yer weddin'?"

"Tell us, Vernon," Sally said with great curiosity.

"Well, a tha giftin' party ova ta tha Palmer House, Miss Savannah Schultz commenced a talkin' ta me real friendly like. She sat by me durin' tha eatin', an asked me ta dance wit her when tha music started up."

"Is there more?" Sally asked leaning in closer to Vernon.

"Yes, Ma'am. Savannah asked me ta sit wit her in church durin' yer weddin', and walk wit her ta tha afta party yes'tidee."

J.W. whistled, "Ya caught ya a beauty thar, my friend."

Sally interjected trying not to show any jealousy, "She is certainly quite lovely being tall with long ebony hair and an infectious smile. Are you planning on spending more time with her?"

"I'd like ta, Miss Sally, but I ain't too good a conversatin 'nor dancin' neither. She'll prob'ly git tarred a me real fast," he replied as he stared at his feet.

"Now listen to me, Vernon. All you have to do is tell her how nice she looks then shut up and listen for most of the evening. She'll think you're brilliant," Sally pronounced.

"Thank ya, Miss Sally. I kin handle tha," he smiled.

"I bin thinkin' bout tha future, an wonda how'd ya like ta 'ave me as yer neighba?"

"Whatcha mean, Vernon?"

"Like you an me talked long time ago, I don't wanna be no blacksmith. I wanna cut trees an grow crops on my own land. I'm gonna talk wit Mr. Graham bout buyin' some land next ta yer place ifen ya don't mind."

"It would be lovely to have neighbors. I would have someone to talk with if you get married. Your wife and I could become best friends," Sally rambled mostly thinking out loud.

"The four a us could hep each otha," J.W. added." I cain't believe I cum 'er wit nutin two yars ago, an now, I got me a wife, a friend, an soon a close neighbor.

Life is good!"

"You boys best get working, and I have a lot to do inside to make this place look more like a home than a barn," Sally ordered them out while looking around the room shaking her head.

As they left the cabin, Vernon smiled and reminded J.W., "What'd I tell ya bout women folk takin' charge a tha livin' space soon as they move in?"

On Saturday, he prepared to take his weekly load to the Henderson Saw Mill. He told Sally that he was going to let her drive the wagon so that she could become accustomed to making the trip to town alone. She hesitated a few moments in doubt but agreed that was the best idea.

"I'll get to see Momma and Daddy while we are there," She remembered excitedly.

After some novice fumbling with the reins, Sally got the feel of leading Jake and Miss Agnes. "Why, I can do this. It's not that hard," she congratulated herself.

"We'll see bout tha when it comes ta parkin' tha wagon in town," he chuckled.

"You men always think you can do everything better than us ladies, but just wait, we'll show you," she replied with her nose in the air.

The following week, Sally, with the help of Miss Agnes, drove the wagon to town, worked at the General Store, and visited with her parents at lunch time.

He worried about her the first few days but she appeared to have developed sufficient confidence by the end of the week.

Life became rather routine for the newlyweds during the remainder of July, August, and into September.

The logging continued with the team of two friends.

The tobacco remained mostly the responsibility of J.W., although he did introduce his bride to the details involved in **this** cash crop.

Sally became familiar with the household duties, and cried privately several times about how rough her hands were becoming from all the cooking, scrubbing, and hand laundry. She tried her best to conceal her exhaustion from her husband, but he could see it in her face.

"Sal, you know I love ya, an I don't wont ya to wear yerself down tryin' ta be tha perfect wife. Maybe it's too much fer ya ta keep workin' a tha General Store," he suggested as he put his arm around her.

"It's just that everything is **harder** than I thought," she answered in between the tears she could no longer restrain.

When he dried her tears, Sally said, "I do want to keep working at the store, at least until winter. It gives me a chance to see Momma, Daddy, and other people. It also gives us a little extra money to buy some of the things we need."

In mid-September, Sally began having bouts of early morning nausea. She didn't say anything to her husband but mentioned it to her Mother during lunch one day.

Eunice looked at Sally and noticed some changes in appearance that led her to believe there might be an addition to the family by spring.

Eunice took Sally aside and explained to her what was most likely happening, and what to expect. Sally was somewhat in shock and asked, "What must I do now?"

"Just take care not to do any heavy lifting or get too tired for the next few months," her Mother advised. She added, "I am excited to think Patrick and I may be Grandparents."

"Should I tell Jay?" Sally wondered aloud. "What about working at the General Store? I was hoping to stay on there until cold weather."

Eunice wisely explained, "Being in the family way is always a little different for each woman; however, you can probably continue working for a few months if there are no complications."

"You should let James know what we think is happening. I would not tell everyone until you are further along, but do let Mr. Frank Graham know that you will be leaving the store before Christmas without any details."

On the drive home, Sally's head was spinning. "How am I going to handle a baby living out in the country side with no close help except Jay who has his hands full?"

As she laid supper on the table, Sally told Jay that she had something to tell him.

"Don't keep me guessin', Sal, what is hit."

She kissed him on the cheek and said, "Jay, there's a good chance you're going to be a Daddy in the spring."

He jumped up from the table, grabbed Sally, swung her around, and let out what later would be called a Rebel Yell.

"Whoo Hoo! I'm gonna 'ave me a son. I'm gonna build us a fam'ly. I'm gonna buy us sum more land an build us a big house. There's no stoppin' J.W. Pressley!"

"Now don't be telling anyone else for a while, Jay. This is our secret for a few months," she pleaded.

"I don't know ifen I kin hold it in tha long, Sal." He tried hard to keep his joy contained, but he couldn't help whistling and strutting everywhere he went.

After a week of that behavior, Vernon said, "What's up wit ye? Yer actin' kinda crazy in a happy sorta way."

"Can ya keep a secret, friend?"
"Shore I kin, don't ya trust me yet?"

"Well, yer lookin' atta proud Daddy ta be," he bragged to Vernon.

"That's jist great. How soon?"

"Sal's not rightly shore, but we're thankin' he'll be here cum spring."

"Oh, it's a boy fer shore huh! How'd ya know tha," Vernon asked chuckling.

"It hasta be a boy, causen I give it my best shot," he boasted sticking his chest out.

"Guess we need to share a sip or two after work t'day in honor of tha comin' event, " Vernon suggested.

"I don't 'ave no corn liquor."

"But I do!" Matta a fact, you an' me needs ta make us a still up in tha woods so as we kin' always 'ave our own supply fer special times."

"Do ya know how ta do tha?" he asked with surprise.

"I know a lot a stuff. Ya ain't tha only man 'roun here wha kin make thangs," Vernon laughed.

On his next delivery trip to town, J.W. was surprised to hear Mr. Graham congratulate him on the coming "blessed event."

"How'd ya know 'bout tha? It was suppose' ta be secret."

"Boy, you've lived here long enough to know that the only way to keep a secret is to keep your mouth shut," Charles Graham guffawed.

Sally was not happy to learn that her condition was already the talk of the town and she scolded J.W. accordingly.

"Jay, I haven't even had time to tell Mr. Frank Graham I will be leaving the store by Christmas time," she said in an unusually shrill tone.

"Well, I guess I saved ya tha trouble, Sal," he replied trying to make her laugh.

It didn't work.

Eunice made a guess as to the expected delivery date of her first grandchild based on the information she could glean from Sally. Taking charge as the knowledgeable person, she laid out a plan for her daughter during lunch one day.

"I'm thinking this baby will come sometime in early May. Since this is your first one, and you will be ten miles out of town with no help, I think you should have James bring you to our house in late April to stay for the rest of your confinement."

"There's a Negro woman, Miss Lucy, working at the Palmer House who has some experience with the birthing process. Mr. Palmer brought her and her husband with him when he moved from Atlanta. We can most likely get her to help us when the time comes."

Sally's could not process all of this immediately, but she said, "I don't think Jay is going to like me being away from home when his child is born."

"Exactly how much help do you think he will be when you start screaming?" Eunice quickly asked. "He'll feel much better knowing you are with people who can help you and make sure both you and the baby are healthy," she added more calmly seeing that Sally was upset.

"After the first week, you can take your baby home. In the meantime, James is welcome to spend as much time as he can take away from his work to visit with you right here."

"You are probably right, Momma," Sally whimpered. "It's all more than I can think about at one time. I'll explain it to Jay and we will both have time between now and then to get used to the idea. Right now, I must get back to the General Store and talk with Mr. Frank Graham, so he will know how to plan for when I'll be leaving."

"It will all work out, Sally. Don't worry too much. That wouldn't be good for your nor the baby," Eunice consoled her daughter with a hug.

The remainder of the fall of 1832 was filled with everyday work at Roaring Fork, Sally's trips to town, visits with the O'Connors, semi-monthly church services, and planning for their first child.

The Presley/Wills team were becoming more productive with their logging. They learned from their mistakes and adapted their process becoming increasingly more efficient.

Graham was pleased with the increased output, and based on the obvious successful working partnership of the young men, had cut a deal with Vernon selling him ten acres adjoining Presley's indentured land on credit. J.W. was thrilled to learn that he and Vernon would be both neighbors and partners.

With her earnings from the General Store, Sally managed to buy a few items she knew would be needed to care for a baby. She also turned her attention to making the small cabin look and smell like Christmas.

She gathered greenery, tied it into wreaths and garlands, and adorned them with scraps of red ribbon from her Mother's sewing shelves. She put bundles of sassafras root in a small crock of water to simmer on the hearth filling the cabin with a cheery aroma.

Eunice surprised the couple one weekend by pulling out an old cradle from storage. "This is what my only baby slept in for a few months," she said with barely disguised tears.

"Oh, Momma, how wonderful. Thank you," Sally said with joy giving her Mother a kiss on her cheek.

Christmas of 1832 was a time of sweet anticipation for the young Presley family.

Leaving her job at the General Store was a mixed blessing in Sally's mind. Excited though she was to be preparing for the holiday and the blessing of a child in the spring, she was also a bit sad to be leaving her friends in town. This would be the first time in her life to be separated from her parents for more than a day at a time.

"This yars bin tha happiest eva fer me," Jay whispered in Sal's ear one evening in front of a blazing fire.

Smiling at him, she asked him for details.

He took a deep breath and began, "I talked tha purtiest gal in town inta becomim' my bride. Cause of ye, I 'rit ta my family in Dublin an my Momma sent me a ring fer tha wedding. Tha town folks had us a special party wit many more gifts than I coulda dreamed. Mr. Graham's happy wit my farmin' an loggin'. My best friend's gonna be livin' next ta us. Best of all, I'm gonna be a daddy."

Sally kissed him softly and responded with a broad smile and a tear falling down her cheek, "I'm happy too, Jay."

Although a bit confused by her smiling tears, he hugged her and promised, "Sal, I'm gonna do tha best I kin to make shore ya stay tha way an' neva regret marryin' a poor dirt farhm boy."

She returned the embrace and added, "Jay, I knew the first time I saw you, there was a prince hiding in those worn out clothes. You just needed the right gal to bring it out."

The next few months flew by as they worked together. Spending all of each day united in purpose deepened their bond.

Vernon and Savannah were becoming more serious and it began to look as if Sally would soon be gaining a female friend living close enough for daily visits.

J.W. reluctantly agreed with the plan Eunice had suggested, and took Sally to stay at her parent's home in late April to await the birth of their first child.

"Don't cry, Sal, I'll be here eva Sat'adee and Sun'dee fer shore."

Eunice tried to console him, "James, we will get word to you as quickly as possible when the time comes."

Late in the afternoon on May 15, contractions began. Patrick walked over to the Palmer house and asked to speak with Miss Lucy. Both Palmer and his manager, Dickenson, had agreed months before to allow Miss Lucy to assist at the time of Sally's delivery.

"How close them pains a comin'?" she asked Mr. O'Connor.

"I'm not in a position to know. All I can say is that both women are highly agitated, and since I don't know nothing about baby birthing, I'm needing you **right now**."

"Ya best be calmin' yerself down, Mr. O'Connor. I ain't be needin' **three** screamin' white folks ta handle this ev'nin'," Miss Lucy said as she gathered some supplies and followed O'Connor across the street.

Inside the O'Connor home, Miss Lucy took charge of the situation immediately telling the expectant Grandparents to stay out of the way until needed. "Lead me to Miss Sally an' keep yerselfs ready ta hep when I calls ya."

"Good ev'nin, Miss Sally, what's all tha squawlin' bout?"

"I'm just scared, Miss Lucy," Sally said as she held her stomach panting between contractions.

"Listen ta me, girl, eva'thang's gonna be fine ifen ya jist does wha I tells ya."

"Have you been through this before, Miss Lucy?" Sally asked hoping that someone could give her the confidence she was surely lacking.

"Ya mite say I's bin, ifen ya count my own six babies plus least ten otha youngins I's heped enter this here world," she said chuckling and singing while arranging the bed linens and wiping Sally's brow with a cool cloth.

"How long does it usually take?"

"Well now, Miss Sally, eva baby has hisen own schedule. First'uns sumtimes ain't in no hurry ta leave tha comfort a Momma's shelter. Cain't say I be blaimin' 'em 'sinderin' tha world they be afacin'."

"The best thang ya kin do is try ta relax tween them pains, breath in deep, an drink sum wata when yer mouth starts parchin' up, "Miss Lucy counseled.

"I'm gonna step outta tha room ta speak wit yer Momma and Papa but I be comin' rite back."

To Mr. and Mrs. O'Connor, Miss Lucy said, "I'm a guessin' this baby won't be cumin' til mornin', but ya mite wont ta git word ta Mr. Presley ta be here afore noon tomorrow."

Miss Lucy's prophecy proved correct. Sally's contractions continued throughout the evening, slowly at first with long intervals during which she was able to talk, ask questions, and even laugh.

The O'Connors were also able to relax under Miss Lucy's calm guidance. As they wandered in and out of the bedroom to check on the progress, they could clearly see that there was no imminent danger and that Sally was in good hands.

Patrick took Miss Lucy's advice and asked Vernon to ride back out to Roaring Fork, inform his good friend that the time was nigh, and remain with J.W. all night until they could ride back together into town early next morning.

When he heard the news, he tried to convince Vernon to ride back to town immediately, but Vernon coached him into getting some sleep.

"Yer bride's gonna need ya rested when we gits thar. T'mora's gonna be a long day fer all of ye," Vernon insisted.

Back in the O'Connor home, things were starting to move faster after midnight. Around four in the morning, Sally, though exhausted, was feeling the urge to push and the space between contractions was becoming extremely brief.

Miss Lucy rearranged the bed and explained to Sally in simple terms what would soon be happening rapidly.
She made certain that Sally had water, that she was breathing more deeply with each pain rather than just panting.

"Jist ya keep alookin' a me, Miss Sally. Take yerself sum slow breathins each time, and hold my hand as tight asin ya please," Miss Lucy advised as she periodically swabbed a cool cloth on Sally's sweating brow.

Just as the sun began peeking its head over the ridge outside Sally's window, the final push brought a healthy baby boy whom Miss Lucy placed in his Mother's arms on **May 16, 1833**.

Sally and J.W. had already decided on a name for a boy child.

"Welcome to the world, James Buchanan Presley," Sally smiled and kissed her first-born son.

He was banging on the front door of the O'Connor house just after sun up.

"Has our son bin born?" he asked excitedly as Patrick opened the door to allow both him and Vernon enter.

"Yes, he made his appearance about an hour ago. How did you know it was a son?"

"I jist knew," he beamed. "Kin I see him?"

"Of course, follow me but be aware that Sally is probably still asleep. She had a long and tiring night," Patrick motioned toward the bedroom. "Vernon, you best wait until James and Sally have a time alone with their baby."

Walking softly into the room, he saw Sally with her eyes closed nestling a small bundle in her arm.

When he looked upon the two of them, it was all he could do to hold back the tears. "Now we're a real fam'ly."

At his voice, Sally opened her eyes and smiled at her husband. "Good morning, Daddy."

"Kin I hold Buck?" J.W. asked nervously.

"Oh, I guess he'll never even know his Christian name," she responded with a slight grin.

"Ta me, he's my son, Buck."

All Things New

Chapter 19

As they had agreed, Sally and the baby remained at her parent's home for another week, during which J.W. made a daily afternoon trip to town. Mr. Graham understood and did not complain at the temporary downturn in logging receipts.

When the day came to take his family home, he put several extra quilts in the wagon to soften the seating for Sally.

Before they set out for the trip home, Eunice had prepared a hearty lunch for the four of them. She also packed a basket of prepared food for their supper.

"Thank ye, thank ea very, very much fer taking such good keer of Sal an Buck," he said with heartfelt appreciation; as he hugged Eunice and shook hands with Patrick.

As he led the mules slowly and carefully over the ten-mile journey so as not to jostle the new mother and babe unnecessarily, he whistled.

"I haven't heard you do that for a long while, Jay," Sally said with surprise.

"I ain't hardly eva bin this full a joy 'septin' our weddin' day. Now I most got ever'thang a man culd ask fer on this side a heaven, Sal" he said as he patted her hand.

One might think that adding a small baby to the household wouldn't disrupt the normal activities very much. One can only take that notion at face value if one has never experienced it.

Everything changes!

The first casualty is sleep deprivation. Sally was afraid to sleep soundly for fear that something would happen to her baby boy. J.W. couldn't get a full night's sleep, so he was dragging himself through each day of logging.

Vernon carried more than his share of work for the first few weeks, as his way of helping his friend adjust to fatherhood.

Sally struggled to care for little Buck, keep meals on the table, and to still be a helpmate to J.W. She worried daily that she might not be doing everything she should to ensure the health and development of their baby. Every strange sound, every prolonged crying spell, every change in behaviour, increased her anxiety.

Without another woman close by, she had no one to consult, and J.W. knew even less than she did about caring for a new born. She found herself becoming irritated with J.W. for no real reason, and occasionally said things that she regretted.

"You're out in the woods all day, and I'm left to do everything in here by myself," she cried one evening when J.W. came in for supper.

He didn't know what to say, so he sat quietly while Sally finished preparing their meal. That made her even angrier, and when she slammed his plate down on the table, he erupted with, "What's got inta ya, Sal?"

He watched her helplessly as she began sobbing. Little Buck echoed his mother with his own loud cries. J.W. walked over to the cradle, picked up his son, then embraced both his wife and baby while they continued to wail.

The next day, J.W. vented his frustration on Vernon, who suggested that a trip to town might cheer Sally and give them both a break from the daily routine.

That evening, J.W. told Sally that he would like her and Buck to accompany him on his weekly trip to the saw mill.

"I'm bettin' yer Momma an' Poppa'll be beside themselves ta git ta hold li'l Buck ag'in."

The excitement about going to town did perk Sally up out of her doldrums, and she tried to show her appreciation by fixing a special breakfast for J.W.

"Thank you so much, Jay, for thinking of taking us with you today."

He hugged her and said, "It's been a big change fer both a us, but ya've had tha worst of hit. Gittin' away from tha cabin fer a day may be jist whatcha need."

The Henderson boys welcomed Sally and little Buck as J.W stopped to drop off his weeks' worth of logging. Sally was beaming as they "o-ohed" and "ah-hed" over her baby.

Next, he stopped the wagon in front of the O'Connor home and helped Sally down to be greeted immediately by both parents who were, due to Vernon's announcement, expecting the visit.

There were smiles and hugs all around. Eunice grabbed little Buck into her arms and began singing to him.

Realizing that he was only an extra in this scene, J.W. said, "I'll be leavin' y'all fer a bit whilst I meet up wit Mr. Graham."

Eunice waved at him and said, "When you come back, we'll have some lunch," then quickly turned her attention to her grandson.

Everyone he passed on his way to Graham's office congratulated him on having fathered a healthy new son.

It would not do justice to his reaction to say that he began to stand a little taller and thrust out his chest just a bit further than usual.

"Welcome J.W. Have a cigar on me and congratulations on the new addition to your family," Graham said slapping him on the back.

"Thank ya, Sir. I feel very blessed ta be wherst I am taday in light a wherst I cum from, an' I'm thankful ta ya fer all yer he'p."

"I brung Sal wit me taday ta visit her folks. She's gittin a bit down wit all tha reg'ler work at tha cabin an tha loss a sleep from li'l Buck's cryin' an' fussin'," he shared wringing his hands and gazing into the distance.

Graham thought a moment and replied, "I'm betting you are also more than a little bit overwhelmed with the changes that a new baby brings."

"Ya got tha right, Sir. I'm full a joy ta 'ave a son, but I'm wondrin' ifen I'm upta tha job," he said in a solemn tone.

"Let me share something with you, Son. None of us know if we are up to the job until we are faced with it, and have no choice but to plow right through as if we know what we are doing. Somehow, it seems to work out in most cases."

"Maybe it's help from above when we need it most, or maybe it's natural instinct, I don't know for sure. But my experience tells me that two people who love each other like you and Sally, and love that baby will get through the hard parts and later remember only the joy.

"I've heard that said about the birthing process, and I think it is also true about the raising process."

"Thank you, Sir, I really needed tha 'couragement," he said shaking Graham's hand. "I think I'll be visitin' my best friend's family for a bit afore goin' ova ta tha O'Connor place."

Eunice and Patrick had been passing little Buck back and forth smothering him with enough hugs and kisses to last a week or more. Sally beamed watching this out-of-character display of affection. She felt great joy seeing how much a grandchild meant to her parents. This was a gift no one else could give to her Momma and Daddy. She was **proud**.

Eunice handed Buck to Patrick and said, "Sally and I are going to start lunch before James returns. You can spend some man-to- man time with your grandson." Patrick chuckled and began singing to little Buck.

In the kitchen, Sally suddenly began to sob. "What is wrong?" Eunice asked leading Sally to a chair by the table.

"Oh, Momma, I am so tired and worried all the time." More tears rolled down her cheeks as she fought to catch her breath and continue.

"I didn't know this would be so hard. I can barely keep up with the cooking, washing, and general housekeeping, let alone carry this baby on my hip most of each day.

"It seems he needs to eat every hour, so that means I have to sit with him then try to catch up with the work I started doing. I almost never get a night's sleep.

"The worst of it is that I get cross with Jay for no good reason." At that point she laid her head on the table and bawled loudly.

Patrick couldn't help but hear and walked in asking what was going on.

"Just stay in the keeping room with Buck. We'll be through in a few minutes," Eunice said waving him out of the kitchen.

Eunice sat next to her daughter, rubbed her shoulders, then took her hand. "Sally, you are experiencing what every new mother since the beginning of time has faced. It is a whole new world and it takes time to readjust your routines and find a new pattern that works for you.

"I know how strong, smart, and loving you are, Sally. You are bound to be a good Mother. I think the loss of sleep and the absence of other people around makes the whole process more difficult.

"Remember that it was your choice to marry James and move out of town. You knew there would eventually be children, and that you would need to do the type of work that was new to you. You made a commitment, and I feel sure that you will honor it.

"I think it may be a good idea for you to come into town every Saturday with James. I could take care of Buck for a few hours and the two of you could visit friends or just wander around. A change of atmosphere and some time for the two of you to be alone will do wonders for both of you."

"Oh, Momma, It is so good to be able to talk with you. I have missed that more than anything. Thank you so much for understanding and not thinking poorly of me," Sally said hugging Eunice and drying her tears.

Roaring Fork Grows Up

Chapter 20

Life in the cabin at Roaring Fork became a continuous learning curve for the Presleys during the first year of Buck's life.

Neither of them had been involved in the developmental stages of a baby in any meaningful way. Sally was an only child without cousins or any babies in her immediate family. Her parents had emigrated from London to America when she was a child herself.

Although J.W. had siblings, sons in that era were not usually assigned child-rearing tasks. With a combined experience of zero, Sally and J.W. laughed and cried together as they made the normal mistakes of first parents.

"Well, he's still alive on his first birthday, so we must've dun sum'thin rite," he laughed as Sally sliced the small cake she had made for the occasion.

In addition to the many changes inside the Presley cabin, other things had happened in Roaring Fork during little Buck's first year.

J.W.'s best friend and right-hand man, Vernon Wills, had built a small cabin on the land Charles Graham allowed him to purchase and repay over time, next door to the Presley land.

Savannah Schultz had set her sights on Vernon when Sally and J.W. were married, and had used her feminine charms to convince him that it was his idea to propose to her.

Sally was ecstatic to have a young female neighbor. Finally, someone close at hand with whom she could talk, plan, even commiserate. Savannah would drop in to visit several times each week and give Sally a small break from chasing after the now toddling Buck.

For Sally, life was becoming more manageable. There was certainly no less work, what with cooking, cleaning, child care, and husband care. Now, she could look forward to a weekly visit with her parents and frequent visits with her new best friend, Savannah.

J.W. was proud that his logging production had increased even with less help from Vernon, who now had his own land to work in order to repay his loan. Charles Graham seemed pleased at his progress as well as the new production from Vernon.

Just as life is feeling somewhat more balanced, Mother Nature hands the Presley family a surprise, in the expectation of a second baby to join them only a little more than twenty months after Buck's arrival. There would be two babies in diapers.

"Don't cry, Sally," Savannah said with her arm around her friend. "I'll be here to help you as often as I can."

Blubbering into her apron, Sally replied, "You'll be having your own babies before long." Then, thinking aloud, she laughed as she added, "Maybe we could get an indentured servant of our own."

During a summer church service in town, Sally struck up a conversation with a woman about her age, who had been looking at the restless little Buck and smiling. She was holding and rocking a new born in her arms.

"Hello, my name's Ruth Johnson and I believe we're neighbors."

"I'm Sally Presley and we live at Roaring Fork near the creek."

Ruth went on, "We're on the next piece of land 'cross tha creek at Old Yellow Creek. I was jist wunderin' the age of yer son?"

"Little Buck had his first birthday in May, so he is almost 15 months old," Sally replied.

"He shore is a pretty little boy and seems so happy too," Ruth smiled.

With pride, she said, "Buck's our first, and he has kept us on our toes since day one. His name is actually James Buchanan, but you'd never know that. His Daddy started calling him, Buck, the minute he first saw him, and everyone fell into line with that."

"How old is your baby," Sally inquired.

"Martha was born in April so she's almost three months. I was looking at your boy and imagining what I'll be dealing with when she starts walking," Ruth laughed.

"Oh, your whole world will change again. You'll need eyes in the back of your head," Sally said chuckling.

"You know, we need to visit from time to time living so close. Why don't you come over for supper some evening. I know Jay would love to meet your husband?"

Ruth smiled, "Yes, we folks outside of town need to know each other better. We're starting to build our own community separate from downtown Graham, and we could be a big help to one another."

Sally, Savannah, and Ruth began visiting on a regular basis, providing a type of support and kinship that only women could appreciate. They understood how much their bodies determined their destiny.

Large families were the norm in those days, and the lives of working-class women consisted mostly of bearing and caring for children during their productive years.

By necessity, they also had the major responsibility for all household chores, cooking, cleaning, laundry, sewing, repairing clothing, and sometimes vegetable gardening. There was little time for any personal pursuits.

The thing Sally missed most about her life in town was the pleasure of getting lost in books. The only book she had brought to Roaring Fork was her Bible. During one visit to her parent's home, she asked, "Momma, if you could find a few books of any kind for me to have at home, it would make me so happy."

Eunice replied, "Before you leave today, I will give you any of our books that you would like to have, and then I will see what I can borrow from folks in town. I doubt that you will have much time for reading with another one on the way, but if it pleases you, I'll make certain you have books around you."

"Oh, Momma, you are so wonderful. If you can find a few books suitable for reading to young children, I would really like to have some of those. I'm planning on teaching my children to read as soon as possible.

"I want them all to love reading and learning. I want them to have other opportunities in life. They may want to be farmers and that is fine. However, they may have other dreams and I will not let a limited education rob them of that pursuit."

A second Presley son, John Marshal, joined the family on January 7,1835. He was immediately nicknamed Johnny. Another blond baby looked a lot like his father who was filled with pride and wanted to show him off around town as soon as possible.

Miss Lucy had been brought to Roaring Fork to assist in this birth, but she insisted that Sally's friends, Savannah and Ruth, be present to learn what to do.

"I hain't gonna be round eva time y'all decide ta pop one out. Y'all best learn ta he'p each otha out 'er in tha country."

This was good advice. With no doctor anywhere around and more babies sure to be arriving for the young families in Roaring Fork and Old Yellow Creek, it would prove to be the normal course of events for them to act as midwives for each other.

Sally joked, "We had best be timing this thing, so there's never two of us delivering at the same time."

When he learned that a third baby would be coming in the summer of 1836, J.W. requested another loan from Charles Graham to start work on a larger house for his family.

His plan was to eventually enlarge the house with a second floor and additional bedrooms at the back of the first floor.

On August 5, 1836, the Presley family welcomed George Wilhelm, who would forever forward be known as Will.

Mr. Graham was very pleased that the population of his farm workers was growing, and he suggested to Preacher Henderson that it might be time to build that second church they had planned in Roaring Fork.

Construction began in the spring of 1840. All the men in the area pitched in to complete the project and a dedication service was held before Christmas that year.

The Presley Homeplace

Chapter 21

J.W. proudly moved his wife and three sons into the initial phase of their new home. Although just the beginning of the final product, it gave them four rooms instead of two.

Sally was so pleased. "Oh, Jay, we have a brand-new place for our family, a place that nobody else ever lived in. It will become the Presley homeplace for our children."

She had great fun arranging their minimal furniture and viewing open spaces for children to play. "I'm thinking that our cabin can be the school room until they are grown. We'll keep it nice so that one of them might live there in the future."

Son number four, William Robert, arrived on October 18, 1839. The family would call him Billy Bob, much to his dislike when he became a man. He would later say, "I hate that nickname. It makes me sound like a stupid baby." His mother would assure him that it showed how much they all loved him.

Vernon and Savannah had two children by this time, Emma and Grace. "Why is hit tha ye keep makin' 'em boys, an all I seem to git is girls?" Vernon asked his friend one morning.

J.W. puffed out his chest and responded with his crooked grin, "Guessin' sum of us got it, an' sum of us ain't."

Vernon had, by this time, built the corn liquor still he had promised. It was out of plain sight in the wooded area between their two properties. The two friends would sneak up there each week to sample their production.

They would sometimes reward themselves for an especially productive day of logging. J.W. found himself looking forward to these occasions and even creating reasons for celebration. He never carried any corn liquor into the house, as he was fairly certain Sally would not approve.

The new church in Roaring Fork was a welcome addition to the families on both sides of the creek. The Johnsons now had four little ones. Savannah and Vernon finally had two boys, Fred and Edward, for a total of four.

By the time two additional Presley boys were born, J.W. had paid off his original indenture contract. Despite the fact that he still owed a small debt for the housing materials, he was emboldened to ask Graham to sell him ten additional acres.

Graham rubbed his chin and said, "Boy, you've really got some grit to be getting yourself back into debt. However, considering you have six yungins to feed, I'm guessing you are not planning on going anywhere, so you've got yourself a deal."

"Thank ya kindly, Sir, ya won't regret hit." They both smiled and shook hands.

Presley boys number five and six were Peter Reed born March 20, 1841 and Andrew Booth born July 14, 1842.

They would be known as Pete and Andy. The final son, Matthew Alexander, entered August 20, 1843. Everyone called him Matt.

Sally was at last blessed with two little girls, Mary Magdalen, November 10, 1844, and Elizabeth Ann, December 1, 1846.

Nine Presley babies born within fourteen years was quite a record even in the days of large families. Both parents were proud of their brood, J.W. took all the bragging rights.

The youngest, Maggie and Lizzie, shared their mother's auburn hair and green eyes, and quickly became their father's little princesses.

.

Dreams Realized

Chapter 22

S ally invited Ruth to bring Martha to the now vacant cabin when she began to teach five-year old Buck to read and write.

As other neighboring children reached the ages of five or six, they were also invited to become part of Sally's unofficial one-room school house.

As the number of young children continued to grow, Preacher Henderson recruited Sally to hold special bible classes for the youth. He didn't have to twist her arm. This was what she was waiting to hear.

"I'm going to be a **real** teacher, Jay, just like I told you before we were married."

Charles Graham donated beginning readers, slates, chalk and other basic equipment in response to Sally's request for the elementary lessons.

"I always knew you were the smartest girl in town," Graham told Sally one Saturday when she dropped in at his office with a list of needs for the classroom.

"I just wish you had that class here in town so others could take advantage of your teaching," he added.

Sally thanked him for his confidence in her and said wistfully, "Maybe someday when all my children are grown."

J.W. was satisfied to leave the small children mostly under the care and guidance of his wife; however, he began training the boys to help with the work of the farm as soon as they were able to walk. There was always something they could do outside.

Over the first decade of life on their farm at Roaring Fork, the Presleys had added chickens, a cow, and a few hogs to their farm, so it was natural for the little ones to begin by feeding the animals.

All the boys loved being outside with their father. It made them feel important to have jobs assigned to them. They sensed that their work was contributing to their family.

By making sure that all the animals had feed, by gathering eggs, by harvesting vegetables, and by helping with the tobacco crop, they gained confidence as well as skill.

When Buck, Johnny, and Will reached the teenage years, they were inducted into the logging business. The younger boys continued with tending the tobacco crop, gathering feed for the animals, and whatever else their father assigned them to do outside.

Maggie and Lizzie, the only girls, began helping their Mother by the ages of three and four. At first, they were assigned very simple indoor tasks such as stacking dirty clothing in a basket to be laundered, or breaking green beans into a cooking pot.

As they grew and became more dexterous, they were assigned duties at all stages of the vegetable gardening season. Sally eased them gradually into the actual meal cooking process when she was certain they understood the dangers of fire and hot utensils.

In that era, there was definitely a well-understood division of labor, at least within working-class families. No one really questioned why girls were not cutting trees, nor why boys were not baking bread. The leisure to question gender roles would come much later even for the aristocracy.

By the time the Presley family numbered eleven, J.W. had added two rooms to the ground floor and completed the second story addition to their home.

Although there was certainly nothing elaborate in either the design or décor of the Presley home, to J.W. and Sally, it was a statement.

Starting with very little other than a contract of indenture, their mutual commitment, and the generosity of friends, they had built a life together, raised a family, worked off debt, and purchased additional land. They were both **proud and grateful**.

Sally continued to teach her own children, and invited her neighbors in the Roaring Fork and Yellow Creek communities to add their children to the classroom in the Presley cabin. She and J.W. were pleased that their small first home was being put to good use.

By the time Lizzie Presley was learning to read, Sally had accumulated quite a library, including the generally accepted Primers and the Webster Speller. She also ensured that there were additional books suitable for both beginning and more advanced readers.

Included in her collection were stories that would capture the interest of boys and girls. It was her goal to inspire life-long curiosity and learning.

With the generosity of the Graham family (at the urging of Eunice O'Connor), the cabin had been visually transformed into a regular classroom.

In addition to the individual student slates, there was a blackboard on which Sally could write instructions, a globe, display boards for illustrations of art and history as well as special student projects, simplified tables/desks of varying heights (fashioned by J.W. and Vernon from scraps), and a few simple science or nature lessons.

Sally's days were full. She was happy to have fulfilled her dream of being a teacher. She adored her husband and their progeny of nine children. She had managed to bring learning, art, and culture into what was initially a rather drab and boring country life for her family and for her community.

Lumber production on the Presley land maintained and even exceeded expectations, with the help of the three eldest boys. Shortly after his fortieth birthday, J.W promoted himself to management.

The friendship between the two original friends continued to be strong. Whenever one of them needed help, the other was always available. J.W. treasured the private talks with Vernon which came in short spurts while the logging was going on.

Sometimes they would sample their latest batch of shine as they were comparing notes on the tobacco and lumber business. It was not uncommon for J.W. to be the one to suggest this sampling.

Vernon sensed that his pal was "taking more than a little liking" to the taste of their product. He would frequently remind him of the dangers involved in combining logging and drinking.

"Slow down a bit, J.W., thars sum thangs don't mix too good. Ye gotta be wide awake an 'ave all yer sense 'bout ye when heavin' an axe."

J.W. just scoffed, "Yer startin' ta sound like my wife or tha Preacher 'stead of my friend. I know what I'm doin'."

Vernon was surprised and asked, "Does Sally know 'bout our special project?"

"Well, not really, but she has asked me wha I bin drinkin' a few times."

"Whatcha tell er?"

"Ah, I jist said ye offered me a taste, an I couldn't refuse my best friend," he laughed.

"That's not **fair**. Now she's gonna tell Savannah I'm leadin' ya down tha road ta Hell."

J.W. laughed again and added, "If hell's got its own supply, I might jist enjoy tha trip."

As Vernon's boys reached their teen years, they also became loggers.

The Wills and Presley farms had become the star producers for Graham, who often reminded his sceptical social peers that he had indeed made better investments than they had.

"Twenty years ago that land was lying dormant, untapped resources. Now look at it. I've got a regular stream of profit and a growing production force."

Buck married his childhood friend and neighbor, Martha Johnson, and their first child, Adam, joined the Presley clan in July of 1854.

Sally and J.W. were overjoyed to welcome their first grandchild. Maggie and Lizzie were likewise thrilled to become doting aunts. They spent much of their time helping Martha with the care and feeding of their little nephew.

When the second grandson, Thomas, arrived fifteen months later, December of 1855, Sally decided that Buck's growing family needed more room.

She asked Preacher Henderson if she could move her classroom to the Roaring Fork Church building to free up the cabin for Buck, Martha, and the babies. They would still be close enough to help out but would have more privacy.

Reverend Henderson said, "That's a fine idea, Sally, let's see what we need to do to make it work."

Garnering the assistance of J.W., Vernon, and several other local fathers, he managed to move a few benches opening up a corner area for Sally's library and teaching equipment.

"Before long, we'll need to have a community project to add onto this church. Kind of like a barn raising except it'll be for child raising, " he smiled.

Sally was so pleased as she thought of what she had started in a small cabin possibly becoming an official school.

"Thank you so much, Reverend for encouraging me to follow my dream. You knew I always wanted to be a teacher, and you have supported that dream all through the years," she said holding his hand while holding back her tears of joy.

Every fall the Presley family joined their neighbors and the town folk in the Graham Harvest celebrations.

For many of the young inhabitants of Roaring Fork and Old Yellow Creek, these excursions into downtown Graham were special events. Since they had their own school and church within walking distance, it was usually only the parents who made trips to town for supplies.

Market Days brought back fond memories to J.W. of his early days in his adopted home. It was during that time that he began to gather equipment and supplies and solidify his relationship with his benefactor and boss, Charles Graham.

It was also when he met his best friend, Vernon Wills. Most importantly, it was when he met and fell in love with his bride, Sally O'Connor.

The annual Harvest Dance gave the proud parents of nine, a time to renew their courtship.

Each time he held his wife in his arms dancing to familiar tunes, he would tell her, "You're still the prettiest girl I've seen all day."

"Oh Jay, you have always made me feel pretty, even when I was at my lowest points," she replied kissing him gently.

"The only reason I say hit, is causen hits true," he said with his always charming smile.

It was during these festive fall events in 1855 that Johnny began to notice Willadeen Eubank. He had been only casually aware of her as a student in his Mother's classes. Since her family lived in the Old Yellow Creek area, their paths did not often cross.

The four-year age difference became insignificant when he noticed that she had become, at age sixteen, a beautiful young lady.

Although rather shy, Johnny, at age twenty, was more than feeling the urge to find a wife. He began visiting her church at Old Yellow Creek, and finding other reasons to talk and walk with her whenever possible.

Buck took every opportunity to tease his brother. "Hey Johnny, who's that purty young gal I've seen ya followin' round like a puppy dawg?"

Johnny turned red, but replied, "What's the matta? Are ya jealous?"

Within the next few years, the relationship between Johnny and Willadeen would become serious, but not until after a major life-changing event occurred in the Presley family.

Unexpected Nightmare

Chapter 23

Tuesday, December 1, 1857, began as most any other day on the Presley farm. The fact that Lizzie would be celebrating her eleventh birthday made it special for the family.

Under Sally's instruction, Maggie, who had just turned thirteen, would be baking a special cake for her baby sister.

After breakfast, J.W. and the boys all headed to the wooded area on the northwest ridge to start their logging duties. The weather was cold, but there was no snow or rain to slow down the work.

Sally would be teaching her usual classes at the Roaring Fork Methodist Church starting at 9:00, and was anxious to get started as soon as it was safe to leave Maggie unattended.

Lizzie was dressed and ready to accompany her Mother. She was so excited to see her classmates and felt certain they would sing to her on her birthday.

Giving his wife a kiss on the check, he wished her a good day, and headed out the door with his boys. Once the seven brothers reached the ridge with their tools in hand, and received the day's instructions from their Father, they were ready to start.

With the Christmas season coming soon, J.W. was eager to take an extra load to the saw mill and collect his half of the receipts. He expected to pick up some special candy and treats from the General Store for his wife and family.

After clarifying his instructions, J.W., who was now the crew manager, made his way deeper into the woods. Finding the jug where he had left it almost full, he decided to take off some of the winter chill with a few swigs. Then he walked back to check on his boys.

"Hey Pop, can ya still handle an axe orya too ole?" Buck asked with a grin. His brothers laughed under their breath.

Taking offense, their father picked up a large axe, and swinging it with all his might made a deep cut in one of the hardwoods.

"I'll show ya whose too ole! I made all y'all, an don't ya forgit it. Now git ta workin', an don't giv me no mor lip," he said walking back into the woods with his chest stuck out.

"Guess he's a bit on tha sensitive side bout being ova tha hill," Johnny observed.

Buck said seriously, "He's got a right. After all, he started all of this by his ownself, and worked twenty-five years ta make a life fer us. We owe ever' thang to him an Ma."

In truth, it had taken all the effort J.W. could garner to swing that axe, and he was paying for it with more than a little pain. He picked up his jug and took a few more sips to lessen the ache, and decided to sit down on a log for a while.

The boys double teamed the big hardwoods. After making the cuts and planning the direction of the fall, three of them would push and the other two would attempt to guide the drop.

They were so focused on their individual duties that they did not see their Father come staggering out of the woods heading down the hill for the house.

Once they spotted him, Buck yelled, **"Watch out, Pop, timber falling!"**

It was too late.

J.W. staggered directly into the path of the falling tree. He was struck on the back of his head, neck, and upper shoulder area.

Screaming, the boys rushed down the hill and attempted to lift the fallen tree but it was too heavy.

Buck and Johnny ran to get the double-sided saws while Will and Billy Bob bent down to check on their father, who was obviously unconscious.

Pete, Andy, and Matt made a run to the house forgetting that their Mother had already left for the school.

After sawing through the portion of the tree closest to the part holding J.W. to the ground, Buck and Johnny pulled their Father out from under the weight. There was considerable blood running from his lower skull and neck area. They could detect no pulse nor obvious breathing.

By this time, Maggie came running out of the house with the three youngest boys to see if she could help. She collapsed on the ground sobbing when she saw her Father lying lifeless.

Everyone except, of course, Sally and Lizzie were gathered at the site of the fatal accident. No one seemed to know what to do.

Finally Buck stepped up and said, "We have ta calm down. Johnny, you and Maggie take the horse to the school to get Maw."

"Maggie, you should stay behind with the class.

"Johnny, bring Maw back with you.

"In the meantime, we'll carry Pop into the house, clean his wounds, and cover him with a blanket."

"What are we gonna tell Maw?" Johnny asked with tears streaming down his cheeks.

"Just tell her ther's been a bad loggin' accident, Pop is hurt, and she needs ta cum home," Buck instructed.

"Maggie, you will need ta stay ther until the students all go home, then you can bring Lizzie back with you."

Sally was startled when her son and daughter walked into the classroom. Maggie said, "Mama, you need to go with Johnny. He'll explain everything to you. I'll stay here 'til everyone has gone home."

Outside, Sally demanded of Johnny, "What's going on?" She could clearly see that her son was crying.

Johnny tried to do exactly what Buck had told him. "Maw ther was an accident. Pop was hurt whilst we was loggin."

Sally was having none of this partial information. "Where is your Father? Is he going to be alright?"

Johnny was having trouble controlling his voice. "I don't know, Maw. He was hurt purty bad. Buck took him inta tha house and told me to come git ya," he sobbed.

It was only a short ride back to the farm. Sally jumped off the horse as soon as they got to their home and ran inside. She fell to her knees beside the body of her husband. The Presley children had never seen their Mother so utterly in despair.

"Jay, Jay, speak to me. Tell me you're going to be alright. I don't think I can go on without you."

Wrapping her arms around his body and dropping her head next to his, she continued to sob at the deepest level of sorrow.

She refused to move from the spot for hours.

The boys did not know what to do or how to proceed. The sight of their Mother, who had always been a rock-solid presence for them, reduced to a paralysis of anguish was more than they could bear.

In addition to their own grief, they were burdened with the feeling that they were responsible. They knew the questions would eventually come. "How did this happen? Couldn't you protect him?"

What would they say? They certainly did not want to tell their Mother that their Father was so drunk he could barely walk and did not hear their warnings.

After several hours of sitting and waiting with no idea of what they should do next, Maggie and Lizzie arrived back home from the school.

They had walked the distance and Maggie had explained the accident to Lizzie so that she would, hopefully, not display her own agony in front of their Mother.

"Lizzie, I'm so sorry that this is the way you'll always remember your birthday," Maggie said holding her sister's hand.

"Is he dead?" Lizzie asked crying.

"I'm almost certain that he suffered a fatal blow when the tree fell on him. There were no signs of life when I left."

"Me and you are goin' to havta be strong for Momma. She'll need us more than ever now.

"Tha boys'll have to carry tha weight of the logging and farming business.

"Me and you'll have to take care of meals, laundry, and other duties around the house until Momma is strong enough," Maggie said stifling her tears.

Seeing that her brothers had managed to do nothing while she was gone, Maggie took Buck aside. "Look, Buck, you're the oldest boy and I'm the oldest girl. Me and you need to get a plan together here.

"There's gonna hafta be a funeral. There's gonna hafta be new arrangements with Mr. Graham for the ongoing logging and farming business. I'll talk with Reverend Henderson regarding a funeral.

"You need to make a trip tomorrow to town. See Mr. Murphy at the livery about a coffin. Talk with Mr. Graham about the finances.

"When Momma has had a few days to think, I'm sure she'll have more instructions for us, but for now, it's up to you and me."

John Henderson and Charles Graham teamed up to handle most of the details for J.W.'s funeral. They had Jim Murphy deliver a casket to the Presley home so that the body could remain with the family until the funeral, which they set for Saturday morning at the Roaring Fork Church.

The parents of Sally's students were informed that classes were suspended until further notice.

Space had been planned for a cemetery behind the church building; however, James William Presley would be the first to rest in peace there. The families in Roaring Fork were all so young, it had not been expected.

Jim Murphy constructed a temporary marker out of a wooden cross with the family name, **PRESLEY**, etched on the horizontal axis. He also arranged to have the grave dug in advance of the Saturday funeral. Vernon's father fabricated a wrought iron urn suitable for planting flowers.

Feeling as if he had lost his best friend, who was as close as a brother, Vernon arranged for pallbearers from among neighbors and town friends. His wife, Savannah, helped prepare meals for the Presley family for the first week.

Eunice and Patrick O'Connor closed the Tailor Shop in order to stay with Sally until she was able to function. They sat with their grieving daughter feeling totally helpless to ease her pain.

Sally sat mostly in silence next to her husband's open coffin occasionally touching his hand and burying her face in a handkerchief.

She was surrounded by her family and many people who loved her, who said wonderful things about J.W., who offered to be there for her, but she heard very little of it.

Her mind was going over that last morning when she rushed off to school with only a peck on the check, without saying, I love you.

The funeral was attended by everyone in Roaring Fork, Yellow Creek, plus many families from town. Sally managed to hold herself together enough to thank everyone for their kindness. Her usually bright and joyful face was drawn and grey.

The remainder of December was a constant haze during which Sally did little, and said less.

The boys were expecting questions and probable recriminations related to the details of the accident, but none had come.

To Sally, all that mattered was that the love of her life was gone . . . . **gone forever**.

Everyone in the Presley family had their daily duties and they handled them as efficiently as possible.

None of the Presley children would allow themselves to openly cry in front of their Mother, but each of them sobbed in their beds at night knowing that **nothing** would ever be the same.

Shortly after the New Year set in, Sally got up one day and headed back to her classroom.

There she met with Rev. Henderson, and told him she was ready to start classes if he had no objection.

Henderson tried to get her to talk with him, to let out some of the pain, but she insisted that she would be fine, and needed to get back to work.

When Spring broke in 1858, Sally announced that she was ready to reinstate the Third Sunday Dinners she and J.W. had hosted for decades. She invited everyone to attend on the third Sunday in May at the usual time.

Harper's Ferry

Chapter 24

Well, I reckon ye boys heerd 'bout tha raid over at Harper's Ferry," Steve Henderson said as the wagons pulled into the sawmill.

"No, I reckon not," Buck replied, "What happened?"

"Where is Harpers Ferry, anyhow?" Will asked. The Presley boys were delivering their Saturday morning load of timber.

"Harpers Ferry's a little town in Virginia over next to where the Potomac and Shenandoah Rivers meet. The armory and arsenal's there. It wuz built by George Washington in 1794. Feller named **John Brown** went in and took it over."

"Why would he do that?" Billy Bob joined the conversation.

"Tried ta git a buncha slaves ta join a rebellion," Steve explained. "Mr Graham said ther wuz twenty-two men with 'im. Slaves refused ta join in tha rebellion. I thank Mr. Graham's gotta newspaper from Raleigh tellin' about it"

"We'll ask him when we go settle up, boys," Buck said.

Buck and Will walked into Charles Graham's office with cash in hand. "Here's our settlement money, Mr. Graham.

"Steve said ye had a newspaper story about a Harpers Ferry Raid. Whatsa goin'on up ther'?" Will quizzed.

"Well, it seems a man named **John Brown** wanted ta free some slaves. He wuz gonna steal a buncha rifles and pistols outta the arsenal and give 'em to these slaves."

"They wuddn't do it." Graham said smugly.

"How come they wuddn't," Will was puzzled.

"Them slaves don't wanna be free. They've got it made. Owners give 'em a place to live, three meals a day, what clothes they need, and doctorin' when they need it.

"Over where they came from in the jungles, they hadda get out and hunt for food. They lived in grass huts and didn't hardly have any clothes at all. Their lives are a lot better here. This whole biz'ness of abolition is a buncha junk."

Will just shook his head in disbelief. Buck nodded in assent and added, "They git ta live here and don't hafta worry 'bout nuthin'. Shore they hafta work, but ever'bidy else does too. We work ever' day our ownselves."

"When did all of this happen Mr. Graham?" Will asked.

"It was last week accordin' to the paper. Let me see, they went in on **October 16, 1859**. Says they were arrested on **October 18th**," he

read. "The Secretary of War ordered a company of soldiers from Fort Whipple to handle the situation. They sent a Lieutenant with them but had to have a higher-rank officer to command.

A Colonel, named **Robert E. Lee**, was vacationing in the area, but didn't have his uniform. Hadda do it in civilian clothes.

"Whadda ye reckon ther gonna do ta 'em?" Buck wondered.

"I reckon they'll hang the whole bunch. Charged 'em with treason and destroyin' government property. There were five blacks in the bunch of twenty-two men he brought with him.

"Says here in the paper a black porter was the first one to get shot. He had a good job with the **Baltimore** and **Ohio** railroad which stopped in Harpers Ferry. He was going to warn the slave owners close to town and Brown's men shot him in the back. These blacks don't want all of this trouble people are causin'. Why can't they just let well enough alone?" he asked rhetorically.

Will couldn't restrain himself any longer. "How'd ye feel if some bidy owned you, Mr. Graham? I wuddn't like it, an' I'd prob'ly be tryin' ta figger out a way ta git out of it. Even if it meant killin' some people."

"Now Will, that kinda talk's gonna get you in trouble," Graham frowned. "If these abolitionists have their way and don't quit this foolishness, there's gonna be war."

"Let's go Will," Buck ordered. "We gotta get back home. Maw'll have dinner on the table."

As they walked to the wagon to go home, Buck admonished Will. "Better keep your mouth shut, boy. Yer gonna mess up a good thang we got with Graham."

"Don't wanna do nuthin' to hurt my fam'ly, but it makes me mad when these big-shots act so high and mighty 'bout ownin' people. Preacher Henderson don't like it neither."

"Well, the preacher's in a li'l bit differen' situation than us. He takes orders from Bishop Cooper. He don't work fer Graham. Jist keep yer idee's ta yerself when yer 'round Graham."

"I'll jist stay away from 'im an' let you an' Johnny deal with 'im," Will promised.

A Call to Arms

Chapter 25

B uck and Johnny drove the front wagon, and Will and Billy Bob followed in the second wagon. Driving to the Graham Sawmill on Saturday morning to deliver the week's crop of timber, they were discussing the war.

It was the year of our Lord 1861, and on Friday of last week, April 12th, soldiers from Sullivan's Island, adjacent to the Port of Charleston, South Carolina, had attacked the United States' Fort Sumpter. The fort was located on a small island at the mouth of the harbor to protect the city of Charleston.

Rebels fired the first shots of what would become the **bloodiest war** in which the United States of America would ever engage.

"Well I wonder what we gonna hear from Mr. Graham this week?" Johnny asked Buck.

"Don't rightly know, Johnny, but I'ma bettin' it ain't gonna be nuthin' good. Them boys down ther' in Charleston, started a damn war last week. Mr. Graham seemed purty upset when he tol' us about it last Sat'adee."

Entering the yard where they would unload their logs, Steve Henderson, came out to greet them. "Mornin' boys good to see ye. Mr. Graham's gonna hold a meetin' at tha Palmer House in tha ballroom. He wants all his tenants ta be ther'. Meetin' starts at 12:00 sharp."

Nervously, Johnny asked, "What's goin' on?"

"A damn war was started last week down in Charleston," Steve answered. "Reckon ther' ahuntin' so'jers to fight Yankees. Ther's a unit called 18th North Carolina Infantry Regiment formin' over 'round Wilmington. They went down to South Carolina and signed up **sum'** boys but need a whole lot more if we're agonna kick Yankee ass, so they come back up here."

"Whatta we gonna do Buck?" Will asked as he and Billy Bob walked up and heard the news.

"Well, I reckon Mr. Graham's gonna tell us to go and join up with that bunch over in Wilmington. That's what it sounds like ta me."

Will, his face contorted and his voice getting louder, exclaimed. "I ain'ta gonna fight and kill people jist so a buncha rich plantation folks can keep people as slaves. It ain't right. Preacher Henderson said, **"A rich man's war is a poor man's fight."**

"Now lower yer voice, Will. Ever'bidy nearer a half a mile 's a gonna hear ye," Buck cautioned.

"I don't give a damn. I ain'ta gonna join no buncha rebels," Will snapped back.

Billy Bob spoke up. "Do ye think he'll want all of us to join up, Buck? Momma's gonna hafta haf' some he'p here on tha farm. She cain't cut no timber. Andy and Matt hasta work tha 'backer crop. Maybe me and Pete can do tha loggin'."

Buck wrinkled his brow and said, "Good thankin', Billy Bob. Don't feel so bad 'bout leavin' Maw and' Martha and my kids knowin' ye're here lookin' afta 'thangs. "

"Does that mean ye're ajoinin' up, Buck?," a wide-eyed Johnny asked.

"Don't know yit. Ain't heerd what Mr. Graham's gotta say 'bout it," Buck retorted.

After they unloaded and settled up with Steve Henderson on the money, the Presley boys drove their wagons the quarter-mile back to the Town Square.

The whole square was full of people and wagons. "Guess we'll hafta park around behind the Methodist Church and walk to the hotel," Billy Bob suggested. "You comin', Will?"

"Yep, I reckon I'll listen ta what he's got ta say, but I don't like it even a little bit."

The boys crowded into the back of the ballroom at the Palmer House. On the raised platform where the band usually set up, a group of prominent townspeople was seated.

Charles Graham sat in the center, and to his right was Ulysses Winslow, the banker, and to his right was Jonathan Mahan, the lawyer. To Graham's immediate left was Conrad Palmer, and next to him sat J.C. Schultz, the sheriff.

Reverend Henderson sat slightly separated from the group on the end of the platform.

At exactly 12:00 noon, John Henderson stood up to address the crowd. (He had been taught by Bishop Cooper, many years ago, to begin all meetings on time and to end them on time.)

"Thank you for attending this meeting. Mr. Graham asked me to begin tha meetin' with a reading from Holy Scripture and a prayer to the Almighty God. Reading from Romans 13:8-10:"

"Owe no man anything, but to love one another: for he that loveth another hath fulfilled the law. For this, thou shalt not commit adultery, thou shalt not kill, thou shalt not steal, thou shalt not bear false witness, thou shalt not covet, and if there be any other commandment, it is briefly comprehended in this saying, namely, thou shalt love thy neighbor as thyself. Love worketh no ill to his neighbor.

" The word of the Lord," Henderson intoned.

"Thanks be to God," the men responded.

"Let us pray," the preacher continued.

"Almighty and Holy God, our Father in Heaven. We come to you today with fear and trembling. Perilous times have descended upon us in this great nation. Division has arisen into our ranks. Strife and killin' are fast approachin' our great land. Stretch forth your healin' hand, and restore us once again as the **UNITED** States of America. All these things we humbly ask in the precious and holy name of Jesus. Amen."

Again, the crowd responded, "Amen."

Henderson returned to his seat, and Charles Graham stood up and walked to the podium. Pausing briefly, he dropped his head, then raised it as he began to speak.

"Men, as most of you know by now, a group of men on Sullivan's Island fired some cannon shots at Fort Sumpter in Charleston Harbor. President Lincoln has ordered U.S. Army troops to *put down the Rebellio*n.

"Governor Ellis has vowed 'no North Carolina troops will aid in this endeavor.'

"South Carolina seceded from the United States of America back on December 20, 1860. In February 1861, they were joined by Florida, Georgia, Alabama, Mississippi, Louisiana, and Texas to form the Confederate States of America.

"My youngest brother, William, over in Raleigh, who as you all know, was a Senator and the Governor of North Carolina, tells me that we will be the next state to secede."

"Hey Mr. Graham," Will Presley yelled out. "What's secede mean?"
"Glad you asked, Will. It means they ain't gonna be a part of the
United States anymore. They're forming their own country."

"So how does that 'fect us here in North Ca'lina?" Will wondered.

"These people are our friends and neighbors down here in the
South. We've got to stick together. There's a unit of soldiers being
formed over in Wilmington. They're calling it the 18th North
Carolina Infantry Regiment. We will fight for our families, for
our land, and for our very own **FREEDOM** itself, " his voice
crescendoed.

"The Damned Yankees cannot be allowed to take these things from
us. **WE, ALL OF US**, have worked too hard and too long to just
give it up to the Yankees. I want to send a large contingent of men
from Graham to join this group. We will also, form a local militia
group to guard us here in Graham.

"The fighting could extend down to us and we need local men to
stay here. Our farms need to continue to produce, so those who stay
at home will have to work even harder. Does anybody else wanna
say anything?" Graham asked.

Schultz, the big guy who was sheriff, walked to the center of the
platform and yelled, "Let's go kick some Yankee ass, boys."

A roar swelled from the crowd. "Yay, hell yes, and we're ass
kickers," could be heard above the roar of the mob. "Look out
Yankees here comes some Ca'lina boys your way."

"A rich man's war is a poor man's fight."

18th North Carolina
Infantry Regiment

Chapter 26

Sally saw the two wagons with her four sons returning from town. Wondering why they were much later than usual returning, she stepped outside to greet them.

"Good afternoon boys, y'all are runnin' late today."

"Yeah, Maw, Mr. Graham called a meetin' over at the hotel," Will spoke to Sally.

With a worried frown she looked at Buck and said, "What's goin' on Buck?"

"Just get ever'bidy in tha house. Ye got dinner ready?" Buck asked. "We got big stuff comin' down Maw."

When everybody was seated at the dinner table, Sally spoke to Buck again. "What's goin' on that's got everybody in town so riled up?"

"Maw, on Fri'dee of las' week, some boys down in Charleston fired some cannons on the Fort out in tha harbor. Lincoln is sending troops down ther to put down tha rebellion. Them's **his** words, not mine. Governor Ellis says we ain't gonna supply no North Carolina so'jers ta carry out his orders."

Pausing to carefully choose his words, Buck continued, **"We're at war Maw."**

"Oh no, we can't be at war. Who are we warring with?"

Will could no longer contain himself. "We're at war with our ownselves, Maw. Ther' wantin' us ta fight and kill and die so them rich guys down south can keep ther' black slaves. Ther' wantin' us ta go ta war with the United States of America."

"Now Will, that ain't tha way Mr. Graham 'splained it, is it , Buck?" Billy Bob piped in.

Seeing the division among his brothers, Buck framed his words carefully. "Mr. Graham said we haf' ta defend our land and our fam'lies from them Yankees who wanna come down here an' take ever'thang we worked fer all these years. and ever'thang you and Paw worked fer too, Maw."

Johnny looked at Willadeen and said, "Ima gonna fight fer my fam'ly an' fer our future. Ain't lettin' no damn Yankees take what's ourn."

"We ain't got no black slaves," Will shouted. That's what this is about. Them big-time plantation owners is tha onliest ones that own other people. Yeah, ther **black**, but ther still human people. I heerd Preacher Henderson say tha Supreme Court said black slaves ain't people. I believe he called it **Dred Scott**, or sum'thin' like that. Said they was jist property, but that ain't right. **I ain't agonna do it.** "Will pounded his fist on the table.

"When's all this supposed ta happen Buck?" Martha wondered with a worried look on her face.

"Don't know fer shore yit. Graham said his brother over in Raleigh is spectin' North Ca'lina ta secede purty soon," Buck answered.

"What tha hell is secede mean?" Pete wondered as Andy nodded.

"Now Peter don't be using profanity here in front of your sisters," Sally admonished.

"**Secede** means we ain't gonna be part of the United States of America no more. We gonna form our own country. I think ther' callin' it tha Confederate States of America," Buck explained.

"Are we **all** gonna join up, Buck?" a wide-eyed Matt interjected.

"No, li'l bru'tha," Billy Bob chimed in. "Sum of us gotta stay here and keep the farm goin'. Ther gonna form a militia to pertect our own town here, too." Anticipating the next question, he continued, "Militia is when ye got yer own local buncha so'jers, Andy an' Matt. You two can he'p with that."

"Can I shoot a rifle and kill me some Yankees? "Matt queried.

"Don'tcha see what's already ahappenin, Buck?" Will was outraged. "These young'uns are wannabe killers."

"Now he don't mean nothing by that," Sally interjected. "He's just a kid talking big."

"Maw, tha rich old men always want tha pore young men ta go ta war fer 'em. Tha plantation owners and big land owners is tha ones apushin' war. **They want us ta kill an' die, while they set back an' jist get richer. Paw used ta say a 'pore man ain't got a chance'**, "Will was yelling. Preacher Henderson said, **"A rich man's war is a pore man's fight. We hafta fight THER' wars."**

"Whadda we gonna do Buck?' Johnny wondered.

"We're gonna jist wait an' see what happens fer now. If North Ca'lina secedes, I guess we'll have to join our frien's and neighbors in the North Ca'lina Infantry."

On **Monday, May 20, 1861**, the North Carolina Legislature voted to secede from the Union. Word quickly spread to all of the farms owned by Charles Graham. In anticipation of the vote, Graham had made some arrangements for his tenants to join the 18th **North Carolina Infantry Regiment**.

Eight wagons with a team of horses had been rented from Fenton Murphy at the Livery Stable in town. Each wagon could haul six men and a driver. Forty-eight men would constitute a platoon. Charles Graham sent word that he expected to field an entire platoon of volunteers from his town.

When the Presley family was all gathered around the supper table, Buck gave them the news.

"North Ca'lina's Legislature jist voted to secede from the Union and join the Confederacy, bru'thas," Buck intoned. "Looks like we're ajoinin' the war. Mr. Graham's got a wagon train headin'over ta Wilmington ta take our men. Wants at least forty-eight of us from here in Graham."

"Who's agoin' from our fam'ly, Buck?" Billy Bob asked.

Buck thought a minute, then spoke, "Well, me an' Johnny fer shore. Will'll haf ta make up his own mind whether he's agoin' er not."

"Hell no, I ain't agoin' ta fight fer no rich slave owners," Will shouted. **"If I fight fer anything. It'll be to perserve tha Union."**

"Now Will, you wouldn't fight against **your own** brothers, would you?" Sally looked him in the eye.

"Well Maw, ya could say ther' traitors agin' the United States, if they join up with them 'rebs' in the Confederacy."

"Don'chu call me no traitor," Johnny argued. "I'ma pertectin' my fam'ly an' my Maw, an' our land from Yankees."

Buck jumped into the fray, "We got 'til Sat'adee ta make up our mind an' git ready. Ther alookin' fer volunteers fer tha militia. Ye younger boys need ta think about that."

Sally and Buck talked about the situation all week long. Since J.W. had died, she relied on Buck to be her adviser and **confidant**.

Johnny and Buck would join the 18th North Carolina Infantry Regiment. Will would just have to make up his own mind.

Billy Bob, Pete, Andy and Matt would work the farm and serve part-time in the militia.

Martha, Willadeen, Maggie, Lizzie and Johnny's son, and Buck's three would work the family's small tobacco patch.

Andy and Matt would work the much larger five-acre patch from which Charles Graham took half the proceeds.

Billy Bob and Pete would continue with the logging business and provide the family with half the proceeds from that.

If Buck and Johnny just took care of themselves, maybe everything would be alright.

At 10:00 a m on Saturday morning, **May 25, 1861**, the Presley family (all of them) loaded up in the two wagons and rode into town. It would take about an hour to drive the ten miles to town, and Buck and Johnny didn't want to be late.

Sally, Martha, Willadeen, Maggie, and Lizzie were crying. Buck and Johnny's kids wondered what all the fuss was about.

A bleak future awaited every member of the Presley family.

Will Heads North

Chapter 27

When the family loaded the wagons to transport Buck and Johnny into town, Will had made up his mind what he would do.

He'd ride into town with his family and say goodbye to his older brothers. While there, he would go to the Livery, buy a horse, and head north. Not knowing for certain what his course of action would be after he settled somewhere, he only knew he could not be involved in defending slave owners and their so-called rights to own slaves.

Crowds of people filled the town square in Graham. The patriarch, Charles Graham, had asked for enough *volunteers* to staff a platoon of men. There was room in the eight wagons rented for their transport to accommodate forty-eight men.

Forty-eight men volunteered.

Family members of all the volunteers showed up to say goodbye and wish them God speed. Consequently, people were everywhere. The transport wagons were lined up in the parking area behind the Methodist church. Will found it very easy to wander into the Livery office and talk to Fenton Murphy.

"Hi Mr. Fenton," Will spoke as he entered the store.

"Hello, Will, they's lotsa folks in town today." Murphy greeted him.

"Yep, I guess ye been purty busy."

"Not real busy. Mosta these folks er here to say goodbye. What can I do fer ye?"

"I'ma lookin' fer a horse and saddle. Whatya got here today?"

"Well I got a roan four-year-old mare that'd make ye a good saddle horse. I'll put ye a good saddle on 'er, and sell ye the whole thang fer fifty dollars," Murphy smiled.

"Now Mr. Murphy, ye know I'm jist a dirt farmer. I ain't got that kinda money'" Will dropped his eyes.

"Will, ye know what they say, 'a forty-dollar saddle on a ten-dollar horse'."

"Ain't ye got a **used saddl**e?" Will pleaded.

"Yep, I got one in tha back room, but it's beat up purty bad," Murphy replied. "I can let ye have it fer **twenty**. Took it in on a trade fer a new saddle. Horse, used saddle, an' I'll throw a blanket inta the deal. Thirty dollars'll put ye on the road."

"Now that's more like it, Mr. Murphy. Let me see the saddle. **Wow it is beat up purty bad**. Would ye take twenty-five fer the whole lot?"

"Ye drive a hard bargain, boy. Give me twenty-eight dollars an' ye got a deal."

"Thank ye Mr. Murphy. I 'preciate it," Will was polite.

OK. I'll git 'er saddled up fer ye. It'll take 'bout five minutes."

"While I'ma waitin', I'ma goin' outside and say 'bye ta my bruthas. Be back in a few. Here's twenty-eight dollars an' I'm purty happy with the deal ye gimme."

As Will walked outside, he saw Buck and Johnny getting in the wagon driven by Vernon Wills. He walked over and hugged both of them. **Garrick**, **Vic**, and **Andre**w, **Steve Henderson's** grandsons, and Reverend Henderson's great nephews got into the wagon.

Fenton Murphy's sons, **Travis** and **Kevin** also climbed in.

Seven of those young men were a tight squeeze, but they all managed to get comfortable. Fenton Murphy came outside to speak to his sons before they left, and told Will he had his horse ready.

Buck and Johnny gave Will a puzzled look, but said nothing. As the wagon pulled out to leave, Fenton and Will stood waving at them.

Both men tried to hide their tears.

"Did ye notice, Mr. Murphy, ther wudd'nt none a tha Big Shot's boys a leavin; jist us workin' people. No Graham's, no Winslow's, no Mahan's. If a buncha people hasta die, it'll be pore folks I reckon."

"Yep, I reckon 'em boys hasta stay here and run the town and the militia. I heerd Graham say that," Murphy scratched his head.

Before the family left to deliver Buck and Johnny to town for their departure, Will wrote a note and placed it on the pillow of Sally's bed.

Dear Maw,

I can't bring myself to go to war
protecting the plantation owners in
their fight to keep slaves. Slaves are people
just like us. They should not be owned by
other people. Preacher Henderson said the
United States of America was founded
on Freedom. People should be Free. I know
my brothers think I'm wrong, but I
think they are the ones who are wrong.
I'm leaving Roaring Fork Farm for now
Don't know where I'm going or what I'm
going to do. I love you and all my family
Hope to see you again someday

Will

Billy Bob and Pete saw Will go into the Livery. After the transport wagons were out of sight., they went inside to get him to go back home.

"Hey Mr. Fenton, where's Will at?" Pete asked.

"He just left here on a horse I sold him. Maybe he's agonna try 'er out."

"Come on Pete, Will'll prob'bly be at home when we git ther'," Billy Bob guessed.

As the family pulled the wagons close to the shed when they arrived at Roaring Fork, there was no sign of Will. Lizzie was the first one to speak.

"Will ain't at home yit Maw. Wonder where he's at? Is he in trouble Maw? Ar' ye gonna bawl 'im out?" she grinned hopefully.

"He's just trying out that new horse, Lizzie," Sally answered. "He'll be along shortly."

Taking off her bonnet and walking into the bedroom to put it away, Sally spotted the note on her pillow. As she read, she began to sob. Maggie was the first to notice and ran to her mother's side.

"What'sa wrong Maw?" Maggie worried.

"**Will's gone!** He's not comin' home."

"Where's he gone to Maw?" Matt came running into the room.

Billy Bob and Pete had unhitched the mules and were entering the door when they heard the loud talking.

"What'sa wrong Maw?" Pete spoke first.

Maggie answered for her mother, "Will's gone an' ain't comin' back."

"How'd ye know that," Andy piped in.

Sobbing, Sally answered, "He left me a note right here on my pillow. Will is really against this war."

Maggie began to cry, "Whatta we gonna do Maw?"

Billy Bob, the oldest male in the room ventured, "Ain't nuthin' we can do, 'cept maybe pray. We'll tell Preacher Henderson an' maybe he'll pray **for us**."

"He don't like this slavery business no more than Will does," Maggie had stopped crying.

"Well, I don't like it much neither, but I don't like seeing my boys fighting over it," Sally declared.

Sadly, many of the Presley family would never see George Wilhelm Presley again.

Camp Wyatt

Chapter 28

O n **Thursday, May 30, 1861**, the Presley boys, Buck and Johnny arrived at Camp Wyatt, North Carolina.

Located very near Carolina Beach and Wilmington, it took a full five days for the Graham wagon train to traverse the entire state. Since no one in the group had ever travelled the entire state from west to east, the timeframe was a huge surprise.

Buck and Johnny had ridden in the wagon driven by Vernon Wills, who had helped J.W. when he first arrived on the farm. They had camped-out on the ground each of the five nights of travel, and Vernon had regaled them with stories of the first attempts that he and their Father had made cutting trees.

Battling copper-head snakes, coyotes, foxes, bobcats, and even a couple of black bears, had made for some memorable stories. Buck made a mental note to share them with his children when he got back home.

After all the men had exited their wagons, the Graham platoon was met by **Sargent Tom Goodman**, a German immigrant who had lived in Knoxville, Tennessee. Goodman had served in the United States Army during the last days of the War of 1812.

His unit was part of General Andrew Jackson's forces who fought in the Battle of New Orleans. Although too old to be a fighting soldier, Goodman was asked to join the Confederate army to train new recruits.

General Lawrence O. Branch was Commanding Officer of the Brigade, and knew Goodman from his days with General Jackson.

Although only sixteen years old at the time he was in New Orleans, Goodman had spent many nights on Bourbon Street sampling the booze and sexual delights offered there.

The battle had raged off and on for over a month, so Goodman had many opportunities. (At least that's the way he told the story.)

Three months of training prepared the country boys from Graham, North Carolina, to be good soldiers. Skillful with rifles from hunting deer and small game in the mountains, Buck and Johnny were promoted very quickly.

Buck, a natural leader as the first-born son, made corporal in five months. Johnny was upgraded to Private First Class. (Both boys listened to Goodman tell his stories, and he liked them.)

Goodman urged the boys to write letters to their mother and their wives. Buck wrote:

Dear Maw,

Hope this letter finds you in good health and doing well. Me and Johnny done got promoted to now-commissioned officers. I'm a Corporal and Johnny is a Private First Class. Our training officer Sargent Goodman is from Knoxville.

We are eating good and training hard every day. We ain't seen no Yankees yet, but will be ready when we do. Heard rumors we might join up with General Robert E. Lee and his bunch very soon, but don't know for sure They just tell us when to move just before we do it. Well I'll go for now. Give my kids a hug and a kiss from their Daddy for me.

Your oldest boy
Buck.

My Darling Martha,

Hope this letter finds you well and happy.
How are the kids doing? Fine I hope. I
love you, Martha. Tell the youngíuns I love
them too. We rode over here with Vernon
Wills and he told me and Johnny some
funny stories about him and Paw when
they first started logging.

Our training Sargent is from Knoxville.
He's a good guy too. Don't know how much
longer will be here in this camp. Probably
through the winter is what some of the
guys are saying. Soldiers kind of lay low
in winter. Fighting will probably start
in the Spring. Word is we will join up
with General Lee in Northern Virginia.

Well, I'll go for now. Will write again
when I get a chance. Kiss the youngíuns
for me. I love you.

Buck

Johnny wrote:

Dear Maw,

How are you? Hope this letter finds you feeling good. How are things going on the farm? I guess Billy Bob and Pete can help Matt and Andy with the tobacco crop. Wish me and Buck could come home and help with it. Is the logging going good?

How are Papaw and Mamaw O'Connor getting along.

Everything is good with me and Buck except we miss home and our family. Well I'll go for now. Write to us when you can.

I love you, Maw.

Johnny

Willadeen,

My sweet and pretty wife. I been missing you. Me and Buck are staying busy with training and getting ready to fight them Yankees. I ain't going to let them take away everything we worked for.

How is my baby boy Johnny Junior? I guess by now he's growing like a weed and keeping you busy watching him crawl all over the place. I hope you ain't been missing me too much.

How are you and Martha getting along? I know she gets bossy sometimes just like Buck. Don't know how long we'll be here, but guess it'll be until weather breaks in Spring. Our Company Commander is Captain Bob Smith. He's from Raleigh and knows Governor Graham.

Most of the boys in our whole regiment is from Carolina. Well I'm going to go for now I love you Willadeen. Kiss little Johnny for me.

Johnny

  The Winter was cold and wet. It rained just about every day
in November, then turned to snow in late December. Sargent
Goodman kept the boys busy training despite the harsh weather
conditions. He told them they needed to know how to fight in bad
weather.

Captain Smith, the Company Commander for "B" Company, sent his mountain boys out to hunt wild turkeys for Thanksgiving Day in November. They killed fourteen turkeys and had a great meal. Lieutenant Tommy Everett had been a Baptist preacher back home and he led their Thanksgiving Day service.

For Christmas Day dinner, General Branch, the Battalion Commander had ordered the cooks to find some venison. Buck and Johnny were selected for the squad to hunt deer on the recommendation of Sargent Goodman.

The squad of ten men came back with twelve deer and the meal was good, but most of the men were missing family and wondering about their wives and children. Once again, Lieutenant Everett led the group as he read the Christmas story from Luke 2, and it seemed more like Christmas to the troops.

News Year's Day came and went uneventfully, but on January 3rd, Buck got a letter from Sally.

Dear Buck,

I hope you and Johnny had a good Holiday season and some good meals. We had a great time with the little ones, and Billy Bob and Pete made some toys for all of them.

Me and Martha made a doll for little Judith. She looked so cute cuddling it and rocking it like a real baby. Pete carved Adam and Thomas two rifles out of some pine wood he had cut. Jedediah got a wooden horse that Billy Bob carved. Little John Jr. got a toy pistol carved by Billy Bob.

Andy and Matt didn't do very good with the tobacco crop this year. They didn't get it cut quick enough, and a lot of it rotted in the field when it rained so much. Mr. Graham wasn't happy, and we didn't get hardly anything out of our little family patch. They done as good as they could, but we sure missed you and Johnny here this year.

Will left home right after you and Johnny did. He left me a note saying he was heading North. We haven't heard from him since.

I wish you all could get some leave time this Spring and come home long enough to get the crop set out. Well we'll just do the best we can with what we got, as your Daddy used to say.

Tell Johnny I love him and hope to see you both soon.

Love Momma

"Johnny, I want you to read this letter from Maw," Buck said as they were eating chow at supper time.

As he read, Johnny's eyes filled with tears. "Buck, what the hell ar' we gonna do? We cain't let our own fam'ly suffer while we're out here hopin' to kill Yankees.

Maybe Will was right. We gotta figger out a way ta git home for plantin' and cuttin'. If we'd been there, we cudda got that 'backer cut an' in tha barn. I'ma 'bout ta decide to tell Jeff Davis and Charles Graham what they can do with this damn war."

"Well let's thank on it, and figger out sum'thin'. If all four of our bruther's can git tha crop set in tha field, maybe we can git ther' ta he'p put it in tha barn.

I'ma gonna write back to Maw and tell her we gonna try ta he'p with gittin' tha 'backer in tha barn."

Dear Maw,

Me and Johnny are sorry you all had such a hard time getting in the tobacco crop. I don't think we gonna get any leave time now. We heard that General Beauregard has whipped a bunch of General McDowells Yankees at Bull Run Creek back in July. Things are heating up now, and we're getting ready to move north to Richmond and join up with Lee.
We'll try to figure out a way to get home around October and help get the tobacco in the barn, but it's going to be hard getting leave time this Spring. Maybe Bill Bob and Pete can stop logging long enough to set out the plants in the Spring. I'm sorry to hear that Will left home, but I'm not surprised. Hope he don't join up with the Yankees. We love you Maw and hate that this damn war has made it harder on our family at home. Tell Martha I love her and the babies. Johnny sends his love to Willadeen and Johnny Junior. Somehow we'll see you all in October.

Your oldest boy
Buck

Washington, D.C.

Chapter 29

Heading north out of Graham, Will rode his horse very hard. A galloping horse could move twice as fast as two mules pulling a wagon, and he wanted to be several miles up the trail from Roaring Fork Creek before Sally found the note he left on her pillow.

Well before sundown, at about 5:30 in the afternoon, he arrived in Asheville. Tired and hungry, he found Rayburn's Tavern on the edge of town. Tying his horse to the hitching post in front of the Inn, he went inside and inquired about a room for the night.

"Howdy sir," he spoke to the young man manning the desk. "Need a room fer tha night, and a place to put my horse."

"OK, we can handle that fer ye. Stable's behind the buildin'. Sixty cents fer a room and a quarter more fer the horse. That includes some hay fer the horse tonight, and some oats in the mornin'."

"Can ye give me a little bit better price than that. I'm kinda short on cash." Will asked pleadingly.

"Well, it is Sat'adee night an' not many folks atravelin'," he mused. "Seventy-five cents is best I can do."

"Shore 'preciate it, pal," Will was thankful.

"Just take tha horse 'round back an' leave 'im with the stable hand. Here's ye a key ta tha room #202 on second floor. Pay when ya check out in tha mornin'. Restaurant's right over ther' if yer hungry."

At seven am on Sunday morning, Will walked down the stairs, and laid two silver coins and the room key on the counter. He was eager to be on his way. Still, he wasn't certain where he would go or what he would do for a living. *"I'll find something,"* he thought to himself.

With a good full day's riding time, he could travel about one-hundred miles before dark. Continuing north through the Shenandoah Valley, he marveled at the beauty all around him. Flashy trillium, mountain laurel, colorful azaleas, and columbine were everywhere he looked, providing a brilliant array. A mother deer with her fawn, birds of every kind that Will had ever seen , and even a black bear with a cub crossed his path.

Just before dark, he came upon a place called Black Bear Lodge, where he spent the night and slept rather fitfully. Arising at daybreak, he wanted to keep moving north, putting as much distance between his family and himself as possible.

Finally, on the fourth day of travel, he arrived in Washington, D.C. This large metropolitan city was overwhelming for him.

Riding through the streets, he saw a sign that read: **Surratt's Boarding House**. A large four-story building, it was operated by a widow, Mary Surratt, along with her three children, Isaac, Anne, and John, Jr.

The house was newly-opened, and well-decorated. Eager to add some new residents, Mrs. Surratt quoted an attractive price - three dollars per week, which included breakfast and an evening meal, which they called supper. Will was happy to have found such a good deal and nice people to share some time with.

It was late May, and flowers and blooming trees abounded.

In preparation for his departure, he had saved some money, but would need to find a job soon. If he could find employment at the average working-man's wage of eight dollars per week, he could get by very well.

Seated at the breakfast table with six other boarders on his first day in the house, he introduced himself. The table was large enough to seat twelve people, so he knew the house was not filled to capacity.

As the conversation began around the table, he asked about opportunities for employment in the area.

"I'ma gonna need ta find a job. Anybody know where a man can find one?" he inquired.

"Well, it depends on what you can do. Whatcha been doin'," an older bearded man asked.

"Born and raised on a fam'ly farm in North Ca'lina. That's 'bout all I ever done."

Chuckling, a younger smooth-faced man spoke, "Ain't too many farm jobs 'round here, 'specially fer Rebs from down south."

"I am from down south, but I ain't no Reb," Will snapped back.

A heavy-set man spoke, "I got an uncle over in Mur'lan lookin' fer a slave overseer. Ye might check with him."

"Ye mean a **SLAVE DRIVER**?" Will got louder. "No Thank ye. I druther dig ditches fer outhouses then whup up on slaves."

"If ye ain't a Reb, and don't wanna drive slaves, ye might join up with tha army. Ther gonna be needing lots of men soon. Lincoln's huntin' some men fer ninety-day enlistments."

"Don't wanna be killin' nobody. That's why I left North Ca'lina." Will quickly answered.

John Surratt Jr. walked in to bring more coffee and heard the conversation. "Sounds like you ain't got very many options, good buddy. I don't like killin' either. You might get a job down at the river dock. Lots of ships sail up the Potomac to bring supplies in - some from down south, and some from England and France. It's hard work but pays 'bout eight dollars a week."

"Yep, that sounds like sum 'thin' I could do. Ye know anybody ther' I can talk to?" Will was eager.

"Nah, just show up in tha mornin' 'bout day light an' ask around. Ther's several ships docked ther to unload."

Will remembered his Paw, J.W., talkin' 'bout loadin' ships in England.

At daybreak, he was on the river dock inquiring about a job. Seeing a man who looked like he might be in charge, he walked up and spoke.

"Mornin' neighbor, I'ma lookin' fer the man who does tha hirin' 'round here."

"That'd be me boy. Wher' ye from?" the foreman asked suspiciously.

"From North Ca'lina, sir," Will was honest.

"Don't want no Rebs workin' fer me. Ain't got no job fer ye boy."

"I ain't no Reb, sir. That's why I left Ca'lina. I wanna perserve tha Union."

"Then ye had best be joinin' up with the army, if that's what ye want. Lincoln thinks it'll only take 'bout ninety days ta 'put down tha rebellion'. Go join the army and stop these Rebs, then come back here. I might have a job fer ye then."

Will moved on down to the next ship unloading. "Mornin' sir. You gonna be needin' any he'p unloadin'?"

"Where ye from boy?" the foreman quickly asked.

"Ca'lina, sir," He answered without thinking.

"Yeah, I thought so by the way you talked. We ain't hirin' no Rebs. Go back where ye come from an' find a job."

Discouraged, Will dropped his head and walked off. "I'ma gonna try one mor' time. 'Three timesa charm' as Paw used ta say."

 Moving on to the next ship, he spoke, "Mornin' sir, how ar' ye taday. " He tried to sound cheerful. "I'ma lookin' fer work. Ye doin' any hirin'?"

"Where ya from boy?" instantly recognizing a southern twang.

"Oh jist here an' ther'. No place in pertic'ler." Will was cautious.

"From the sound of yer talkin', I'd say sum'wher' down south."

"Yes sir, " Will admitted. "Ca'lina."

"Well I'll be damned, an' ye wearin' shoes, too?" he snidely remarked. "Ain't got nothin' fer ye boy. Now move along, I'm busy."

After six weeks of facing this kind of rejection, Will gave up. "Guess I'll jist hafta go join up with Lincoln's army."

Will had just made a monumental decision.

Army of Northern Virginia

Chapter 30

General Lawrence Branch sent orders to **Major John W. McGill** to muster his Regiment. As soon as **Captain Smith** got the word from the Major, he informed Company "B" they would be moving out to Richmond. The thought of joining General Lee in the Army of Northern Virginia was exciting for the Presley boys.

General Pierre Beauregard and his able assistant **Thomas J. Jackson** had previously won a decisive victory in the **Battle of Manassas on July 21, 1861** near **Bull Run Creek**. The Confederate troops were stationed there to protect their Capital city, Richmond.

General Jackson had distinguished himself there and earned his nickname, **"Stone Wall,"** because his troops had stood "like a stone wall" (as one of his cohorts, General Bee had described him). While other Confederate troops were retreating, Jackson's troops ensured the victory for Beauregard and the Confederate army.

This battle changed the minds of leaders on both sides. Believing the "rebellion" to be short-lived, Lincoln had called for volunteers to enlist for ninety days.

Likewise, Jefferson Davis and Robert E. Lee thought they could make short work of the Union Army. Thinking that by inflicting heavy casualties on them, Lincoln would give up the fight.

The Rebels were so lightly esteemed by the residents of D.C., that when news of the Battle at Bull Run Creek was about to start, huge crowds came out to witness the Union victory.

The shock of watching the Rebels defeat a much larger force of Union soldiers, sent them scurrying back to the safety of their fine lodgings in the city.

Although this first battle took place in **July 1861**, the final truce would not be signed until **April 26, 1865, almost four years later**.

On **March 1, 1862**, the 18th North Carolina Regiment moved north to Richmond. This group, originally organized with eleven hundred men, would suffer massive casualties in the sixteen months leading up to the Battle of Gettysburg.

Buck and Johnny experienced their first engagement with the Union Army near the Hanover Court House on **May 27, 1862**.

Under the command of General Lawrence O'Brian Branch, the 18th North Carolina was positioned at Peake's Crossing (about four miles from the court house) to guard the Virginia Central Railroad. Accompanied by several other Infantry units from North Carolina, and one from Georgia, they numbered about four thousand men.

General Fitz John Porter was dispatched by **General George McClellan** to engage the Rebels, because they were a threat to reinforcements coming from Fredericksburg, led by **General Irvin McDowell**. Porter's unit was composed of Infantry, Cavalry, and Artillery, and numbered about twelve thousand men.

"Johnny, you stay right beside me when 'em Yankees git here. We both has got to re-load when we shoot. When I shoot, you wait while I reload, then I'll wait while ye re-load. 'At way we'll take care of each other," Buck reasoned.

"Hey, 'at's purty smart, Buck," Johnny smiled. "Reckon I'll tell **Travis**, **Kevin**, **Garrick**, **Vic**, and **Andrew** to do that too. We gotta try and take keer of our boys from Graham. We all wanna git back home 'afore 'backer cuttin' time."

"Look out boys, I seen Yankee Cav'ry comin' up on our left side," Garrick yelled.

"Yep, I seen 'em too," Travis said.

"Now you boys wait an' take time about shootin'," Johnny knowingly advised. "At way one kin be a reloadin' while the other 'un is a shootin'."

"Hey Johnny, ye ain't as dumb as ye look," Vic grinned.

Corporal Buck Presley addressed his fellow soldiers from Graham. "Fix bayonets an' git ready fer close combat if need be."

Captain Smith spoke to his Company, "Here they come. Wait until I give the order to fire, we don't want to waste powder."

As the Union cavalry drew close, Smith gave the order. **"FIRE."** A volley of shots rang out. In about twenty seconds, a second volley was heard. Reload, shoot, then reload again.

The cavalry retreated, and the Infantry attacked. Once again, the Confederates repeated the pattern of shoot and reload.

Confusion reigned among the Union forces. Instead of sending his vastly superior numbers of troops to attack, Porter sent small groups to the Confederate lines and they were repulsed.

But even after successfully beating back the Union forces, Branch's forces exhausted their supply of ammunition, and were forced to retreat.

When the Southern soldiers retreated, Porter ordered his men not to pursue. He wanted time to assess his losses. As they counted their casualties, orders came from D.C. for **them** to retreat.

"Stone Wall" Jackson had just inflicted a resounding defeat to Union forces in the **Shenandoah Valley**. McDowell's troops were recalled to Fredericksburg.

General Porter's forces suffered three hundred ninety-six casualties. These were big losses, but Branch's casualties numbered nine hundred thirty, almost one fourth of his men - a big win for the Union Army.

General McClellan proclaimed it "a glorious victory for the United States of America."

Almost exactly one month later, McClellan's forces would suffer a major defeat at the hands of General Robert E. Lee.

The **Seven Days Battle** began on **June 25, 1862** and ended on **July 1, 1862**. Union troops numbered 103,000, while Confederate troops numbered 92,000. Losses were heavy on both sides - McClellan lost 15,500 and Lee lost 20,000.

Americans were slaughtering each other in huge numbers.

Exactly one year later on **July 1, 1863**, the most decisive battle of the war would occur at **Gettysburg, Pennsylvania.**

Robert E. Lee   George B. McClellan

Army of the Potomac

Chapter 31

"Hey Will, I heard that **General Ambrose Burnside** is starting a new brigade of U.S. Army soldiers," **Isaac Surratt** spoke as Will sat down for breakfast.

"He's the guy with them whiskas' that start at tha bottom of his ears and grow all the way down and make a moustache. Funniest thang I ever seen. They call 'em 'sideburns'."

"Yep, I heerd of him. He's got them new guns they call carbines. You can shoot five times without re-loadin', " Will responded.

"Heck, I cain't find no other job."

"They just pay a private thirteen dollars a month, but ye git 'three meals an' a place ta sleep' as they say. Course ye also git uniforms an' boots," John Surratt added.

"Think I'll go over ther' to them recruiters taday," Will mused.

Ambrose Burnside was a graduate of the U.S. Military Academy at West Point, and served on the Western Frontier, and in the **Mexican War**.

Leaving the military, he invented a breech-loading weapon, which was called **"Burnsides Carbines."** A fire totally destroyed his factory in **Providence**, **Rhode Island**, and left him financially ruined.

His carbine was replaced by a multi-shot lever-action carbine called Spencer's carbine. Designed by Christopher Spencer, and, before the fire, was manufactured by Burnside Rifle Co. It was widely-used by cavalry units because of its' smaller size.

He then formed a militia of Rhode Island men in answer to Lincoln's call for ninety-day volunteers. As its Colonel, Ambrose's unit fought without distinction in the **Battle of Manassas** - an ignominious defeat for General Irvin McDowell's Union troops.

After the defeat at **Bull Run Creek**, near **Manassas**, **Virginia**, Burnside's ninety-day volunteer unit was disbanded. He, then, returned to Washington, D.C., and was promoted to Brigadier General. On August 6, 1861, he began to recruit and train a new unit.

Will Presley was one of those recruits.

As a new recruit, he quickly made some friends. From **Knoxville, Tennessee**, a young man named **Norville Hill** had joined Burnside's volunteers. **David** and **Tony Stansberry**, brothers from **Morristown, Tennessee**, and **Darrell Hensley** and **Clyde Coker**, brothers-in-law from **Union County, Tennessee** were among the men in Will's unit.

East Tennessee voted not to secede from the Union, thus its people were Union loyalists.

"Hey Will, word is we're aheadin' to Ca'lina to fight Rebs, " Norville Hill announced. "Guess yer' glad ta be goin' home."

"Not really, Norville. Got bruthers fightin' fer the Rebs. Maw was upset thinkin' we might be fightin' each other. Don't know where ther' at, but hope they ain't 'round the coast nowhere."

Carolina Expeditionary Force

On **September 1, 1861**, Burnside was given command of the Coast **Division of the Carolina Expeditionary Force**. As Commander of a Union Naval Crew as well as his ground troops, he led a successful battle for the seaport town of **Elizabeth City, North Carolin**a. This victory led to the Union Army effectively controlling **eighty percent of the Carolina coast-line**.

Later, at the **Battle of Roanoke Island** and **New Bern**, Burnside's victories won him a promotion. Promoted to **Major General**, he was offered the job as **Commander of the Army of the Potomac**.

General George McClellan, a long-time friend of Burnside, had suffered a severe defeat at the hands of Robert E. Lee's smaller-numbered forces in the **Peninsular Campaign**, and the **Seven Days Battle**. Because of this friendship with McClellan, Burnside declined the offer.

McClellan retained control of the Army of the Potomac, and Burnside was assigned the job of commanding the right wing. They moved north for the **Maryland Campaign**, and on **September 17, 1862**, engaged Lee's forces at **Antietam Cree**k, near Sharpsburg, Maryland.

Although unbeknownst to each of the Presley brothers, all three were involved in this battle - Will in Burnside's volunteers of the IX Corps, and Buck and Johnny in the 18th North Carolina Regiment of Lee's forces.

Antietam

McClellan's battle plan involved separating Burnside's IX Corps from the 1st Corps making it difficult for Burnside to achieve any major victories (or glory). Realizing that Burnside had been offered the command of the Army of the Potomac, he was reluctant to give him much leeway.

Outraged by the restrictions placed on him, Burnside refused to relinquish command of 1st Corps. He continued to issue orders, and relayed them to **General Jacob Cox**, taking McClellan out of the command loop. This cumbersome command structure enabled Lee's smaller army to repel the attacks of Burnside's men.

Realizing he had vastly superior numbers of men, McClellan planned an aggressive strategy His men numbered more than 75,000, but he estimated Lee's numbers at about 38,000, half as many as he had.

Determined to take advantage, McClellan sent orders to Burnside to cross the creek and attack, hoping to overwhelm Lee on his left flank.

Attempting to cross a small bridge over Antietam Creek with small groups of cavalry units, proved difficult.

Captain Bob Smith of "B" Company placed a squad of North Carolina sharpshooters on a hill overlooking the bridge.

The squad of twelve men included Sargent "Buck" Presley, Corporal Johnny Presley, Sargent Garrick Henderson, Corporal Vic Henderson and PFC Andrew Henderson, Corporal Kevin Murphy and PFC Travis Murphy.

As they continued to shoot Union Cavalry soldiers, the crossing was averted.

Once again, McClellan ordered Burnside to cross the creek and attack. Ignoring the command, Burnside persisted in sending cavalry across the bridge only to have them shot.

Impatiently, McClellan sent a note, **"Even if it costs 10,000 men, I command you to cross and attack."**

During a break in the action, Buck noticed some Union horses standing at the base of the hill. He whispered to Johnny, " Follow me, we're agoing home."

"Whadda ye mean, Buck?" Johnny was surprised. "We cain't go home."

"See them two horses down at tha bottom of tha hill? We gonna jump on 'em an' go he'p Maw git that 'backer crop in tha barn."

"That's **desertio**n, Buck. We could git a firin' squad fer that," Johnny worried.

"Jist follow me an' agree with whatever I say," Buck ordered. "Come on let's go."

As they prepared to leave, Buck looked at Garrick and said," We'll be back shortly." Then they slipped down the back side of the hill, mounted the Union horses, and headed South.

Sargent Will Presley, seeing his fellow soldiers in the cavalry unit unable to cross the creek, and hearing about McClellan's orders, took a small squad of his men along the creek bank. Being careful to stay out of sight behind some trees, he found a shallow spot where they could wade across.

Approaching from the side of the hill where the sharpshooters lay, the Union squad attacked. Burnside's carbines, breech loaders, gave them a distinct advantage over the muzzle-loading single-shot rifles used by the rebels.

When they began to cover the hill with rapid fire, Captain Smith ordered his Rebel squad to retreat.

At the retreat of the snipers, Burnside's men crossed the bridge and began to force Lee's troops into retreat.

The long delay, however, allowed **General A.P. Hill's** forces to arrive from Harper's Ferry as reinforcements for Lee's troops.

McClellan refused Burnside's request for reinforcements. Even with the vastly superior numbers of Union forces, McClellan chose not to pursue Lee's retreating Army of Northern Virginia.

With over **23,000** total casualties including Union and Confederate forces; this was **the bloodiest single day in the Civil War**.

McClellan's army suffered **12,401** casualties counting **2,10**8 of them dead and an additional **225** reported missing.

Lee's forces reported **10,310** total, with **1,540** dead and **306** missing. (**Buck and Johnny Presley were among those reported missing**).

The battle ended in a stale-mate, (although McClellan proclaimed it a **"glorious victory"** for the Union army), and caused Lincoln to replace McClellan as Commander of The Army of the Potomac, because he failed to pursue Lee's retreating men.

On November 1, 1862, Burnside was appointed Commander of the Army of the Potomac.

Ambrose Burnside

Buck, Johnny, and Will Presley lived to fight another day.

"A rich man's War is a poor man's fight."

"First" Emancipation Proclamation

Chapter 32

David Hunter, as a graduate of West Point in 1822, was appointed a Second Lieutenant and assigned to an infantry division. Serving eleven years in this position, he eventually was promoted to Captain.

In 1838, he briefly resigned from the army, and moved to Chicago where he worked as a real estate agent and speculator. There

he met and married his wife, Maria Kinzie, whose father was the first permanent white citizen to settle at Fort Dearborn (which would become Chicago, Illinois).

Rejoining the army in 1841, he was promoted to Major, where he worked as a paymaster.

He served in the Seminole War, then the Mexican War.

Moving to Leavenworth, Kansas in 1860, he began a correspondence with Lincoln.

Focusing on his strongly-held anti-slavery beliefs, Hunter became close friends with Lincoln. In **February 1861**, he was asked to join Lincoln's inaugural train ride from Springfield, Illinois to Washington, D.C.

Shortly thereafter, he was promoted to **Major General** in charge of volunteers.

Assigned to the Department of the South as it's Commander, Hunter issued what came to be known as "General Order Number 11."

As a strong advocate of arming black men who were freed slaves, he formed the First Regiment of black soldiers in the Union army.

This unit was formed in South Carolina and was called **1st South Carolina (African Descent)**. Initially ordered to disband this unit, he ultimately won approval from Congress to continue.

Then, Hunter took a major controversial step.

General Order No, 11

"The three states of Georgia, Florida, and South Carolina comprising the military department of the south, having deliberately declared themselves no longer under the protection of the United States of America, and having taken up arms against the said United States, it becomes a necessity to declare them under martial law. This was accordingly done on the 25th day of April 1862. Slavery and martial law in a free country are altogether incompatible; the persons in these three states - Georgia, Florida, and South Carolina – heretofore held as slaves, are therefore declared forever free."

Maj. Gen. David Hunter Department of the South, General Order No. 11, **May 9, 1862**

Fearing political repercussions from slave owners in border states, Lincoln immediately, rescinded the order. Advocating, instead, a policy of gradual emancipation, with government compensation for the slave holders. Despite Lincoln's fears that border states might be driven to join the Confederacy, the national mood had turned very strongly to anti-slavery, especially in the army.

Congress, with the strong urging of the President, had already enacted several laws to inhibit slavery, beginning with the **First Confiscation Act in August 1861**, and culminating with Lincoln's own Emancipation Proclamation on **September 22, 1862**.

Scheduled to take effect on **January 1, 1863**, concerned Confederate slave owners reacted very strongly.

Confederate President, **Jefferson Davis**, issued an order declaring that General Hunter was a "felon to be executed if captured."

Controversy continued to envelope Hunter. Disregarding Lincoln's reluctance, he once again gave black soldiers in South Carolina the opportunity to serve and to fight for their own freedom.

A Representative from border-state Kentucky, John Wickliffe, introduced a resolution condemning the action, and incensing other border-state Congressmen.

Responding to the resolution, Hunter wrote a sarcastic letter to the Congressman from Kentucky reminding him of the authority given to field commanders by the Confiscation Act.

No regiment of "Fugitive Slaves" has been or is being formed in this department. There is, however, a fine regiment of persons whose late masters are "Fugitive Rebels" – men who everywhere fly before the presence of their National Flag leaving their servants behind them to shift as best they can for themselves.

So far, indeed, are the persons comprising this regiment seeking to avoid the presence of their late owners, that they are now, one and all, working with remarkable industry to place themselves in such a position as to go in full and effective pursuit of their fugacious and traitorous proprietors.

The instructions given to Brig. Gen. W.T. Sherman by the Hon. Simon Cameron late Secretary of War and turned over to me by succession for my guidance – do distinctly authorize me to employ all loyal persons offering themselves in defense of the Union and for the suppression of this rebellion in any manner as I might see fit.

In conclusion, it is my hope there being no possibility of other reinforcements owing to the exigencies of the Campaign of the Peninsula to have organized by the end of next Fall, and to be able to present to the government forty-eight to fifty thousand of these hardy and devoted soldiers.

First Confiscation Act

The Confiscation Act enabled Union Generals to confiscate any and all personal property acquired in defense of the United States of America. When confronted with black slaves whom they freed in small skirmishes with Rebel plantation owners, these people were declared contraband to be used for the war effort.

Hunter began to use them as soldiers. Also, he used them as teamsters, livery stable operators, and wagon makers.

Encouraged by these efforts, slaves began to escape and join the Union forces in trickles, then, gradually, in droves. By mid-1862, the public perception of slavery changed. More and more it was considered **immoral**.

The war effort was not going well for Lincoln and his generals; so, encouraged by the audacious actions of David Hunter, a decision was made to change the focus of the war.

Instead of *putting down the rebellion to preserve the Union, the total abolition of slavery* **became the goal**.

It was believed that the Proclamation should not be issued until after a major Union victory, but to expedite the action, the marginal victory at **Antietam on September 17, 1862** provided the impetus needed.

Lincoln's Emancipation Proclamation

On **September 22, 1862**, Lincoln stated that slaves in the United States of America ..... "then, thenceforward, and forever more, free" - effective **January 1, 1863**.

13th Amendment

Realizing that laws and proclamations can be easily changed, a movement began to amend the Constitution. Passed by two-thirds of the Senate in 1864, it was finally ratified by the House **on January 31, 1865 .... "neither slavery nor involuntary servitude shall exist within the United States of America."**

More than 3,000,000 slaves would be freed.

News of Lincoln's action quickly spread to Union and Confederate soldiers alike.

Captain Curtis Kintner, Will's Company Commander, summoned him to his tent, along with **Lieutenant Joseph Barkley**, second-in-command of "D" Company.

"Just got some big news from General Burnside. President Lincoln has just issued a Proclamation freeing all the slaves in territory we now control. You can share this with the troops. This will be a great, inspiring action for our men. The freeing of all slaves is a noble cause for which to fight," the captain smiled. "Makes me feel better about this gol'- danged war."

Will wryly smiled, "I been tellin' my fam'ly this fer a long time now – me an' Preacher Henderson back home."

"Where is home for you, Will?" Lieutenant Barkley inquired.

"Little town down in North Ca'lina, Lieutenant."

The Captain spoke, "How are your folks gonna react, Sargent Presley?"

"Cain't rightly say Cap'n. I reckon Maw'd be happy if this war wuz over. She didn't much like it ta start with. My bruthers wuz all 'bout 'state's rights', they never said much 'bout slavery 'cept Buck. He said slavery wuz in the Bible."

"In my opinion this whole business of war is about slavery. I never wanted to see the Union split up, but I hated the thought of men being slaves," the Captain mused. "I'm glad the President said it straight out."

"A rich man's war is a poor man's fight."

A.W.O.L.

Chapter 33

Quickly, Buck and Johnny mounted the Union horses and galloped away from the battlefield. As they neared the troops from General A.P. Hill's advancing forces, they slowed and waved as they passed.

"Stay cool, Johnny, 'em boys 'er on 'er side," Buck spoke softly. "Jist keep riding south. If any'bidy asks, we wuz ordered to retreat."

Almost unseen by the **officer**s of Hill's units, the Presley boys nodded and waved as they passed. Soon they were far enough south of the reinforcement troops that they returned to galloping.

"If we keep a steady pace an' don't dilly-dally, we kin be home in three or four days," Buck was confident.

"Woo Hoo, I cain't hardly wait ta see Willadeen an' my young 'un," Johnny was exuberant. "Hey, it shore is good ta be back home ag'in," he spoke to Buck.

"Yep, we bin gone over a year, but it seems longer," Buck replied.

Nearing the confluence of Roaring Fork Creek and the Nantahala River, the Presley boys saw Billy Bob, Pete, Andy, and Matt working in the tobacco field.

The rich, fertile soil along the river bank was the perfect spot to grow tobacco. A water ditch had been dug to divert water from the river and from the creek into the field in dry weather. A wooden gate stopped the water flow when necessary.

"Hey, there's Buck and Johnny," Matt was the first to see them. Running to greet them, he stumbled twice.

"Hello Baby Brutha. Ar' ye glad ta see us?" Buck yelled.

"Mighty glad, mighty glad."

The other three brothers stopped working and hurried to greet and hug the two soldiers.

"How'd ye guys git off long 'nuf ta come home?" Pete inquired.

"If I tol' ye, I'd hafta ta kill ye," Buck joked with a curled-lip grin.

"Aww, yer jist like Paw," Andy piped in. "Always tryin' ta be funny."

"We come home ta he'p ye boys git tha 'backer cut and in tha barn." Johnny volunteered. "Guess ye'll need he'p with fam'ly crop too."

"What kinda 'backer ye set out this year Billy Bob?" Buck asked.

"Well, of course, we're araisin' Burley here in Mr Graham's field ta sell at Market, but I 'cided ta raise Bull Head in the fam'ly patch. Hit makes better chewin' 'backer and snuff fer tha girls." Billy Bob replied. "**An'** I thank we kin sell sum' of hit on Market Sat'adees in town. Town folks don't raise no 'backer fer ther ownselfs."

"Me an' Johnny better git on ta tha house. I wanna see Martha an' my kids, an' Johnny wants ta see Willadeen an' li'l Johnny," Buck declared.

"We're agoin' ta tha house too," Andy spoke up. "It'sa 'bout dinner time. Hope Maw's got it ready, I'm hungry."

Stepping out onto the back porch to ring the dinner bell, Maggie saw her four brothers walking up the road toward the house. Two men wearing Confederate uniforms and leading horses were walking with them. **Her heart skipped a beat**. *"Why wuz them so'jers escorting her bruthas?"* she wondered.

As they drew closer, she recognized Buck and Johnny. "Maw, Martha, Willadeen, lookee who's here," she yelled.

Everybody in the family ran outside and rejoiced at the arrival of their soldier boys. Adam and Thomas, Buck's two older boys raced to greet their father.

Adam, now eight years old, outran Thomas who was only six. Jumping into his arms, Adam almost knocked Buck off his feet. Thomas ran up and jumped into Buck's arms too.

Holding both of them, he looked to see Jedediah and Judith running toward him. Setting the older boys down, he scooped up the two smaller children into his arms.

Martha waited until her children had finished with her husband before she approached. Grabbing him and kissing him very deeply, she smiled and blushed. "We didn't know ye wuz comin' home. Why didn't ye let us know so I could've fixed myself up a little bit," she complained.

Willadeen , carrying little Johnny in her arms, ran out to greet Johnny. "Hallelujah, I'm so glad ta see ye. How come ye got ta come home?"

"It's a long story. Me and Buck'll tell y'all 'bout it at tha dinner table. Have ye got dinner ready? I'm hungry."

Sally and Lizzie waited their turn to hug Buck and Johnny. Then they all went inside to have dinner.

Sitting down at the table to eat the noon-time *dinner*, every member of the family gathered around. The women and children (as was the custom) stood, and allowed the men to be seated and eat first.

Maggie and Martha continued the final preparations for the meal, and everybody else was asking questions of the soldiers.

Billy Bob wondered, "How'd ye boys git leave time right now? I heerd tha fightin' was getting' *hot 'n heavy.*"

Buck grinned, "Sometimes it's easier ta git forgiveness than permission. I heerd Preacher Henderson say that one time."

Johnny added, "We knew y'all had a hard time gettin' tha 'backer crop in tha barn last year. Wanted ta be here ta he'p this time, **an'** I wanted ta see my purty wife an' baby boy, too."

"Maw have ye heerd anythang from Will?" Buck wondered.

"No, not nothing since he left me a note the day he left home. I wrote you a letter and told ye about that. He left here the same day you boys did and didn't know where he was going," Sally said to Buck with a worried frown.

"I shore hope we see 'im again' when this is all over," Buck wished. "Jeff Davis an' General Lee keep sayin' them Yankees er goin' git tarred of this an' jist give up."

"I don't know, Buck, I just have a bad feeling about this whole mess," she was glum.

Johnny interjected, "Them Yankees has got a lot more men an' guns an' horses an' cannons than we got, but 'er generals is a lot smarter. I thank we can whup "em Maw."

"I jist wish tha whole thang wuz over an' ye wuz back home wit us," Willadeen said.

"Yeah, me too. I shore miss havin' my man home wit me an' tha kids," Martha spoke.

"We jist gotta keep it quiet 'bout us bein' home rite now, ever'bidy," Buck directed. "Nobidy in town, an' specially Mr. Graham don't need ta know. We're goin' back when tha 'backer's in tha barn. Jist keep yer mouth shut."

"O.K., boys, let's go finish 'suckerin' that 'backer." Pete said. "Buck an' Johnny's hada long ride an' 'er tarred. Tomorrow's Sun'dee, an' they can have another day ta rest."

"How much more ya gotta do, Pete?" Johnny asked.

"I'd guess 'bout two more weeks of 'suckerin' then start cutting. Maybe 'bout second week of October, we can cut it."

Billy Bob took charge, "Should have it in tha barn by first of November."

"If we git it in tha barn by first of November, can ye boys get it ta Market without me an' Johnny? "Buck questioned. "We gotta git back ta 'er unit."

"Yep, ain't no problem gittin' it ta Asheville ta sell it. We got two wagons wit trailers ta haul in. Us four boys here kin do that. Ye two so'jers kin go back to killin' Yankees," Matt piped in.

"Now Matthew, I've told you about talkin' of killin' son," Sally warned, "don't let me hear you sayin' that agin'.

Beautiful weather prevailed with only three days of rain from September 20, when the boys got home until October 11.

Completing the job of removing the small offshoots from the stalks of tobacco (**suckering**), the cutting of the stalks, and separating the leaves from the stalks finished their work.

With Buck and Johnny assisting Andy and Matt in the tobacco field, the job went quickly and smoothly. The younger boys had a tendency not to stay focused on the task at hand, but Buck took charge and kept them working well together.

Billy Bob and Pete worked in the woods cutting timber and made their weekly trip on Saturday to the sawmill. Being careful not to mention Buck or Johnny, they came home with **terrible news on October 4**.

Vic Henderson had been shot in his right shin and calf. Some Yankees had sneaked up on their left flank and attacked from the unprotected side of the bunker. This squad of Yankees had diverted the attention of the sharpshooters and allowed the Yankee cavalry to cross the bridge. Hearing the bugle play the retreat signal, Company "B" began their flight. As he left, Vic was wounded.

Taken to a field hospital to be treated, doctors decided **to amputate his leg** to prevent gangrene. He was now in a hospital in Richmond. Soon, he would be coming home when the infection healed. Steve was already crafting an artificial leg for him.

When they returned from town and told this story to Buck, Johnny, Andy, and Matt, they were shocked and surprised.

"Gosh, I never thunk 'bout Vic getting' his leg shot off," Pete mused. "Him an' me 'er bout tha same age."

"Yep, an' they say them docs 'er quick ta cut yer legs an' arms off, if it ain't ther' own," Buck added.

Johnny grimaced, "I wuz goin' by tha hospital one day an' seen a guy haulin' a wheelbarrow load of legs an' arms out ta be burned. It'sa God-awful smell when they burn 'em."

"Yeah, I tol' Johnny not ta let them take me ta no field hospital. I'll take my chances wit a bullet still in me," Buck shook his head.

"We're getting a lotta boys killed too. They said we lost over 20,000 in tha **Carolina Coast Battle**, an' I reckon we lost a big bunch at **Antietam**, too," Johnny responded.

"Ye boys can talk 'bout that at supper time. Let's git this 'backer in tha barn now, " Buck ordered.

On Friday, October 17, Buck spoke to Sally as they sat down for dinner, "Maw is Preacher Henderson gonna be eatin' dinner here on Sunday?"

"No, this is his Sunday to eat with Martha's folks over at Old Yellow Creek, but he'll be preachin' here at Roarin' Fork, why'd you ask?"

"Don't want him ta know me an' Johnny's here, Maw. We gotta go back ta 'er unit in 'bout two more weeks."

"Yeah, I thought about that."

"Y'all go on ta church, but make shore none of tha kids say anything 'bout us bein' home."

After church on Sunday, Matt burst into the house an' yelled, "Hey Buck guess what?"

Startled, Buck asked, "What is it boy?"

"Tell 'im Maw, tell 'im," Matt was excited.

"Buck and Johnny, President Lincoln has issued a Proclamation declaring all the slaves are free from now on," Sally nervously explained. "Preacher Henderson told us at church."

"How'd tha Preacher feel 'bout it?" Johnny asked. "He's been preachin' agin' it fer a long time."

Willadeen answered Johnny, " He thanks it shudda happened years ago. Talked 'bout Jesus sayin' ye otta treat people tha way ye want them ta treat ye."

Buck interjected, "Supreme court said slaves wuddn't people; they's property. Preacher Henderson called it Dred Scott decision."

"Well it ain't gonna 'fect us much, Maw," Pete joined in. "Ain't no slaves round these parts."

Martha wondered what Buck thought about it. "Whatta ye thank 'bout it Buck?"

"Pete's right, Martha, but it might make tha war go on longer," Buck guessed. "Them plantations cain't work without slaves. It'll put them big-time cotton growers outta business."

Maggie, usually quiet, joined the conversation, "Why cain't they run them plantations like we run our farm?"

Billy Bob answered Maggie, "It takes a whole lot more labor ta work them big fields a cotton, an' them darkies kin stay out in tha hot sun a lot longer'n white men.

Wide-eyed, Lizzie spoke, "Bet not manya them'd stay there if they hadda chance ta leave. I wuddn't. Would ye Matt?"

"Heck no, I'd git outta ther' quick as lightnin'." Matt grinned.

On November 2nd, the Presley tobacco was cut, handed off, and hung in the barn. If it stayed dry, the tobacco would cure by December 1st, and could be sold. It was a big crop and a good harvest this year. Hard-wood timber was bringing a good price, so the Presley family should be in good shape for the winter.

Dreading the thought of leaving their family again, Buck and Johnny prepared to leave. After dinner on Sunday afternoon, they mounted their horses and set out for Richmond.

"A rich man's war is a poor man's fight."

Fredericksburg

Chapter 34

A rriving in Richmond on November 5th, Buck and Johnny found their Company's encampment on the outskirts of town. Quickly, they reported to **Captain Bob Smith**, their Company Commander.

"Where in tha Hell have ye boys been? It wuz over six weeks ago when I seen ye last time. Cudn't account fer ye afta Antietam."

Buck had told Johnny to keep quiet and let him do all the talking. "We got captured by Yankees as we wuz retreatin', Cap'n."

"Where'd they keep ye, Buck?" the captain wondered.

"Don't know the name of it, but I thank it was in Maryland jist outsida D.C."

"Well, I'm glad to have ye back. The First Sargent will write a report, and ye'll have to give him a statement. Welcome boys. We're glad yer here."

General Burnside was informed by the Commander of "D" Company, **Captain Curtis Kintner**, that Will Presley had taken the initiative to lead his squad to the left flank of the Confederate snipers. Presley's maneuver had enabled Burnside's troops to cross **"Burnside's Bridge"** and force Lee's troops into retreat at Antietam Creek.

Although General McClellan had chosen not to pursue Lee's soldiers in their retreat, Burnside had prevented a defeat. Recognizing Will's role in this battle, Burnside summoned him to his tent.

"Sargent Presley, it has come to my attention that your squad enabled us to cross the bridge at Antietam Creek. You have my sincere thanks and congratulations. I wish we had more soldiers like you. To reward your actions, I have ordered that you be promoted to First Sargent, and that you be awarded a medal for 'Meritorious Valor'.

"At morning roll call your Battalion Commander will present your award. I've, also, been informed that you were one of my first recruits when I formed the unit in D.C. Thank you for joining with me and thank you for your act of bravery."

Will respectfully responded, "Thank ye, sir, happy to be servin' with ye, sir."

As he saluted the general, Burnside returned the salute, and dismissed him. Being promoted to First Sargent meant that he would now be third-in-command of his Company, behind the Captain and the Lieutenant, **Joseph Barkley**. "It's kinda funny," he thought, "now I'm in the same position I wuz in our fam'ly, Buck, then Johnny, then me."

Hoping for a quick end to the war, Lincoln took an active role as Commander-in-Chief. Not happy that **McClellan** had declined to pursue Lee's retreating forces at Antietam, the decision to replace him was made.

Once again, **Burnside** was chosen to take over command of the Army of the Potomac. Hearing that if he refused the command, **Major General Joseph Hooker** would be offered the job, he reluctantly accepted the appointment.

Even though he lacked confidence in his own ability to command at this level, he was convinced that Hooker was even less-qualified than he. As a classmate of Hooker at West Point, Burnside despised him, and didn't want his less-qualified acquaintance to inherit the position.

Rumors abounded that Hooker had recruited some less-than-honorable females to hover around his encampments to provide pleasure and contentment for his men. Some people were calling them **'Hookers'**.

On **Monday, November 10, 1862**, Burnside assumed command of the Army of the Potomac. Lincoln encouraged him to attack Lee's army and take over the Confederate capital of Richmond.

Devising a brilliant plan, he presented it to Lincoln who very quickly approved it. Unfortunately, brilliant plans are ofttimes poorly executed.

The plan was to cross the **Rappahannock River at Fredericksburg**, then march on to Richmond.

Arriving on **December 1st**, well before Lee, the Federal forces could easily have captured the city. With a delay in the arrival of pontoon bridges to cross the river, Burnside opted to wait for them, and stick with his plan.

When the pontoon bridges finally arrived, and assembly began, Rebel snipers kept the Union forces on the other side of the river, and Buck Presley's squad was again employed to keep them there.

"All rite boys, when a Yankee cav'ry horse starts inta tha river, shoot quick. Don't let 'em git mor'n ten 'er fifteen feet out. Take time 'bout shooin', then, reloadin'. Ther's fifteen of us here, so let's make all of 'er shots count," Buck instructed his men.

On the morning of **December 11th**, Garrick Henderson pointed out to Buck that pontoon bridge segments were being floated into the river. Wading into the river, soldiers attached another segment onto the one further out in the water. Standing close to the bank, segments were added, then, pushed further into the water. Eventually, they would span the entire waterway.

"We gotta keep 'em from gittin' all tha way across as long as we kin. When they finish 'at bridge, all ther' infantry boys'll come across," Buck directed. "Keep shootin' 'em boys out in tha water."

First Sargent Will Presley directed his men from Company "D" as they assembled the pontoon bridge. Bringing three squads of his men to the river bank, he ordered them to "provide cover" for the engineers' assembly efforts.

For a day-and-a-half, Buck's plan worked. Then Burnside gave orders to use the artillery. In an attempt to destroy the snipers, 150 cannons were deployed on the city, almost completely destroying every building therein. Finally, two cannon balls hit the building Company "B" was occupying and it began to collapse.

"Let's git outta here boys," Buck ordered. "We're afixin' ta join our Company on tha ridge outsida town.

With 120,000 soldiers at his disposal, Burnside saw no need to hurry. Intelligence told him that Lee's army was divided, so he waited almost two weeks until the bridge was completed.

Two divisions of Rebel soldiers arrived before the completion of the bridge, even though Lieutenant General **Thomas "Stonewall" Jackson's** forces were a week's march away in the Shenandoah Valley. That delay allowed Jackson's division to arrive before they were attacked.

After the long delay on, **December 13th**, Burnside ordered his forces to cross the river and take the town of Fredericksburg. Lee's main body of troops were dug in on the high ground outside the town in strong defensive positions on Marye's Heights.

Attempting a diversion, Burnside sent 60,000 men to strike at Lee's left flank. At the base of the ridge, a stone wall bordering a sunken road, provided a 'natural' bunker for the Rebels. Strike after strike after strike was repelled.

Burnside then attempted a surprise attack on the center of Lee's entrenchments. Although surprised, Confederate forces inflicted heavy casualties on their Union attackers, and they eventually retreated - ending the fight on **December 15th**.

The **Battle of Fredericksburg** involved more soldiers than any other battle in the war - more than **190,000** Union and Confederate fighting men.

Heavy losses occurred on **both** sides, with Burnside losing over **12,000**, and Lee losing over **5,300**. Once again, much-smaller numbers of Confederate troops were victorious over Union troops.

Smart Confederate Generals and bumbling Union Generals were the deciding factors.

One month later, desperate to turn the tide of the war, Lincoln fired Burnside, and replaced him with his despised classmate **Joseph Hooker**.

Brigadier General George Meade was assigned to Hooker's command, and eventually would replace him to lead the "most decisive battle of the war" - **Gettysburg**.

"A rich man's war is a poor man's fight."

Chancellorsville

Chapter 35

Resting and recuperating from the heavy battles, Buck and Johnny took time to write letters to their wives.

March 10, 1863

My Darling Martha,
We been real busy fighting Yankees, but got a little break right now. I'm missing you and the yung'uns a lot. Wish me and Johnny was home.

Lee keeps saying Lincoln's gonna give up soon and the Confederates can have our own country. I'm not sure he's right. We are hoping to get home again in the fall to help get the tobacco crop in the barn.

Maybe this war will be over before then. Tell Maw and my brothers and sisters I miss them too. I'll go for now. Write me back soon. I love you.

Buck

March 11, 1863

Willadeen,

We finally got time to rest some. Me and Buck both decided we need to write home and let you know we are all right.

Hope ever thing is good at home. I miss seeing little Johnny growing up. I know he's growed a lot since we was home in November.

We are going to come home again in September or October. Don't know if we can get leave time, but we are coming home to help with the tobacco crop.

I love you Willadeen and can't hardly wait to see you soon. Tell Maw I love her too.

Johnny

March 22, 1863

Dear Buck and Johnny,

Hope this letter finds both of you in good health. Everybody here is doing fine.

Lizzie is going to move to town and stay with Momma and Poppa O'Conner. They're still operating the tailor shop, but I keep trying to get them to quit. Momma keeps saying, "We've worked all our lives and wouldn't know what to do with our self if we quit."

I worry about them, and Lizzie wants to live in town with them where lots of things are going on. Frank Graham said he needs someone to work in the fabric department in the General Store. She can go over and check on them occasionally, and stay in their house at night.

I hope you boys can get home to help us get the tobacco in the barn. It was a big help having you both here last year.

Willadeen has a surprise for Johnny,

Love,
Momma

March 23, 1863

Dear Johnny,

Do you remember Lawyer Mahan's son, Doug? Well, he just finished up his studies at Atlanta Medical School and opened an office here in Graham. Maw took me to see him last week, and he told me we are "in the family way"

He thinks it'll be sometime about middle of August. I'm hoping for a little girl this time. Hope you want one too

My grandmother was named Catherine and Martha's was named Louise. I'm thinking Catherine Louise if it's a girl. If it's a boy I would like to name him James William after his grandfather, J.W. What do you think?

If you can come home this Fall, maybe we'll have a new baby for you. I am soo happy Johnny, I love you.

Love,

Willadeen

March 23, 1863

My Dearest Buck,

I was very happy to get a letter from you last week. The children made me read it to them three times.

All of us are missing you every day and wish you was home with us. Jedediah and Judith especially miss you. Almost every day Judith asks, "When's Dada comin' home?"

Being as how Willadeen's "in the family way," our children are excited too. They're eager to have a new cousin.

Please come home as soon as you can. I hate this war. Hope to see you in the Fall. I love you, Buck Presley

Loving you,

Martha

Finishing the letter, Buck quickly brushed the tears rolling down his cheeks. *"Damn this war, and Damn Abraham Lincoln. If the Yankees had just left us be, and not tried to tell us what to do, this war wuddn't a happened,"* Buck thought to himself.

"Hey Johnny, I jist read tha good news 'bout Willadeen. Ye didn't waste no time in tha six weeks we wuz home," Buck grinned.

"Aw, I wuz jist pokin' a little fun at her, an' she took me serious, I reckon," Johnny retorted.

Soon after his promotion to Commander of the Army of the Potomac, Major General Joseph Hooker planned an excursion into Virginia. Knowing that Lincoln was expecting him to be more productive than the Generals who preceded him, he planned to take the Capital city of Richmond.

On **April 27, 1863**, he ordered **Major General George Stoneman** to cross the Rappahannock River at Fredericksburg, with his Union Cavalry. Stoneman was planning to disrupt Lee's supply lines, but his men were repulsed by Lee's troops.

Entrenched, once again, on **Marye's Height**s - the high ground gave them a distinct advantage. Company "B" was positioned directly at the point of crossing, and Sargent Buck Presley's squad was instrumental in sending Stoneman's cavalry into retreat.

Lee had left one Division of his troops to defend Fredericksburg, (about one-fifth of his total), commanded by **George Pickett**. He, then, moved the main body of his troops on down near the **Rapidan River at Chancellorsville**.

"Great job men," **Captain Bob Smit**h addressed his soldiers. "**General Pickett**, our Division Commander, summoned **Lieutenant Everet**t and myself to his tent. He wanted to congratulate us on driving the Union cavalry into retreat. Asked us to extend to all of you his personal thanks, and planned to mention it to General Lee."

Lieutenant Everett spoke. "I especially want to recognize Sargent Presley's squad of 'sharpshooters'. General Pickett inquired about the great group of riflemen at the center of our forces. He personally watched your efforts, and complimented you."

"Well, we wuz jist doin' our job, Lieutenant," Buck replied modestly.

With their ranks thinning due to casualties, the 18th North Carolina Regiment had been merged into General George G. Pickett's Division. In a few short weeks, they would become part of an infamous Civil War operation.

Devising a plan to attack Lee simultaneously from the front and the rear, Hooker sent his infantry across the Rapidan River - a small tributary of the Rappahannock. Crossing at **Germanna** and Ely's **Ford on April 30th**, he met unexpectedly heavy opposition. On **May 1st**, ignoring the advice of his subordinates, Hooker made the decision to withdraw to defensive positions around Chancellorsville.

The withdrawal gave Lee the initiative in the battle. On **May 2nd**, dividing his troops again, Lee sent **"Stonewall" Jackson** on a flanking maneuver. Surprising Hooker's Xl Corps, he totally routed them.

Leaving a small cadre of men led by **Major Jubal Early** at Fredericksburg, Pickett was ordered to rejoin Lee's main force at Chancellorsville. Positioning his men like pieces on a chess board, Lee was the consummate battlefield tactician.

Elated with his victory, Jackson went on a personal reconnaissance mission. Accompanied by ten of his subordinate officers, he made a night-time excursion to survey Hooker's Xl Corps. Satisfied with his findings, he returned to his encampment.

Company "B" was standing guard duty. Among those guards were **Johnny Presley**, **Garrick Henderson**, and **Travis Murph**y. As Jackson's entourage approached, Presley yelled, "who goes there?" Answering quickly. Jackson yelled, "It's General Jackson, Stand Down."

The Major in charge of the sentries yelled, **"It's a Yankee Trap. FIRE, FIRE."**

Six shots rang out loudly, as all of the sentries fired their rifles. When the smoke cleared, the awful truth was learned. **General "Stonewall" Jackson was severely wounded**.

With a bullet in his right leg and two in his left arm, he was rushed to a tent-enclosed field hospital. The standard operating procedure was to amputate any limbs with multiple wounds.

Using only a large shot of whiskey for anesthesia, and a large knife as a surgical instrument, Jackson's left arm was amputated.

Extremely unsanitary conditions prevailed in field hospitals, both North and South, and as a result, infections were common.

Eight days later, on **May 10th**, **"Stonewall" Jackson died of pneumonia**. News of his death quickly spread, and the reactions were varied and mournful.

Lee said, "Jackson lost his **Left** arm, but I lost my **Right** arm."

Johnny Presley said to Buck, "I wuz jist following orders, brutha. I wuddn'a shot Gen'ral Jackson fer nuthin'."

"Yeah, I know, Johnny," Buck answered," but don'cha ever let them take me to no field hospital. I'll take my chances with a bullet still in me."

General J.E.B. Stuart, a cavalry officer replaced Jackson on Lee's command team. **General Richard Ewell**, Jackson's Junior Officer, took command of the left flank.

Along with **General James Longstreet**, Lee still maintained a formidable team of experienced officers.

J.E.B. Stuart   James Longstreet

Longstreet's unit fought a successful delaying battle at Salem Church and on **May 4th**, drove Sedgewick back to Bank's Ford. Sedgewick retreated across the Ford on **May 5th**.

Hooker withdrew the rest of his men on the night of May 5th. This battle finally ended on **May 7th**, when Stoneman's cavalry reached Union lines near Richmond.

Large numbers of troops were deployed in this important battle. Union troops numbered **97,764**, while Confederate generals utilized only **57,352**. Casualties were high on both sides. Hooker lost **1,694** killed, **9,67**2 wounded, and **593** missing in action.

Confederate losses were **1,724** killed, **9,233** wounded and **2,503 missing in action**.

The Battle of Chancellorsville has been called **"Lee's Greatest Victory."** With fewer men and less munitions he had won another decisive victory.

As Lee piled up the victories over much-larger forces, he began to feel **almost invincible**.

Adhering to his belief that if he could inflict heavy casualties on the Union army, Lincoln would just "give up the fight" and quit.

The next big battle at Gettysburg would prove the fallacy of Lee's idea.

"A rich man's war is a poor man's fight."

Gettysburg

Chapter 36

Retreating from Chancellorsville, Hooker moved his men to Harper's Ferry. The Armory and Arsenal were located there; so, it was possible to re-arm his forces with weapons and powder.

Will, speaking to Captain Kintner said, "Cap'un, Sir, I know only officers are allowed to carry side arms, but I would feel a lot more safer if I had a repeater pistol. My breech-loading rifle is faster than a musket, but it's still just one shot at a time. Them revolving pistols shoots six times. Can you get me one from the Arsenal?"

"Tell ye what I'll do, Sargent Presley, I'll give ye mine and requisition a new one fer myself. If anybody asks, I don't know wher' ye got it."

"I won't tell if ye won't, Cap'un. I can always say I picked it up on the battlefield at Chancellorsville. Thank ye, Sir."

In 1861, when Virginia voted to secede from the Union, the western counties of Virginia voted overwhelmingly against secession. Soon after, a movement to form a separate state called **West Virginia** was started. On **June 20, 1863, West Virginia was admitted to the Union**.

Buoyed by his two most-recent victories in Virginia, Lee made plans to invade the North. He would move through the Shenandoah valley into Pennsylvania, and engage the enemy on their territory.

Moving the battle lines northward had several advantages. First, it would allow the Southern residents a respite from the effects of the war. Secondly, it would position his troops to move on to Philadelphia, and, then later, to Washington, D.C. Thirdly, he believed that if he could choose the battlefield, he could land a knock-out blow to Union forces, and, thereby, convince Lincoln to give up the fight.

When he lost General "Stonewall" Jackson at Chancellorsville, Lee turned to Lt. General **James Longstreet** to be his close confidant. As Lee outlined his plan to Longstreet, a controversy erupted between the two generals, that would prove to be decisive in the upcoming battle.

Longstreet, seeing the massive Confederate casualties in the victories at Fredericksburg and Chancellorsville, espoused a plan to fight defensively rather than attacking aggressively. Find a position on high ground, and establish defensive positions. Entice the Union Generals to take the offensive, then wipe them out with a much smaller number of Confederate casualties.

Lee, along with his late commander, **Thomas Jackson**, believed an aggressive attacking strategy worked best. With smaller numbers of men, the last two battles were decisive victories for the Confederates. Lee reminded Longstreet that the defeated Union generals had used this defensive approach.

Finding a Shakespearian actor by the name of **Henry Thomas Harrison** to act as a spy, Longstreet sent him to Washington, D.C. As a close friend of **John Wilkes Booth** and well-known among Washington elite, Harrison patronized the bars and taverns. Plied with alcohol, the legislators and staffers for Lincoln gave much information which was funneled back to Lee through Longstreet.

Garrisoned at Cash Town, only eight miles from Gettysburg, on **June 28th**, word came that General Hooker had been replaced by General George Meade as commander of the Army of the Potomac. Meade was traveling from Washington to assume command.

Meade had been summoned to the Department of War offices of Secretary Stanton on **June 28th**. Told by Lincoln that he would replace Hooker as commander of the Army of the Potomac, he was given three orders. First, assume command, then, inform Hooker of the change, and immediately engage Lee at Gettysburg. Hooker had already been made aware that Lee was near Gettysburg and had started moving from Fredrick, Maryland where they were garrisoned.

With this news of Meade's replacement of Hooker, the decision to move forward to Gettysburg was made on **June 28,1863**.

Following the advice of Longstreet, high ground was located just outside town at a place called **Seminary Ridge**, where a **Lutheran Seminary** was located.

Lee set his headquarters tent at a position toward the center part of his forces. Moving 72,000 men is quite a cumbersome process; so, it took two days to get all the soldiers in position stretched out over two miles.

"Al'rite men, we're moving out. Get yer shit tagether an' let's move," Captain Smith ordered his men of Company B.

"Damnit Buck, I jist now got my boots dried out from marchin' in all that mud comin' here," Johnny griped.

"Yeah, all these Yankee roads is jist mud holes, I reckon," Buck answered.

Seeing the Lieutenant standing nearby Buck approached. "Lieutenant, sir, wher' 'er we aheadin' out to, sir?"

Everette quickly answered, "Bout eight more miles down tha road to a l'il town called Gettysburg. Seems ther's a buncha Yankees headed this way, an' we 'er gonna be waitin fer 'em."

An advance force of Meade's cavalry led by General John Buford arrived in Gettysburg on **June 30th**, and encountered some of Lee's men in town. (They had entered the town in search of shoes.) A brief skirmish ensued, and the cavalry retreated to high ground on **Culp's Hill** along **Cemetery Hill**.

Believing them to be a small local militia group, the encounter was not reported to Lee. The position on Culp's hill would become the headquarters when Meade arrived to assume command.

JULY 1, 1863

Marching up the muddy road that was the Chambersburg Pike from Cash Town, combatants were still arriving in the early morning of **July 1st**. A unit of A.P. Hill's Third Corps met some of Buford's dismounted cavalry soldiers. As the fighting grew more intense, a unit of John Reynolds' infantry - the First Corps - arrived to reinforce Buford's cavalry. The Confederates were repulsed, but General Reynolds was killed.

By early afternoon, the Union 11th Corps commanded by **Major General Oliver Howard** had arrived, and the their position was laid out in a semi-circular form that resembled a fish-hook. Will Presley and his fellow members of Company "D" were in the center of the fish-hook on Cemetery Hill.

Confederate General Richard Ewell's forces were positioned on the right flank east of the Lutheran Seminary on the ridge bearing the "Seminary" name.

Pickett's division, a part of Longstreet's Corps, was still in Cash Town, and was the last division to move out to Gettysburg . They didn't arrive until the evening of **July 2nd**.

JULY 2, 1863

"Hey Buck, didja heer 'bout all tha stuff that happened yes'tidee an' taday?" Garrick inquired.

"Yeah, I heerd ther' wuz a lotta fightin on Wednesday, an' we kicked Yankee ass."

Captain Smith wandered by the position where the Graham soldiers had settled (they always tried to stay close together.)

"Well, ther wuz sum Ca'lina boys down ther, in Herbst's woods yes'tidee but nun from 'er bunch," Smith replied. "I just got a report that they put tha Yankees to retreatin' toward town, and 'er boys took a buncha prisoners. Hate ta say it, but a buncha townspeople wuz killed too. As they say, ya gotta expect sum losses ina war."

Buck spoke up, "Yeah, but it's better them than us, I reckon."

Captain Smith continued, "We lost a lotta men taday, an tha Yankees did too. Over in tha Peach Orchard an' in tha Wheat Fields. It wuz mostly Ewell's men."

When the Union forces retreated, they headed for Cemetery Hill with their main units. Lee gave orders to General Ewell, "to attack the hill if at all practicable."

Apparently, this order wasn't clear; so, Ewell took it as a suggestion, and not an order. Right then all of the Union soldiers had not arrived - including their commander, General Meade.

An opportunity for the knockout blow was missed.

"We whupped 'em yes'tidee, but not so much taday," Smith surmised.

Lieutenant Everette walked up and excitedly started blabbering, "General J.E.B, Stuart jist got here an' Lee's mad as hell."

"Wher' tha hell has he been?" Smith wondered.

"Somewhere fiddle-fartin' aroun' down in tha Shenandoah Valley huntin' Hooker."

"Hell, Hooker ain't even in charge anymore. It's Meade now," Smith answered.

"Yeah, that's why Lee's so damned mad. He depends on Stuart's cavalry for information 'bout tha enemy troops, an' he's been operatin' blind since he wuz'nt here."

"Didja hear 'bout that fight this af'ta noon at Devil's Den and Little Round Top," Captain Smith asked Everett and Buck.

"Naw, what happened?" Buck asked.

"General John Hood's bunch wuz supposed to attack tha left flank at 9:00 this mornin'. Didn't git 'em ready 'til 4:30 this evenin'. Seems like the Yankees got a lot more reinforcements in taday.

Lee blames it on Longstreet and his defensive strategy. They almost overrun Little Round Top, but some Colonel from Maine name of Chamberlain, an' his bunch ended up fightin' with bayonets. Said they run outta powder. But they held that hill and pertected the flank.

Hate Yankees, but ye gotta respect that kinda fightin', " Smith shook his head wryly.

JULY 3, 1863

At 2:00 a.m., Lee rode over to Longstreet's tent to discuss his battle plan for the day. Lee's plan was to attack the center of the Union lines on Cemetery Hill with Pickett's men. They had not seen combat in Gettysburg and were at their full strength of 13,000 troops.

Longstreet, sticking to his strategy of fighting defensively, strongly opposed the maneuver, citing the three-quarters of a mile open field to be traversed, but Lee prevailed. Hoping for a knockout blow for the win, Lee ordered the attack on the middle of Union lines to begin at 9:00 a.m..

Longstreet gave the orders to Pickett, who also, strongly opposed, believing that most of his division would be wiped out. **He was right.**

The day dawned with steady rain falling, and by 8:30 a.m., puddles of water lined both hillsides and were flowing into the valley.

Precisely at 9:00 a.m. all of Lee's cannons were unleashed on the central point of Meade's line. Watching the cannon fire, Meade rightly anticipated Lee's plan to attack the mid-point, and moved most of the men from the flanks to the center.

Will Presley was positioned squarely in the middle adjacent to the booming Union cannons as they returned fire.

"Hey Johnny, git all our Graham boys over here. I've got a plan," Buck yelled.

"Alright boys, do ye see tha grove a trees at tha bottom of tha hill? When we move out, run fer them trees We can use 'em fer cover an' be able ta re-load ever time we shoot. It'd be hard to re-load right out in tha middle of tha field. Watch out fer 'em puddles, and try not ta fall when ye start runnin'."

Garrick and Andrew Henderson, Kevin and Travis Murphy, and Buck and Johnny Presley made it safely into the tree grove.

"Hey Buck, 'atsa purty smart plan ye come up with," Travis admired.

At the front edge of the grove, Buck's squad found trees with an open view of the Union lines and steadied their rifles against them.

"Boys, 'em Yankees is hunkered down behind tha little short stone wall. Watch close, an' when one of 'em raises up ta shoot, git 'im," Buck directed.

Andrew's rifle rang out. "Got me one," he exulted. "Just like shootin' deer back home."

"'Cept that ain't deer he'sa shootin'," Garrick thought.

Buck's squad continued to inflict damage on the Union soldiers from the grove. Finally, Will Presley spotted the fire coming from the trees. Motioning to Captain Kintner, and pointing to the grove, they directed ten cannons to fire into the cluster of trees.

A cannon ball whizzed by Travis Murphy's head. "I'ma gittin' tha hell outta here Kevin. Let's go," he yelled.

Re-loading their rifles first, both Murphy brothers raced into the open field. Halfway up the hill, Kevin fell. Stopping to help his brother get up, Travis was shot twice and fell dead. Getting up quickly screaming the rebel yell, Kevin fired his rifle and charged with his bayonet poised. Ten feet short of the stone wall, he was shot four times.

Two Graham boys lay dead in the mud of Cemetery Hill.

Seeing the Murphy boys go down, Garrick and Andrew moved about twenty yards to their left. As they ran, a cannon ball landed on Andrew's foot, and he fell. Screaming in pain, he tried to walk, but fell to the ground.

Watching from twenty yards away, Buck yelled, "Git him ta tha back side of tha grove, an' prop him up agin' a tree. You stay here with 'im and use both rifles if ye haf to pertect yer'selfs. Andrew can re-load while ye shoot. Jist stay here 'til ever'thang dies down."

Buck noticed that the left edge of the cluster was closer to the top of the ridge, and believed that a spot on the fringe would be safer from cannon fire. "Let's jist set here fer a while, Johnny. We'll let 'em Yankees thank they killed us all. Then, we'll sneak up on 'em."

Will Presley hunkered down behind the stone wall, and chose his targets carefully. The breech-loading rifle was easily re-loaded while lying on the ground.

Sounds of cannons being fired were deafening; so, he decided to move toward the rear, rest a while and get more ammo.

"Come on Johnny, let's go," Buck spoke softly. "Tha shootin's died down. We'll run out there and fall down beside some of 'em dead boys. Move just a few yards at a time then duck down again. They won't see us 'til we get ta tha wall. Make yer shot count then git yer bayonet ready."

Seeing Will sitting on a rock, Norville Hill joined him. "I thank we done killed us a bucha Rebs taday, Presley."

"Yeah, and I hate killin', but I reckon it's them 'er us," he responded." I got fam'ly in the Rebel army. Don't know where ther'at or even if ther' still alive, but my Maw wuz really ahatin' this war. And Preacher Henderson back home did too."

As they rested, Captain Kintner walked over toward them. "Sounds like tha shootin's slacked off some boys. Maybe them Rebs 'er gonna give up, an' go home."

"Well I shore hope so, Cap'un. I've had enuff killin' fer taday," Will answered.

The steady rain that had been falling all morning on the soldiers suddenly turned into a downpour. Arising from the rock, Will started to return to his position at the wall.

Looking up, he was startled by a Rebel soldier stepping over the wall. Raising his rifle, he shot him in the chest. Will, threw down his rifle and drew his pistol. As the Rebel soldier moved and groaned, Captain Kintner shot him with **his** pistol.

As they moved toward the dead soldier, suddenly another Rebel stood and aimed his rifle. Will, with his pistol in hand, shot twice. The Rebel soldier fell dead on top of the wall.

Kintner, then joined by Lieutenant Barkley, rushed over to Will and shook his hand. Gushing profusely as he complimented Will, Barkley proclaimed him a hero. "You saved our lives Presley. I'm mighty grateful to ye."

"Just reaction, Sir. Nothin' special," Will dropped his head.

"Nothin' Special, Hell. You saved our **lives Sargent**. I'm gonna take you to General Howard. He needs to promote you to Lieutenant," Kintner declared.

"Hell, I think he deserves the Medal of Honor for what he done. Let's go see the General now. It'll be an excuse to git outta this heavy rain fer a while, too," Barkley grinned.

"Well, it looks like the Rebs 'er retreatin' anyway. Guess ther' givin' up," Kintner added.

Will reluctantly agreed to accompany them. "Guess I can bury them two Rebs in tha mornin'."

General Howard was eager to promote Will (casualties had thinned the ranks of company-level officers), and promised to recommend him for the Medal of Honor.

Arising at dawn and finding a shovel, Will returned to bury the two Rebs. He couldn't tolerate the thought of leaving their bodies to be ravaged by wild animals.

"Oh my God, that's Buck," he screamed. Rushing to the body lying on the wall, he immediately recognized Johnny.

"Dear God in Heaven, what have I done? Maw will never forgive me. Hell, I'll never forgive myself," he sobbed.

As he started to dig the graves, a heavy downpour of rain swept over him.

"A rich man's war is a poor man's fight."

War Comes Home

Chapter 37

Friday, **July 24, 186**3, dawned at Roaring Fork Farm. It was going to be another hot, muggy, July day in the mountains of North Carolina. Cool nights, and humid air, brought a morning fog, and heavy dew on the ground.

As Sally Presley awoke, she felt a deep foreboding in the pit of her stomach. Something *bad* was going to happen today. Sally could "feel it in her bones."

Hearing Maggie busy in the kitchen, she arose and joined her. "Mornin' Maw, I got the coffee ready, want some?"

"Yeah Honey, thank ye. I need some coffee this mornin'. I woke up with a bad feeling."

"Are ye **sick** Maw?" Maggie worried.

"No, Honey, not sick, just got a bad feelin' about things. Sometimes things just don't **FEEL** right."

"Maw, I know yer aworrin' 'bout them three boys of ourn, but twon't do ye no good," Maggie was dispensing wisdom. "Worryin' ain't gonna change nuthin', Paw used ta say."

Martha joined the other women in the kitchen, just as Willadeen and Little Johnny came in from the log cabin.

"What can I he'p ye with Maggie?" Martha asked.

"Not nuthin', jist about got it all ready. The men'll be here in a minnet to eat afore they go ta work.

Billy Bob and Pete walked into the kitchen and poured themselves a cup of coffee. Andy and Matt quickly followed.

"Why's ever'bidy so sad an' gloomy 'bout?" Matt wondered.

"Now don'cha go gettin' sassy boy," Maggie admonished him.

"Come here and give Maw a big hug, Matthew," Sally urged.

"Yep, Maw's baby boy gets all her attention," Andy was jealous.

"You can hug your Maw, too, Andy."

"What about me and Billy Bob?" Pete grinned.

"Yes, I wanna hug all you kids this morn'. Just wish Buck, Johnny, and Will were here so I could hug them too."

Working in the tobacco field near the river, Andy looked up and saw three men riding up the road from town. As they neared, he could see two Confederate soldiers and what looked like Preacher Henderson.

"Hey Matt, looks like we got company. Is 'em two so'jers Buck and Johnny?"

"Naw, I don't thank so. One of 'em's too fat an' tha other one's too tall."

"Is that Preacher Henderson with 'em? Wonder why he's comin' here on Fri'dee?"

"Don't know, but it cain't be good." "Maw wuz kinda thankin' this wuz gonna be a bad day," Andy remarked.

"Mornin' boys," Henderson spoke as they drew close. Y'all need ta come ta tha house. These fellas needs ta talk ta tha whole fam'ly."

"Oh Shit," Pete blurted out. "Sorry Preacher, didn't mean ta say no bad words in front of ye."

"Go on ahead and see if it's alright fer me ta brang these men inta tha house."

Running the quarter-mile to the house, Matt was out of breath when he burst into the kitchen. The women and children were all there preparing the noon-time dinner.

"**Maw, Maw**, Preacher Henderson's got two so'jers with 'im an' wants ta brang 'em ta tha house." Matt blurted out.

"Maggie go ahead and ring the dinner bell. That'll get Billy Bob and Pete down here to the house. **I knew** something bad was going to happen today."

As Henderson and the soldiers rode into the yard, the logging brothers came down out of the woods. "Mornin' Preacher," Billy Bob spoke first. "What'cha doin' here on a Fri'dee?"

"These gentlemen got some news about yer bruthas, boys. Let's all go on in tha house."

"Hello Sally. This here's **Captain Joe Shelto**n and **Sargent Tom Goodman** from over at Camp Wyatt. Is ever'bidy here?"

"Yes, I believe ther all here Preacher," Maggie spoke up. "What's this all about?"

Captain Shelton removed his hat and spoke. "I'm afraid we got bad news, Mrs. Presley. On Fri'dee July 3rd, both of yer boys wuz killed. It wuz a big battle an' we lost a lotta men."

"I knew something bad was coming today," Sally was screaming. "Why **MY** boys Preacher? They've always been good church goin' boys and men. Why, Preacher, **WHY?**"

"Wher'd it happen, Preacher?" Billy Bob sobbed.

The Captain answered, "Ina little town in Pennsylvania called Gettysburg. Fighting went on for three days, and we lost more men in that'un than we ever lost before. Buck and Johnny went down on tha third day. Died pertectin' ther land an' fam'lys. Sorry ta hafta ta tell ye folks tha bad news, but they died doin' ther duty."

"What about ther duty ta he'p raise ther chil'dern?" Martha sobbed.

Willadeen could contain herself no longer, "Johnny ain't never gonna git ta see this'un Ima carryin', an' he won't git ta see Li'l Johnny grow up. Damn this war. Sorry, Preacher Henderson I jist cuddn't he'p it," she wailed uncontrollably.

Billy Bob and Pete silently sobbed, while Andy, Maggie, and Matt wept openly. Sally took each one individually in her arms and tried to comfort them.

Henderson spoke to the family. "We lost Kevin and Travis Murphy too. Some thangs jist don't have a good an'ser, folks. We jist gotta trust tha Lord an' keep on tryin' ta live fer Him. Tha Bible says 'Now we see thru a glass darkly, but then face to face'."

"What about ther buryin' Cap'n?" Billy Bob inquired. "Er they buried up ther in Pennsylvania?"

"Yeah, Ima 'fraid so, Mr. Presley," the Cap'n answered. "Ther aplannin' a big new cemetery, but I don't know that they'll bury any Southern boys ther."

"Cap'n kin I say sum'thin," Sargent Goodman asked.

"Go rite ahead Sargent."

"Jist want ye folks ta know I trained 'em boys over at Camp Wyatt when they first come in. 'Em boys wuz real good shooters an' good so'jers. I heerd 'bout ther shootin' at Antietam an' Fredericksburg. They wuz good so'jers and good men. Ye can be proud of 'em."

"God bless ye Sally an' all of ye Presleys an'yer young'uns. We'll be aprayin' fer ye in ever church on this circuit," Henderson hung his head.

Maggie spoke up, "Will ye pray afore ye go, Preacher?"

"I shore will Maggie. Let's all bow our heads." Pausing a few seconds, he began,

"Almighty God, our Holy Father in Heaven, with heavy hearts and tears we humbly approach your throne. We give you the honor of welcoming our loved ones into your Holy Presence. Today, we don't know why you chose to take them from us at this early age, but we trust that you don't make no mistakes. Give us Peace and Comfort in this time of sorrow fer all of this fam'ly. We pray in tha Holy an' precious name of Jesus. Amen"

The family members repeated. "Amen."

On **August 20, 1863**, Willadeen Presley gave birth to her second child, a baby girl whom she named **Catherine Louise**.

"A rich man's war is a poor man's fight."

Gettysburg Address

Chapter 38

Thursday, November 19, 1863 had finally arrived. Today, President Lincoln would be here to dedicate the new cemetery. Will Presley was excited on two accounts. He would get to see and hear Lincoln, and, also, to honor the memory of his two brothers who died here on July 3rd.

Will Presley, Norville Hill, Darrell Hensley, Clyde Coker, and Tony Stansberry, along with several hundred other Union soldiers from **Fort Whipple**, had been assigned the duty of identifying bodies.

Hastily buried dead soldiers were placed in shallow graves very close to the spot where they fell. The new **Gettysburg Memorial Cemetery** had been constructed to give a "proper burial" to these casualties of war.

Originally scheduled to be dedicated on **October 27th**, the opening was delayed. Many more unmarked graves had been discovered, and more time was needed to identify and move the bodies into the new cemetery. The Southern Union soldiers were chosen to help with the task. (Consequently, a few Confederate soldiers were buried there.)

"Hey Will, did ye git them two boys ye knowed from Ca'lina moved to new graves?" Norville Hill asked.

"Yeah, I did, Norville. Thanks fer askin'."

"Who wiz 'em boys anyway?"

"Aw, jist a coupla guys from Graham named Buck an' Johnny." Will tried to hide his tears.

"I kinda noticed ye wuz takin' it purty hard. Didya know 'em very good?"

"Yeah, Norville. Can I tell ye sum'pin ?" Pausing, he then added, "I don't want nobidy else ta know." Will was cautious.

"Ye know me an' you are almost close as bruthers. Ye can tell me anythang," Hill assured him.

"Them two boys wuz my two oldest bruthas, Buck an' Johnny Presley," Will sobbed.

"Oh shit," Hill exclaimed. Sure am sorry ye had to identify an' bury 'em."

"Yeah, me too. Keep remem'brin' when Maw said; I don't want ye boys warrin' with each other."

"Where wuz 'em two boys buried, Will," Norville was curious.

"Right in fronta tha short stone wall up on Cemetery Ridge where we wuz stationed."

"Did ye see 'em go down, Will?"

"Afraid I did," Will was openly crying now.

"Oh Shit, did ye see who shot 'em?"

Without answering, Will began to cry uncontrollably and fell to his knees.

"***God Damn it,*** Will. Don't tell me ye shot yer own bruthas," Hill was yelling.

As he stood up and looked at Norville, the only thing he could say was, **"Maybe."** "Don't tell that ta nobody," Will pleaded.

"I won't, but Hell Far. Ain't that some Shit."

Sobbing, Will cried," I cain't never forgit this, Norville ."

Printed programs had been prepared for the dignitaries attending. Eight sections of ten chairs each were placed near the raised Speaker's Platform. Several of Lincoln's cabinet members, including the Secretary of War, Edwin Stanton, had accompanied him to the dedication.

All members of the government of the City of Gettysburg, the Governor of Pennsylvania, and several of the state legislators were in attendance.

Completely surrounding the cemetery, the military people who had handled the identification and re-burying of the soldiers stood at attention.

ORDER OF PROGRAM	
Brigfeld's Band	"Homage"
Prayer	Rev. T.H. Stockton, D.D.
Marine Band	(Old Hundred) Director Francis Scala
Orator	Edward Everett
Music	Baltimore Glee Club
Dedication	Hon. Abraham Lincoln
Dirge	"Oh it is Great for our Country to Die"
Benediction	Rev H.E. Baugher, D.D.

After Everett had given a two-hour oration, Lincoln rose and spoke these words:

"Four score and seven years ago, our fathers brought forth on this continent a new nation, conceived in Liberty and dedicated to the proposition that 'All men are created equal'. Now we are engaged in a great Civil War."

As Lincoln spoke, Will thought to himself, *"Yeah we're afightin' with our ownselves. God knows I wuddn'ta killed my bruthas if I cudda hep'd it."*

"Testing whether **that** nation or **any** nation so conceived and so dedicated can long endure."

"My bruthers didn't long endure, but them plantation owners 'er still endurin'."

"We are met on a great battle-field of that war."

"Yeah, a lot of people wuz here killin' each other, but not any of you all wuz here."

"We have come to dedicate a portion of that field as a final resting place for those who here gave their lives that that nation might live."

"Uh huh, my bruthers 'er layin' over yonder in their graves. At least they got a good buryin'."

"It is altogether fitting and proper that we should do this."

"Yer damn rite. That's tha least ye can do fer 'em."

"But in a larger sense, we cannot dedicate - we cannot consecrate - we cannot hallow this ground."

"Words don't mean much, when thousands an' thousands a people died."

"The brave men, living and dead, who struggled here have consecrated it far beyond our poor powers to add or detract."

"Why is it the ones who pay tha biggest price, 'er tha ones who git tha least out of it?"

"The world will little note nor long remember what we say here, but it can never forget what they did here."

"My Maw an' my fam'ly don't keer what ye say, but they do keer 'bout Buck an' Johnny layin' ina grave."

"It is for us the living, rather, to be here dedicated to the unfinished work which they who fought here have thus far so nobly advanced."

"How long does this damn war hafta go on before it stops?"

"It is rather for us to be here dedicated to that cause for which they gave their last full measure of devotion."

"Yeah, an' ther's gonna be a whole lot more of 'em, Mr. Lincoln."

"That we here highly resolve that these dead shall not have died in vain."

"Resolve HELL. Just stop tha killin' sir."

"That this nation, under God, shall have a new birth of Freedom."

"Ther is a new freedom for 'em slaves."

"And that government, of the people - by the people, and for the people, shall not perish from the earth."

"I reckon a lotta pore people'll hafta die ta keep it agoin', but maybe it'll be here if I ever have any children or gran' children or great gran's."

Lieutenant Will Presley assembled the men from East Tennessee who had accompanied him on this mission, and spoke. "We heerd a good speech from tha President taday, an' I feel better 'bout givin' 'em boys a 'proper burial'."

Darrell Hensley spoke, "Lieutenant ye shore took it hard at that funeral."

"Yeah, Sargent Hensley, I knew summa 'em guys from my hometown. Thersa lotta Ca'lina boys in Pickett's bunch, an' we killed almost all of 'em."

"I seen sum Tennessee boys in tha Rebel bunch, too." Tony Stansberry chimed in. "Coupla boys from Morristown."

Arriving back at Fort Whipple, the headquarters for the Army of the Potomac, Will Presley went immediately to the Administrative Office.

"Sir, Lieutenant Presley, sir," he saluted smartly.

Returning the salute, the Major in charge of the office; **Jack Williams**, smiled and asked, "How can I help you Lieutenant?"

"I've completed tha ninety-day extension I signed up fer, sir. Finished my two-year enlistment in August, sir. Now I want ta request my discharge."

"Well Lieutenant, I'm sorry to hear that. Didn't you just recently get a promotion to Lieutenant?"

"Yes sir, I did, but I've finished wha I come here ta do. Took care of sum biz'nus in Gettysburg, an' now I'm ready ta quit. Had my fill of killin', sir. Don't wanna do tha no more."

"OK then, Presley. I really hate to lose you. You've been highly decorated and done an outstanding job. I'll start the paper work today. You should be a civilian in a coupla days.

"What are you gonna do when you become a civilian, Presley," the Major inquired.

"Don't know fer shore, sir. Gonna go back downtown in D.C. and try ta git a room at **Surratt's Boarding House**. I lived ther when I signed up fer the Army," Will replied.

"There might be a job here at Fort Whipple for you. We have some civilian maintenance workers at this Fort. I heard they're lookin' for a Foreman. You were with General Meade at Gettysburg weren't you?"

"Shore wuz. He's tha one who give me a promotion. And I wuz one of tha first so'jers ta sign up when General Burnside organized his bunch rite here at Fort Whipple. It'd be almost like goin' back home."

"Where is home, Presley?"

"North Ca'lina, Sir, a little town named Graham."

"Are you goin' back home?"

"No Sir, when I joined up with tha Union Army, I knowed I cuddn't ever go home agin'."

"Well, if you're interested in that maintenance foreman job, I'll put in a word for you," Major Williams volunteered.

"Thank ye, Sir. I'd shore 'preciate it."

Will Starts Over

Chapter 39

A s he walked in the front door at Surratt's Boarding House, Will was greeted by Anne Surratt. "Hello, sir, how may I help you?"

"Lookin' fer a room, ma'am. Got anythang available?"

"Yes, we do have one room empty, but it's up on the fourth floor. You hafta climb three flights of stairs. Didn't you stay here once before?" she smiled.

"Shore did ma'am. I'm surprised ye remembered me."

"Couldn't forget that crooked smile. You have a funny way of curling your lip when you smile."

"How much for that fourth-floor room?"

"Still just three dollars a week. We ain't gone up none."

"Them three flights of stairs otta make it cheaper."

"We're still servin' two good meals every day and three on Sunday. Where do you work? Can you afford to stay here?"

"Supposed to git a job in maintenance over at Fort Whipple. Pays twelve dollars a week."

"In that case the price is **four dollars a week**," she grinned."

"Ye done already said **three dollars**, Miss Anne. My Paw used ta say ye can come down but ye cain't go up once ye price sum'thin.

"Is Miss Mary and Isaac and John, Jr, still here, Miss Anne?" Will asked.

"Yeah they're all still here. It takes all of us to run this place," Anne answered.

"Does me being here fill up yer house?" Will was curious.

"Yes, we've got six rooms on each floor and three floors of rooms to rent. We save the ground floor for family. There's fifteen men and three women staying here now?"

"Don't guess ther's much chance of me a catchin' a wife with just three women here."

"Are you lookin' for a wife, Mr. Presley?"

"Maybe," Will grinned..

On Monday, **November 30, 1863**, Will received a hand-written note from Major Williams.

> "Mr. Presley, Can you come to my office at Fort Whipple tomorrow? I have an offer to discuss with you. I talked about your desire for employment with General Meade and General Burnside. They both were highly complementary of you and gave great recommendations. Be here at 900 a m if you're interested."

At supper that night, Will mentioned his appointment with Major Williams. **Ralph Davis**, a fellow boarder from **Knoxville Tennessee** and **Joe Butler** from **Maryville, Tennessee** got excited.

"Can ye he'p me git on over ther, Will? That's a good payin' job," Davis asked

"Yeah, me too, Will. Been tryin' to git on ther for nigh on to two years now," Butler implored.

"Gotta git my ownself a job first. If I git tha job I want, I might be able ta git ye boys on over ther. Ye Tennessee boys 'er good workers."

As they talked, the three women residents entered the dining area. Amelia Lowe, a tall, slender girl with brown eyes, ash-blond hair, and a quick smile sat down next to Butler. Lenora Parker, a shorter auburn-haired girl with green eyes, smiled demurely and sat next to Will. Rebecca Haynes, a brunette with an impish grin, sat next to Davis.

Davis introduced all the new arrivals to Will. "Pleased ta make yer acquaintance, ladies," Will flashed a smile at them.

Speaking first, Lenora spoke to Will. "Well I do declare, Mr. Presley, I believe you are from the South, too. Where are you from?"

"From all over ma'am," Will quickly replied - remembering the initial reaction from local residents, "But I was born in North Ca'lina. Where 'er ye from?"

"Born right here in D.C. Work in an office for Secretary Edwin Stanton at the Department of War."

"It shore is a small world, Miss Parker. I'ma goin' over ta Fort Whipple in tha mornin'ta see about workin' ther."

"Oh I know Major Williams. Met him one day in Secretary Stanton's office. He sure is a handsome fellow," she smiled. "But he's a married man and off-limits for me."

"Well I'll tell him I know ye, Miss Parker. Maybe it'll he'p me git tha job."

"Yeah, an' if he gets a job, maybe he'll he'p us git one," Davis volunteered.

"It'd be nice ta have a lotta folks livin' here workin' for the Union and the war effort," Butler added.

At precisely 9:00 a m on Tuesday, Will Presley walked into the office of Major Williams at Fort Whipple. "Good mornin', sir," Will addressed the major. Standing tall and erect, he started to salute, but remembered he was now a civilian. "I was happy to get your note yesterday."

"I'm happy you showed up Mr. Presley. Secretary Stanton likes for us to hire veterans to work here at the Fort."

"Speakin' of Secretary Stanton, one of the ladies in my boardin' house works fer him. Said she knowed ye too."

"What's her name, Presley?"

"Lenora Parker, Sir."

"Oh yes. She's a pretty red-head with an alluring smile. She'd be a good match for you, Will. Be a big help to me, too, having a connection in Stanton's office."

"Major Williams, I'm definitely interested in the job. How much does it pay?"

"Well there is a sliding scale for entry-level foremen, and since you were discharged as an officer; we can start you at fourteen dollars per week. In addition, you can eat in the mess hall with tha officers. Then too, Army doctors will treat any health problems you have. You will have all the advantages of being a soldier, without most of the disadvantages."

"Sign me up! I want in," Will smiled broadly. "I can start tomorrow."

"Alright, work hours are 7:00 a m 'til 5:00 p m. Monday thru Friday, and 7:00 a m thru 12:00 noon on Saturday."

"Mr. Presley, I'd like for you to meet **Carl Fain**. He's our crew leader, and a retired Sargent from the Union Army," Major Williams introduced Will.

"Well are you it?" Fain asked with disdain in his voice.

"Yep, I reckon so, Mr. Fain," Will answered nonchalantly.

"You can just call me, Carl." Fain growled

"OK, and you can just call me **Mister Presley**," Will shot back.

Will had been a Sargent, and then a Lieutenant in the army; so, he understood the dynamics of "being in charge".

"Alright Carl, give me a tour of the facilities, and show me what we are maintaining taday." Will directed.

Walking, first, to the stables, they encountered **Thaddeus Jackson**, a black soldier from Kentucky. "Private Jackson, this is Mr. Presley. He's from North Carolina. He'll be our new boss," Fain explained.

"Happy ta meet ya Massa Presley," Jackson bowed his head slightly.

"You can call me Will, Private Jackson," Will volunteered. Fain looked at him in disbelief, but said nothing.

"How long ye been in the army, Jackson?" Will inquired.

"A little over a year, Sir. Worked on a hoss farm in Paris, Ken'tuck'. They raised and trained thura breds fer racin'. I tuk keer a tha stables ther. Joined tha army when Gen'ral Hunter started signin' up black so'jers. He said they'sa gonna need stable workers an' I'sa already trained."

"Happy ta be workin' with ye Jackson. Let me know if ye need anything," Will turned to leave.

Moving then, on over to the wagon shop entrance, Fain softly asked Will **the question**, "How come the **darkie** can call ye Will an' I hafta say Mister Presley?"

"Have ye ever heerd of a thang called **respec**t, Fain?" Will looked him in the eye.

"Yes, Sir, I have, Sir," Fain was apologetic.

"Good, now ye can call me Will, too.

"Will, I want ye ta meet **Theotis Robinson**," Fain said as they entered the wagon shop.

"Hello PFC Robinson. Pleased ta meet ye," Will extended his hand.

"Yas, Sur, happy ta make yer 'quain'unce, Sur'," Robinson lowered his eyes as he took Will's hand.

"Where ye from Robinson?" Will was friendly.

"Cartersville, Jaw'ja, Sur, down close ta At'lanta. Worked ona cotton plantation. Tuk keer of tha hosses, mules, an' wagons, Sur. Jined tha a'my when Gen'ral Hunter signed up African so'jers."

"Happy ta be workin' with ye, Robinson. If ye need anything let me know. I'll be seein' ye aroun'."

Entering the boarding house after work, Will saw five men sitting in the parlor. Isaac Surratt motioned for him to come in. "Will Presley, I want you to meet some friends of mine."

All the men stood, and Isaac introduced them one at a time "I think you know my brother, **John, Jr**. Meet **George Atzerodt, Lewis Powell**, and **John Wilkes Booth. Mr. Booth** is an actor, and frequently stars here at **Ford's Theater**," Isaac bragged.

"Will is from North Carolina, and still has family there."

Booth spoke first, "I understand you just left the Union army and you're working at Fort Whipple."

"Yep, just started taday as a matter of fact," Will replied.

"Why'd you leave the army, Mr. Presley?" Lewis Powell inquired.

"Just got tarred of tha killin' and dodging bullets," Will was direct.

Atzerodt then spoke, " Yeah, Lincoln said this wouldn't take but ninety days, and it's been well over two years now. Them Rebs don't give up easy. Got relatives in Virginia myself. I know 'em."

Cautiously listening to the banter, Will remained silent, then excused himself. As he walked the three flights of stairs to his room, *he had a bad feeling about these men.*

When Will left, Booth spoke to his companions, "Presley could be a good source of information. I'm certain he hears conversations at Fort Whipple that Lee would find interesting. And the girl who works for Stanton at the War Department would, too. How well do you know them Isaac?"

"Well the girl has been here about a year. Moved in right after she got the job with Stanton. Presley was here for about two months before he joined the Union army. I understand he was some sort of hero at Antietam **and** Gettysburg. He's a strong Abolitionist," Isaac replied.

One week later, when Will arrived from work, the quintet of men was again seated in the parlor. Again, Isaac motioned for him to join them. "Hey Presley, Booth here is starring in a show down at Ford's Theater. Do ya want some tickets for Saturday night? John's got enough free tickets for you and your whole bunch of dinner friends - Miss Parker, Davis, Miss Lowe, Butler, and Miss Haynes. You can take all of them with you."

"Gol'lee, Mr. Booth that shore is nice of ye," Will grinned. "Been lookin' fer a excuse ta ask her out. She'll be more likely ta go if all her frien's ar' agoin', too. I'll ask 'em tanite at supper."

Will sat down at the supper table and looked around. Lenora wasn't there. Looking at Amelia Lowe, Will inquired, "Wher's Lenora tanite? Is she not feelin' good?"

Answering him, she replied, "Oh no, she's alright. She told me she would be right down in a minute." As she finished, Lenora walked into the dining room.

"Good evening, everybody," she smiled and lingered in her glance at Will.

"Evenin' Miss Parker," Will returned her smile.

"Mr. Booth give me some tickets ta tha play he'sa starrin' in down at Ford's Theater. Got enuff fer ever one of us ta go Sat'adee nite. Says here it's called The Marble Heart, and it's starrin J.B. Wilkes. I reckon 'at's his stage name."

"Wow, he's a big-time star. He's ahangin' out rite here in our place," Butler exclaimed. "I understand he's got lotsa women writin' him letters."

"Yes, I think that'd be a lotta fun," Rebecca Haynes exulted. "Looks like those seats are Orchestra section, fourth row."

"Nuthin' but tha best fer **my frien's**," Will bragged.

Lenora looked at Amelia and Rebecca and winked.

Two weeks later, Will came home, and, once again Isaac and John, Jr. were talking in muted tones to Booth. "Come on in Will, John's here again."

"Yeah, I just wanna thank ye, Mr. Booth, fer 'em tickets ye give us. Ye wuz real good in 'at play, an' we all had a good time."

"Glad ye liked it, Presley. How are things at Fort Whipple? Anything exciting going on over there?"

"Naw, jist same ol' stuff, but diff'runt days."

"How are you and Lenora getting along?" Isaac asked.

"Fair ta middlin', I reckon," Will smiled.

"Well, she'd make you a good match, Will. I think she likes you, too," Isaac advised.

Will walked out and climbed the stairs to his room.

When he was out of earshot, Isaac observed, "He ain't gonna tell you nothing, John. That boy ain't as dumb as he looks."

As he ascended the stairs, Will thought, *"'Em boys is up ta sum'pin' no good."*

War Continues

Chapter 40

Settling into the job at Fort Whipple, Will was happy to be contributing to the war effort without being placed in the position of killing people.

Major Williams worked very closely with him as he maintained the facilities at the fort. Carl Fain very soon began to respect his leadership, and made Will's job much easier.

Seeing Lenora Parker every day at breakfast and supper, their relationship flourished. Because they worked at different locations for the Department of War, each had different perspectives on the events of the day.

When he ate his daily meal in the Officer's Mess Hall, Will gleaned a lot of information about activities taking place on other fronts of the war.

Major Williams was a long-time friend of **General Ulysses Grant**. They were classmates at West Point; so Williams followed his career closely.

Williams shared an interesting tidbit of information about the General. His birth name read **Hiram Ulysses Grant**, but when he enrolled in West Point, he listed his name as **Ulysses S. Grant**. Asked what the "S" stood for, he answered, **"nothing"**. It was noted, however, that his mother's maiden name was **Simpson**.

Will was fascinated to hear of Grant's victories at **Fort Henry, Fort Donelson,** and **Shiloh Church** in Tennessee, and at **Vicksburg** in Mississippi. These battles and subsequent Union victories were happening at about the same time Will was involved with battles at **Antietam** and **Fredericksburg** and **Gettysburg**. The battle of **Vicksburg** ended on **July 4, 1863,** the very next day after Meade's victory at Gettysburg on **July 3, 1863**.

The Vicksburg victory resulted in Grant's promotion to command the **Military District of Mississippi**. Later, in 1863, he was moved to **Chattanooga**, a Confederate stronghold. Once there, he defeated the Rebel Forces at **Signal Mountain** and **Lookout Mountain**, and drove them back into North Georgia.

"Hey Will, did you hear about General Grant gettin' promoted again," Major Williams asked.

Eating lunch in the Officer's Mess Hall with Williams and some other men, Will was pleasantly surprised. "No Sir, I hadn't heerd that. Gen'ral Grant's a lot more aggressive than some of the Gen'rals I served under. What rank is he now?" Will inquired.

"He's now '**Lieutenant General**', a rank that only **George Washington** had ever been granted before. Lincoln made him **General-in-Chief** of the whole army."

"Well good. Maybe he'll be able to git Lee and Jeff Davis to give up this crazy war. Ther's been too mucha killin' a'ready," Will spoke out.

At supper that night, Will informed Lenora what Williams had told him.

"Yeah, I heard about it two weeks ago right after Mr. Stanton and Lincoln decided to promote him, but I was told not to talk about it," Lenora cautioned.

Will glanced up and saw **John, Jr** standing in the doorway listening intently. "Yer rite Lenora. Sorry I brought it up," he was embarrassed.

The next day at the Officer's Mess table, the conversation continued. "Grant has moved here to oversee the **Army of the Potomac**. He left **Major General William Tecumseh Sherman** in charge of the Southern District. I knew him at West Point too," Williams bragged. "He's a lot like Grant - a bit too ruthless for me, but he means to win."

"I want to win too," Will interjected, "but a lot more lives ar' gonna be lost in tha winnin'."

Colonel **John Turner** joined the conversation. "That's tha kind of decisions Officers hafta make, Presley. Nobody ever said it was easy, just that it's necessary."

Turner was a medium-height, stocky, man with broad shoulders, dark hair, and a gruff demeanor.

"Did they learn ye that at West Point, Colonel?" Will wanted to know.

"Yes, they did, Presley. Ye gotta be tough to be an officer."

"Glad I never went ta West Point. Don't like killin' ner watchin' people die. 'Specially if it's yer own kin," Will choked up.

He excused himself, left the table, and returned to work, not wanting the officers to see the tears rolling down his cheek.

After supper that night, Will and Lenora wandered into the parlor and sat on the couch. Looking very deeply into her eyes, Will whispered, "Lenora, yer tha prettiest girl I seen all day."

Blushing she answered, "Don't reckon ya seen many girls over at tha fort, did ya?"

"Not many, but yer the prettiest one of 'em all," he smiled.

Moving closer, he allowed his eyes to linger on her lips and bent down to kiss her. Raising her chin to meet him, their lips touched very gently, then deeper. As he withdrew his lips, Will smiled once again and Lenora blushed.

"I was wondering how long it was gonna take you to do that," she smiled as her eyes sparkled.

"Been wantin' to fer a long time, but didn't wanna seem too forward. Wuzn't shore how ye'd take it."

"Well it was nice. I've liked you ever since I saw that special smile of yours."

"Have ye heerd any more about Gen'ral Grant," Will was curious.

"Yes. He is directing the entire war effort now. He has General Meade and General Burnside under his command here in Virginia."

"Yeah, all of 'em have offices at Fort Whipple. I served under both of 'em two gen'rals and ther' good. Major Williams thanks we're gonna whip 'em purty quick now."

"Lincoln and Stanton and Grant have been meeting every day for the last two weeks. They're making plans to coordinate everything around here with Sherman and his bunch down South. At least that's the word going around in the office.

"We must be careful what we say. The Surratt's and their friends are Confederate sympathizers. I heard Mary criticizing Lincoln and praising Jeff Davis when she was talking to Booth one day. She quit talking when I walked in the room."

Will added, "Well it seems like Grant's made a big diff'rence since he moved here," Major Williams was sayin'. "He's personally commandin' tha troops opposin' Lee."

"I've said all along that we need to be more aggressive with Lee," Colonel Turner answered.

Will, sitting at an adjacent table in the Mess Hall, just listened as the officers spoke. Feeling unqualified to offer an opinion, he remained silent.

"Sherman is giving it to them Rebs down there in Tennessee and Georgia," Williams suggested.

"Yep, and Florida and South Carolina too," Turner added.

"Grant has been more aggressive. When them Rebs retreat, he goes after them," Williams replied.

"Lincoln has been saying that from the beginning, but our other Generals worried too much about casualties," Turner exclaimed.

"Yeah they keered 'bout 'em people dyin' out ther'," Will thought silently. *"Guess nun of Turner's kin has went down,'er he wuddn't be so unconcerned 'bout it. Guess I wuzn't cut out ta be no officer."*

"We lost a lotta men in that battle in 'The Wilderness' down next to Chancellorsville, didn't we, Major?" Turner inquired.

"Yeah. Grant didn't really wanna fight there in them woods. He wanted a more open spot where his big guns could be used, but Lee attacked before they could move. He fought for three days, then pulled out and moved to Spotsylvania County, where it was more open," Williams informed him.

"I heard they had a lotta problems with wet gunpowder at Spotsylvania. Their guns wouldn't fire; so, they hadda fight with knives and bayonets. Is that right, Major?"

"Well, that's the report I got. Heard we lost over 12,000 men there. It got pretty bloody," Williams reported.

"Major Williams likes ta make ever' bidy thank he knows ever thang 'bout whatsa happenin'," Will thought. *"Shore glad I don' hafta kill people no more. Why don't they end this dang thang and let ever'bidy go home?"*

"Grant moved all his troops over to Petersburg, and set up a **sie**ge. That's the way he won the Battle of Vicksburg," Turner responded. "If it worked once, it'll work again. Maybe he'll starve out Lee and his men, and they'll surrender."

Over the weeks and months of 1864, Will shared his thoughts with Lenora. She, for the most part, just listened as he ranted and railed against the war.

Making certain that nobody heard their conversations, they drew closer together, and slowly **Fell In Love**.

Will Meets the Family

Chapter 41

S unday morning dawned, and Will had made a firm decision. Today, he would broach the subject of marriage with Lenora.

Descending the stairs from the fourth floor, he glimpsed her entering the dining area. When he entered, Lenora was seated between Amelia and Rebecca in the center chairs. The only available chair was at the head of the table; so Will sat there.

Glancing at Lenora, he saw she was engaged in conversation with the girls on either side of her. "Maybe this ain't a good time," he thought. Then Lenora glanced at him and smiled.

"Man, that shore is a purty smile. I do believe she likes me. Paw always said, 'Ye don't know 'lessen ye ask'."

Mornin', Will," Ralph Davis spoke. "Yer runnin' late this mornin'."

"Yep, I'ma havin' a slow-movin' mornin'. It is Sun'dee."

Mary Surratt came in with a plate full of hot biscuits and a bowl of sausage gravy - Will's favorite breakfast. Before he had finished eating, Lenora and her two friends arose and walked into the parlor.

As soon as he finished eating, Will got up to follow them. Joe Butler spoke, "Hey Presley what's yer hurry. I ain't seen ye all week. Ye been leavin; afore I got down here."

"Yep, we been busy at the fort. Lotsa stuff goin' on over ther'," he responded.

"What's tha latest news from Grant and his boys?" Davis asked. "We don't get much information down at tha loadin' docks."

"If I tol' ye, I'd hafta kill ye," Will smiled. "I need ta catch Lenora an' talk ta her this mornin'." Davis looked at Butler and winked.

Will went into the parlor and found a chair adjacent to the couch where the girls were seated. Seating himself he spoke," Mornin' Ladies, how ar' y'all this fine day?"

"Fair to middlin'," Rebecca spoke first.

"I'm just fine and dandy, Will," Lenora smiled. "And how about yourself?"

"Well my Paw used ta say, '**Any** day above groun'sa **goo**d one'."

All three of the women laughed and Lenora's eyes lingered on Will's smile.

"Would ye like ta take a walk, Miss Lenora? It's such a purty day," he suggested.

"That sounds like a good idea, Will, where are we going?"

"Aw, I thought we'd walk down by the crick. Ther's lotsa flowers and purty stuff ther. It'd be a fine place ta have a picnic some time."

As they walked, Will felt his hand brush against Lenora's. Glancing out the side of his eye, he detected a slight smile on her face. He reached and took her hand and squeezed it. **She squeezed back**.

Holding hands and walking by the creek, Will began to speak, "Lenora, I ain't much for purty words, but we seem ta have some special feelin's fer each other. Ye don't know nuthin 'bout my fam'ly, an' I don't know nuthin' 'bout yers. All I know is I'm fallin' in love with ye."

"Will, I do have special feelin's for you too. We seem to have a lotta things in common to talk about, and it's easy for me to talk with you. I love it when you hold my hand, and I really liked it when you kissed me."

"Where does yer fam'ly live?" he asked.

"My Momma and Poppa live over on a small farm near Falls Church. It's just about ten miles from here. Poppa sells produce and pork meat to the War Department. That's how I got my job over there. When the war started, they needed a lot more suppliers. We were raising enough to feed ourselves pretty well, but not enough to sell. Momma told Poppa we needed to do something to help the war effort."

"My fam'ly's farmers too - down in the mountains of North Ca'lina. Had two bruthas in the Rebel army. Got four bruthas and two sistas who stayed at home ta he'p Maw run the farm. I think my younger bruthas wuz gonna join the local militia."

"How come you decided to join the Union army, when all your family were Rebels?"

"Didn't like tha notion that people wuz bein' held as slaves. Preacher Henderson back home didn't like it neither. Don't thank my Paw wudda liked it much his ownself.

"Paw wuz killed in a' accident. We wuz in tha loggin' bizness, and a tree that me an' Buck an' Johnny cut down fell on him. It wuz 'bout seven years ago; back before tha war.

"Paw come ta this country as a 'dentured servant, an' hadda pay tha land owner. Took him twenty years ta pay hisself outta de't, but he done it - him an' Maw togetha. Two people workin' togetha can do a lotta thangs that just one cain't by therself," Will was philosophical.

"Yes, that's right, Will. I watched my Momma and Poppa build up our little farm into a productive business. I kinda helped 'em get more business when I started workin' for Secretary Stanton. One day I might take it over, when Momma and Poppa retire."

"Don't reckon I'll ever go back home 'lessen I change my mind. My **whole town** wuz Rebels - even Mr. Graham who started tha 'hole thang," Will remembered. "I don't wanna seem pushy ner nuthin', but I'd like to see yer farm an' meet yer folks."

"I usually go home about once a month, and go to church with my folks. There's a little Episcopal church there close to 'the Falls' in the Potomac River. That's how the area got its name **Falls Church**. I'm going next weekend. You can go with me if you want to."

"Sounds like a lotta fun. I'll see about borrowin' a buggy from the fort for the weekend."

On Monday morning Lenora made sure she was in the loading dock area where the vendors unloaded. She knew her father would be driving the delivery wagon from his farm.

"Good morning Poppa," Lenora smiled as her father drove up to the dock.

"Well hello, pretty Princess," **Harry Parker** spoke to his daughter. "I didn't expect to see you down here at the dock."

"I hadn't seen you in two weeks, and I wanted to remind you I'm coming home next Sunday. Tell Momma I've got a young man who wants to come with me. He's a resident of my Boarding House, and was raised on a farm in North Carolina. Poppa, he's got the cutest little curled lip smile. You and Momma are gonna like him," Lenora gushed.

"Whoa, slow down a minute here. You tellin' me you wanna bring a Southern Rebel to our house?"

No Poppa, he's not a rebel. He was a Union soldier who got several medals fighting for our Army. He fought with McClellan, Burnside, Hooker, and Meade in some big battles. He works now at Fort Whipple as the Maintenance Director. We're coming early so we can go to church."

"Well, I'm glad to know he's a church-going man, Princess. That's one thing in his favor," Harry replied.

"Yes Poppa, and he sings and plays fiddle in church with his two brothers. Talks a lot about the Methodist minister who preaches there. They both are abolitionists, and hate the idea of slavery," she assured her father. "That's why he joined the Union Army."

"I guess Methodists ain't too far removed from Episcopalians. **John Wesley** was a priest in the **Church of England**," Parker agreed. "Will you be there in time for breakfast?"

"Probably not, but we will stay for dinner. I'm eager for Momma and you to meet him," she exclaimed excitedly.

"OK. This is the first time you've brought a young man home to meet us. He must be pretty special," Parker was cautious.

Sunday morning dawned with a beautiful sunrise. Will glanced out the window and thought, *"That'sa good omen. I believe God'sa smilin' down on us. I really hope so,"* Will was nervous.

Descending the stairs, he saw Lenora coming out of the kitchen. "I went in and asked Mary for a coupla biscuits and two apples. Thought we'd eat breakfast as we ride. It takes over an hour to get there, and I wanna be there in time for church."

"I put a jug a water in the buggy yes'tidee afore I left the fort," Will informed her. "Let's git amovin'."

As they rode, Will thought, *"It shore is nice being seen out in public with a purty girl. I hope her Maw and Paw like me."*

"Does your Paw have a spring house to keep milk an' butter cold?" Will wondered. "We had one back home, and a smoke house too."

"Oh yes. He's got apple and pear trees, grape vines, a huge vegetable garden, and a big hog pen. He usually kills hogs in the fall when it cools down. Keeps the meat salt cured and smoked in the smoke house. Carries some of it in every week to the commissary at the War Department."

"Does he hafta do all that work by hisself?" Will wondered.

"Oh no. He's got some hired help. People working for him."

"He ain't no slaver is he?" Will was hopeful

"Absolutely not, " she answered firmly. "He's selling food to the Union Army, and pays his helpers very well. Some of them make more than the Army pays your helpers at the fort," she declared.

"It's gonna be inter'stin' for me to see a farm that big. We had a big fam'ly and done all tha work our ownselfs," he explained.

"Well, Poppa and Momma started out with a family farm, but had to make it bigger when they started to supply the Army. They have about twenty workers, now. Poppa makes sure all his helpers have plenty of food for their families plus decent wages."

"We're getting close to the house now," she informed him. It's just around that next bend."

As they pulled up to the house, Lenora's parents came out to meet them. Will helped Lenora out of the buggy and turned to greet them.

Speaking first to his daughter, Harry Parker said, "Good mornin' Princess. Y'all made good time."

Alice Parker hugged her daughter and cautiously eyed Will. She was a tall woman with ash-brown hair, hazel eyes, a ready-smile, and a peaches-and-cream complexion. Will thought, *"Now I know why Lenora is so purty. She looks a lot like her Maw."*

Harry Parker was a tall, slender man with gray eyes, curly blonde hair, and rough hands. He turned to Will and shook his hand with a firm grip. "Howdy, young man. Pleased to meet ya."

Will removed his hat, and took Parker's hand. "Pleased to meet ye, sir. I'm Will Presley" Turning to her mother, he said, "Mrs. Parker, now I know why Lenora 's such a purty girl. She looks just like her Maw."

"Oh, how you **do go on**, Mr. Presley. What a nice thing for you to say. **I** can easily see that **you are a charmer**."

"Just call 'em like I see 'em ma'am. That's what my Paw learnt me," Will grinned "You can call me, Will. Mr. Presley wuz my Paw."

"Come on in the house, Son," Harry Parker directed. "Let's sit a spell and chat before we go to Church."

"See Momma, I knew you'd like him," Lenora whispered to Alice.

"Like you said, he is **a charmer**."

After they sat down in the parlor, Harry Parker spoke first. "Lenora told me you are a war hero, Will. Tell me about that."

"Well I don't know about bein' no hero, sir. I did get a coupla medals. One wuz at Antietam, and one wuz at Gettysburg. Got two battlefield promotions too. I wuz promoted ta First Sargent after Antietam, an', then, to Lieutenant afta Gettysburg."

Nodding as he listened to Will, Parker spoke, "I served in the Navy during the Spanish War. Thought about becoming a career sailor, but when I met Alice, I didn't wanna be gone for months at a time. Didn't win any medals, but got promoted to Petty Officer-equivalent to Sargent in the army."

"Well, I reckon we got some things in common, sir. We're both military veterans, and we both thank yer daughter's a purty girl."

"How long have ye known her, Will?"

"I guess several months, sir. We live in tha same boardin' house, an' see each other ever' day at breakfast and supper. I work at Fort Whipple an' she's at the War Department. We got lotsa thangs ta talk about, an' we enjoy talkin' ta each other."

"Are you gonna keep workin' at the Fort after the war is over, or are you going back home to Carolina?"

"Don't 'spect ta ever go back home, sir. Don't know how tha folks in Graham'd take ta me.

"Lincoln's talkin' bout Reconstruction, an appointin' some retired Gen'rals ta be in charge. I served under some of the best un's, an' thank it'd be good ta he'p fix all tha stuff that's been tore down."

"Well there's certainly gonna be a need for that, and a smart young man could probably find some things for himself in the process. I like your thinking, Presley," Parker observed.

"It's time for church," Alice reminded the men. "Let's go."

Walking to church, Harry kept Will at his side and they continued to talk. Alice walked with Lenora following the men, and they softly chatted.

"Don'cha just love him Momma? He's so handsome and smart too. He's gonna amount to something someday."

"Well I can certainly see that you are smitten with him. **I do like him**, but don't rush things, honey."

As they approached the church, Will was impressed by its size and the brick construction. The ornateness of the interior was like nothing he had ever seen before. Speaking to Harry he said, "**Wow**, we ain't got nuthin' like this in Graham."

"It is a beautiful building, Presley. **George Washington** and **George Mason** were two of the first vestrymen here. There's a lot of history in that building," Parker bragged.

After church and dinner and conversation with the Parkers, the couple started back to the Capital city. "It was a nice day with your folks, Lenora. I really enjoyed talkin' with 'em," Will remarked.

"Yes, it was Will. Thanks for coming with me. I think Momma and Poppa liked you, too."

After several minutes of silence, he slowly began to speak. "Lenora, I have something to say. Now ye just lis'n and thank about what I'ma gonna say ta ye.

"I love you, an' I wanna spen' tha resta my life with ye. I wanna marry ye. I thank me an' you can make a good life tagetha, an' raise a fam'ly.

"Don't make up yer mind rite now. Ye can thank about it fer a while, an' let me know in a few days."

"I appreciate your givin' me time to think about it, Will. It's something you only do once, and, I wanna get it right. I do love you, and think we would make a good team.

"Momma said 'don't rush things' and I think she's right."

"One other thang I want ye ta know. Lincoln's already talkin' 'bout Reconstruction. I wanna be a part of restorin' the country, and fixin' what's been tore up. I'ma gonna do this, an' I'd like ta have ye with me."

"Those are very noble ideas, Will. I admire your aspirations," she mused.

The rest of the ride back to Washington was made in silence.

Grant Changes Strategy

Chapter 42

Entering the Surratt House on Monday after work, Will noticed Lenora sitting in the parlor chatting with Mary and Anne.

"Good afta'noon Miss Mary, Miss Anne, Miss Lenora. Have you ladies had a good day?" Will smiled.

"Very good, Mr. Presley," Mary answered. Anne only nodded and smiled.

Lenora, with a big smile, rose and hugged him. "We were really busy in the office today."

Mary looked at her with curious eyes. "What's goin' on in the war effort Lenora?"

"I really don't know much about the war effort, Miss Mary. All I know is we had a lotta paper work today. Will, I saw Poppa today, and he was braggin' on you," Lenora smiled broadly.

"Oh, does Will know your parents?" Anne questioned.

"Oh yes, he met both of them last Sunday. We rode over to Falls Church and attended church services with them."

"Sounds like you two are gettin' serious," Anne snapped.

Will just grinned, then said, "Maybe."

"Supper will be ready shortly folks. Come on Anne and help me finish up," Mary directed.

After supper as they rose to leave the table, Will looked at Lenora and asked, "Wanna take a walk."

"Yes, that sounds like fun," Lenora grinned.

Taking her hand as they walked out the door, he had a serious expression on his face. "Looks like we are in for some major changes from Grant."

"Yes, I heard some of that today too," she replied.

Will continued, "Colonel Turner and Major Williams were talking at lunch today. Grant moved over to Petersburg. That's just thirty miles from Richmond. He's bringing General Benjamin Butler's boys over from the James River area."

"General David Hunter's **Freedmen African** soldiers are ther' too. Ther' diggin' trenches around the edge of town so they can shoot from bunkers."

Lenora questioned, "How's that gonna affect his plans?"

"Well, this might be 'tha beginnin' of tha end' of this war. Lee's got a dwindlin' Army of Northern Virginia, and Beauregard's bunch is just a lotta old guys and amputees a defending' Richmond," Will explained.

"Ther's five railroads comin' tagether at Petersburg, and, tha Appomattox river joins the James River ther'. That's how Lee gits supplies. If they can take over that li'l town, Lee'll hafta give up when he runs outta ever thang."

"Gen'ral Sherman's gonna take over At'lanta, then go all tha way across tha state. Hit might take a while, but I thank we might be gittin' closer to tha end."

"Well I certainly hope so," Lenora sighed.

"You know, At'lanta'd be a good place ta start with Reconstruction. It's rite smack-dab in tha middle of tha South, and not too far away from Graham. We might be able ta find us a little place down ther, if we git a job. Secretary Stanton's yer frien', an' Colonel Turner an' Major Williams like my work."

"Will, the war isn't over yet," Lenora smiled and squeezed his hand.

"Yep, I know. Jist thankin' ahead and dreamin', I guess," he grinned.

On Monday, **September 14th**, Will was chatting with Major Williams, when Colonel Turner walked into the office. "I just got the news that Sherman has captured Atlanta. He has the whole city under control. Comin' across Alabama, he burned everything in sight - houses, barns, cattle, sheep, and hogs. A lot of plantation owners have been shot, too. Said he didn't want them to have anything left to continue fightin' with."

"Have you heard where he'sa goin' next Colonel?" Will wondered.

"I would guess he'll go all the way to the ocean - probably Savannah. It's a big port city, and he wants to stop the Rebs from getting' supplies," Turner retorted.

"Well Grant is diggin' more trenches toward Richmond from Petersburg. I heard General Hunter's **Freedmen Blacks** are makin' him really good soldiers," Williams added.

"Yeah 'em Black boys has got a reason ta fight," Will interjected."

"I expect with Sherman burnin' everything in the South, and Grant cuttin' off everything around Richmond, Davis and Lee'll give up sooner rather than later," Turner offered.

"I don't wanna see a lot more people die, but I hope Grant and Sherman git Jeff Davis and Gen'ral Lee to give up this war," Will thought to himself.

When he got home after work, Lenora was sitting by herself in the parlor reading a newspaper. Looking up when Will entered the room she smiled. "Hello Mr. Presley, did you have a good day?"

"Yes, it wuz jist 'nother typ'cal 'day in Paradise," he joked. " I heerd some disturbin' stuff 'bout Sherman an' At'lanta. Seems he's burnin' the 'hole city down."

"I was just reading about that in the paper. There's a reporter from the Washington newspaper following Sherman and writing about him. He's been sending his stories in by telegraph, but he said Sherman had eliminated all the telegraph communications around him. One of his men anonymously told me that he doesn't want anybody to know what he's doing."

"I heard in the office today that Secretary Stanton is fuming mad. He has no way to know what Sherman's plans are, nor to pass orders down to him from Grant or Lincoln. Lincoln said that Sherman goes into a hole and nobody knows where he'll come out," Lenora shared.

As he sat down for lunch, Colonel Turner said to Major Williams, "Did ya ever wonder where Sherman got his middle name?"

"Yeah, but I never heard anybody say. **Tecumseh** is a strange name for a white boy," Williams observed.

"I ran into a friend of mine from West Point while I was over at the War Department this morning. Of course, all the talk is about Sherman, and where he is, and what he's doing.

"My friend said, 'He's like an Indian on the 'war path'. I guess he's trying to live up to the name his father gave him. There was a Pawnee chief in Ohio who was a fierce warrior. Sherman's father wanted him to grow up to be a warrior, so he gave him that name," Turner observed.

"Yeah I fought some of those Plains Indians out West. When they conquer a village, they loot it and take what they need, then burn everything else. Apparently, Sherman isn't leaving anything behind that the Rebs might use. I heard somebody call it **Scorched Earth**," Williams replied.

"The National Republican newspaper called it a **March to the Sea**."

Continuing to skirmish with the Rebs' occasional excursions out of Richmond, Grant's men kept digging the trenches toward the Capital city. By mid-November, they were within a few miles of the outskirts. At this point, Grant took a less-aggressive stance, and decided to just wait for Lee to surrender.

Reading the November 15th, edition of the National Republican aloud to Will, Lenora recited the head-line story of Sherman leaving Atlanta in flames. "Most of the commercial buildings were burned to the ground.

"Railroad rails were removed from the tracks and heated over hot flames. Bent around trees, local residents call them **Sherman neckties**," Lenora read.

"All of the cotton bales in sight were taken by Sherman's troops. Many houses of the lower classes were left standing, but most of the plantation manors and stables were torched. Horses, mules, hogs, and, cattle were taken to feed the Union soldiers, along with vegetables and fruit. Sherman did ensure that enough was left so the Atlanta residents wouldn't starve."

"I'm shore glad them At'lanta folks wuzzn't all killed," Will interjected. "A lotta tha people in Graham come from At'lanta, and ther' fam'lies still live ther'. We bought a lotta stuff from com'nees down ther', and I reckon it'll be hard on tha Graham folks fer awhile."

Entering the office at Fort Whipple the next morning, Will encountered Turner and Williams in the office. "Mornin' Colonel and Major, how ar' y'all taday."

"Fair to middlin'," Williams answered him. "How 'bout you Presley?"

"I'ma li'l bit upset, Major. Me an' Lenora wuz readin' 'bout Sherman an' At'lanta. He shore done a lotta damage ta property an' people."

Turner spoke up, "You can't win wars without damagin' property an' killin' people, Presley. You gotta be tough to be a soldier."

Will dropped his head and turned to leave. "There's gonna be a lot more damage an' killin;' before this war is over, Will," Williams commiserated. "Word is that Sherman's headed for Savannah. There's a lotta property and people between Atlanta and the coast."

Savannah Surrenders

Leaving Atlanta on November 16th, Sherman, with 60,000 men, headed toward Savannah. Abandoning his supply lines and all communication with Washington, it became necessary to confiscate food, horses, mules, and feed for his animals. A three-day supply was all they could handle, so frequent stops were made, and the Georgia residents were terrorized.

A strategy of destruction was, also, part of his plan. Attempting to show the residents of Georgia the power of the Union Army, and the impotence of the Confederate Army to protect them, houses and barns were burned even in rural areas.

"I'm exercising **Statesmanship**," he told his subordinates. "I want these Rebs to know they can't win; so, they had better just give up."

On **December 21,1864**, a regiment of Sherman's 20th Corps neared the Savannah river and spotted the rear flank of Confederate General Hardee's men on the South Carolina side of the river heading north. Seeing the abandoned defensive earthworks with fires still burning, they knew there were no defenders in the area.

"Apparently them Rebs heard we wuz comin'," the Union Colonel boasted to his men. "I guess we skeered the pants offa them boys. Look at 'em runnin'."

Resuming their advance on the city, the Union soldiers were met by a group of men from Savannah. The mayor, **R.D. Arnold** and his staff rode out to meet them.

Proposing terms of surrender, he asked to speak to Sherman. Addressing him he said, "The Confederate military last night evacuated our city. We are now defenseless. As the chief magistrate of the city, I respectfully request your protection of the lives and private property of the citizens and of the women and children.

"Trusting that this appeal to your generosity and humanity may favorably influence your action, **I have the honor to be your obedient servant**."

Sherman accepted these terms, and immediately set up his headquarters in the Green Mansion, the finest house in Savannah.

On **December 22, 1864**, Sherman sent a telegram to Lincoln.

"It is my honor, sir, to offer as a Christmas gift to you, the City of Savannah."

On Christmas Eve, 1864, there was much joy in the White House, the War Department, and at Fort Whipple.

"A rich man's war is a poor man's fight."

Thirteenth Amendment

Chapter 43

"Lenora, what's the 13th Amendment?" Ralph Davis asked. Sitting down at the breakfast table she paused, then answered him. "It's a way of changin' the Constitution, Ralph."

The eyes of everyone at the table looked and listened as she spoke.

"It takes a vote of two-thirds of the Senators and two-thirds of the Congressmen, plus a vote of three-fourths of the states to ratify it."

"What's ratify mean?" Joe Butler looked puzzled.

"It means to approve it, Joe," she replied.

"Sounds ta me like it'd be purty hard ta do all of that," Will spoke up. "What's tha purpose? I thought Lincoln done issued his Emancipation Proclamation."

"Well, yes he did, Will," Lenora explained. "But it's not a law, and can be easily changed. If we can get an amendment to the Constitution, it can't be so easily changed. That's the point."

"How come you know so much, Miss Smarty Pants?" Amelia Lowe snapped.

"I heard Secretary Stanton talking to Mr. Seward about it. President Lincoln is making it a major issue in his re-election campaign."

"The election ain't 'til November is it?" Rebecca Haynes chimed in.

"Yeah, but with this dang war draggin' on, he wants ta git it done,"

Will mentioned. "I heerd Turner and Williams talkin' about it Fri'dee."

Anne Surratt came in with extra biscuits and gravy, and coffee. " I read in the **National Republican** that Lincoln's gonna have a hard time getting' re-elected. We have fam'ly in Maryland that think so too. This amendment biz'ness ain't gonna help him."

"My opinion, Miss Anne, is tha slavery ain't rite. And this war needs ta be over. If Lincoln can do them two things, I'ma gonna vote fer 'im. I heerd somebody say tha Senate already passed the amendment on April 8th, but it'sa gonna take longa in the House."

"Yes it will, and they might never get enough states to ratify it," Anne snapped back.

Butler nodded in agreement and Davis spoke. "I'ma gonna vote fer him too. Maybe he'll give me a job at tha War Department or at the post office. I think 'em things is important, but I want me one of 'em gub'ment jobs."

"Me too," Butler chimed in.

"Well, if you want a job, I suggest you go sign up to help the campaign," Lenora advised.

"Ooh, is **that** how ye git a gub'ment job?" Davis grinned.

"It certainly don't hurt none if ye know somebody, too," Butler opined. "Will you recommend us, Miss Lenora?"

"When you volunteer for the campaign, tell them I sent you over," she grinned. "It's all about helping each other."

"Do you wanna go Saturday, Joe?" Ralph asked.

"Yeah. We'll get up early and go over to campaign headquarters. Looking at Amelia and Rebecca, he inquired, "Wanna go with us girls?"

"Yeah, That sounds like fun. I've never worked in a campaign before."

"OK, it's a date for early Saturday morning.," Butler reminded them.

"Are ye gonna work in tha campaign, Lenora?" Will inquired.

"Yes, I've already signed up. Momma and Poppa are gonna work over in Falls Church. They'll try to get all their workers to vote for Lincoln."

With a slight grin, Will responded, "Reckon I otta sign up too, if I want one of 'em Reconstruction jobs. Don't want nuthin' ta git in tha way of 'er future. Think I'll go over Sat'idee an' sign up too."

As the group from Surratt House travelled to volunteer for the campaign, Will spoke to Lenora. "It's really important that Lincoln gets re-elected. If he don't, the amendment ain't got a chance ta git three-fourths of the states ta vote fer it."

"You're right, Will. The opposition is insisting on 'States' Rights'. They want each state to decide for themselves whether to allow slavery," Lenora sighed.

"Ain't that what this 'hole gol-danged war's been 'bout?" he lamented.

"Yes, yes it is. I don't know what'll happen if Lincoln doesn't win."

"This dang war"ll jist keep goin' on I reckon. I'ma gonna tell ever'bidy I work with who I'ma voting' for. We gotta stop this killin' and fix this country back like it wuz. And me an' you 'er gonna he'p make tha happen."

At the **Re-elect Lincol**n headquarters, some interesting information emerged for Will and his friends from Surratt House. In order to get enough support for his re-election Lincoln had formed a new political party.

Taking the National Republican Party and adding some Democrats who desired the preservation of the Union, this new coalition was formed.

He called it the **National Union Party**. Joining him on the ticket as his Vice-Presidential nominee was **Andrew Johnso**n, a Democrat, from Tennessee.

Two women from Seneca Falls, New York, had mobilized a large group of women. Calling themselves **Women's Rights Movement, Elisabeth Cady Stanton** and **Susan B. Anthony** were promoting Abolition, along with some other important issues to women - right to own property, right to keep their own money, right to sue for divorce, and the right to vote.

Taking one thing at a time, abolishing slavery with the Thirteenth Amendment was the first thing on the agenda.

Supporting Lincoln in his re-election and passing the amendment, they expected Lincoln and the Republican Party to assist them with the rest of their crusades.

Lincoln's opponent, running as a Democrat, was retired General George McClellan. Democrats were still insisting on States' Rights, and opposing the Thirteenth Amendment, which would forever abolish slavery.

On **November 8, 1864**, Lincoln and Johnson would be elected to lead the nation for four more years. Receiving **212 electoral votes and 55% of the popular vote**, It would be a land-slide victory.

January 31, 1865 would bring the Congressional approval of the Amendment, and on **December 6, 1865**, the final state would ratified it.

Carolina Campaign

Chapter 44

L eaving Savannah on **January 6, 1865**, Sherman marched his men northward. Ordered by Grant to put them on ships and hurriedly move to reinforce the Army of the Potomac in their siege of Petersburg, Sherman had other plans.

Convincing Grant to allow him to march his units north, he knew that a **greater legacy** could be achieved by destroying the remnants of the Confederate army in the Carolinas. On **January 5, 1865** he said, **"I do think that in the several grand epochs of this war, my name will play a prominent part."**

Instructing his officers to demolish only military installations, and to take *only* what they needed to supply their troops, they spread out and headed north. Feigning a move toward Goldsboro, his primary target was the Capital city of Columbia.

Three different groups of soldiers were deployed as they moved into South Carolina - the Army of Tennessee, the Army of Ohio, and the Army of Georgia. Fanning out over a wide-spread area, very little of the territory was left untouched by Union soldiers. Regularly receiving reinforcements, their numbers quickly swelled from 60,000 to over 88,000.

Opposed by a Confederate unit commanded by **General Joseph Johnston**, and his **Army of Tennessee** which numbered at the start **15,000**, it was an easy task to destroy them. By mid-April their ranks dwindled to **9,500**.

Very loosely supervised, Sherman's commanders reverted to their *scorched earth* tactics from the *March to the Sea* in Georgia.

Because South Carolina had fired the first shots of the war and had been the first state to secede, Sherman wanted, especially, to make an example of them. Terrorizing defenseless towns and villages, they pillaged and burned their way north.

Occasionally engaging small local militia units and some regular Confederate troops, they left bodies lying in the streets, and listened to the screams of women and children as they watched their homes and barns burning, their cotton fields, and all livestock destroyed. The stench of burned bodies - both animal and human filled the air for miles around.

As the Capital city of Columbia burned, Union General Slocum observed, "A drunk soldier with a musket in one hand and a match in the other is not a pleasant visitor to have around on a dark windy night."

A controversy arose about who started the fire. Union soldiers claimed the Rebs started it to destroy bales of cotton, and the high winds fanned the flames. The end result was that everything of value in the entire central district was wiped out.

As reports trickled in to the War Department and Fort Whipple back in D.C., Will and Lenora talked. "I just can't believe what Sherman is doing to those people in South Carolina," Lenora lamented. "I can almost see my own parents and their workers, if it wuz Rebels doing that to us."

"Yeah me too," Will replied. "My folks 'er prob'ly gonna get sum'thin like that if 'em boys git all tha way over ta tha mountains."

As they walked in the front door at Surratt House, John Wilkes Booth was ranting about Sherman's atrocities. "Them Damn Yankees are gonna pay for what they done to them people in Georgia and South Carolina. Come Hell or high water, I'll make 'em pay for this."

John, Jr. nodded his assent. Mary had a concerned expression on her face as she said, "Now don't get too loud, John. There's other people in the house."

Will and Lenora continued up the stairs to the second floor where her room was located. "Whadda you think he means by 'makin' 'em pay for this,'?" she asked .

He replied, "Don't rightly know, but I don't like tha sound of it." "I've felt like for a long time tha they wuz up to something." "Well, let's jist keep 'er ears open an' 'er mouths shut." Will advised. "We'll find out sooner or later I reckon."

At dinner the next day, Will listened as Turner and Williams discussed the war effort. "Man, ol' Sherman's really puttin' it to them Rebs in Carolina;" Turner exulted. "He's gonna make short work of whatever's left of tha Rebs in both Carolinas. Gonna make a name for hisself, too."

"Yeah, I heard it's awful bloody down there. Lots of civilians dyin' too. Hey Presley, ain't you got people in Carolina?" Williams asked.

Looking toward their table, Will answered. "Yes sir, I do. All my fam'ly lives in North Ca'lina."

"Are they anywhere close to where Sherman's boys are?"

"Don't rightly know fer shore, but from what I hear, Sherman's boys 'er ever 'wher'," Will replied.

Williams continued, "Have you heard from any of your folks?"

"Ain't heerd nary a word since I left in '61. I don't even know if any of 'em's even still alive. Lots of people an' property's been destroyed."

"They're just now movin' into North Carolina. It's the **first of March**, and I think this thing's gonna be over before the end of April," Turner speculated.

"What makes ye thank that, Colonel?" Will wondered. "I'ma shore hopin' this killin' stops soon."

"You know, of course, that Sherman's whipped just about ever'bidy in tha South – Tennessee, Alabama, Georgia, Florida, and now the Carolinas. His Generals are spread out all across the state of North Carolina now. From Goldsboro in the east, to Asheville in the west; they're all converging on Raleigh.

"Grant's siege has closed off Lee's supply lines, and they can't hold out much longer. I sincerely believe that it's now just a matter of weeks, maybe just a few more days."

"I shore do hope yer rite, Colonel Turner. Ther's been way too much killin' a'ready," Will was hopeful.

"Me and Lenora are gonna try to get a job in Reconstruction. We'd like ta he'p build back some of tha tearin' down that's been dun."

After a major Union victory at Bentonville, Confederate General Johnston met with Jefferson Davis in Greensboro in Mid-April. He told the Confederate president, "Our people are tired of the war, feel themselves whipped, and will not fight. Our country is overrun, its military resources greatly diminished, while our enemy's may be increased to any extent desired. My small force is melting away like snow before the sun."

On **April 18th**, just four days after Lincoln's assassination, Johnston signed an armistice with Sherman at a farmhouse near Durham Station. Agreeing, under the terms of surrender, to many political conditions, as well as military, without prior approval from Washington, Sherman was reprimanded by Grant.

The confusion was sorted out, and on **April 26th**, Johnston agreed to purely military terms, and formally surrendered his army and all Confederate forces in Georgia, Florida, and the Carolinas. It was the second significant surrender that month.

On **April 9th**, Robert E. Lee had surrendered the Army of Northern Virginia at Appomattox Court House.

The war was over, but it took several days for the news to filter down to all the scattered troops. On Saturday morning, **April 29th** a company of Sherman's cavalry rode into Graham.

Completely filling the Town Square, they were met by opposition from the Graham Militia Unit. Gunfire erupted just as the Presley wagons rolled into town to deliver the week's load of timber to the sawmill.

Hearing gunfire, Matt Presley grabbed his rifle and ran into the square. Stopping in front of Graham's General Store, he fired his musket and killed a Union soldier.

Three shots rang out, and Matt fell to the ground mortally wounded. One shot hit him in the right leg, one in the right side of his chest, and the third shot caught him just below his cheek bone.

Seeing her brother lying in the street, Lizzie ran out of the General store. Kneeling down and lifting her brother to her chest, she held him, and screamed uncontrollably.

As she did so, the captain of the Union cavalry rode up and shot her four times with his pistol.

Two Presley children lay dead in the street.

At three o'clock that afternoon, news came from Raleigh that the war had ended on Wednesday three days before.

"A rich man's war is a poor man's fight."

EPILOGUE

After services On Sunday, **May 17, 1**868, Reverend Henderson sat with Sally Presley, her four remaining children, two daughters-in-law, and six grandchildren outside the two-story Presley home and offered a blessing before their meal.

This tradition of gathering for the Third Sunday meal began in 1840, shortly after a new church was built in Roaring Fork to serve the growing families who found it difficult to make the trip to First Methodist in town with their small children.

Everyone in Roaring Fork looked forward to this day. It was a welcome break from their daily labors, a chance to socialize, and a leisurely opportunity to catch up on local gossip as well as news from town and the wider world.

Neighbors from adjoining farms shared in the preparations, each providing their specialities. Vernon, his wife Savannah, and their children were always part of the group.

Since losing Jay, Sally cherished her friendship with Savannah. They had shared all the joys and sorrows of motherhood.

When their stomachs were full and the ladies had cleared the tables, neighbors sat in small groups to chat, while the younger children romped through the yard making up games.

Preacher Henderson spotted Sally sitting alone, looking wistfully toward the old cabin.

"May I join you, Sally?" he asked softly.

"Most certainly Reverend. I'm pleased to have your company," she replied.

"May I be so bold as to ask your thoughts, Sally?"

"I was just remembering that it has been almost five years since two of my boys died on the same day fighting for a lost cause, and just over three years since my two youngest babies died for no reason, due to misinformation," she answered in a tone that combined grief and rage.

"Tell me, Reverend, where is the sense in all that has happened to my family, our friends, our town, and this country?"

He thought it best to continue listening instead of commenting as she obviously had more to say; therefore, he gently touched her hand and looked into her eyes.

Sally swallowed hard trying to control her emotion and continued, "All of us honest, hard-working, God-fearing folks had dreams of building a better life for our children. We just tried to do the right thing.

"It wasn't the folks like us who started the fight. We were too busy with the everyday work of raising our families to get involved in politics."

Sally's voice became louder and a few tears escaped as she continued. **"It was those people who never get their hands dirty, and have the leisure to sit around thinking how to make sure they are always on top of the heap.**

"Then, when they work themselves up to a fever pitch, who do they send to fight their futile battles? **Why it's always the working folks, of course."**

Breaking his silence, Henderson added, **"The rich man's war is the poor man's fight."**

He took the liberty of putting his arm around Sally's shoulders to comfort her, and she did not protest this sudden show of affection.

"If you will allow me to speak for a moment, Sally, I would like to summarize your remarkable life as I have witnessed it."

Gazing at him in utter surprise, she responded, "There's nothing remarkable about me, Reverend. I'm a shopkeeper's daughter who married a tenant farmer, had a passel of young'ins and did the best I could with what we had."

"Sally, I must disagree with you. I watched you grow into an intelligent and compassionate young woman. I saw how you honored your parents, how you respected people of every kind. I heard from others how you helped them make the most of their resources when you were working at the General Store.

"I saw you turn a young almost illiterate stranger into a man of confidence and determination. I watched with some envy as you built a family with him overcoming many hardships, while always retaining a loving presence and an optimistic attitude toward what the future could hold.

"I marveled as you taught not only your own children, but your neighbor's children to read, write, think, and to believe they were worthy of an ever-improving future if they worked for it.

"I sadly watched you grieve for the loss of your beloved husband, and still hold the family together, always pursuing his original dream.

"In the horror of this war, I saw you lose four children in violence, and one who disappeared to an unknown destiny."

With her jaw dropping a bit, Sally said, "I don't know who that gal is you are talking about, but I would sure like to know her."

They both laughed, hugged, and the dark cloud that had hovered over the day of remembrance seemed to be replaced by filtered rays of light seeping through the trees on the ridge behind the big house.

"Sally, I have something else to discuss with you if you will give me a few more moments of your time," Henderson said taking her hand in his.

"Would you like something else to eat or drink first?" she asked.

"No, thank you, Sally, I just want your attention."

"This sounds serious, Reverend, should I be worried?"

"No, but I would like you to stop calling me Reverend; my name is John. We have known each other for more than thirty years. I have shared most of the important moments of your life with you. And you were there for me when I lost my Nellie. We are certainly more than friends.

"Sally, you and I are now facing the latter years of life without the partners we thought we would always have. If you are worried about disloyalty, I believe that both J.W. and Nellie would want us to be happy and would be glad for us.

"Billy Bob, Pete, and Andy are strong young men who can carry on the work at the farm, They will look after Martha, Willadeen and the children. Maggie has married and moved to town."

Sally was listening intently with puzzlement. "All that is true, John, but I feel there is something more on your mind."

John replied in a soft voice, "Sally, I would like you to consider becoming my wife, and moving back to town.

"You don't need the heavy labor of farm life at this stage, and you could spend full time teaching more children in a larger school in town. With the recent loss of your Father, you would also be close enough to care for your Mother in her golden years."

"I don't know what to say to all of that. Those ideas never even entered my head."

"Don't worry, Sally, you can take all the time you need to think about the possibility. Just know that I have always loved and respected you at a distance. I, also feel, that we would be good partners.

"You and I share many concerns about what has happened in the recent past and what may happen in the future. It would be rather presumptuous of us to believe that we could change the world.

"However, as a team, we could use our remaining years to act as a positive influence on our community. As a teacher, you can inspire the next generation to strive to become their best selves.

"Hopefully, I can continue to provide pastoral care and to challenge our friends to listen to their better angels.

"It only takes one or two people in a group to steer people toward the light instead of the darkness. I want us to be those two people for the community of Graham, Sally."

"I am honored, John, but I do need a little time to absorb all that you have said," Sally answered touching his hand gently.

Suddenly her attention was shifted to the sound of a carriage pulling up the road and into the lane past the cabin. "Who could that possibly be?" Sally thought.

As the carriage neared the site of the gathering, she spotted a young couple and the woman was holding two small children.

The man stopped the horses and stepped down. Going to the passenger side of the carriage, he lifted two toddlers to the ground and then took the woman's hand to help her down.

Sally and John walked toward the carriage as other people were beginning to form a line in the same direction to see what was happening.

As Sally approached the man, he smiled at her with a very familiar curled lip crooked grin.

"Oh, I cannot believe it but that is my long-lost boy, Will," she said running and crying at the same time.

Will grabbed his mother in a tight embrace, "I've missed you so much Momma."

John came closer and said, "We have all missed you, Will. Now who are these beautiful folks with you?"

"Momma, this is my wife, Lenora, and these little tykes are your grandsons, Ronnie and Randy."

Sally bent down to hug the little boys, and then took Lenora by the hand.

"Let's all go inside and sit down. You must be hungry.

"After I fill you up, we'll be having a long talk, because **you've** got a lot of questions to answer, young man."

Acknowledgments

The authors are indebted to a variety of institutions and sources whose missions are to preserve historical information in detailed but understandable formats.

Special thanks to:

- The Museum of the Civil War in Harrisburg, Pennsylvania.

- The town of Gettysburg preserving a living reminder including the battlegrounds, museum, and Cyclorama.

- The Museum of Appalachia in Norris, TN.

- PBS and Ken Burns Civil War documentaries.

- Chris Cawood for his inspiring class, his beta reading, and his advice and suggestions.

- Sylvia Sheh for her artistic rendering of our cover idea.

- Al Gore for the "vast information highway."

About the Authors

 Ronald E. Pressley is a native of Knoxville, Tennessee.

Ron enjoyed two successful careers spanning fifty years. Travelling the southeast, he represented a diverse variety of products both at Trade Shows and directly with customers.

Simultaneously, he served as a Minister of Music for multiple East Tennessee Baptist congregations.

As a life-long learner, he retains intense curiosity and interest in history, philosophy, and politics Ron is now deeply involved in making his goal of sharing his experiences, thoughts, and inspirations through the written word a reality.

Blood Brothers, 2019, written with his companion, Nancy P. Holder, is his third book and first novel.

Straight Outta Lonsdale, 2017, Memories of a Working-Class Family (A Memoir)

Straight Outta Lonsdale II, 2018, Voices from Lonsdale (An anthology)

Coming soon in 2020, **Out of the Ashes** (a sequel to Blood Brothers)

All are, or will be, available on Amazon.

You may also contact Ronald Pressley by email. ronaldpressley12@gmail.com

 Nancy Parker Holder was born in Washington, D.C.

After graduation from Carson-Newman College in 1965, she enrolled in additional studies at the University of Tennessee and East Tennessee State. For most of her life, East Tennessee has been home.

Her professional career, first as a Social Worker and later as a Human Resource Manager/Consultant, afforded many opportunities to put words on paper explaining the missions, programs, and policies of numerous companies, institutions, and organizations.

Now retired, she is enjoying sharing observations, perceptions, and inspirations in her own voice.

Blood Brothers, 2019, written with her companion, Ronald E. Pressley, is her first novel.

The Fourth Quarter, 2018, Reflections of a Septuagenarian, (A Memoir)

Coming soon in 2020, **Swamp Girl**, Babblings of a Beltway Baby, (a collection of essays)

All are, or will be, available on Amazon.

You may also contact Nancy Holder by email.
nancypholder@gmail.com

CPSIA information can be obtained
at www.ICGtesting.com
Printed in the USA
LVHW081546310122
709862LV00022B/341